A
Time
To
Live

A Time To Live

Chana Stavsky Rubin

CIS

C.I.S. Publications
Lakewood, New Jersey

ISBN 0-935063-48-X h/c

Published by C.I.S. Publications,
a division of C.I.S. Communications, Inc.
674 Eighth Street, Lakewood, New Jersey 08701
Tel: (201)367-7858/364-1629

Book and Cover Design by Ronda Kruger Israel
Cover Illustration by Gregg Hinlickey
Typography by Chaya Hoberman and Shami Reinman

Printed by Gross Brothers, Inc., Union City, New Jersey

This book is dedicated to
my children and grandchildren

Always be united in familial love and loyalty
Hashem's guiding Hand is there always
May we be *zocheh* to recognize it

There is a time to be born,
And a time to die . . .
A time to weep,
And a time to laugh.

(Koheles 3:2-4)

chapter one

The shrill sound of the bell penetrated the silence of the house. Two rings were all it took. Just two rings and our lives were irrevocably changed.

"Marian, answer the doorbell, please," Mother said.

"Is this the Asher household?" the young man asked.

In response to the affirmative shake of my head, he handed me a telegram addressed to Mr. J. Asher.

"Daddy, telegram for you," I called out after tipping and thanking the messenger.

My father's fingers shook as he ripped open the telegram. Mother stood next to him, her inquisitive birdlike face showing signs of fear. Telegrams, registered mail and blue coated policemen fall into the category of officialdom and cause trepidation in our household. At that time, I just couldn't understand why. I now realize that most of the traumatic events of my parents' lives revolved around official-looking documents.

My father held the telegram with two fingers, delicately, and away from his body as if the paper were burning hot. He walked to the couch and put his head in his hands. There was a tremor in his voice.

"Papa is gone," he said.

My mother's face turned ashen. The tears ran down her face.

"May I?" I asked as I took the telegram from my father's hands.

"We are sorry to inform you," the telegram read, "that your father passed away in the Sunshine Nursing Home this morning. Rabbi Isaacs and I attempted to contact you by phone but your phone was out of order. Please call or come to the home to make arrangements. Tom Layner, Administrator."

We had taken our phone off the hook after midnight because we'd

11

been receiving crank calls. I suppose that is why they couldn't reach us.

I took the list of names and phone numbers to call which my father had given me before he and my mother had left for the nursing home. My mother had called my Aunt Leah, my father's sister in Israel. There were no other relatives to call on my father's side. It was ironic that at a time like this, I couldn't cry. Instead, a panorama of uncontrollable thoughts passed through my mind.

I wondered why my grandfather had never gone to live with his daughter in Israel. Why had he stayed in America, living alone so many years? I seemed to remember him saying, "I want to be near you, little one. I must be near you. In you lies the future of our family. In you, I will live." Or was my mind playing tricks with me?

I shook my head to sweep away the cobwebs of my imagination. I shut my eyes and then opened them. Putting my emotions into a controlled corner in my mind, I went to make the telephone calls my father had assigned me.

The funeral was to be held the same day. I learned that Jewish law required burying a body as soon as possible. My father said that since my grandfather had been a pious man, he would carry out his wishes.

A black shiny car pulled up. My father was sitting in it. My heart was pounding in my chest. I just knew that my grandfather was in that car.

The steamy air of this hot summer day surrounded us as we walked to the car. It only added to the heaviness and gloom. I sat down in the car. My palms were sweating and my tongue was thick. Reality hit me with an uncontrollable loneliness. Grandfather, I'll never see you again!

My mother put her hands over her face. Her body shook as she sobbed. My tear ducts were dry. I could not cry.

Images revolved in my mind . . . Grandfather, strong, with his long, black curly sideburns. I remembered him playing hide-and-go-seek with me. I remembered his lilting voice as he sang songs to me.

"Why does grandfather have curls?" I had asked with childish innocence. Was it really so many years ago? Oh, how easy it was to change the subject and steer a child's mind and imagination in other directions. I never remember receiving an answer, nor was there any continuation of the subject. It just faded away as did so many similar childhood thoughts and questions.

I recalled my grandfather lying in the nursing home, sick and helpless; my strong grandfather was gone. His pale face grew even whiter when I told him about the new boy I had met who was going to be a doctor.

"Who are his parents?" he asked.

"Dr. and Mrs. Brennan," I answered.

"The name . . . it doesn't sound Jewish. Is he Jewish?"

"No," I answered with the blindness of youth. "But so what? It doesn't matter."

How much I have learned to understand in these few months. Grandfather, please forgive me. Oh dear Grandfather, please forgive my lack of sensitivity and understanding.

Like a hammer chiseling away at wood, the sounds of my parents voices reached me. I listened to their conversation.

"I'm sorry your sister Leah could not be here," my mother was saying. "I know what Papa meant to her. She urged him so many times to come to spend his last years with her. I remember the letter she wrote him. How she begged him to come, telling him that he'd love Eretz Yisrael and that her husband Moshe couldn't wait to spend the days learning with him. Do you remember Papa's answer? 'My heart yearns to come,' he replied, 'but within Malka lies our future. Our family will live through her.' "

"Yes, he had his plans," my father said. Was that a note of sarcasm I detected in his voice? "I could never change him, but I didn't let him change us."

"Too bad that now, of all times, Leah cannot be reached. When I called Israel, it took quite a while to find Moshe. He was giving a *shiur* in his *Yeshivah*. He is a good man, Leah's husband. He told me that it would be impossible to reach Leah, because she's *en route* to Poland. He would have to wait for her to call. How ironic! She most probably will be standing near your mother's grave at the same time Papa will be buried."

The cars stopped and we walked a short distance. I was bewildered at the group of strange faces of older people.

"Who are these people?" I asked.

"Grandfather's friends," my father answered.

I remembered him once laughingly saying that he was going to his *chavrusos*.

"What's that, grandfather?" I had asked.

"They are my friends who keep the well full of water," he had said. "They help me find the fountain of youth. Without it, our old brains would get rusty. It gives us the vitamin injections that help us live." Noting my puzzled expression, he had added, "I hope one day you too will understand that Torah is life."

We gathered around a gaping hole in the ground. I looked around me. There were tombstones lined up in a precise row. Each one marked off another life in this sea of grass.

It was still. Now I understand what is meant by the stillness of death. No one spoke. There was no movement of feet. The only sound we heard was the cawing of birds flying overhead.

One of the men separated himself from the others. He had a kind face. He looked a little bit like grandfather as I remembered him.

He spoke in English. I can't understand why I had a strong feeling that he would have been more comfortable speaking in another tongue, that he was speaking English for my benefit. Perhaps it was because he seemed to be looking in my direction. Perhaps it was just my imagination.

I heard someone whisper, "Rabbi Isaacs," so I understood that he was the Rabbi.

"I knew the *niftar*, the deceased, Reb Mordche for sixty years," Rabbi Isaacs was saying. "We were childhood friends in Poland. His life was a difficult one. As a young boy and the oldest in his family, he was battered by poverty. He had to work hard to help support his family. But at night, the entire *shtetl* saw the candle burning until daylight. Yes, he worked hard all his years, but Hashem was good to him. He prospered and became wealthy. Throughout everything, he was always an honored and respected man. He married and had children . . . and then came Hitler.

"Friends, how can I describe the strength of this person? There were times I saw him sitting quietly, perfectly still, his eyes and hands tightly shut as if to ward off the blows of life, but his faith always remained strong.

"The angry swell of the dark, furious sea of hatred swept over Poland. The waves rose to gigantic heights and then crashed around him, but the thunder of the waves did not break him. Above the roar of the storm, he heard another sound and saw another sight."

I heard soft sobbing. I turned around to see who it came from. It wasn't one person. It seemed as if all my grandfather's friends were sobbing together in unison.

14

The Rabbi continued, his voice louder, pleading, and at the same time, harsher.

"*Ribono Shel Olam*! What makes one man see the rays of the sun and brightness rising on the horizon while another sees only the setting of the sun and gloom? Mordche, my friend, Mordche, teach us. Teach your child, your grandchild, all of us that are still living, that are present here today. Teach us how to go on when you, our ray of light, has been extinguished. How will I go on without you, dear friend?

"Oh, what your eyes have seen! You saw your baby son torn from your wife's hands and thrown in the air to be caught on the rifle bayonet of a laughing Nazi. Oh, what your ears have heard! I was there when they told you how your Malka, your dear Malkala died; the peals of hysterical, insane laughter torn out of her throat when one child after the other met death in those heinous inhuman concentration camps.

"And yet," the Rabbi's voice grew softer, he was crying softly, "and yet, you were always firm in your faith. You bolstered mine. 'There is a reason for everything,' were your favorite words.

"Relatives and friends," the Rabbi's voice grew stronger and louder. "I saw him waiver only once, and that was when he was rebuffed when he pleaded for someone close to him to come back to Yiddishkeit. 'Please, Hashem!' he cried. 'Don't let this be the end of my family, because then this would really be the end of my life!'

"My dear friend Mordche," the Rabbi cried. "Be a *gutter beiter* for *uns alle*, be a good pleader for all of us where your are going. In *Gan Eden* may you find peace. There, you will intervene and your prayers will be answered. I'll never forget your last words to me. You told me that you were ready to accept whatever Hashem has in store for you.

"Dear friend, you accepted your fate all your life. When you said *Vidui* and the *Shema*, you looked at peace. Yes, those were your last words. 'Listen Yisrael, Hashem is our Lord, Hashem is One.' "

I heard someone scream and cry out loudly, "No! No!" I looked around to see where the crying was coming from. I hadn't far to go. The voice had been torn from inside of me. I didn't want to believe it. His life couldn't be over. My grandfather couldn't be gone.

I heard my father say some words in a foreign tongue. My mother mumbled the word, "Kaddish."

I looked at the deep hole in the earth. Is that the end of life? We are born, we live, we die. Thud, thud. I heard the clods of earth fall on the

15

coffin. I remembered the words I had heard somewhere in the past . . .

There is a time to live and a time to die.

A time to cry and a time to laugh.

When is there a time to live? When is there a time to die? What is life!?

I don't think I'll ever forget the sight or the smell of the earth or the realization that one day a person lives and the next day he is gone.

On the drive home from the cemetery, my father was quiet. I saw my mother glance at him surreptitiously, but my father's lips were drawn tight. There was no conversation, and there was no way for me to know my father's feelings or thoughts.

When we arrived home, I watched as Rabbi Isaacs put white sheets over all the mirrors. My father had put on sneakers at the cemetery. He now sat down on the floor. Rabbi Isaacs gave him a hard-boiled egg which he dipped into ashes. I was mystified at all these strange happenings.

I followed my mother into the kitchen and questioned her. She told me that this was the Jewish ritual for mourning.

"Daddy is following it out of respect for grandfather," she explained.

The entire week, the house was filled with people. There were old men, friends of my grandfather, wearing black hats or little black skull-caps on their heads. Some of them spoke English, others Yiddish. My parents' friends and business associates also came. They talked about the old country and sacrifices parents had made so that they could receive a proper education in the new world. They discussed how the doors opened to the professions and the business world because of their parents' relinquishment of pleasures. Some looked guilty and others fidgeted uncomfortably. I wondered how often they thought about their parents and grandparents. I was curious whether they visited and took care of them. I made a mental vow to be different.

I tried to keep the youthful image of my grandfather in my mind, but it became intermingled with the last picture I had of him in the nursing home, a sick, withered old man without any teeth. I erased it from my mind and thought of the pictures Rabbi Isaacs had painted of my grandfather and then I felt better. I realized that Rabbi Isaacs had not buried my grandfather. That was just a box and a body in the ground. Rabbi Isaacs had really brought him to life for me.

16

chapter two

Fortunately, school was over. I hadn't had a complete night of sleep since the funeral. I kept thinking about my grandfather. It was wonderful for a person to have so much faith, but what had made him have it? What caused him to believe there is a purpose for everything? How could he accept the death of his three children? I felt that perhaps I could learn some answers from Rabbi Isaacs.

It was a brutally hot Monday when I decided to drive over to his synagogue. Broadway looked like a street that had tried very hard to stay awake but finally had to close its' eyes at 4:00 p.m. Most of the stores were shuttered and the barricades were up. The heat of the day kept customers in their air-conditioned homes and few would venture outdoors.

I parked the car near the synagogue. From my safe sanctuary, I viewed the building. There was writing in Hebrew on a sign over the door. I had never been inside a "*shul*." The windows were opaque with the dust of the summer. They seemed like eyes that looked at me with half-shut lids.

Across the street, a grossly obese woman was sitting on the stoop. Her bleached red hair was streaked with gray. Even from this distance, I was able to see the sweat stains under her armpits. She was drinking something out of a can. Two children were tossing a ball to each other. It was so quiet that the bounce of the ball cut the silence like a knife. I seemed to be standing in front of the building for hours, but it was only seconds. When I looked across the street, the redheaded woman was still drinking from the can.

Rabbi Isaacs startled me.

"Come in, child," he said. "I'm glad you came."

Rabbi Isaacs was an old man. I realized he must be as old as my grandfather, but he didn't look as old. His beard still had streaks of black in it, and his hair under the black skullcap he always wore also had touches of black.

I walked the two steps down to what looked like an office. There were some people in the outer room. I closed the door to his office. The air conditioner made an undercurrent of noises but they were muted. Rabbi Isaacs stood up from his seat and opened it a few inches. I wondered why.

I looked around the room. The whitewashed walls were lined with thick, heavy books.

"What can I do for you, Malkala?" Rabbi Isaacs asked.

Malkala? I wondered why he called me that. I'm sure he knew my name was Marian. Malka was my grandmother's name. I wondered whether he was growing senile. I had an urge to get up and leave, but something kept me glued to my seat.

"Rabbi Isaacs," I said. "I'm here because I want to know how my grandfather kept steadfast in his beliefs after witnessing the deaths of members of his family."

"Did you ever ask your father?" Rabbi Isaacs asked me.

"My father said that belief in the Lord is only for old people who need straws to cling to. 'Religion,' he said, 'is a crutch for cripples!' My grandfather and father were on two different sides. How could people of the same flesh be so different? I need to understand my grandfather, and I want to understand my father."

"That's understandable," Rabbi Isaacs said. "There was a famous American saying during the Second World War. 'In the foxholes, there are no atheists.' During war, when shooting and death constantly surround a person, it is then we all cry out to the Lord. Inside ourselves, we know that there is a greater Being, but when life is secure, we want to continue with our own life styles. It is then that many people forget the Lord. They make Him a convenience. It is only when you have faith that you can have compassion for one who thinks he has no faith.

"Malkala, in order to appreciate your grandfather, you must understand his very soul. You must learn the history of our people. Your people. You must learn of your heritage. I would like to be your teacher, but my words do not come easily. I am used to thinking and speaking in Yiddish. How old are you?"

"Eighteen," I answered.

"I have a granddaughter close to you in age," he said. "Her name is Naomi. Should I make an appointment for you to meet her?"

His hand reached for the telephone. I quickly shook my head in the negative. Rabbi Isaacs looked at me. I felt as if his eyes pierced me, as if he understood my every thought. He didn't say anything. He just gave me a slip of paper with her name, address and telephone number. His eyes glistened.

"You are your grandfather's granddaughter, Malkala," he said softly. "You are. You'll see."

The brightness of the sun hit me as I opened the door to the street. I cupped my hand over my eyes against the sun. The redheaded lady was gone. The children playing ball were gone. The only thing in sight were the tears on my cupped hand as I left Rabbi Isaacs and his synagogue.

chapter three

*I*t was a glorious day. I knew I would want to hold on to the warmth for the bitter cold winter months ahead. Neal, Janet, Joe, Carol, Kurt and I found room in the crowded park for a game of dodge ball.

"Throw the ball, Marian," Janet said. "Throw it to me."

"Okay," I said. "That's enough for me."

"I'll get the franks," Neal said. "Want to come, Marian?"

"No, I'm lazy," I replied. "I'll sunbathe a little."

"Lazybones," Janet said.

I watched Neal's progress through the crowd. When he disappeared from sight, I shifted my eyes to the group playing ball. They frolicked like seals at play.

I lay back on the grass. The sun bathed me in its warmth. The muted noise of the crowd was like a soft lullaby. I closed my eyes and felt my relaxed body succumbing to sleep. And then . . . as if I had been stung by a bee, my thoughts came fast and sharp. I jumped up with a start. What gave my grandfather the ability to be able to make a statement that he was ready to accept whatever Heaven had in store for him? Why? What made him feel like that? Why didn't he scream at life? Since my grandfather's funeral, these thoughts, like a carousel, kept going around and around in my mind.

"With mustard or without?" Neal asked.

I had met Neal at Carol's party last year. We hit it off immediately. He was pleasant to look at and easy to talk with. It wasn't only his fair hair and blue eyes that attracted me but also a dreamy quality he had. We did not articulate our feelings, but I knew he felt the same way about me. Janet, my best friend, said she didn't think we would wait to get married until after Neal graduated. I looked up at Neal. His bronzed face made the sun shining on his blonde hair even whiter, and once again I admired his looks. Although not handsome in the traditional sense, he had great charm. I felt fortunate to have Neal for a friend and could only hope his application and acceptance to medical school in another state would not change our status.

There were a few occasions when I had almost opened up to Neal. I wanted very much to talk to him about the mixed up feelings I had about my grandfather, but my mind was in too much chaos to share my thoughts clearly with someone else.

"A penny for your thoughts," said Neal.

"They're not worth it," I answered. "I'll take one of those franks with mustard, Neal. Look! Here come the others for theirs."

"What should we do tonight?" asked Janet.

"Let's go to Coney Island and do the rides," Kurt answered.

Before piling into Neal's car, a time and place of meeting was agreed upon.

The last one of our friends to be taken home was Janet. I waved goodbye.

"You've been very quiet all the way home, Marian," said Neal. "You okay?"

"Do you think we really should go tonight?" I asked.

Neal looked surprised. "Why not?"

"It's Kurt. He frightens me with his wild ideas and plans."

"He's an okay guy, Marian. He just likes people to think he's tough."

Somehow, I was not convinced.

That evening, Neal's broad smile reassured me that I looked good in my new white skirt and navy blue blouse.

"Don't come home late," my mother said.

"I won't."

We found parking in front of Janet's house. Joe was already there.

"Hi, Janet," said Neal. "How are you, Joe? Where are Carol and Kurt?"

Janet shrugged her shoulders. "I don't understand. I called Carol's house, and her mother said they left at 7:00. I'm worried. It's 9:00 already, and they're not here yet. Oh, look. There they are."

Kurt pulled into the parking space behind Neal. He seemed to have a lot of difficulty maneuvering into the space. He opened the door of the car and wobbled out, practically stumbling over his own feet. His words were slurred.

"Come on," he said. "Let's go. I'm ready to celebrate. We'll use my car, because it is much larger than yours."

"Maybe we shouldn't," I whispered to Neal.

"Come on, Marian," he answered. "Let's go."

"Don't be a spoil-sport," said Janet.

The others chorused her remark. I felt alone and detached from my friends. Usually, it was I who was the life of the party. I felt my cheeks flush with anger when Kurt whispered "Jew coward" into my ear. I looked at the others. No one had heard. Why had he singled me out? Was it because one day last year he had seen my grandfather, an unmistakable picture of a Jew?

I held back as the group walked to his car with Kurt swaggering in the lead.

"Come on," Neal pleaded. "Please."

"Okay." I bowed to the pressure and followed. My nerves tightened in fear when I saw a few six-packs of beer on the floor of the car. Kurt must have had some before picking up Carol.

The sounds of Coney Island reached us even before we were out of the car. As we came closer to the arcade, the noise of the rides and the hawkers was deafening. I looked at the faces about me. The smiles looked painted on, and there was real fear in some eyes. Did people enjoy this or did they just pretend?

Kurt took the lead. There he was, the Great Manipulator. He pulled the strings, and like puppets, we did whatever he wanted. We went on all the rides he chose.

On the drive home, my earlier fears were realized. He handed beer cans to everyone. I objected, but it was a losing battle. Neal took the wheel of the car. I was grateful for that.

"Please, Neal. Don't drink."

I was ignored. We passed under a street lamp, and I saw that his face was flushed and his eyes glittered. The car took the turns on two wheels. I held on to the side of the car tensely. I was angry. The hysterical sounds of laughter and singing were all around me. Once in Queens, when he cut off the expressway and drove through quiet, tree lined streets, I felt more secure. Two months ago, I too would have reacted exactly like my friends. What was the matter with me? Could I blame Neal for behavior I would have been a part of? I was glad to finally arrive home, and it was with a sigh of relief that I left the car.

A TIME TO LIVE

My house was quiet. My parents had gone to bed. I breathed a little easier. I would not have to pretend it had been a pleasant evening.

I went up to my room and sat down with my pencil and pad. I wanted to put my thoughts into words while they were still fresh in my mind.

The Mad Escapist

The gaudy tinsel of Coney Island
The shoving, milling crowd
Packed nightclubs and firehazard movies
A whirling, stamping frenzy
Is happiness found?

Nature's best handiwork
Calmness of a soul
Peace of mind and of heart
Beauty of a moonlit night
Lost

Conformers, follow the milling crowd
Your smiles are sneers
Laughter grates and clinks
Metallic sounds in the night
Insane glee

Ludicrous people
Drunk on superficial joys
Following artificial devilment
Pouring money into grime-stained paws

Seek
Happiness
Ultimate satisfaction
In a bottle
Through a penny arcade

Reached . . . by whom?

I reread what I had written; it reflected my feelings. I made a few corrections, then washed up and fell into bed, exhausted.

chapter four

*T*he morning turned out to be unusually dull, humid and cloudy, as some summer days can be. I tried to forget my problems by burying myself in a good book. I thumbed through the pages of three books but found nothing I could sink my teeth into.

I felt irritable. My skin was prickly and tight. The sky looked dark and depressing, and I felt the same way.

"Marian, you seem so restless," said my mother, looking concerned. "What's bothering you?"

"Nothing you can help, Mom," I replied. "I think it's just the weather making me feel uncomfortable. Could you use some help?"

"Well, now that you ask, if you really feel like it, Marian, I could. We've had an ant problem this summer. Would you take everything out of the closet, check the shelves and rewash the pots?"

I shuddered and scratched my hands at the thought of ants but swallowed my aversion, put on an apron, and got down on my knees.

"Marian, I really appreciate your willingness but I don't think today is your day," said my mother a short while later. "That's the second thing that has fallen out of your hands in five minutes. Why don't you call Janet and see whether it's okay to go to her house?"

"Janet left early this morning," I said. "She's going to spend a few days with her aunt and cousins in their bungalow in the country, and Neal is following up on his application to medical school. Will you need the car today?"

"No. But if you have plans to go any place, you had better leave soon because it looks like it's going to pour."

"I'll call Sandy. Perhaps I'll spend the day with her."

"Sandy?" my mother asked. "Who is she?"

"Don't you remember? The girl from the nursing home."

"Oh, yes. I never met her, but from what you told me she seems like a charming girl."

I went to call Sandy. She answered after the first ring.

"You couldn't have called at a better time, Marian," she said. "I also feel *uchie*. My mother and father are doing some renovations in the basement, and my little brothers are making so much noise I feel as if my eardrums will burst. Come over, and let's have some adult conversation."

I took the car keys from my mother and went to the car. Driving on the highway, I thought about Sandy. I like her. There is a uniqueness about her. I have tried to narrow it down and isolate what it actually is. She has a wonderful sense of humor and is pleasant to be with. Although there is sadness in her eyes, I still get a feeling of serenity about her. She seems fragile, as if there is something within her that is hurting. Her voice is low, and there is a faint trace of distinctiveness in her pronunciation of words. I don't think she is a New Yorker.

I met Sandy last year when I visited Grandfather in the nursing home. It wasn't usual to find young people there. Grandchildren do not find a nursing home a pleasant place. Although cleanliness is stressed, the rugs, drapes and beds become impregnated with the odors associated with old age. The usual visitors are the sons and daughters of the bedridden who try hard to convince themselves that what they've done for their parents is really in the parents' best interests. But they walk around looking guilty.

One late afternoon, as I was leaving the nursing home, I heard footsteps behind me. It was a young girl I'd seen visiting with some of the patients.

"Hi," I said. "My name is Marian. I've seen you here before. Is it your grandmother or grandfather you come to visit? I think I saw you here last month."

"I've seen you many times, too," she replied. "Your grandfather is such a wonderful person. I've spoken to him a few times. No, I really didn't come to visit any relatives. My grandparents are not living."

"Then . . . I don't understand. Is it a neighbor? What are you doing here? I can think of better ways to spend a Sunday afternoon."

"The truth is I don't come to visit a particular person," she said. "I spend a few minutes with anyone who looks lonely."

"I don't believe it! You have no one here, but you just come to visit?"

"Yes. You see, some of the people just don't have any relatives at all. It is important not to feel forgotten."

"And the staff permits it?"

"They are really very cooperative. It helps morale to feel someone is interested in you."

"How often do you come?"

"As often as I can. At least twice a month."

"You've shamed me," I said. "I think now, whenever I visit my grandfather, I'll make it my business to talk to someone else as well."

"Forgive me," she said with old world courtesy. "My name is Sandy."

We found a bench under a grove of trees that was shaded from the sun. The only sound was the buzzing of two small flies playing tag. It was depressing to see the three elderly people sitting across from us. They stared silently ahead, their hands clasped tightly on their laps.

We talked. Sandy told me that, unfortunately, she never knew her grandfather. She remembered her grandmother who had left an indelible impression on her even during the short time she had known her.

"Although she was old in years, I never really felt that she was an old lady," she explained. "There was a youthfulness about her. I look at the people in the home. They too were once young, just as we are now. They had dreams, raised children, laughed, danced. People forget that. Although their interests have changed, they still have needs. We all pray to live to be old, but none of us wants to be alone and neglected."

Sandy amazed me with her depth and maturity. I appreciated how she opened my eyes to things I had just taken for granted.

She lived on a quiet, tree-lined street in Brooklyn. It took me a long time to reach her house as I kept getting lost in the unfamiliar territory. I finally had to stop the car and ask directions. When I looked up at the sky, it looked threatening. I hurried to race the storm. I breathed a sigh of relief when I finally found the address and was lucky to find parking directly in front of her house.

I pressed the bell and its sound was a harsh and broken cry as in the quiet before the storm.

Sandy opened the door. She enveloped me with her warm welcome. There was genuine concern in her eyes.

"I was worried about you driving and hoped you would get here before the storm," she said. "I was almost sorry I hadn't told you not to come because of the weather. But I'm glad I didn't. I'm so happy to see you."

She took my coat and hung it in the hall closet. I looked searchingly at her to see whether she knew about my grandfather.

"How is your grandfather?" she asked, as if she'd read my thoughts. "I haven't been able to get to the nursing home these past few weeks. My father is on vacation, and he's spending every available moment renovating the basement. It has really become a family project, and if there is nothing I can help with, I'm assigned to babysitting."

Tears filled my eyes.

"Sandy, my grandfather's gone," I blurted. "I can't believe it. I can't believe I'll never see him again."

And then, like an overflowing well it came. The tears gushed down my face. Her arms went around me, comforting me.

"I'm so sorry, Marian," she said. "He was such a special person. I wish I could find the words to help you. I understand what you lost. There was something about him that made you feel you were the most important person in the world. He really cared. I also felt close to him. We had some interesting conversations together."

"You did, Sandy? What did you talk about?"

I saw a shadow cross her face.

"About you mostly. Marian, he loved you. He loved you so much."

I felt my throat constricting and the tears continued to run unrestrainedly down my cheeks.

"And I loved him very much, too," I said. "Unfortunately, it is only now, day by day, that I realize how very much."

I wiped my eyes when I heard footsteps approaching, but I wasn't fast enough. Two boys appeared.

"Why are you crying?" asked the shorter one. He was slight of built and very dark skinned.

"This is Azriel, my little brother," said Sandy. "The older one is Ovadia."

I wiped my eyes.

"How do you do?" I said. "My name is Marian. How old are you?"

The older one answered for both.

"I'm six and Azriel is four," he said. "How old are you?"

I laughed. "Why do you want to know?"

He looked up at me with his black eyes sparkling and answered, "Why do *you* want to know?"

27

"*Touché*," I said. "You got me."

"Huh?" he questioned.

"You win," I said. "I'm eighteen."

"Just like my sister," the little one answered.

"Now let's see whether I can remember who is Vodya and who is Azrel," I said.

They broke into peals of laughter.

"Let me try it again," I said, but again I could not pronounce their names.

Sandy laughed and explained that these were typical Israeli names.

"Is your family Israeli?" I asked. "Were you born in Israel?"

"My family was born here," she answered. "Oh, I hear my mother and father."

"Time for a coffee break," a woman's voice said. Then she saw me. "Hi, you must be Shaindee's friend Marian. I'm her mother and this is her father, Mr. Josephs."

My mouth fell open. I must have looked like a fool. Her mother and father really looked young enough to be her sister and brother. I could see Mrs. Josephs was expecting a baby. Sandy's parents were dark-skinned and dark-haired, just like the boys.

"Where do you get your red hair from, Sandy?" I asked. "You must have been adopted!" I was embarrassed at my remark when I saw the red flush start on the white skin of Sandy's neck and slowly creep up until it covered her face.

"Everyone asks that because of Shaindee's red hair," her mother quickly answered. "It comes from a great-grandfather. I'm making some drinks. Would you like hot cocoa? Or maybe ice cream soda? That's the boys' specialty."

"I'm not dieting this week," I answered. "Ice cream soda will be fine."

I felt myself folded into the warmth and friendliness of this family. I liked the mutual respect between Sandy and her parents. When we finished our drinks, Sandy's mother said it was Sandy's time off from the "brats." She seemed to mispronounce Sandy's name. I assumed that she most probably was not a New Yorker, and therefore, the dialect was different.

"Go ahead, Shaindee," said Mrs. Josephs. "I'll take over."

"We're not brats," the little boys said.

"I'm just kidding," their mother answered. "You definitely are not

28

brats. I love you . . . and you," and she bent forward and kissed them both.

"Come," Sandy said. "I'll show you my room and then the room being built downstairs."

Sandy's room was simply furnished in American colonial maple. The furniture was polished to a high gloss. It was like the rest of the house, clean, solid and dependable.

There was a picture on her dresser of a man and a woman. It had been made from a snapshot and enlarged.

"May I pick it up?" I asked.

Sandy nodded. The man had a long black beard and the woman had a kerchief covering her head. The lack of any hair showing from her kerchief made her eyes the outstanding feature. They were striking.

"What an interesting couple," I told Sandy. "Her eyes are extraordinary. If her hair were red, I would say that you have a remarkable resemblance to her. Your grandparents?"

"Relatives," Sandy changed the subject. "Now I want to show you the basement room. We expect the baby in a few months, and that's why we want the room finished as quickly as possible. My room upstairs will become the baby's room. It was too small for me to have any friends overnight, but the basement room is much larger and really lovely."

It was a large, surprisingly airy looking room. There was a hi-riser against the wall and a white triple dresser.

"I told my parents I would be only too happy to share my room with the baby so they would not have to go through any expense, but they wouldn't hear of it. They felt we would need an extra room," Sandy blushed as she added, "for when I get married."

"How exciting," I said eagerly. "Tell me all about him."

"There is no him at present. My parents are just preparing for the future." She looked around the room. "Funny, isn't it? My parents bought the bed and the dresser before putting in the heating and the floor. We hope to have it finished by the end of the month. Dad is having a contractor in to rush the job because Mom is due to have the baby soon, and then we won't have time to work on the room."

"Your mother looks so young," I remarked. "Actually, she looks more like your sister than your mother."

Sandy looked at me strangely.

"Yes, everyone says that." She continued as if I hadn't interrupted.

"This is going to be the playroom. We will put a hi-riser here and one over there. That will give us plenty of sleeping space. I plan on covering it to resemble couches. Like it? Isn't it terrific?"

I caught her enthusiasm, and we sat down and verbally spent thousands of dollars decorating the room.

Sandy laughed. "Now that we have finished spending all this money, I'll show you how we really intend to do it."

She proceeded once again to amaze me. She showed me her sewing machine and the drapes and hi-riser covers she was in the process of making.

I enjoyed the afternoon very much and was sorry when it drew to a close. I thanked Mr. and Mrs. Josephs for their hospitality. I was about to leave when Sandy's brothers came in.

"Please say our names," they teased.

I tried but was still unsuccessful. They were adorable as they sat down on the floor, bent over with laughter.

Sandy walked me to my car. She looked at the sky and said, "Watch how you drive home. It's not raining yet, but it is still threatening. I hope you make it home before it starts pouring. Please call me as soon as you get in to let me know you arrived safely."

I told her I would, and we promised to keep in touch.

I drove quickly in the waning daylight, trying to keep my mind concentrated on the road. It kept wandering back to the pleasant afternoon. I loved her family. I tried to identify what was special about it. Everyone really cared about each other. There was something, an elusive picture that kept appearing and disappearing. Suddenly, I remembered. Mr. Josephs and the children had worn skullcaps, just like my grandfather and his friends. But Mr. Josephs and the children were young. Somehow or other, I had always associated skullcaps with old people.

As I walked to the house from the car, the trees and flowers exuded a delightful aroma. I remembered I had once read that as the air pressure drops before a storm, flowers emit more perfume, a signal that the weather is about to change. I wondered whether that was true.

The threatening storm did not come. The sky remained dark and dismal with the moonlight breaking through for a brief instance. The air was thick and heavy. I forgot the delightful afternoon and the beautiful fragrance of the flowers. My edginess returned. I recalled reading in that same article that the possibility existed that if the moon could exert pulling power on water and regulate tides, perhaps the gravitational power of the moon pulls the liquids in our bodies up towards our heads, causing temporary swelling of brain tissues and constricting cranial blood vessels and the supply of blood to the brain. Maybe that was producing my sluggishness. But then again, how could I explain my cheerful mood of the entire day?

chapter five

"Hello. Is this Naomi? My name is Marian Asher. Your grandfather, Rabbi Isaacs, told me to call you. When? 2:00 o'clock. Okay. I'll be there."

Well, I'm finally going to do it. I'm taking the first step. Why am I doing it? Coney Island and its shallow glitter doesn't hold any satisfaction for me. The drinking and the need for artificial stimulation, the pretending I'm having a great time, disturb me. Sandy's house and her family, their concern for others, the extra something there and their beautiful warmth aroused a hunger in me. Rabbi Isaacs' words at my grandfather's funeral are constantly on my mind. Sometimes I feel I'm being manipulated by forces beyond my control. There are things I need to know and so . . . I called Naomi.

I couldn't use the car because my mother needed it, so I took a taxicab. Naomi had told me she lived near the ocean in Far Rockaway. I asked the driver to stop a few blocks from her house. I wanted to walk the remaining distance. I felt I needed time to be alone. The taxicab had barely drawn away when the sky, as if in mockery, started to darken. I looked up and saw a canopy of gray clouds. The weather report was finally accurate this time.

There were a few hardy people standing along the boardwalk's rail viewing the ocean. I walked along the boardwalk tasting the salt spray on my lips. A big white bird flew majestically overhead, in sharp contrast against the gray sky. I listened to the crash of the waves. The wind started gusting. I felt a shudder pass through me. Perhaps my blood had thinned as I acquired my tropical summer tan.

I was afraid; it is much easier to be complacent and not upset the routine of life. Would my visit to Naomi open foreign doors or close the ones I was peeking though? I pulled the collar of my jacket up and held it tightly around my throat. The deafening crescendo of the waves accompanied me. With a burst, the threatening rain came down. I started to run.

Naomi was a tiny girl. I don't think she reached five feet, but her diminutive build did not take away from her self-composure or stature. Her large brown eyes showed compassion as she welcomed me, took my dripping jacket and led me into the kitchen. The cup of hot cocoa was an elixir, warming my chilled body. I watched Naomi. Her movements were delicate. I noticed that even the sound of the cup as she put it on the table had a daintiness about it. It made a slight tinkle.

We went into the living room. The windows were covered by a soft gold gauze curtain. She led me to a damask, gold tweed sofa which blended with the curtains. I looked around the room. The walls were lined with books. It was a comfortable room. It reminded me of the girl sitting across from me. She also gave me a feeling of comfort.

I listened as Naomi spoke. I felt some of the tension leave me. She told me that her parents were born in Europe but that she was an American. It was interesting that we had much in common. We were both children of parents who had lived through the Holocaust, but there our paths separated. There was an open door between Naomi and her parents, and they had communicated to her some of what they'd seen. My parents never discussed their youth. Her parents were fully committed to Judaism and had given her a thorough education in the Orthodox tradition, belief and faith. My parents had raised me without any religious beliefs. They seemed to want me to melt into the American melting pot.

It wasn't necessary for Naomi to ask me questions. She had an innate ability to grasp feelings and thoughts before they were expressed. With a smile she said that "roots" was currently the "in" thing and the best way to start would be for me to find my roots. Did I have any questions? Had I any preference as to where I would want her to begin? I shook my head.

"Do you believe in G-d?" She shot the question at me.

I thought for a few minutes and then answered, "The truth of the matter is that I had never thought of it one way or another, but when my grandfather died . . . You know, Naomi, death makes us re-evaluate our lives. It started me thinking. It was incredible that a person could be made of the earth. Basically, the same components are contained in man and in the earth, phosphorus, calcium, oxygen, hydrogen, carbon, magnesium, iron, potassium and so on. But logically, I couldn't fashion a human being out of earth. There must be . . . someone . . . who breathed that little something special into that piece of clay to make it into a living human being."

"That makes everything much easier," Naomi said. "Can you believe, Marian, that there was a time when people would not accept this? The idea of one G-d was revolutionary. The world was steeped in superstition and idolatry. The land which we call Eretz Yisrael and to which the Romans gave the name of Palestine, was then known as the land of Canaan. The Canaanite religion was polytheistic, and they had gods or goddesses for different things. As an example, there was a god for the worship of the sun and one for the worship of the moon, and they weren't the only ones who believed this. Worship of the sun and the moon was imported from Babylonia, and besides the chief gods, they had lesser ones also. Their celebrations, if you think about it, are not that dissimilar from today. Changing seasons, harvest seasons and so on were celebrated with boisterousness, hilarity, dancing, drinking and orgies. Magic and sorcery were the accepted pattern of life. Witchery and the fear of demons were rampant. Children were offered by parents as human sacrifices."

I gasped.

"Yes, human sacrifices and depravity was a way of life," Naomi continued. "And into this atmosphere, Abram, the light of the Jewish nation and the world was born to parents who worshipped and sold idols. He was completely surrounded by idolaters."

Naomi had a flair for dramatics and as she continued, I was able to visualize everything clearly. She made ancient history seem contemporary, and I felt as if I were living through it; as if I personally had been present during this era. I thanked her before I left for giving me her time, and we talked about meeting again in the future.

As soon as I arrived in my room, I threw my coat on the bed; a move that I knew would irritate my mother, but I felt I had to work quickly. I was keyed up with feverish excitement.

I had had a dream since I was a little girl. Some day, I would be an author. I would write great books which would be read with enthusiasm by the young. I realize that dreams without the work remain just dreams. Now would be the best time to begin, while Naomi's words were still freshly imprinted in my mind. I could write a chapter here and there, not necessarily in any specific order, and put it all together at some future time. Besides, memory can become an elusive agent, and writing would help me remember and clarify for myself what she taught me. Who knows, I thought, perhaps someday it would be material for a book. I would call it *My Life* by Marian Asher or perhaps, *My Search*. I took a pencil and pad, noted the poem I had written previously, *The Mad Escapist*, turned over the page and wrote a story.

I awoke with a start. My sleep had been a deep one so I felt groggy and disoriented. I thought back to the previous day. It was the beginning of a new era in my life. I was treated as an adult and permitted to attend the special services.

I'll never forget the sight of King Nimrod. He had a cold smile. I can still see his eyes and the expression in them, so cruel and calculating. My father had explained to me that he was a divine power and we must bow down to him.

I was thrilled at the laughter, dancing and singing. The excitement stimulated me as did the constant chanting, chanting and chanting. I couldn't grasp the words, but the rhythm was intoxicating. I searched the faces around me and saw my reaction mirrored in them.

The chanting had begun softly and then it became louder and then still louder. The rhythm was continuous, and the multitudes were bowing in unison. It reached a crescendo, and I felt as if my ears would burst. And then, suddenly . . . silence. The silence was deafening after all that noise.

I looked around to see what would happen next. Everyone turned to the right, so I also turned to the right. A little boy was held firmly by his parents. The parents prostrated themselves in front of the king and pulled the little boy down with them. I was fascinated at the mass of faces around me and the aura of exhilaration and anticipation in everyone's expression.

"Eeeeeeeeee." The little boy's blood curdling scream tore through me. I had to suffocate the scream that rose in my throat at the sight and sounds that filled the huge hall. I couldn't believe it . . . I just couldn't believe how happy everyone looked at the terrible sight of the little boy thrown into the fire by his parents.

I thought that perhaps the king would issue orders to pull him out, but he had such a look of gloating and satisfaction that I shuddered.

Murderers! Murderers! Cold-blooded murderers! I wanted to yell it at the top of my lungs, but to whom? The frenzy which had been there and the chanting were gone. In its place, they looked placid, relaxed.

Will I too eventually also grow to accept this way of appeasing the gods? I must. I dare not think differently from everyone.

I got out of bed and tried to focus upon what had awakened me. I tried to forget yesterday and think only of today. I heard the murmur of voices, words. King Nimrod, Terach and Abram. I couldn't connect anything into a complete sentence.

I dressed quickly and ran outside. There was an obese, pompous man standing next to my father. His thin, cruel mouth appeared incongruous and belied his girth. I heard words like "he smashed them and created havoc," but I couldn't hear more.

Wherever I focused my eyes, I was able to see small knots of people in conversation. Something terrible had befallen Terach, who was one of the most honored noblemen at the court and the seller of idols. He had left his son Abram in charge of the idol gods. The son had discouraged all customers from making a purchase. He had asked a customer how old he was. When the customer answered that he was fifty years old, Abram retorted, "Isn't a man of fifty years old ashamed to worship an idol that is one day old? My father just made it the previous day." If that wasn't enough, Abram brought food to the room containing the idols. He smashed all the idols except the largest one. When he finished, he put the hammer in the hand of the one remaining idol.

"What happened . . . oh my, what happened?" Terach asked.

His son answered that the small idols had dared to eat before the large one, and the large idol became angered by their lack of manners and shattered them all.

His father raged at him and accused him of being a liar and an upstart. He said that the idols were not alive and could not have done that.

"After all," he said, "they can't eat, talk or move."

"In that case," the young Abram asked his father, "why do you worship them?"

Terach was so angered by his son and so frustrated that he complained to the king. Today was the big day. The king was going to have Abram brought to him for punishment.

Now I understood why everyone was excited. They wanted to see how the king would handle the situation. There was great enthusiasm in my house. My father was one of the chosen few to be permitted in the palace. I pleaded with him to take me, and reluctantly, he agreed.

My eyes absorbed everything. I didn't know where to look first. The palace was beautiful. The king looked awesome sitting on his high throne.

"Are you Abram, the son of Terach?" the king demanded "Did you destroy the gods?"

There was no fear in the young man's voice. "Yes."

"Don't you know I am the master of all creation," said the king. "Everything obeys me, even the sun, moon and stars. Bow down to me and worship me and my underlings. Bow!"

Abram did not bow.

"Don't you believe I am a god, as are the sun, moon and stars?" the king asked him.

"There was a time when I did," Abram replied. "I thought that maybe the sun was a god and there was nothing greater. After all, it is because of the sun's warmth and light that the world exists. So I prayed to the sun. Then, along came the night, and the sun disappeared. Perhaps the moon and the stars were divine? But then came daylight, and the sun reappeared. I then thought I should worship the earth. It is the earth's products that sustain us. But I soon realized the earth could not be god, because it cannot produce without rain. You see, each and every process has a purpose, and sometimes, they even have multiple purposes."

"Since I control all the things you have spoken about, then you have to worship me," the king stated.

"There was a time I might have considered that," said Abram, "but you require food. No mortal can live without sustenance which is produced in the earth. The soil cannot produce without rain and rain depends on the wind and the clouds. How can I worship you? You are mortal. You must eat in order to survive. Your body needs nutrition. No! There is a Higher Being."

"Enough! Enough!" the king exclaimed. "How dare you!"

"Traitor! Traitor!" the people shouted.

The king's face turned purple in anger.

"Imprisonment," he said.

The years passed rapidly for me. I married and became the mother of a daughter. Forgotten was that young boy languishing in prison and his heretic thoughts. But today there was excitement in the air. The rush was on to witness the spectacle . . . the entertainment of the century. How would the king handle Abram's refusal once again to acclaim him a god and to bow down to him?

Oh no! He is to be thrown into the fire for his sacrilegious remarks. I tried to harden myself not to cry. It was a poignant scene, pregnant with emotion. Amatala, Abram's mother, pleaded with her son, "Bow down, my son. Bow down just once. That is all you have to do. Please, dear child, so you can be saved from the flames." But the stubborn young man refused.

I looked at the fire. The flames were growing hotter and hotter. The red tongues were licking the edges. I could almost feel the heat scorch my face and sear my nostrils. I could actually taste its acridity. I heard the roar of anticipated pleasure from the crowd.

I flinched. I couldn't watch. I hid my eyes behind my hands, but that didn't help. I ran out. I ran away as fast as my legs could carry me. I had heard and seen enough. I know that the King is correct in everything he does but . . .

Three days later, I saw my father. Or was it my father? He frightened me. He moved his lips, but there was no sound.

Finally, in a low throated, fearful cry, he said, "He lives. He lives."

I stared at him. I didn't understand.

"Yes. He lives. Three days and three nights in that roaring inferno, and he walked out alive."

"There is a G-d," I said to my father. "Abram is right. I knew he made sense. I must know more about this G-d, the Lord of the Universe of whom he spoke. I must know about this Hashem who he felt was more important than his own life." These things I told my father, and I felt the words floating in the air in the early morning breeze.

I stopped writing. My hand was tired, and I sat back to review what I had written. I wondered whether it was really possible people could believe a piece of wood or a human being was God. I knew God had created man, and therefore, things could really be simple. But man is forever seeking the complicated. Philosophies become so involved in a maze of theories that they often miss the simplicity of the point; just as a house does not evolve from nothing, this beautiful edifice of our universe also needed a Master Builder.

I thought about Carol's brother Michael, an all American boy, a product of an American household and schooling. His disappearance and police involvement came back to me. Was it foul play, or was he just another runaway?

Months passed and there was no word and then, just a short time before my grandfather's death . . . My thoughts stopped. I seemed to think of events and time as occuring before or after my grandfather's death. It happened when Janet and I were in Carol's house. The bell rang. I recalled the conversation as if it had occurred today.

"Mr. Young, please."

"Dad, there is a policeman here to see you," Carol called to her father. She turned to the policeman.

"Can I help you?" she said.

"Can we come in?"

Sudddenly, Carol let out a scream. "Michael!"

I ran to the door. I felt Janet beside me. There was a tall boy standing next to the policeman. The boy's head was shaven. He wore odd clothing, and there were sandals on his feet and no socks.

"Carol? What seems to be the problem?" Mr. Young came to the door.

"We found him soliciting in the streets," the policeman answered. "He is part of one of those movements. Although he looks somewhat different, I detected a resemblance to the picture at the Missing Persons Bureau. I brought him here for your positive identification." In a soft, gentle voice, the officer added, "I'm sorry, Mr. Young, but he didn't want me to bring him home. He said he doesn't live here, that he now lives with his real family."

Tears glistened in Mr. Young's eyes. He raised his hand and in a soft, pleading voice asked, "Michael . . . why? Please excuse me, officer. Do come in," he added.

Mrs. Young ran over.

"Mikey!" She hugged him. He pulled away.

"You are not my family. You are not my parents."

"Mikey," she cried. "It's me. Mommy. This is Daddy."

Robot-like, he answered, "You are not my mother. You are not my father. You are not my family."

"Please, Mikey," she cried.

"You are not my mother," he repeated. "You are not my father. You are not my family."

Carol tried. "Mikey, it's me. Your sister."

"You are not my mother," Michael repeated. "You are not my father. You are not my family. My family is not here. I want to go back to my family."

"We really can't hold him," the policeman said. "He is over twenty-one."

Michael stared straight ahead as if we were talking about someone

39

not in the room when Mr. Young asked, "What has happened to him?"

The policeman looked pityingly at the Youngs.

"Mr. Young, our religions might differ but in one thing, we can agree," he said. "The cults have claws, and they grasp and hold. Children who have something to believe in have the resistance to fight. These cults are very experienced. They are all over the college campusus. When youth do not have a religious upbringing, they find their lives empty. They search for something to cling to. Your son found it in this movement. Other children find it in other movements or forms of escapism. I'm sorry for your son but even sorrier for you, the parents."

Although my sheltered room was warm and cozy, I shuddered as I thought about Carol's brother. I remembered Janet telling me that some cults actually worship the cow. If, in this day and age, there are people who still believe in this form of idol worship, it is not difficult to visualize that there were people who held the beliefs of those unfortunate heretics during Abram's time, until Abram brought light to a dark world.

chapter six

I have no sister or brother. Perhaps that is why Janet and I were so close. Sometimes, I felt she was my alter ego. Many times we'd start a sentence and, realizing we were actually going to say the same thing, break out in laughter.

I knew my parents had wanted more children. In fact, I was considered a "miracle baby." I recall lying on the couch one evening, listening to the murmur of adult voices in the kitchen. I had seen the purple number on my parents' arms, but the visitor frightened me. He had only the stub of an arm with a number in purple imprinted on it. I cried when I saw him and my mother put me to sleep on the couch. I listened closely from my bed to the adult conversation.

"How old were you when she was born?" the visitor had asked.

"Forty-two," my mother replied. "I'd given up hope completely. The doctors told me it was an impossibility."

"Then what happened?"

"I wasn't feeling well so I went to the doctor. He thought I had a tumor and said it had to be removed immediately."

"You must have been terribly frightened."

"You can imagine," she answered. "It brought everything back."

"Yes."

"As they were doing the preparations for the operation," my mother continued, "an intern put an instrument on my abdomen. He jumped back and ran to bring other doctors."

"You can imagine the thrill we had at her birth, our little tumor . . . a miracle!" my father added.

I often wondered what my mother was frightened of and what she meant by it bringing everything back. This may be one of the reasons my parents have always been oversolicitous of my welfare. It may also

41

account for our mutual dependency.

I once remarked to Janet that I wondered how it would be to grow up in a large family, surrounded by many brothers and sisters.

"Noisy," she laughingly answered.

It was also lonely growing up without friends. People my parents' age did not have small children. I found it difficult to communicate with children in school and in the neighborhood. I often wondered why. I now know it was because I was mature for my age, having grown up in an adult household, with my parents, my dolls and my books for friends.

When I was twelve years old, we moved to Far Rockaway from Riverdale, and it was then that the world first opened to me. I met Janet.

I found myself next to Janet when the teacher seated us alphabetically. Abikoff and Asher. Living just three blocks from each other helped to seal our friendship.

We are alike in everything. Even our physical appearance is similar except for the coloring of our eyes and hair. It wasn't until our mid-teens that our gangly legs and skinny bodies filled out. Janet had long blond hair and dark brown flashing eyes, a strong contrast to my black hair and blue eyes.

I heard the peal of the bell.

"I'll get it, Mommy," I said.

It was Janet.

"Let's go to my room, Janet," I said as I let her in. "I have so much to tell you."

She dropped on my bed. I watched as she looked around my room for the umpteenth time.

"I love your room, Marian," she said. "In a strange way, it is you."

I looked around the room trying to determine what Janet meant. The morning sunlight was slanting through a chink in the drawn blinds and curtains. It muted the bright yellow colors and gave the room a mellow softness. The wallpaper had yellow and brown marigolds with a blue butterfly perched on top of the flower. The butterflies looked ready to fly. The rug is my favorite. I love the rug. I believe it is because my mother and I had gone together to choose it. She had been like a young girl that day, bubbly and efflorescent, her sentences lyrical. We giggled like two young conspirators as we looked at the rows of carpeting. I felt guilty because of the expense I was putting my parents through, but my mother told me that parents always want their children to have more than they had. Today, two years later, I wonder why that had only material connotations. What about spiritual wealth?

I looked at the rug. The blue wool had a twist of a yellow strand in it. The combination of colors made it seem as if it had been made to order for this room. My furniture was white with blue handles. The yellow ruffled bedspread seemed to add to the total look, tying everything together.

"Okay, Marian. Talk. I can't leave you for a short time before you take off on mysterious excursions."

"I don't even know where to begin," I said. "I guess I'll start from the beginning. Remember my grandfather's funeral? Well, it wasn't until then that things started to fall into place. I had never thought about the conflict between my father and my grandfather. I knew it existed, but I just thought it was a generation gap."

"They *were* from different generations, Marian."

"No. It was much more than that. When the Rabbi spoke at the funeral, I began to realize this, and then when my father said *Kaddish*, I heard him read it in Hebrew. He spoke it fluently. I wondered why he had never taught it to me." I paused. "There was such a marked contrast between my father and grandfather. My grandfather was a very pious person, but my father was hostile to anything that touched religion. Why?"

"Did you ever ask your father?"

"I tried. I remember that now. At that time I was too young to understand. I recall asking him why grandfather wore a skullcap while he didn't. As young as I was, I realized that I had irritated him."

Janet looked puzzled. "And so?"

And then I blurted it out. "I can't find my place. I don't even know what to narrow in on. I was unhappy when we went to Coney Island, and I went to see Rabbi Isaacs and his granddaughter and I wrote this chapter—"

"Hold it," she said. "One thing at a time."

I told Janet about my meeting with Rabbi Isaacs and his granddaughter Naomi. I explained the reason for the chapter I had written.

She looked at me incredulously, unbelieving. "You're not getting religious at this late date, are you?"

"Don't be silly, Janet," I answered. "I only want a sense of identity. At least your parents have taught you to be proud you are a Jew, even though they didn't teach you ritual. My parents remind me of frightened animals who slink away with tails between their legs at the word Jew. Why? Why?"

"Don't be so melodramatic, Marian."

"Look, Janet. I know my father loved my grandfather, but for some reason, they could not communicate their feelings to each other. I know there was love between them. I saw it. But they also hurt each other. Each wanted the other to accept his way of life, and in trying to accomplish this, they were pulling each other apart. Some day, I hope to marry and have children. What if my children come to me and ask me questions? I don't want to turn away. I want answers."

"Come on, Marian. Don't make such a big deal out of it. Read books. I have."

"And what have you found?"

"Well, there's a piece by Mark Twain that was printed in *Harper's Magazine* a long time ago," she said. "It's quoted very often. I memorized it once. Would you like to hear it?"

"Of course I would," I replied.

"Well, I'm not sure I can get it word for word, but it goes something like this: If the statistics are right, the Jews contribute but one quarter of one percent of the human race. It suggests a nebulous dim puff of stardust lost in the blaze of the Milky Way. Properly, the Jew ought hardly to be heard of, but he is heard of, has always been heard of. He is as prominent on the planet as any other people and his importance is extravagantly out of proportion to the smallness of his bulk.

"His contributions to the world's list of great names in literature, science, art, music, finance, medicine and abstruse learning are very out of proportion to the weakness of his numbers. He has made a marvelous fight in this world in all ages, and has done it with his hands tied behind him. He could be vain of himself and be excused for it. The Egyptians, the Babylonians and the Persians rose, filled the planet with sound and splendor, then faded to dream stuff and passed away. The Greeks and the Romans followed and made a vast noise, and they are gone. Other peoples have sprung up and held their torch high for a time, but it burned out and they sit in twilight now, or have vanished.

"The Jew saw them all, survived them all and is now what he always was, exhibiting no decadence, no infirmities, no dulling of his alert and aggressive mind. All things are mortal but the Jew; all other forces pass, but he remains. What is the secret of his immortality?" She stopped to catch her breath. "Well, that's it. How do you like it?"

"What does it tell you?" I asked.

"It tells me I'm proud to be a Jew."

"So . . . and what is the secret of his immortality?" I asked.

Janet shrugged irritably and didn't answer.

"I want that answer," I insisted. "Inside myself, I feel my grandfather had it. I want it also! I want it for myself. I remember once when I was a little girl and we went to visit my grandfather. He was much younger then and had his own apartment. We didn't have school that week. It was during the December vacation.

"There was an interesting candelabra burning. It was on the window sill and had a place for eight candles. I was used to seeing trees in windows and not candelabras. 'Grandfather, what is that in your window?' I asked him. 'It's Chanukah, my child,' he said. 'Sit down while I tell you the story about the miracle of the oil.'

"But just then, my father walked into the room and didn't let him continue. Now that I'm grown, I understand why their eyes locked. It was quiet in the room. I don't know whether I imagined it or if I really heard the sputtering of the candles and if the room really darkened as they flickered. My mother broke the silence. 'Happy Chanukah, Papa,' she said. 'Here is a gift for you.' He smiled at her and said, 'Thank you. Come, let's sit down and have some Chanukah latkes. I made them myself.' The tension broke."

"What happened after that?" Janet asked.

"We spoke about nothing really important. When I kissed my grandfather goodbye, he gave me this locket which I still wear around my neck. He held my hand in his for a long time. I always felt his love for me, and at the same time, I was always aware of the love he and my father had for each other. But there was always that undercurrent of tension present. It's only now that I am able to realize what it was."

"Sounds like your grandfather was a very special person," Janet said. "Still, it must have been difficult for your parents and for you, too, to be caught in between."

"It was. I remember leaving my grandfather's house that evening. I was holding my father's hand. I looked up at the sky. The branches of the trees were bare of leaves but heavy with snow. Only fragments of the sky could be seen through the treetops. Every so often, I was able to catch a smattering of stars. I kept looking at one of the stars and tried to follow it with my eyes. 'Daddy,' I said. 'Don't the stars twinkle like grandpa's candles? Why don't we have the same candles too? Why does grandpa have them?' I was bubbling over with questions.

"I felt a stillness like the lowering of a thunderstorm. I looked up at my father, and the network of veins on his temple stood out, ropelike. Even in the dark, lit by the moonlight, I saw his face blanch. I remember that on this cool, quiet street, my father picked me up in his arms. We stood under the shadow of a tall tree. I could hear the stirring and rustling of the snow on the tree branches.

" 'Grandpa is an old man,' my father said. 'He lives in the past. Mommy, you and I are young. We live for today.' And then with a smile, he said, 'Why do we need candles? We have electric lights.' I was too young then to realize that my grandfather had candles and electric lights, too.

"There is another time that stands out vividly in my mind. This happened during the springtime. I don't remember whether it was the same year. Janet, have you ever experienced the sensation that you had forgotten something that happened in the past, and then because of circumstances, it comes back to you as vividly as if on a screen?"

"Yes, I know what you mean," Janet answered.

"Where was I? Oh yes. It was springtime then, and it was also a time that we didn't have school."

"Passover?" Janet asked.

I nodded.

"We were in the midst of dinner. There was a knock at the door. It was my grandfather. I still remember how happy I was. I was jumping with excitement. I grabbed his hand and led him over to the table. I'll never forget his face. It turned ashen. He seemed to age ten years. My mother rushed to the table and, in an unexpected flurry of activity, commenced to clean the table of the dishes, food and crumbs.

"My grandfather sat down on the chair. He did not talk. He just sat quietly and stroked his beard. There was no anger on his face. He rocked in his chair, forward and back, forward and back. When he finally spoke, his voice was sad, poignant with emotion.

"He said, 'Yankel, my son, if we don't eat the bread of affliction, Hashem has other ways to make us taste affliction. Good and evil are at war in a man's soul, in your soul. Please, I beg you, remember, you cannot escape from your past or from your people.' That was all."

"Whew, Marian, that was real heavy."

"I was only a child but I was uneasy. I searched my mother's face for some answers, for a feeling of security. The soft smile that had been pasted on her face as she rushed around in a flurry was wiped off. Her eyes filled with tears. She extended her hands. 'Please Jack, Please Papa,' she pleaded.

"Tap, tap, tap. My eyes were drawn to my father's hands. I was fascinated by his fingers on the tabletop. Tap, tap, tap, they went, the staccato sound beating rhythmically in the silence of the room. 'Papa, I'm an empty shell,' he finally said. 'I can't believe. Perhaps—' He shrugged his shoulders and put his head in his hands.

"I looked at my grandfather. He leaned back in his chair and closed his eyes. There was a smile on his face, and his voice was drowsy with remembered pleasure. 'You were such a lively boy, full of *chein*,' he said. 'I remember how you charmed whomever you met. And your voice—I can still hear it in its melodious childlike sweetness. *Tatte, ich vill dir freigen die feir kashes.* Yes, I remember it well.'

"My grandfather loosened his shirt collar and took a great gulp of air. His voice rose as it came out charged with emotion. 'Yankel! Listen to me! If you are sick, crippled, why make her sick? If you cannot believe, why close life to her?'

"He picked me up in his arms. There was such tenderness in his movements. He held me close and kissed me. As he left the house, he appeared to be in a daze. I heard his footsteps going down the steps. They had lost their springiness. They sounded like the footsteps of an old man."

"That's some story," said Janet. "Heavy. Heavy."

"Janet! I can't help it. I need answers. I must find them."

Janet looked at me searchingly.

"I don't understand you, Marian. Your grandfather was a religious Jew while your father rejected it. What is so difficult for you to grasp?"

"It's much more than that, Janet. It's hard for me to explain. I feel as if I'm caught in a long dark tunnel. I can't make peace with myself."

"Have you spoken to Neal?"

"No. He has his own problems right now," I said. "At first, he couldn't make up his mind which school he wanted to go to, and finally, when he decided, it was very late to register. School opens shortly, and he hasn't heard anything. So why add to his worries?"

There was no sound in my bedroom. Janet didn't say anything, and I couldn't. I felt totally drained. There was sympathy in Janet's voice when she spoke.

"How can I help you, Marian? You know I'm with you in whatever you do. I'm with you all the way."

I sighed with relief. I knew I needed a vessel to fill when my feelings would spill over. I knew I would need support as I began to dig.

"Thank you for always being here when I need you," I said. "Something tells me I'll be needing you a lot from now on."

When Janet left, I sat on my bed looking at the photograph on the mantle. It was a picture of Neal and me. I was smiling in the picture. I thought back to the day the picture was taken. It was at Carol's party on the night I met Neal. It was wonderful to have been so lighthearted. I wanted to hold on to the pleasure of a moment of nostalgia.

Marian, I said to myself, there are just a few days left before school starts. Be your cheerful old self. Once I made this decision, I felt carefree and relieved. As I prepared for bed, I realized I was singing.

I felt stimulated and needed a good book to help relax me so that I could fall asleep. I chose a soft, light melody to put on the record player and climbed into bed with a new book. Just as I was beginning to doze off, I had to jump out of bed to close the record player. The needle scratched and scratched. My euphoria vanished with the sweet melody.

chapter seven

I heard the door close, and then I heard Neal's voice. He was talking to my parents in the hallway. Wisps of conversation floated up to my room.

"Hi, Mr. and Mrs. Asher," he was saying. "How are you?"

"We're fine, Neal. You look dressed for a special occasion."

"I'll be down in a minute, Neal," I shouted as I put a few finishing touches to my hair.

I looked in the mirror. My white dress with the gold belt looked nice. Neal had asked me to dress up for this evening so I didn't wear my usual sporty attire.

As I walked down the steps, I listened to Neal's conversation with my parents. He really sounded in high spirits.

"Let's go," he said, excitement in his voice. "I feel exhilarated and alive. I have some good news to tell you."

"Tell me quickly, Neal."

"Nope," he teased. "I'm saving it for dinner."

Neal parked the car a block from the boardwalk. The boardwalk was crowded with people. I heard my heels make a click-clack noise as they hit the wooden slats. A sudden shift of the wind whipped the salt spray in my direction, and I tasted it on my lips. We stopped at Luigi's, and I showed my surprise.

"Luigi's, Neal? It is so expensive." Luigi's specialized in seafood platters. It was known as the exclusive place on the boardwalk, with its showy and ornate decor. It was not the usual spot for our crowd.

"Yes, Luigi's," Neal answered. "This is a special evening."

We followed the waiter to our table and sat down on the gilt chairs covered with maroon upholstery. He gave us each menus.

"Tell me, Neal," I pleaded. "Stop keeping me in suspense."

"Not until we finish our main course."

We made little conversation during the meal. I could feel Neal's excitement increasing as he finally blurted it out.

"They accepted me in Harvard Medical School."

"Neal, how wonderful," I cried. "I'm so happy for you. You wanted it so badly. It's your dream come true."

There were beads of perspiration on his forehead. When Neal finally spoke, his voice seemed to come out of a throat caked dry. He groped for words.

"Now comes the hard part," he said. "I have to leave for Boston immediately. Tomorrow, in fact. Kurt is there already. He also received his acceptance notice, and we have a lead on an apartment. Living quarters are at a premium there."

I drank the hot searing coffee. It was something for me to do so I didn't have to make any comment. I noticed that Neal also drank long and hard from his cup.

"Excuse me," the waiter said. "Can I get you something else?"

We shook our heads and watched as the waiter methodically cleared the table. There was a dour expression on his face. He wanted us to leave to accommodate the waiting line that had formed outside.

Neal left a tip on the table and paid the bill. We walked in silence. Finally, we found a secluded bench on the boardwalk and watched the sun. It was a ball of fire as it was setting, giving the water its own special halo.

"Marian," Neal said. "You know I hope we will eventually marry, but I promised my parents I wouldn't make any formal commitment until after I graduate from medical school. I cannot give you an engagement ring now, but you would make me very happy if you accept this charm as a sort of understanding between us."

"Thank you, Neal. I'm proud and happy to accept it."

I undid the chain on my neck and slipped it next to my grandfather's locket, unaware then of the irony of my grandfather's gift and Neal's gift next to each other.

We sat on the bench talking until it grew dark. I watched the water shimmering in the moonlight and the constant motion of the white capped waves as they kissed the shore. We could hear the murmur of voices, but they were distant enough for us to feel isolated, as if the bench was our private island.

"Marian, will you come to the airport to see me off?" asked Neal. "My parents will be going along, and it could be an informal way for you to meet them."

"If you are sure your parents won't mind."

"Good. We'll pick you up at noon."

"Have you ever travelled by plane before?" I asked.

"Many times," said Neal. "We've been to Europe a few times, and I went along when my father and mother flew to medical conventions."

"Do you like to fly?"

"Love it. How about you?" he asked.

"I have a fear of flying. Actually, I have really only had one experience in an airplane, but that was enough to last me a lifetime."

"What happened?" Neal asked curiously.

"I think I must have been about nine years old. My mother has an only brother who lives in Florida. I had never met him or any of my cousins. Their oldest child was going to be married, and we were to fly to Florida to attend the wedding. Neal, I looked forward to it for weeks. That was all I talked about—the excitement of the plane ride and meeting my cousins. I must have tried on the dress I was to wear to the wedding at least ten times. My calendar was full of pencil marks as I crossed out each day until that special one.

"The night before we were supposed to leave, I tossed and turned in bed. I couldn't sleep most of the night. I kept jumping out of bed to see whether it was daylight. Finally, dawn came. I watched the thin light of day, so narrow it barely broke through where the shade met the sill. I jumped out of bed and dressed rapidly. My parents were asleep so I stayed in my room but as soon as I heard their footsteps going softly down the steps, I was up and running.

" 'Good morning, merry sunshine,' my mother said. 'I wonder how much sleep you had last night?'

"I smiled in reply.

"My father was glued to the radio. 'Ssh,' he said. 'Let's listen to the weather report.'

" 'New York is preparing for another winter snowstorm . . .' the commentator was saying.

" 'Oh no,' my mother said. 'It won't interfere with our flight, will it?'

"The commentator continued, 'There is a possibility that air transportation may be discontinued. Do not take your automobiles. I repeat, do not take your automobiles. This storm threatens to be the worst one in a century. If you can, stay at home. If you have booked a flight, check with the airlines.'

"It seemed as if my father sighed with relief when he said, 'Well, I guess we won't be able to go.'

" 'Jack, I must go,' my mother replied. 'I haven't seen Meir since Marian was born. We have so few relatives. This is the first wedding in the family. We all shared so many tragedies together. Let us share in this happy occasion.'

" 'Then that's it,' my father said. 'We'll go. Get your things downstairs, Marian. We'll leave a little earlier, just in case getting to the airport is difficult.'

"Although the radio commentator had specifically asked people to stay home, traffic to the airport was dense. The streets were still slippery from the previous snowstorm, and the taxicab slid on the icy snow.

"The sky was darkening. Ominous clouds formed overhead. Traffic was a confusion of cars, each driver wanting to reach his destination before the storm would begin.

" 'Look! Airplanes!' I jumped up and down in the cab when we passed some hangars. It was the first time I had seen an airplane on the ground.

"My father paid the driver and we went inside. The airport terminal looked like a beehive. Thousands of passengers from delayed or cancelled flights were milling about. My father stopped someone and asked about our flight. The man pointed to a board.

" 'So far, so good,' he said. 'The flight has not been cancelled.'

"I pressed my nose against a large plate-glass window where I could watch the airplanes on the ground.

" 'Daddy! Look! The snow!'

"My father looked out the window and together, we watched the snow come pelting down with a fury.

" 'I'm going to check about our flight at the desk,' he told my mother. 'Stay here with our luggage.'

" 'We're lucky,' he said when he returned. 'Our flight was not cancelled because our route will be away from the storm. I'm going to check the baggage.'

"We boarded the large plane. My parents gave me the window seat. I looked out the tiny window. The sky continued to be dark and turbulent, and the snow kept falling against the sides of the airplane in masses.

"I was thrilled to button my seat belt but the stewardess' announcement of safety precautions frightened me.

" 'Why aren't we going, Mommy?' I asked. 'What's taking so long?'

" 'They have to remove the snow from the runway,' my mother replied. 'That's the path the plane has to travel down before it goes up in the air.'

"I watched the massive snow removal machines operating, and then the mighty plane started to taxi.

" 'We're off!' I said excitedly, jumping up and down as much as possible strapped in. 'We're off. We're off!'

"I peered out the window but couldn't see anything except a white haze. I remember having a blurred impression of some movement and hearing a harsh scraping sound just before the plane began its climb into the air.

" 'There will be some turbulence due to the weather conditions, but there is no reason for concern,' the stewardess assured us.

"I watched through the window as the lights of the airport receded and then became dimmer and dimmer.

"Suddenly, there was a violent, shimmying movement. It felt as if the plane would fall apart. I was frightened. 'Mommy, Daddy,' I screamed. I tried to get out of my chair but I was locked in. I gasped and felt paralyzed, unable to breathe. Neal, it was such a terrible feeling. My head was thrown to one side. There was a mist in front of my eyes from the impact. I felt my mother's hand reaching for me, but it did not give me comfort. I was terrified. I looked at her. Her face was chalk white. I heard a baby whimper and my mother murmuring, 'Dear Lord, help us.'

"There was a sound like rushing wind as the plane maneuvered into a turn and circled the airport. The lights of the airport were barely visible through the window. I bent forward to see my father in his aisle seat but my seat belt did not give enough. The economy class section was filled to capacity and the narrow seats were made even more uncomfortable by the lurching of the plane. The darkness in the plane did not help morale. It gave everything a macabre effect.

"What can I tell you, Neal. We first realized what a miraculous landing we had gone through when we saw the fire trucks and ambulances lined up on either side of the plane."

"So I guess you didn't make the wedding?" Neal asked.

"That's right," I said. "And it was my only experience with flying."

"Did your mother ever get to see her brother or his family?"

"Yes, a few times but she never took me along. My father and I stayed home. I never met my aunt, uncle or cousins." I felt my forehead crinkle. "In fact, we never even wrote to each other. I wonder why?"

The silence between us became impregnable. Now there was a problem that Neal and I had to face together, and Neal revealed an uncanny sense of knowing what was flowing through my mind.

"I'll be home in December," he said as if to reassure himself as well as me. "The time will pass quickly. We'll write."

To change the tone of our conversation, I asked Neal to describe his parents to me.

"Well, my mother is very elegant looking," he said. "She has black hair which she wears pulled back sleekly into a soft chignon. The society pages describe her as having aristocratic features. In the words of one of the write-ups, 'Mrs. Brennan carries herself in a manner that bespeaks monied gentility.' " Neal laughed. "To tell you the truth, she is a little bit of a snob."

"Are her parents, your grandparents, alive?"

"No. My grandparents from both sides are dead."

"Do you have uncles and aunts?"

"There is a maternal great aunt whom I love," said Neal. "Some people resent it, but I love the fact that she is outspoken. You know exactly where you stand with her. Now, my Uncle Nickie is another story. He is my father's brother, and the black sheep in the family. I call him Uncle B, because he reminds me of a butterfly. He flits from wife to wife. I can't keep track of how many he has had. At one time he was a very successful surgeon. You've heard the expression that the operation was a success but the patient died. Well, that was Uncle Nickie. He was tormented by it for years. Finally, he left medicine and used the millions he had made and inherited to help him become the dapper, debonair, mindless society boy you see today."

"Interesting," I said. "Wait. You didn't describe your father."

Neal paused. It was obvious he was trying to pull his thoughts together.

"He's difficult to describe. No . . . not his looks. He has iron-gray hair and is considered a very handsome man. It is not that but you see . . . he is more of a physical person than a mental one. Actually, he was a tennis star when my mother met him. I guess he felt overshadowed by my grandfather's medical success, and at that time, Nickie was well known so my father steered clear of the medical profession. When my grandfather died, my father was twenty-two years old and totally involved in sports." Neal stopped talking, and I saw it was difficult for him to express himself. "I guess you could say my mother made him a doctor. She had the money and managed the connections."

"Is he happy with it now?"

"Yes. I'm sure he is."

"You know my parents are not wealthy, Neal. I'm not crying poverty, but we have a totally different life style. Do you think your parents would have objections?"

"Don't be silly, Marian. Once they meet you, I know they'll admire your qualities as much as I do."

We got up and walked to the car. The boardwalk was full of a motley mass of teenagers. Faded blue jeans and bare feet in ragged white sneakers seemed to be the mode of dress. Hand-held radios and tape recorders blared their music. Conversation was impossible.

The trip home went quickly. When we arrived, we didn't find parking in front of the house and had to circle the block and park on the corner. We walked the narrow streets slowly, passing the well-lit manicured lawns and making ridiculous conversation, trying to prolong the evening. With a feeling of emptiness and with a sinking heart, I wished him a good night, then reluctantly, I went into the house.

My parents were sitting in the living room when I came in. I showed them the charm Neal had given me. My father looked pleased, particularly so because he had previously voiced his satisfaction that Neal was going to be a doctor and that Neal's father was one. My mother's expression was inscrutable.

I went up to my room, a room that held both the comfort of solitude and the frustration of loneliness.

chapter eight

I t was five minutes before noon when I heard the melodious tune that Neal's horn played. I ran out to the car before Neal even had time to get out of the driver's seat. He opened the back door and introduced me.

"Mom, Dad, this is Marian."

"How do you do?" I answered.

Neal opened the front door for me and I sat down. There wasn't much conversation with Neal's parents on the way to the airport.

Neal parked the car in the parking lot and handed the keys and registration to his father. We walked in pairs into the airport. The trip was shorter than Neal had anticipated, and we had time to keep Neal company until his takeoff time.

Neal's description of his parents proved to be accurate. His mother's hands were white and delicate with long, tapered fingernails. She held a cigarette loosely between her fingers. I was to find out that this was her constant pose as she was an incessant smoker, but no description could convey the coldness of her blue eyes set above her high cheekbones or the chill I felt as she looked down at me from her patrician nose.

"Now that we are seated, I must tell you that I am really glad to meet you, Marian," she said. "Neal has told me quite a bit about you. Why don't you tell me something about yourself?" Although her words sounded warm, I had a feeling of an instantaneous dislike of me. Her social poise however, was so well cultivated that she managed to mask it.

"Well, I'm an only child and, as you know, we live in Far Rockaway."

"Where were you born and where were your parents born?"

"I was born in New York. Both my parents are from Poland."

There was a restlessness about her and she constantly crossed and uncrossed her legs. She seemed ill at ease in her conversation with me. Dr. Brennan took over.

"What does your father do for a living?" he asked.

"He has an electrical appliance business."

"When did he come to America? What is his educational background? Does he have any brothers or sisters?" Between the two of them, I was pelted with question after question.

"Hold it," Neal said. "You're making Marian feel as if she is being interrogated. Leave her alone." And he smiled as if it was all a great big joke.

Neal's description of his father was also accurate. He was a tall, heavy-set man with a few patches of grizzled gray hair, interspersed with black. He had a persistent habit of absently having his fingers wander through his thick short hair. Neal had a strong physical and facial resemblance to his father, but Neal's eyes were warm and kind.

I felt relief when the announcement came over the loudspeaker that it was time to board the plane. Neal bade his parents goodbye.

"Remember, Marian," he said. "Write."

With a wave of his hand, he was gone.

I sat in the back of the car, and Dr. and Mrs. Brennan sat in the front. Mrs. Brennan asked me what my plans were, and I told her I was starting college. There was little conversation, and we were soon in front of my house.

I invited Dr. and Mrs. Brennan in for some coffee and cake.

"My mother makes a very special apple pie," I said. "Please come in and have some coffee and pie with us."

"No, thank you," Dr. Brennan said. "We have to get home. By the way, the name Asher, what nationality is it?"

"Jewish," I answered.

"Does Neal know?" Mrs. Brennan asked.

"We've never discussed it, but I'm sure he does."

As the car drove away, Neal's parents were not aware that the open window and the breeze carried their words back to me.

"Jewish! The match is preposterous."

The puzzlement I had felt at Neal's parents behavior and dislike towards me changed to a vague feeling of uneasiness. They had calmly stripped me of my self-esteem.

My hands were shaking so much from the tension that I found myself fumbling in my pocketbook for the keys. My parents must have been listening for the car because my father opened the door before I could find the keys.

He craned his neck to look over my shoulder. His eyes searched in back of me. I pulled my eyes away from the disappointment I saw on his face when he realized that Dr. and Mrs. Brennan were not there. I had to control my tears when I saw the table set in the dining room with my mother's best China cups and silverware and her famous apple pie in the center.

My mother misunderstood my tears.

"The time will pass quickly," she consoled me, "and Neal will be home for midwinter vacation. Don't look so disappointed. You knew he would have to leave."

"No, Mom. It's not Neal's leaving that disturbed me. I expected it to happen sooner or later. It was his parent's rejection of me. They didn't give me a chance."

"Marian," my mother explained. "I can understand his parents. They did not want him to become interested in a girl as long as he was still attending school."

"No." I shook my head. "It's not that. I don't think they would have felt like this about any other girl. It has to do with the fact that I'm Jewish."

My mother dropped the plate she was putting away and quickly spun around. She looked anxiously at my father. His shoulders sagged as he walked slowly to the window overlooking the garden, and stared unseeingly outside. The only sound in the room was the faint, soft creaking of the floorboard as he shifted from one foot to the other.

"It follows us where we go. There is no escape," he said as he put his hands to his face. If I didn't know better, I would have thought he was silently crying.

chapter nine

I thought time would pass slowly after Neal left, but surprisingly, it passed quickly. School was such a delightfully new experience. There was prestige in being a "college girl." Janet and I managed to take English and Philosophy of Education together. Our paths separated during Creative Writing, but we were together again for Secondary Education.

I was pleased with school, but I was very disappointed with many of our classmates. It seemed there were few students really interested in the educational part of college. Most were attending college for the social aspect. Others attended just to accumulate credit. Many times, I felt there was a conspiracy not to learn. The professor started his lecture, a student would ask something not pertaining to the curriculum and a discussion would ensue which would consume the rest of the period.

"I just don't understand," I remarked to Janet. "If these kids are not interested, why do they go to college?"

"You said some of it yourself. They go for social reasons and because it is the thing to do. There is also parental pressure, because parents feel they've failed their children if they don't send them to college. Unfortunately, the business world courts the college graduates with promises of good positions and prospects for advancement. Can you see a school hiring a teacher without a college education?"

I laughed. "I had plenty of teachers through my years of schooling who were incompetent, and they all had college degrees. I don't think you can be taught to be proficient in teaching. You can learn skills and formal methods, but the actual spark has to be within you. When you stand in front of the class and a discipline problem arises, what do you do? No one can train you to handle each and every incident. It is then that you sink or swim."

"That reminds me of something cute," said Janet. "Listen. A college professor was saved from a shipwrecked boat by an illiterate sailor who made a makeshift raft.

"The college professor asked the sailor, 'Can you read?' The sailor replied, 'Nope.' 'Oh my,' the college professor said. 'You lost half your life. Have you heard any quotations of any philosophers?' 'Nope,' the sailor answered, 'and before you say anything further, let me ask you a question. Can you swim?' 'No,' answered the college professor. 'Well,' the sailor drawled. 'We just sprung a leak. I guess you lost your whole life.' "

"It's true," I said, laughing. "We really have to accept the fact that a person can be competent, intelligent and creative even without a formal education. So . . . why are we going?"

"So . . . why are you going?" she countered.

"I like saying that I go to college," I said. "It means a lot to my parents. And I think Neal would feel I'm not with it if I didn't. And as for his parents, oh my! I don't even want to think what they would say. Sometimes I wonder why a doctor needs to learn liberal arts. Is it to make him a well rounded individual? If I had to have surgery, I wouldn't care if the doctor had a taste for a piece of Mozart or could recognize a Rembrandt. All I would be interested in is that he should know how to hold that knife and perform surgery expertly."

Janet, who was very good at mimicry, gave an imitation of a doctor painting a portrait as he was doing an operation.

"Brush . . . I mean scalpel. Paint the area henna. Oh, I mean with antiseptic."

I laughed. "Okay. Let's get serious. Do you think high school prepared you for college?"

"Prepared me!? I think the total aim of high school was a preparatory course for college. I pity the kids who went through high school and did not want to go to college. Most of their education was geared to prepare them for something they never really wanted in the first place." Janet looked thoughtful. "Sometimes I wonder what education really is and who educates? Who are the educators? It seems we are brainwashed by the authors of textbooks who teach us what they feel is important. It is they who determine what we should believe in and they even twist history around."

"What do you mean?"

"I remember," Janet continued, "how upset my father was when we learned about the Dark Ages engulfing Europe. The history book left us with the impression that all cultures and civilizations were intellectually at a much lower level than in the days of ancient Greece or Rome, but my father said that the books did not mention that for the Jewish nation it really was a glorious intellectual time. And my father pointed out to me that there really are two sides to everything. We think of the American Revolution as heroic; others feel that America was actually made up of a bunch of discontented colonists who took advantage of a European war to free themselves of taxation."

"I think that one of the things I would teach my students when I become a teacher is to keep an open mind and not accept every new educational theory, because what is accepted today might be considered ridiculous in the future."

"Hear ye! Hear ye!" Janet said. "But really you are right. I know what you mean. Did you see how many kids in college can hardly read or do math? They had to set up special programs of tutoring. Oh, here's our stop. Call me or I'll call you. Hope you have a letter from Neal."

I got off the bus and ran up the stairs to my house.

"Hi, Mom," I called as I entered the house.

"How was school today?" she asked.

"Interesting. How was your day? Any mail?"

My mother smiled and said, "I was waiting for that million dollar question. There are two letters on your dresser top."

I ran upstairs quickly. I was breathless when I reached my room. There was a letter from Neal and one in an unfamiliar feminine handwriting. I turned it over. It was from Naomi.

Although Neal had called twice since he left New York for Boston, this was the first letter I'd received in the three weeks since he had gone. With excited anticipation, I tore open the envelope.

September 21

Dear Marian,

It is really very difficult to talk on the telephone. When I call from the apartment, Kurt or Jeffrey are usually there. If I call from the outside, it is not that convenient, so if I sound a little stilted or if my answers or questions are worded somewhat discreetly, you'll understand why.

It was good to hear your voice on the phone. I guess things went okay with my parents. I hope you like them as much as they like you.

When I arrived in Boston, Kurt, who had arrived before me, met me at the airport as we had planned. He explained the difficulty in finding an apartment and how fortunate we were to be able to get one.

"We were lucky," he said, "because I had gone to the newspaper office for the paper as soon as it was off the press and followed through on every ad immediately."

At first, I wondered why he made such a big fuss, but now, after being here for a while, I realize the problems involved in getting apartments so I can understand his pride in this accomplishment.

It's a comfortable apartment. There are five rooms. Oh, I forgot to tell you, the apartment really belongs to a fellow named Jeffrey. When we were driving from the airport to the apartment, I had asked Kurt to describe this fellow. Kurt answered me that he was slightly odd, like all people of his race. I couldn't imagine what kind of beast we would be rooming with. But he is really a nice, quiet guy who comes from the West Side of New York. You know Kurt can be nuts sometimes. He pointed to his head as he described Jeffrey and said he had special plans for him. Well, Kurt is a kibitzer and has to be taken with a grain of salt.

Back to the apartment. I have one bedroom, Kurt and Jeffrey each have their own room and there is a living room and an eat-in kitchen.

School is hard, hard, hard. We are really packed with work.

How are your parents? Janet? School?

Write soon.

Neal

I opened the other letter. It was short.

Dear Marian,

I am writing this letter and hope I have the courage to mail it.

It is a sultry hot day. The sky was gray a half hour ago, but now the rays of the sun have broken through the mists of the sky, lending a glow to everything. It reminded me of you. The rays of warmth are

beginning to penetrate, adding life where once was darkness.
I am here whenever you need me.

Sincerely,
Naomi

I pulled open the blind and looked out. A restless breeze rustled the branches, and I watched as a small gray squirrel scurried up the tree. He looked fearful and in an urgent rush to escape. I felt a kinship with the squirrel.

My feelings were a curious mixture. I was glad to hear from Naomi but hesitant about seeing her again. To continue to see her would be a lonely road with no return. I wanted to tread only familiar pathways.

"Marian, dear." My mother's voice broke into my reverie. "Dinner. Dad is home."

I was glad my father was home a little earlier this evening. I wanted so to cheer him up. I didn't know whether it was the intense heat of this particular summer that made his movements so languid or a moroseness due to my grandfather's death. Had it all changed with the incident with Neal's parents? Was he feeling ill? It was difficult to go back in time and pinpoint exactly when it had started.

"Hi, Dad. How was your day? I received a letter from Neal," I blurted out all in the same breath.

My father's face brightened. Later, as we sipped our coffee after dinner, he really seemed to be his old self.

"What did Naomi write?" my mother asked.

"Wait. I'll get the letter," I answered and ran upstairs to my room.

"Who is Naomi?" I heard my father ask.

"Remember? Rabbi Isaacs' granddaughter."

I read the letter to my parents.

"You're not going to pursue this friendship, are you?" my father asked. "You really are worlds apart."

"I like her," I said. "She is a terrific person, but I have loads of work. I don't think I could manage the time."

I thought my father looked relieved. I couldn't say the same for myself. I felt an insistent urge pulling me towards Naomi, but I was using my workload as a good defensive barrier.

"Come, Marian," said my mother. "Let's finish the dishes and relax."

"Mom," I asked. "How did you meet Daddy?"

Her face lit up. "I met Aunt Leah, Daddy's sister," and then her face darkened as she added, "in the concentration camp. The most miserable years of our life brought us together. Actually, I think it was about a year before the war was over. They had closed her camp and moved everyone to our camp. Moved? What a euphemism. She came limping into the camp with bleeding feet. Her shoes had completely disintegrated on the long trek of miles and miles she had had to walk.

"We were both very young, taken at a time when we should have been experiencing girlish pleasures and conversations. We became old very young. We clung to each other and to our past lives as the only sanity in a world gone insane. I told her everything about my family, and she told me about her family. We did not know from day to day whether on the next day we would still be alive, but Leah insisted that her brother was just the perfect match for me and that she was sure one day we would marry. Can you imagine, Marian? We didn't know what the next minute would bring, and yet, she introduced me as her future sister-in-law."

She stopped talking, and I watched as painful memories flitted across her face.

"We went through so much together. The weariness penetrated our bodies and tried to invade our souls, but something kept us going, something kept us alive. And then the Americans came, and we were rescued."

She told it short and sweet, but her sigh told me that much had happened before the Americans rescued her.

"We were taken to a hospital to recover," she continued. "The Americans had found out for us that Uncle Meir was alive, but they weren't hopeful about the rest of the family. Leah had heard that her grandfather was in a hospital, but of Daddy, her brother, there was no news. Leah stopped everyone and asked for word of Yankel Asher from Galicia. Leah refused to lose hope; refused to give up. And then, like a storybook ending . . ."

My mother paused and couldn't continue.

"Please, Mommy," I pleaded. "Tell me the rest."

"Well, when we recuperated a little and some of our strength came back, the doctors recommended taking walks," she said. "At first, we had so little strength that half a city block would leave us exhausted and breathless, but little by little, we were able to increase the distance.

"Oh, I remember it clearly. Dawn had come with a crispness. It was a beautiful autumn day. We had risen early and watched the sun come up through our window. The field looked like a beautiful painting with lovely wild flowers nodding in the sun. Leah suggested we try to walk across the field. We walked though an ocean of grass, appreciating every minute of freedom, stopping every few minutes to breath the fresh, crisp air into our lungs.

"Suddenly, Leah stopped in her tracks. Her hand was on her chest, and her breath seemed suspended. It was as if a form of paralysis swept over her. Her mouth moved, but I heard no words.

"I was terrified. Poor Leah. My poor Leah. Her overworked, over-wrought nerves had not healed. 'Is it? Is it?' she shouted. I watched stupefied as she ran towards the stranger. I tell you, Marian, to this day I get chills when I picture that scene."

"It does seem like a scene out of fiction," I said. "What happened next?"

"I didn't realize how horrible Leah and I looked. The mind is an amazing organ that can forget at will. He also looked terrible, totally emaciated with the look of a hunted animal in his eyes. He hadn't eaten in days as he had been hiding in the forest. In the concentration camp, he had been on a starvation diet to begin with, and now, he was in such a weakened condition, he could hardly stand up."

"Did he recognize Aunt Leah?"

"Not at first. He looked at her with hostility and mistrust."

"Why was he in the forest?" I asked.

"Everything was done as a hoax by the Nazis. You went to death camps thinking you were going to work camps. You went to death thinking you were taking a shower, so when the Americans came to liberate the camps, this seemed just another hoax. Your father saw an opportunity and escaped."

"If that was the case," I asked, "then what made him finally come out of hiding? Was it the hunger?"

"No. I think he would have taken his chances in the forest. When Leah asked him, he answered that the world seemed to be standing still. There were no sounds of gunfire and no airplanes dropping bombs from overhead. 'I began to believe,' he said, 'that maybe they were really American soldiers.' He came out of hiding. And Marian, G-d led us to him. It was a miracle."

"Poor Daddy."

"But you know, Marian, your father was broken physically, but the Nazis did not break him spiritually or emotionally. He still maintained his fighting spirit. And that, my dear child, is how your father and I met."

"Please. Please tell me more," I begged when I realized this was to be the completion of the story.

"It took quite a while for your father to recover, just as it had taken most of us," my mother said. "It took months to grow flesh upon the skeletal body, months to heal, months to learn how to eat and to become a human being once again."

"What did you and Daddy have in common?"

"Marian, everyone who ever was in a concentration camp had something in common with the next person. You ask me what we had in common?" My mother paused and then said, "Hell. We had both lived through Hell. That was our common bond."

"What made you decide Daddy was the person you wanted to marry? Was it love at first sight?"

"My dear daughter, contrary to what your magazines and books tell you, that is not love."

"How about what I think I feel for Neal?"

"Marian, you just answered your own question by saying the word think."

"Then what made you marry Daddy?"

"I liked Leah."

"I don't believe it, Mom. Because you liked Leah, you married Daddy?"

"Almost, but not exactly as it sounds. You see, I liked Leah. She was compassionate and full of faith. There is a Jewish expression that an apple doesn't fall far from the tree. I felt that since your father came from the same stock, he couldn't be much different. I liked that. Leah told me stories about your grandfather. I was impressed with the kind of person he was. I felt I would find all this in your father."

"Did you, Mom? It is so difficult to know a person before you live with him. How can a person know so they don't make mistakes?"

"Well, let me put it this way. If your backgrounds are similar, your goals in life and interests are similar, and the person is of good character, you have a good chance of a happy marriage."

"Mom, is Aunt Leah like Grandfather, an observant Jew? All I know about her was that she had gone from Europe to Israel, while you and Daddy left Israel and came to America."

"Yes, she is."

"Then isn't it strange?" I asked. "Grandfather was religious and Aunt Leah is, but how come Daddy isn't?"

We had completed the dishes. Instead of seeking a seat and continuing the discussion, my mother opened the cabinets in the kitchen and moved things around. One of the things she did when angered or troubled was to attack the closets with a vengeance.

I knew she was loath to continue, but I was persistent. A hollowness inside me was tormenting me and tearing me apart.

She was on her knees, cleaning the cabinet under the sink. Slowly, she took out the scouring powder, the soap, the steel wool. Each item was handled delicately, like the finest crystal.

"Please, Mom," I insisted.

She looked dishevelled and dusty. There was a smudge on her face and a straggle of hair sticking out of her usually well-coiffured hairdo.

"It is too complicated to go into now, and maybe very difficult to understand."

"Was it the concentration camps?"

"The disillusionment that came afterwards were what caused his embitterment."

I looked puzzled. I could understand the concentration camps, but what could have happened afterwards?

I watched as my mother shook her head. "I'm sorry, Marian. I just can't go into it now. Besides, I think it is something for your father to explain, not me."

"Then tell me about yourself."

"What is it that you want to know?"

"I want to know about the kind of home you were brought up in and about Uncle Meir in Florida and about my cousins and why I have never met them or never write to them or anything?"

"Whew, hold it, Marian. One question at a time. Start over."

"Please come to my room, Mom, and let's talk."

Without any further discussion, I sat there and watched as my mother put each item back into the cabinet under the sink.

In order to go up to the bedrooms in our home, it is necessary to go through the living room. The staircase is on the side of the living room and leads upstairs. We had to walk past my father who was sitting in a chair in the living room, his head down, engrossed in a book. We walked silently up the staircase. I gave my mother a chair, and I sat down on the bed.

"Tell me about your family and the home you came from in Europe."

"We were four children," she began. "I was the youngest and Uncle Meir the eldest. There were two other children. Boys. They didn't make it through the war. I was born in a small, close-knit village. We attended each other's happy occasions and shared unfortunate happenings. My home wasn't rich, but it wasn't poor either. We had whatever we needed, and our house always had an open door and an open hand for whoever was in need. My father was a *shochet*."

"What's that?" I asked, puzzled.

"He slaughtered animals to make them kosher."

"I don't understand," I said.

"In order to make meat ritually fit for a Jew to eat, it has to be slaughtered in a special way established by Jewish law."

"Mom. We don't eat kosher. How come?"

My mother put her hands over her eyes and rubbed them as if she was very tired.

"It is a very, very long story, Marian, and something I'm not up to tonight."

"Do you feel okay?" I asked my mother. She had turned pale.

"Yes and no, Marian. Yes, in that there are things that are becoming clearer to me after so long, and no, because I just don't know what to do about it."

"Perhaps I can help. Tell me what is bothering you."

"Interesting, Marian. We are now going to reverse roles. You'll be the mother, and I'll be the daughter. I'm afraid I can't. Not yet."

"Please continue."

"When my brothers were little, a *melamed*, a teacher, used to come into the house to teach them. When they grew older, they went away to school, to a *Yeshivah*. That's a place of higher learning."

As she continued talking, I detected an intense and pathetic longing in her voice for things that had been.

"I remember going to sleep and waking up to the musical sing-song sounds of learning," she said. "Sometimes, I get such a strong yearning to hear it again. I feel torn inside, as if my heart will break."

"I understand what you mean, because I too sometimes feel like I'm being torn into a million pieces."

"You, Marian? You are too young to feel that way. Why, my darling?"

"I don't know what it means to be Jewish. I feel different, not belonging anywhere. Grandpa, my uncles and aunts, you and Daddy, all have different backgrounds than you've given me. Why? Why? Why?" I stamped my foot in anger.

"Because . . ." She hesitated, then shrugged her shoulders and continued. "Because your father felt that by escaping, he could help you avoid the trauma he himself had gone through."

"Well, as you can see, obviously he was wrong," I said. "You don't escape from life. Things have a habit of catching up. It has caught up to me now." And then I was pleading, "Help me. Can you help me? Should I go back to Naomi and find out more about Judaism? What should I do?"

With a deep sigh, my mother said, "What can I say to you, Marian? I know it would upset your father, but I also understand your need. The truth is that as your father's wife, I really cannot condone it, but as your mother, I cannot condemn you for searching to see if this is really what you want. But there is one thing I must tell you. You must realize that if you do go on, remember my words, you are threatening your relationship with Neal." I heard that sigh again, but this time I wasn't sure I heard her whispered words correctly. I thought she said, "I hope it does."

"What did you say?"

She pretended not to hear.

"At this point," she said, "you have never really had a Jewish identity. Actually, you are Jewish by birth only. I want you to be aware that there are risks involved if you go further."

"Please believe me, Mom. I'm not interested in changing my life or my way of living. I just want to understand some things that are puzzling me. No," I shook my head. "No! I definitely do not want to change or reconstruct my life in any way."

"Marian, all living changes us. All knowledge changes us. Every type of exposure makes a dent. Look what your grandfather's death opened up to you. Are you the same person you were the day before the funeral? Is your father the same person? Am I? No! You are wrong. If you go, you will change. I only want you to be prepared for it."

"Do you have any pictures of Grandfather and Grandmother?" I asked, changing the conversation.

She left the room and returned shortly with a picture in her hand. She gave it to me. It was a picture of a man and a woman. It reminded me of the picture I had seen on Sandy's dresser.

My mother took back the picture and held it in her hand with a delicacy and reverence. "My parents, your grandparents," she said.

This poignant, touching moment, this rare closeness my mother and I had achieved, was interrupted by a knock on the door. It was my father. I couldn't believe the change that came over my mother. She stood still, eyes fixed on the door. She held the picture behind her back, her face an image of guilt.

"What's going on here?" my father asked. "Girls' night out? You have a phone call, Marian."

"Thanks, Dad," I answered. "I'll be right down."

My mother put the picture under my quilt and then went out to join my father. I walked down behind my parents. Down the staircase we went, downward and downward, slowly bringing me back to today and reality.

It was Sandy on the phone. I invited her to my house for the weekend. I told her I would like her to meet my friends Janet and Carol. There was a slight hesitation before she answered.

"Marian, i don't think this is the time for me to leave the house for a weekend," she said. "Ovadiah has a bad cold and the baby is due soon. How about Sunday? This way I'll only be gone for the afternoon, and my parents know where they can reach me by telephone."

"Terrific, Sandy," I answered. I hung up and called Janet and Carol to make sure they would be available Sunday.

With the calls completed, I went back into the living room. My parents were sitting there, engrossed in their own activity. My father was reading his book again, and my mother was knitting. The click-clack of the needles was the only sound in the room.

My eyes were drawn towards my mother. Our eyes met. Hers were pleading. I understood the message. No discussions now in front of my father. The message traveled from mother to daughter. There was a bond between us which was stronger than the natural bond between mother and daughter.

"Who called?" she asked.

"It was Sandy. She's coming over Sunday afternoon. I also invited Janet and Carol. Okay?"

My mother gave me a grateful look and answered, "Certainly. Should I prepare lunch or just bake some cookies or a cake?"

"Perhaps just a light snack," I answered. "I'm going upstairs to do my homework. If you get a chance, come to my room. Okay?"

She didn't answer me. I understood her silence. It said: Pause. Moratorium. Not tonight.

I went up to my room and looked under the quilt. The picture was there. My eyes were drawn to them like a magnet to metal. My ancestors. My grandparents. My family.

I looked out the window. It was dusk outside. The familiar scene had an unfamiliarity about it, like a painting viewed for the first time. The sun was setting, and everything was edged in a reddish glow. The sun was dipping towards the west, and for the moment, I experienced surcease from the turmoil within me.

I went to my desk, took out Neal's letter and read it once again. I reread Naomi's letter. A sound in the street drew my attention. I looked out. A woman was walking hurriedly down the street, a small crying child in tow. The child tried to keep up with her mother by trotting along with the mother's long steps. When they reached the corner, the mother dropped a letter in the mailbox. The breeze and stillness of the evening carried the sound of the closing of the metal mailbox. The mother walked back slowly; the child skipping along by her side. The mother looked relieved. That's it, I decided. I would write to Aunt Leah and ask her opinion.

I took out a piece of paper and began writing.

Dear Aunt Leah,

I suppose you are quite surprised to hear from me. Frankly, I am surprised to be writing this letter. It is unfortunate that family doesn't get to know each other. Life is really so short and passes by so quickly. I am sorry for the years I did not get to know you. But really, I am not to blame. I wonder why you never wrote to me or why my parents never asked me to write to my aunt in Israel. Is it because we have different life styles?

I don't know how much you know about me so let me put you up-to-date. I am eighteen years old and in my first year of college. I'm going with a boy who is in his first year of medical school. His name is Neal. He is not Jewish.

Aunt Leah, it is really hard to write to someone I have never met. Things would be so much easier if I knew you. I wish I could have the opportunity to meet you. Just this evening, my mother told me how the two of you met and how she met my father.

I guess you are wondering why I decided to write now. I have a problem and need some advice.

At Grandfather's funeral, my eyes were opened to things I had been shielded from and blinded to all these years. I guess I should not use the word "blinded." It was there for me to see, but I wasn't mature enough to realize what I was seeing. I knew there was a major difference between Grandfather's way of life and my father's because they conflicted many times. These things were just a shadow in the recesses of my mind. But now I realize that Uncle Meir, my mother's brother, also shares the same beliefs as you and Grandfather.

Why, I ask myself, and what, I ask myself, made my parents take such a different path from their parents? And what bothers me most of all, why does my father try to erase that he was born a Jew? It is not natural. And, of course, therefore, he raised me without any tradition.

Dear Aunt Leah. I'm hoping you can give me answers. Although we don't know each other, somehow, lately, I feel a stronger kinship.

I met an interesting girl who is very knowledgeable about Jewish history. She would like to open doors for me, but I'm afraid it would cause my father great unhappiness. My mother has told me to do what I feel I have to do.

You are my father's sister. I know you do not want him to be hurt. You are also my aunt, and I know that whatever advice you give me will be what you feel is best for me also. Please, write soon and give me guidance. I am impatiently waiting for your answer.

Regards to Uncle Moshe.

> With love,
> Marian

P.S. Do you know Rabbi Isaacs? He presided at Grandfather's funeral. Would you know why he calls me Malka? I know that it was your mother's name. I really can't ask my father or mother.

I sealed the letter and put it in my purse. I would have to get the address tomorrow and sufficient postage for airmail.

I looked at the blue butterflies on my wallpaper and at their wings poised as if in flight.

No, I decided. I'm not running away from decisions. I'm facing them. I'm not a coward if I seek help. A coward is one who refuses to face his fear. A brave and honest person faces his inadequacies and looks for help.

I prepared for bed. My homework was forgotten. Totally exhausted, I climbed into bed. I took out the picture. The picture became dim and misty as my eyes filled with the tears that brimmed over. I went to sleep holding the picture under my pillow like a baby clutching a teddy bear, a security blanket, not wanting to let go.

chapter ten

The late September day came upon us with surprising reminders of the hot sultry summer that had just passed. The humidity and airlessness made breathing difficult. I couldn't believe autumn was just around the corner.

Janet and I met at the bus stop. I had looked forward to the ride on the air-conditioned bus, but unfortunately, the air conditioning was out of order. There was no breeze, and the open windows offered no relief. The congested bus made everyone quarrelsome. A fight over a seat was in progress as we boarded. I held tightly to a seat back as I found myself swaying to and fro at the whim of the bus. Just as the air was thick, the traffic took its cue and also thickened. The heat made the passengers bleary eyed. My eyes were droopy with drowsiness, but I forced myself to be alert. I managed to keep my balance, holding the back of a seat with one hand and my books with the other.

Finally, the crowd thinned, and we found seats. With a sigh of relief, I finally sat down. I felt so weary that for the first few minutes I just didn't want to talk. Soon, my natural gregariousness returned, and I told Janet what had transpired between my mother and me. I wanted Janet to really understand my mother, her feelings and longings and to share in my tumultuous emotions. I tried to paint a vivid picture for her.

"And you know what, Janet," I said. "My mother's father also had a long beard and resembled my other grandfather, and he wore a skull cap. I can't understand why the picture is not on display in our house. It bothers me. The only conclusion I reach is that my father's father was a presence here, an Orthodox man in the flesh, and that could not be avoided, but I guess what Marian didn't know about the others didn't matter." Even I was able to detect the irony and sarcasm in my own voice.

"Dirty Jews!"

At first, I thought it was only my imagination but I saw my horrified reaction mirrored in Janet's face. Was that remark made to us? Was it directed at Janet and me? I turned around and stared right into the eyes of two pimply faced, dungaree clad boys. It was obvious they had listened to our conversation and heard everything.

"Ignore them," Janet whispered. "It won't be the first time ethnic slurs are made against Jews."

I saw we had arrived at our destination. I pulled the cord for the buzzer to ring, and the bus stopped.

"Janet. Look!! They are getting off the bus. Oh no, I hope there is no trouble."

They stopped in front of us, blocking our way. When we moved to the right, they moved to the right. When we moved to the left, they moved to the left. The taller of the two went in back of us. I looked around for help. It was broad daylight and people were all around us, but no one came forward. No one saw anything adverse in their behavior.

"Please move," I said.

There was a smirk on his face as he continued to block our path. We tried to walk around him, but like an immoveable mountain, he was wherever we went.

"Hi, Jew girls," he said. "Going somewhere?"

"Get out of our way or I'll scream," Janet said.

Quickly and with animal cunning, Janet was shoved. As must have been preplanned, the one in front put his foot out and Janet fell forward.

With a loud "Ha, ha," they ran away, their gleeful laughter piercing our ears.

"Here, I'll help you up," I said as I dusted her skirt. "Are you hurt?"

"I'll live," Janet answered, biting her lower lip in pain.

As we collected her books, I said sarcastically, "I guess this is what is known as an anti-Semitic incident."

"I guess."

"But why?" I continued angrily. "We did nothing to harm them. We didn't even talk to them. Since Judaism is the father of all religions, we should get appreciation, not hatred."

"I guess they just can't accept the thought that we rejected their beliefs, that we are different," said Janet. "You know, Marian. I think insecurity may be at the root of anti-Semitism."

"It's weird," I said. "My mother said the concentration camps were Hell. Why? If we're supposed to be a civilized world and the Germans the symbol of culture, what happened? Don't people value a human being? But, you know, you're probably right. I guess that is why they try to convert us. To prove the validity of their own beliefs."

Janet laughed. "Now I'm beginning to understand why the Jews are known as the people of the book. They search into the depths. It's true. I really find it difficult to understand what incited these boys. What harm were we doing? All we did was talk."

"You know, Janet," I said. "Everything that has been happening lately seems to form a pattern for me, and the pieces all add up to finding out more about our source."

"There's the bell, Marian," Janet said as its clanging noise signified classes would begin. "Let's run."

On the way home later, we continued our conversation.

"My father was born in America," Janet said. "His parents came from Europe at a young age and married in America. Actually, the Second World War did not affect them or their relatives. My father is practically a Yankee."

"But your parents knew, I'm sure, what was happening to the Jews in Germany."

"People knew, but no one wanted to believe it. Look, Marian. Imagine yourself living in America and you hear about the man with the comic moustache and goose-step controlling the minds of the most educated, cultured nation of the world. Would you believe it? Would you believe that the best scientific minds of Germany, that cultured nation, would develop the best method of mass murder? After all, the twentieth century is known for its humanism as well as its technology.

"Marian, there is something my father taught me and I just can't understand some people because of it. My father fought in the Second World War. He had to go because he was drafted, but he said he would have gone anyway because he was one of the few who believed the rumors of the Nazi's plans for genocide. He felt it was the enemy of the Jews he was fighting."

"What is it you can't understand, Janet?"

"How can people buy German-made goods, Marian? During the war, afterwards and up to today, my father refuses to buy any German-made goods. Do you know what china dishes are made of?"

76

I thought for a while and then answered, "Earth, I think."

"That's right. The German china dishes people admire are made out of earth. They're eating their elegant meals on plates made of Jewish blood."

"You're crazy, Janet. How can dishes be made of blood?"

"Think about it. The earth in Germany ran with Jewish blood, and if china is made out of earth, then dishes made in Germany can have Jewish blood in it. Gory, isn't it?

"My father says," she continued, "that a nation that made lampshades of Jewish skin and soap of Jewish body fat should not receive a penny of my money."

Janet continued to shock me. "I don't understand, Janet."

"The Germans didn't waste anything," she answered sarcastically. "They really took the skin of our people and made it into lampshades, and they melted our bodies to make fat for soap."

I shivered. "Unbelievable. I can't believe it. I don't want to believe it. We are a cultured and educated people, not barbarians."

We walked in silence for a few minutes. Every direction my thoughts took carried me into pain. I couldn't understand the brutality dormant in human beings.

Somehow, Janet's words rang a bell. I remembered an incident at my grandfather's house.

"My grandfather was a soft spoken intellect," I recalled. "Once, when I was in his house, I heard him raging uncontrollably at a man sitting at his table. My grandfather used to buy material and buttons from this man for the suits he made at home. I was shocked.

" 'Grandpa, what's the matter?' I took his arm.

"He shook me loose and pointed his finger at the man. 'Go!! Get out of my house and never cross my doorstep to sell me buttons or material again.'

" 'Sit down,' my mother said. 'Calm yourself. What happened?'

" 'Did you see that . . . that . . . that.' He stuttered and couldn't complete the sentence. 'That man, that animal limps. Do you know why? Because he lost a leg in a Nazi concentration camp. He was one of a group of Jews chosen for a special mission for the German army. It was his job to walk through minefields. Only after the Jews were exposed did the Germans send dogs, who, of course, had more value than Jews. If both the Jew and the dog passed safely, it was considered safe for the army.

That was how this man lost his leg; it was blown off.' "

"But why was your grandfather so upset?"

"Because this man tried to sell him German made goods. When my grandfather asked how he could possibly do that, he answered, 'Business is business.' "

"It's a crazy world," Janet said. "Here is the turnoff for my house. Take care. See you."

As I walked the short distance to my house, I thought of what my parents had gone through. Although I was able to feel pain and compassion, I knew that living through something is much different from only visualizing it.

I quickened my pace. I wanted to see my mother, to hold her and show her how much I really cared.

"Hi, Mom," I called. "I'm home."

Silence. No answer. No response.

"Mom. Mom?" I raised my voice and then called again, "Mom, Mom."

I heard only the hollow echo of my voice as it returned to me. I opened the door to the basement. Perhaps she was doing laundry.

"Mom?"

No answer.

I ran up the staircase.

"Mom, Mom, where are you?" I cried plaintively.

The muted silence of an empty house greeted me. Reluctantly, I walked into my bedroom. I knew with certainty what I would find. I put my hand under my pillow. My hand met the silky smoothness of the sheet. The picture, of course, was gone. I had really known it all along.

It was a rare occasion that I would arrive home after school and not find my mother home. Today, she returned five minutes before my father. I was certain it had been planned by her. No questions from Marian. Under the external coverings of her makeup, I was able to discern that her face was colorless. While my father went upstairs to wash, I went into the kitchen to help my mother prepare supper. She seemed thousands of miles away. I watched as she fumbled about the kitchen, taking out the salt, then asking me, "Marian, did you see the salt? I'm sure I took it out." It was directly in front of her.

She dropped the pot. It hit the floor with a thud, the metallic sound breaking the silence of the house. I looked searchingly at my mother, but she avoided my gaze.

My father came into the kitchen, the fresh, clean smell of soap preceding him. He was bright and cheerful.

"Let me give you a hand," he said. "Did you go into the city to shop today?"

"It was such a hot day," my mother answered. "I went to relax and sit on the boardwalk and watch the water."

I needed no further explanation. One major thing my mother and I had in common was to utilize the therapeutic value of the ocean. There was something about the magnificence of the ocean, the wildness of the waves or, at other times, its soothing calm. The white, frothing bubbles as they hit the sand would give me a serenity I received in no other place. If I feel lonely or crowded, if I have nothing or too much to do, the ocean gives me a feeling of comfort and peace. I sit there for hours. I read or just meditate. The ocean always impresses me. I am enthralled by its magnificence. I like to watch the waves hit the edge of the sand, and then marvel how the water recedes.

With an effort, I pulled my mind to the present. My mother was disturbed. Her complacent lifestyle had been shattered. Her past was filled with too many submerged memories, and her future was insecure. She had run to the oceanside, hoping to find tranquility for her troubled soul.

My father, so innocent and insensitive at this time, was humming a song as he helped me set the table. He was completely removed from the drama being enacted.

I stared at the yellow-orange of the cantaloupe. Its color facetiously lent a festive look to the table. I couldn't talk. My father broke the silence.

"How is school?"

"So, so," I answered.

"What do you mean?" he asked.

"I'm not impressed."

"Why? It's a wonderful opportunity to learn. I wish I had had that opportunity."

"It really isn't what it is blown up to be. Maybe it will get better." I quickly stood up and returned to the kitchen.

While my mother served the soup, I was tempted to tell my parents about the incident with the two loathsome boys, but my father's reaction to Dr. Brennan's remarks about the Jews had caused him unhappiness. I didn't want to cause him further pain.

My mother looked tired. She seemed limp and weary.

"I'll take care of the dishes, Mom," I offered. "You look tired. Perhaps you want to go to bed?" I was warmed by her grateful look.

"Thanks, Marian. I think I'll take a bath and go to bed early. I do feel exhausted."

"Are you okay?" my father asked solicitously.

"Don't worry," she answered. "I'm just tired."

I watched her climb the stairs. It seemed to take a tremendous effort on her part to lift her feet. She saw me watching her and smiled a wan smile as she threw me a kiss. I threw one back and then went in to clean up.

The week passed quickly, and before I knew it, another weekend arrived. On Friday, when I returned from school, I found my mother showered and dressed. The table was set festively, and there was a candelabra on the table.

"Are we having guests?" I asked.

"Not exactly . . . and then again, you can say yes. A *Shabbos* guest," she answered.

"What is this?" I asked, waving my hand to include the candelabra and the cooked meal.

"I had an early start," she answered.

"Good. So now you have time to relax," I said as I went upstairs to put my books away.

I heard the door close, a cheerful hello from my father and then his voice raised in anger. His words were unclear, but my mother's voice attempting to placate him came through.

Again, I head the closing of a door but this time, it was slammed closed. I went downstairs. My mother was standing in front of the table, crying, her face and body looking totally dejected. My father was nowhere to be seen.

"What happened?" I asked. "I heard loud voices. Where's Daddy?"

"He'll be back soon."

"What happened?" I asked again.

"The Satan is still present. Too bad," she said. "It is just too bad."

Like a mechanical doll, her head went to the left and right as she shrugged her shoulders. She mumbled something I didn't understand. She seemed to be pleading with someone for help. I had never seen her like this.

My father returned. His face was red, livid in anger.

"Please," my mother begged.

"No!" he answered.

I looked from one to the other. What is going on? I wondered. I had never seen my parents like this.

The telephone rang and I ran to pick it up. It was Carol, confirming the appointment for Sunday.

I returned to the room. Both my parents were gone. I heard appeasing voices from upstairs, no longer raised, no longer in anger but as if each was trying to make the other understand.

"I'm going for a walk," I shouted. I had decided to give my parents the complete freedom of the house.

When I returned, it was as if nothing had happened. The table was cleared of the silver. My father looked at ease and so did my mother. I realized it was a pretense, an act arranged for my benefit. I became the third member of the troupe and performed outstandingly. I deserved a tremendous ovation.

chapter eleven

Were there only the four of us at the table? There was so much chatter, it was hard to believe. I was pleased that Janet and Carol accepted Sandy so readily.

Although we were gorging ourselves on the lunch my mother had prepared, I noticed that Sandy was not eating.

"I'm sure it is not because you're dieting, Sandy," I said. "First of all, you need one like I need a hole in my head, and second of all, everything is dietetic. Come! Help yourself!"

"I ate before I left home," she answered. "But I'll take a fruit."

"But I thought I told you it would be a light lunch," I said. "Oh well, I guess I forgot."

I had left Carol and Janet listening to records in the living room when I went to the station to meet Sandy. I watched as she walked down the staircase of the train station. There was such a refinement about her demeanor. I don't know whether it was the way she walked or the way she talked. Perhaps it was the manner in which she carried herself. The brashness of many of my acquaintances wasn't present in Sandy. I made a mental note to emulate her in some ways.

She was dressed in a long sleeved blouse. The soft pink and light blue print and blue pleated skirt had a crisp, clean look to it in contrast to the usual dungaree and washed out colors of my group.

"How is your mother doing?" I asked.

"So so," she said. "A little tired, I guess. The boys are driving her crazy with questions about when the big day will be. They just don't have the patience to wait."

I could imagine their mischievous eyes sparkling when it would finally happen.

"What do you do with yourself, Sandy?" I asked as I pulled the car out of the parking area. "It's funny. We've spoken about many things, but I never did ask you. Do you go to college?"

"Yes and no," she answered.

Puzzled, I asked, "Meaning? Either you do or you don't?"

"I go to a Hebrew Teachers' Seminary," she said. "It's similar to a college except that it is for Jewish studies."

"Are there really such things?" I asked excitedly. "What do you learn? What does it prepare you for?"

Sandy looked puzzled. "Marian, you never heard of a post high school for Jewish studies?"

"Really, I didn't," I answered.

"Well, seminary or post-high has a triple purpose," she said. "It reinforces all the values of what I've learned in my twelve years of education, and I also learn new things. At the same time, I am being prepared for a teaching career. Where did you go to school, Marian?"

"I attended public school, and now I go to college."

"More and more, I find a huge chasm separating you and your grandfather," she mused. "The very first time I saw you, I was certain you were a *Yeshivah* student since you had such a pious person for a grandfather."

"Oh, you mean that my grandfather was an Orthodox Jew," I said. "Yes, he was. But my parents aren't, and I wasn't raised that way."

Suddenly, things became clear.

"Sandy," I said. "Your family is Orthodox. How terrific. Now I have another friend besides Naomi."

"Naomi?"

I explained my visit with Rabbi Isaacs.

"Should I tell you?" Sandy murmured.

"Tell me what?" I asked. "Here we are. Home sweet home."

In the excitement of the afternoon, I forgot completely about this conversation with Sandy.

"Sandy, do I detect a slight trace of an accent?" Janet asked. "Where is it from?"

"Almost international," said Sandy. "Or shall I be fancy and say, very cosmopolitan. Actually, it is a little of this and a little of that."

"What is this and what is that?" Carol asked.

"Well," said Sandy. "There is a dash of Polish, a large smattering of Yiddish, a big heaping of Hebrew, a drop of German and a large dose of

English. Mix all the ingredients together and you have Shaindee."

"Shaindee?" My voice echoed my surprise. "All this time I thought your name is Sandy."

"No. It is Shaindee. That is the correct pronunciation."

"What kind of name is Shaindee?" Carol asked.

"It is a Jewish name."

"Well, what is your English name?" Janet asked.

"I don't have one. My name is Shaindel, and the nickname is Shaindee."

"How come your accent is so international?" Carol asked. "Have you travelled so much?"

"Not really. Well, I guess everything is really comparative. Some people would say I have. My Polish accent is from my father, the Yiddish is from my grandmother, German from my mother and Hebrew became my native language when we lived in Israel. And of course, English from America."

I looked at Sandy, I mean Shaindee, wide-eyed. There was much more here than met the eye. Shaindee's father did not have a Polish accent nor did her mother have a German accent. Rain came pouring down in a windy sheet on the trust and friendship we had established. I felt deceived. Was I really so naive? It was difficult for me to play act, but I seemed to pull it off.

We played Scrabble, and before I knew it, it was time for Shaindee to leave. After Shaindee said goodbye to Carol and Janet, I said, "I'll take you home."

"Thanks loads, Marian," she said. "I really appreciate your offer, but the train takes me close to home. I don't want you to go out of your way. I'll call my father when I leave, and he'll meet me at the train station. If you'll take me to the station, that will be fine."

I couldn't look at Shaindee. My voice quivered in anger when I spoke to her, and although I tried to control the frost in it, I knew I was hiding nothing from her.

"I know you are angry and that you have many questions," she said. "I'm being unfair by not answering them."

I stopped her and did not let her continue.

"Look, Shaindee," I said. "It is your life and what you want to tell me and what you don't want to tell me is your privilege." Words, just words.

Shaindee changed the subject. "I like your friends. Janet impressed me as a very intelligent girl, and Carol is warm and friendly. This is a totally new world for me, meeting girls who are Jewish but don't act as if they are."

"I know," I answered bitterly. "And of course, I'm in that category. How does it feel to visit the zoo?"

"Please, Marian," she said. "Let's continue to be friends. Life is full of choices. I stood at the crossroads, reading the signpost when we met. I simply felt it just wasn't the time to open my life to you. Not yet."

It was true. What right did I have to infringe upon Shaindee's privacy?

"Have you all been friends for a long time?" Shaindee asked.

There was a strain in our conversation, but we did try our best.

"I've known Janet for a while, and I met Carol through Kurt," I said.

It took me a second to realize there was a part of my life unknown to Shaindee. Our lives together had been pretty much centered around the nursing home.

"And Neal is . . . I guess you would say the boy I am going to marry."

"How wonderful, Marian!" she exclaimed. "You never told me. When? What? Oh, I'm so excited for you."

"Right now he is in medical school, so we have to wait. Here's the station. I hope we'll keep in touch. Call me or I'll call you."

I couldn't help but wonder about Shaindee's past. I had realized that Mr. and Mrs. Josephs seemed too young to be her parents and that Ovadia and Azriel's dark complexions were so totally different from Shaindee's, but she did call them Mother and Father. Could Mr. Josephs be her brother? Or perhaps Mrs. Josephs her sister? But then, why did she call them her parents? It was all very strange.

I guess everything that happens to us in life has a purpose. There must have been a reason for me to become enmeshed in all these tangled webs. In my childhood, I was always impatient as well as curious. When I was bothered by something, I couldn't let go. "Remember, curiosity killed the cat," my mother would always say. As I grew older and a bit wiser, I used to end the expression with "but satisfaction brought it back." I am indeed curious, and I am surely looking for satisfaction.

chapter twelve

The sun was streaming into my room, the warmth of its rays bringing a pleasant feeling of languor. The musical sound of children at play was broken occasionally by the solid crack of a bat hitting a ball. It all added to my feeling of laziness this Saturday morning. Since there was nothing pressing, I turned over and tried to go back to sleep. From the distance, I heard the rhythmic sounds of the wheels of the mailman's cart as he came up our walk. My peace and contentment were interrupted by the realization that it wasn't as early as I pretended. I yawned and stretched my arms over my head. Reluctantly, I turned over and looked at the yellow and white clock standing on my dresser. Unbelievable. 11:00 A.M.

"Get out of bed, you lazybones," I told myself. Slowly, I put one foot out and then the other.

I jumped. Reality hit me. The mailman! I hadn't heard from Neal in over a week. Perhaps there was a letter for me.

"Mom," I shouted down. "Do I have any mail?"

"Good morning, Marian," my mother answered. "Did you have a good sleep?"

"Yes. I slept like a log."

"Would you like some breakfast, Marian?"

"Not right now, Mom. Was there any mail?"

"Yes," she answered. "There is a special sale brochure from Acme's Department Store, a telephone bill, a gas bill and, oh yes, what is this? The electric bill?"

I hastily washed up and put my robe on. I ran down the steps. My mother was standing at the foot of the staircase.

"And a letter from Neal."

"Oh Mom, why didn't you tell me that right away?"

She laughed and handed me the letter. I ran up the stairs to read the letter in the privacy and quiet of my four walls.

Dear Marian,

How are you and how is everything on your side of the world? How do you find school? We are overwhelmed with work, but I had to squeeze in these few minutes to write to you. You wanted a complete description of the apartment, so here goes.

As I told you in my previous letter, there are three bedrooms. We each have our own room but share the kitchen. The rooms are large, nice and airy. Jeffrey has a cleaning person who comes in once a week, so the place is kept up and our sloppy housekeeping is remedied. I'm not very good at this, so I must be repeating myself.

Human nature is peculiar. You can have two people, each special in his way, and yet, they just don't get along. Kurt and Jeffrey are like fire and water. They are having problems and just do not hit it off. To be really honest, I can't blame it on Jeffrey. Kurt hounds him. Jeffrey is Jewish, and Kurt keeps making nasty remarks. You would think that in this day and age people would have outgrown this silly hatred. To be honest, Kurt is an anti-Semite, and I just don't know what to do with him. After all, it is really Jeffrey's apartment, and we're subletting the rooms from him. I'm afraid he will ask us to move.

In my previous letter, I wrote that Kurt had some odd plans which he disclosed to me. I thought he was just talking through his hat, but I'm beginning to believe he really meant what he said. He thinks he will make Jeffrey so disgusted and frightened that he will move out. I keep warning him that his plans may backfire, and we will be the ones to be put out on the street. With the tight apartment market, this is a definite possibility.

It is really unbelievable! Kurt made a blueprint of a plan which he has already initiated. I saw it in writing, and I'm at a loss as to how to deal with it. It goes something like this. He calls it The Kurt Smith Ten Commandments. It is almost heresy. The entire plan is a strategy to get rid of Jeffrey. But, of course, he doesn't say how to get rid of Jeffrey, but how to get rid of "that Jew."

The Kurt Smith Ten Commandments:

1. Thou shalt initiate constant arguments about anything and everything with the Jew.

2. Thou shalt butter up the owner of the building so that he should prefer us as tenants.

3. Thou shalt send assorted hate letters: Ku Klux Klan mail, etc.

4. Thou shalt organize fellow students on the campus to make nasty Jew remarks.

5. Thou shalt make noise, turn on radio, play records when he is trying to study.

6. Thou shalt talk about how wonderful the Nazis were, the P.L.O. movement and all enemies of the Jews.

7. Thou shalt have friends make threatening phone calls.

8. Thou shalt intercept his phone calls when he is not home and not give him messages.

9. All of the above will lead to: Thou shalt say a pleasant "Bye Bye, Birdie" to him.

10. Thou shalt be extremely helpful in making him move.

Kurt claims he is now working on steps one and two. Although I feel compassion for Jeffrey, it really is none of my business. I am too busy to get involved.

My parents called me last night. They are planning to call you to invite you to our house. I'm letting you know so you won't be surprised when they do call and so you'll be prepared. I told you they like you!!

Take care of yourself and write, write and write.

Neal

I sat holding the letter in my hand for an indeterminate amount of time. There was a dull ache in my body, and my head was throbbing. What had started out for me as a bright and shining day had changed dramatically.

I got up and put the letter on my dresser. I moved around the room like a sleepwalker, stumbling over everything. My knees were shaking, and when they buckled under me, I threw myself on my bed. I looked up at the ceiling, staring at it but not really seeing it. It seemed as if hours passed, but it was only minutes.

"Marian, come down for brunch," my mother called to me. "Since you are too late for breakfast, we'll make it a combination breakfast and lunch."

"Thanks," I answered. "I'm not hungry. I'm not feeling too well. I think I'll just go back to sleep."

My mother came into my room.

"What's the matter, Marian?" she asked anxiously, placing her cool hand on my forehead. "You don't seem to have a fever."

"It is really nothing to worry about, Mom. I guess I'm feeling the results of a heavy week. I'd just like to rest."

I heard her footsteps as they went softly down the stairs. I got out of bed, brushed my teeth, showered and went back to bed. I reread Neal's letter. I wanted to return to the innocence of my childhood when adults were perfect and the only villain I knew was the wolf in *Little Red Riding Hood*. But I wasn't five years old. I was eighteen, and the world was made up of all kinds of people. There was no golden aura, and there were such things as evil people. The innocent of the world do suffer.

I spent the rest of the day secluded in my room. It must have been around 3:00 A.M. before I finally fell asleep.

It was a long night, a night of nightmares and restless half sleep. In the morning, I looked in the mirror and saw my red-rimmed eyes. I used makeup to try to hide the redness from my mother.

"My, you're up early today. Do you feel better?" She looked at me piercingly. "No, you don't look better. What is bothering you, Marian? Talk it out. Maybe it will help."

"I'm fine," I insisted. I knew I looked terrible and that my sullen mood did not help alleviate my depressed state of mind. "I'm okay, Mom. Please don't worry. I guess I'm just a little under the weather."

Ah, the selfishness of youth. Little did I think she might be having problems of her own.

"I think I'll spend the day at Janet's house," I said.

We drank our juice and coffee in silence. I washed my cup and then went into the bathroom to run a comb through my hair.

Even nature tried to placate me on my walk to Janet's house. It had been a hot summer that had extended itself into early fall. The leaves were just turning reddish-brown. They made a canopy of russet to walk under all along the avenue. The excited voices of children at play mingled with the street noises; all created a background of lulling peacefulness.

The screeching of brakes as a car stopped short overpowered all the other sounds, interrupting the tranquility of the moment. There was a sudden stillness. It was as if the world stopped, the silence broken by the sounds of running feet and a mass of moving bodies. I followed along. The driver of the car sat white and still, his eyes almost unseeing. I watched two pedestrians pick up the little boy who seemed unhurt. They dusted his clothing. He smiled, thanked them and skipped away.

The man in the car put his head in his hands. His sobs could be heard in the solemn quiet of the street. I saw the heaving of his shoulders as he tried to move from fright to thankfulness. Someone brought him a glass of water which he took with trembling hands.

I overheard two women talking as I reached the corner. One said, "Life and death. Minutes apart. How lucky the little boy was that the driver's brakes were in good condition."

I thought about her remark. We are in control of some of the brakes in our own life, and we too may be called upon to stop short. How important it was to keep them in good condition and to know when to use them.

Mr. Abikoff opened the door to my knock. He was a tall man who looked even taller because of his angular frame. His thinning blonde hair was streaked with gray. It was difficult to tell where the blonde hair ended and the gray began as the hair covered his head so sparingly.

"Sit down, Marian," Mrs. Abikoff said when I came in. "Janet and I were just telling Mr. Abikoff about the shocking incident you and Janet encountered on your way to school."

I looked at Mrs. Abikoff, and it seemed as if I was looking at an older and heavier version of Janet.

"We think," she continued, "that as the world becomes more educated, anti-Semitism will lessen. Unfortunately, it just doesn't work that way. 'Give me your tired, your poor, your huddled masses yearning to breathe free.' You know that that was written by a Jewish woman named Emma Lazarus. It is inscribed on the first thing a person views upon entering America—the Statue of Liberty. But even America doesn't always want the tired and poor huddled masses."

"We are taught that America was founded to be a haven for all religions. What happened?" I asked.

"What happened, Marian?" Mr. Abikoff replied. "People happened. People make a country and people influence people. In fact, Peter Stuyvesant did not want to permit Jews to come into New Amsterdam. It was only because of the tremendous pressure that he finally conceded. He tried to limit the rights of Jews by not permitting them to observe their Sabbath or worship publicly."

Mr. Abikoff awed me with his tremendous knowledge and Jewishness. It was only afterwards that I realized something bothered me. It was when he spoke about Peter Stuvysant and how he tried to limit the rights of the Jews when they came to America by not permitting them to observe their Sabbath. Who is *them*? *Them* includes Mr. Abikoff, Mrs. Abikoff, Janet, her brother, my parents, all of us . . . each and every Jew. It is not *them*. I was becoming more aware of innuendoes, inflections in conversations. *They* were not permitted. Why couldn't he say, *we* were not permitted.

"They may hate Jews, but they can't live without Jews," Mr. Abikoff was saying. "Jews were expelled from Spain, from England and other countries, but not before they built up the financial standing of the communities where they lived."

"But something like the Nazis could never have happened here in America?" I asked.

"Do you know, children, here in America, in 1939, there was a Nazi party called the German-American Bund?" he said. "At meetings in Madison Square Garden, they filled the place with twenty thousand men, women and children. They decorated the room with giant black swastikas hanging next to a figure of George Washington, the first President of the United States."

"I can't believe it, Mr. Abikoff," I said. "Here in America? In this democratic country people would be interested and become part of such a movement?"

"That's right, Marian. Have you heard of Henry Ford?"

"Is that the man after whom the Ford car is named?"

"That's the man," Mr. Abikoff answered, "and to this day, I will not buy a car manufactured by Ford because he was pro-Nazi."

"Henry Ford?" I asked, astonished. "Impossible!"

"No, my child, not impossible," he said. "He was also a publisher of newspapers, and many articles against Jews were printed in these papers. The international Jew was used as a derogatory term, and many of his articles were slanted to cause anti-Semitism."

"And why don't you tell them about *The Protocols of the Learned Elders of Zion*?" I turned around to see who was talking. It was Janet's brother Abe.

"What was that?" I asked.

"You explain it, Abe," Mrs. Abikoff said.

"It was a fabricated collection of minutes of a meeting of Jewish leaders which the anti-Semites claimed was held in 1897," he said. "They claimed that this meeting outlined a plot for world domination. It was a fake, but it gave rise to many pogroms in Czarist Russia. The Nazis used it, and it is still being used to this day."

"That's enough for today," Janet interrupted. "Come, Marian, let's go up to my room."

"I'll see you later," I said to Mr. and Mrs. Abikoff. "And thank you for the discussion."

We went into Janet's room.

"You know, Janet," I said, mimicking her. "I love your room. It's really you."

"Cut it out," she answered. "Let's talk. You look terrible. What's the matter?"

I told Janet about Neal's letter.

"I don't know what to do," I said. "I don't know whether to be angry at Neal for being so passive or to forgive him for his blindness. I guess I'm also frightened because Neal wrote me to expect a call from his parents."

Janet tried hard all day to reassure me that everything would be fine at the Brennans, but the queasy feeling in the pit of my stomach just would not go away.

chapter thirteen

I t came just as I expected, a cool wind followed by frost. The phone rang and it was Mrs. Brennan on the line. She wanted to speak to me.

"Hello. Is this Marian? This is Mrs. Brennan. How are you? Dr. Brennan and I would like to invite you for dinner Saturday night. We'll send our chauffeur to pick you up at six o'clock." Her voice was cold and condescending. I was not asked whether I would like to go. I was commanded, left no choice. I thanked her for the invitation.

My father was ecstatic; my mother's expression was inscrutable. I was wary and a little frightened, but I kept quiet and did not transfer my worry and apprehension to them.

I had never tried to hold back time as much as I tried that week. Things were proceeding at a rapid pace. I felt like a child who had climbed to the top of a huge slide. As I put each foot down slowly, I knew I eventually had to let go and move. The only way to finally move on a slide is downward, either by the steps I had just climbed or down the slide.

Saturday arrived, and for me, it was much too soon. I think it was one of the rare times that I watched the hands of the clock move and my heart met each tick of the clock with a strong beat of its own.

The bell rang promptly at six. My father opened the door.

"She'll be out in a minute," I heard him say, his voice cheerful.

"Miss Asher?" the chauffeur inquired when I came to the door. There was a crisp elegance in his clothing and manner. He tipped his cap and helped me into the long, black Cadillac standing at the curb.

I looked about me. The seats were covered in red velvet. There was a long red velvet carpet on the floor. Even the walls had plush coverings. I pressed a button next to me. A mini make-up table appeared. I looked at my reflection in the mirror. I saw a pale face and frightened eyes.

"Pull yourself together, Marian," I told myself. "Your dress is tasteful, and you did what you could. The rest is out of your hands and that is that."

It had taken me hours to decide what to wear. I had pulled one dress after another out of my closet, and in the end, I had purchased a new dress. It was powder blue with a pleated skirt. I wore a strand of pearls and pearl earrings. My mother had given me her set. It was a present from my grandfather to her. I hoped it would bring me luck.

The car ride was smooth. In fact, I couldn't even feel the car moving. I shivered. It wasn't because the evening was chilly.

I raised the window shade on the window. I had never seen this on a car window before. I looked outside. The night was crisp and clear. The stars were shining brightly.

If I could have a wish tonight, what would I wish for myself? I almost laughed out loud at the first thought that came to me. My wish should have been that Neal's parents like me, or perhaps that the evening would be pleasant. Instead, the first thought that had entered my mind was to wish the evening over.

The car made a left turn under a grove of trees, and we were there. The sight was breathtaking. The entire place was lit up. I caught my breath. I was awestruck at the beauty. Green, green, green. Wherever my eyes alighted, I saw green shrubbery. It was totally unexpected at this time of the year when the leaves were beginning to turn colors and fall from the trees. Shrubbery, trees and lawns all met my eyes as if painted by an artist's hand. Centered within this scene was a stately house of incredible beauty. It looked like a palatial estate, the white columns giving it a Grecian effect and the broad portico an air of dignity and self-assurance. We drove up a long path lined with exotic flowers, which led us to the house.

The chauffeur opened the car door and helped me out. I walked up the white marble steps which fanned out on either side of me. The front door was opened by a white-aproned maid even before I reached the top step. She ushered me in and led me to a room lined with books. It was an immaculately clean, gleaming wood panelled room. I sat down on the edge of my chair, hoping my tenseness would not show. I heard light footsteps approaching.

"How are you, Marian?" Mrs. Brennan said with a smile which she immediately discarded. "Welcome to our home."

"How are you, Mrs. Brennan?" I answered. "And how is Dr. Brennan?"

"Dr. Brennan was delayed, but I expect him shortly."

She lit a cigarette and held it loosely between red, manicured fingertips.

"Have you heard from Neal?" she asked me.

"Oh, yes."

"Did he call or write?"

"Both."

"Often?" she asked with raised eyebrows.

"I have received two letters from him."

"I see." Pursed lips.

Quiet. No conversation. I was searching for something to say to make conversation when I heard the sound of a door closing.

"That must be Dr. Brennan." Relief. "Good evening, dear. We are in the library."

Through the archway, I saw Dr. Brennan give his hat and medical bag to the maid.

"Good evening," he said to his wife.

He walked to her and gave her a peck on the cheek. He then turned to me.

"Good evening, Marian," he said. "It is Marian, isn't it? Do excuse me. I'll just wash up, and then we'll go in for dinner."

Well, Marian, I thought to myself, this evening has started with a real bang! Could it get much worse?

We walked into a magnificent dining room. It was almost as large as my entire house. It was furnished in French decor. The panels on the wall were inset with a soft water-silk taffeta which matched the coverings on the chair. The rug was of an oriental design and it was coordinated with a slightly darker shade of blue than the chairs. If I had not felt so threatened, I think I would have laughed, because even my dress seemed to fit into the monochromatic color scheme of the room.

The breakfront was awesome. It covered almost one entire wall, and it was inset with hand-painted blue, pink and beige flowers. I looked at the table. It was set with gleaming silver and shining crystal on a beautiful soft eggshell lace tablecloth. It all added up to a picture of total elegance.

Dr. Brennan sat at the head of the long table and Mrs. Brennan at the foot. The maid seated me in the center. I felt uncomfortable and very small. Now I understood the expression of wanting to "sink into the woodwork." There was no conversation during the meal.

I was astounded. Neal had never told me he came from such great wealth. I knew his parents were financially comfortable, even rich, but I had never envisioned this. I looked up at the ceiling. I had never seen a chandelier with so many crystals. Their blue-white sparkle threw designs on the ceiling. The opulence of the place was overwhelming.

I hardly touched the food. The maids served and cleared away quietly. Their footsteps were so cushioned I did not even realize they were at my elbow until I saw the dishes being removed.

"Let's go into the living room," Dr. Brennan said when we finished the meal.

He led the way, and Mrs. Brennan followed behind me. I felt surrounded by two predatory animals. We passed a graceful circular staircase. The oriental rugs in muted colors covered the floors and gleaming polished wood bordered the rugs.

The living room had a white couch. Of course, there were no plastic covers. The three chairs were covered in soft blue velvet. In one corner, I noticed a chair covered in a beautiful tapestry. All the colors of the room seemed to be blended into this chair in a successful effort to tie the room together. The coffee table was inlaid with brass. Everything looked expensive, and I felt as if they had labels on them which said, "Look! Don't touch!"

I stood awkwardly to the side.

"Sit down, Marian," Mrs. Brennan said.

I looked from the chairs to the couch, not knowing where she wanted me to sit. Mrs. Brennan nodded towards a chair, and I sat down. She took a seat opposite me to the right, and Dr. Brennan took one to my left. I was closed in. I felt a tingle begin at the bottom of my backbone and slowly travel upward. My hands were cold and I had to control the tremble. I knew there was a purpose for this invitation, and I waited. What choice did I have?

"Marian," Mrs. Brennan began. "You are a sweet girl. Dr. Brennan and I are really happy Neal showed such good taste."

Was I wrong? Her voice and manner were sugar sweet. Were we going to establish a casual, easy rapport? Her words had a ring of sincerity and truth, but why was her face a frozen mask and her eyes two points of ice? I looked for support from Dr. Brennan, but he avoided my gaze. He looked uncomfortable, shifting restlessly in his seat. He opened the bottom closet of the end table. His surgeon fingers placed three glasses on the table. I seemed to be in a trance as I watched his movements; everything seemed to be happening in slow motion. He poured a drink for himself and one for Mrs. Brennan.

"Would you like a drink, Marian?"

"No, thank you," I answered.

As if there had been no interruption, Mrs. Brennan continued.

"However, now you can understand why Dr. Brennan and I have asked you here tonight. We wanted you to realize the differences in your backgrounds. You realize Neal was born into luxury, and you come from a more modest background. And you do have a problem of differences in religion."

"Mrs. Brennan," I answered. "If you are referring to the fact that my parents are Jewish, please be assured that I have been raised without religion. It has never become an issue between Neal and me, and I cannot see it ever becoming one in the future."

"Foolish child," she said. "It does not change the fact that you are Jewish, and we would never permit our child to marry anyone who is Jewish."

"Please try to understand, Mrs. Brennan," I said. "I do not consider myself Jewish as you see it. I am an American. There really is basically no difference between us."

I heard Dr. Brennan clear his throat, and I looked at him, hoping that succor would come from that source.

"It cannot be!" he said emphatically. That's all. Just those three words.

I reeled back as if I had been hit. I was stunned. The room was spinning. Bursts of dull light grayed the room. Fortunately, this sensation did not last long, and not only did my senses return to me but also my pride.

"Dr. and Mrs. Brennan," I said politely and bravely. "I had hoped that you would like me. I mean *me*! If you had said that you didn't like me for some particular reason, I think I could accept that, but to feel like this because of an obsession against Jewish people is something I cannot accept. Neal knows I am Jewish, and he does not feel that way. How can you handle your son's happiness in such an impersonal manner?"

"I'm sorry, Marian, that you don't understand our feelings," said Mrs. Brennan. "We are a cultured and well-bred family and I have tried to reach you through kindness, but you don't seem to comprehend. We cannot and will not permit this friendship to develop and will do every-thing within our power to discourage Neal."

I looked directly at Mrs. Brennan and then at Dr. Brennan. A feeling of fatigue and weariness overcame me. I thought I would choke on my humilation. It took me a while to realize that this was a plan to do just that, to deliberately humiliate me. I decided to bear this indignity with dignity.

"Thank you for your hospitality," I said. I lifted my head high and walked proudly towards the door.

"You won't see Neal again, will you?" Dr. Brennan asked.

It hit me. They were really two frightened, insecure people. I didn't answer at first, but waited until I reached the door. I turned around and looked slowly at one and then at the other. I was amazed at my calmness and control.

"That, Dr. and Mrs. Brennan, will be our decision, mine and Neal's," I said and closed the door firmly.

I walked down the marble steps and looked at the lit landscape. Yes, it was a beautiful house peopled by less than beautiful souls. The chauf-feur was standing at attention by the car. He moved as soon as he saw me coming. He went to the passenger side and opened the door for me. I thanked him but told him I wanted to walk a little and that I would find a taxicab to take me the remainder of the way. He stared at me oddly. I couldn't tell him that I wanted no favors from the Brennans.

The sky was dark; it was an inky blackness which matched the feeling I had around my heart, but the darkness on the path was broken by the floodlights. I was frightened to walk alone, but my pride prevented me from asking for assistance. I walked rapidly.

A new world had been presented to me during these past few weeks, a world full of hatred. I was being sucked into a man-made labyrinth of evil. I felt shock and revulsion, and my heart filled with resentment against the Brennans and all the Brennans of the world. They thought they belonged to the upper crust of society, but with all their money and so-called breeding, they were not different from the guttersnipe, pimply faced boys who tripped Janet on the way to school. Each one tried to demean a person; the boys' method was through physical force, and the Brennans' method was masked in silk gloves. The basic difference was that the Brennans' method took years of cultivation, but ultimately the aims were the same.

I saw a taxicab and ran.

"Taxi, taxi, taxi," I shouted. I was panting audibly when he finally stopped.

"Where to," he asked.

"Home," I answered. "Please take me home."

chapter fourteen

I was a bundle of nerves. I questioned my future and my feelings about Neal. The uncertainty made me feel insecure. As much as I tried to control my feelings, I just couldn't cover it up. I was full of hostility and resentment at my parents. I pestered them with questions which they avoided answering. I taunted them for not having at least given me the education and opportunity to make a choice, and then I felt guilty about it. I found myself with one leg strongly planted in one world and the other leg inching into another. It was splitting me apart.

The weather, at least, was kinder. The last sultry summer heat completely disappeared. I welcomed the youthful springiness of fall and the kaleidoscopic colors of the green leaves turning russet and yellow. I enjoyed the sounds and the feel of the crunchiness when I stepped on the fallen leaves that cushioned my footsteps. It was unusual, but we also had our first snowfall in November, and I viewed it through the warmth of the window in my room. My breath, as it hit the window, formed smoke clouds against the cold. I watched the snow falling softly, each flake like cotton, each snowdrop individually shaped. The snow, with its freshness, radiated an aura of cleanliness as it covered the grounds in front of my house.

Just as I watched the changing of the seasons, I also watched my father's transformation from day to day. The attempts I had made at initiating discussions with him about my grandfather, my mother's family, the war or issues to which I had been newly exposed met with opposition. We stared at each other combatively. I knew I was hurting him, but I was also hurting.

It was too much for the both of us to bear. This was my loving, devoted father, and under my very eyes, minute by minute, he was changing. He looked ill. His face grew thinner. His cheeks became sunken, and the furrows on his brows deepened. Even his hair seemed scantier. Only his eyes were still alert, but they looked like two furies trapped. There was a defenselessness about him, and so, as if by mutual agreement, we established a pact of silence on controversial issues. Our discussions became a pattern of impersonal talks. My mother completed the threesome which dashed any hope from that quarter. I was also worried about her. She too seemed restless and indecisive, my dear mother who had been a source of strength.

One Sunday morning in late November, my father asked me if I would like to take a ride into the country. I thought I detected a plaintive note in his voice, and when I saw a pleading look in my mother's eyes, I said I would love to go. I did so want to bring them some happiness.

It was a beautiful fall day. My parents made an effort to recapture our former family closeness, and I too really tried very hard. We all tried. It turned out to be a refreshing afternoon. The cerulean sky was clear with frothy white clouds, a beautiful backdrop for the austere mountains.

We ate a picnic lunch, sitting on a blanket under the open sky. After lunch, we opened the beach chairs, and I can't even recall of what we spoke. It was just inconsequential banter.

In the evening, on the drive home, we stopped to watch the sunset turn a small stream into shimmering copper. It was nature at its best. My parents kept looking at me, urgently seeking signs of approval. Our life had become like this autumn day with vague remnants of summer's warmth. But we all knew that outside, close by, lay the winter darkness with the constant menace of blizzards and the threat of bitter cold weather.

Neal's letters were coming with regularity. Slowly, I was able to detect a change in his outlook. Kurt had made inroads on him, and he seemed to be in agreement with Kurt's plans for the persecution of Jeffrey. Jeffrey was at the top of his class, and Neal's fierce drive of competitiveness added fuel to his feelings of bitterness.

I looked forward to Neal's return in a few weeks. Too many things lay concealed under the surface. I kept telling myself, "Anticipate, anticipate," but what was it I wanted to anticipate? I felt myself standing on a precipice, one wrong step and I'd fall. Only, I really didn't know which was the wrong step.

I received a letter from Aunt Leah. She was warm and sympathetic.

Did she help me? Tears rolled down my cheeks as I read and reread the blurred words.

Dear Marian,

Grandfather did not come to Israel. His heart yearned to walk in the footsteps of our great men, to tread the streets of our holy city, to kiss the stones of the Wailing Wall, to pray at the graves of our Rabbis. But no. He did not come. He felt his place was with you.

You asked why Rabbi Isaacs called you Malkala. You are named after your grandmother. In our religion, we name a newborn after a deceased relative. That is why you have the same name as your grandfather's wife, your grandmother, my mother, Malka. Malka means a queen. I know you'll be the queen of the family and that through you, our family kingdom of Judaism will once again flourish. Then grandfather's sacrifice will have meaning. No one likes to feel his life was in vain.

I guess that answers how I feel about Neal.

As to your question about my brother, all I can tell you, my dear niece, is that the measure of a person is how he reacts under pressure. Your father did not fall apart under pressure but under disillusionment. I'm confident he'll come back.

Your loving aunt,
Leah

P.S. You must come to Israel, and stay with us. We really have to get to know each other, Malkala. You are the only one left from whom we can hope to see *nachas*. You represent our future generations, our own flesh and blood.

chapter fifteen

The news media was shocked. The headlines blared the horror story of the People's Temple in Guyana. It hit the public with the violence of an explosion. It was on everyone's tongue. People spoke about it in the streets. It was all you heard on the bus. Classes were impossible in college. The media went wild. Was it possible that one person could have such powerful charisma to be able to influence nine hundred people to commit suicide?

Many of my classmates in college were personally involved, because the tragedy touched someone they knew or were related to.

I bought a newspaper on the way home from school and passed the paper to Janet when I had completed reading the front page.

"Oh no!" Janet suddenly screamed. "It can't be."

I grabbed the paper from her and went down the list of names. There it was, at the bottom of the page, Michael Young, Carol's brother.

"Those poor parents," I whispered. "Poor Carol. Poor Michael. How? Why?"

Janet shrugged her shoulders and answered, "Who knows? I guess one cult led to another, and after all his searching, this was unfortunately, his end. How confused and lonely he must have been to seek family relationships and meaning in such a cult."

"I can't get over it," I said. "He had a family. Why did he turn away from them? They were his blood relatives. What makes a person go this far out?"

In a feature story, I read about one of the leading cult members, and I guess, that answered my questions. Her name was Mara Leator and her son Larry was charged with the murder of Congressman Ryan. I read about the history of Mara Leator.

She was the daughter of Hugo and Beverly Farkas of Hamburg,

Germany, a well known family of Jewish bankers. When Hitler came into power, they were already assimilated Jews, but Hitler found them out. He made Jews recognize they were Jews even if they tried to hide behind a gentile facade. They were deported to a concentration camp. Eventually, they came to America.

In America, Mara enrolled in Pennsylvania State University where she met and married Dr. Leator, a famous scientist. Her assimilated life did not satisfy her. As was the pattern for many others who had joined cults, she divorced her husband and turned over a quarter of a million dollars to the cult leader.

"You see, Janet," I told her. "You asked what I'm searching for. I told you I need answers for myself and, eventually, for any children in my future. Here was a girl, born of Jewish parents, who denied her heritage and ancestry. Believe it or not, I can understand this girl. She was confused, lonely and searching for something her assimilated parents refused to give her. She needed the strength of traditions, but her parents failed her. They kept her ignorant about her Jewishness."

"What does this have to do with you?" Janet asked.

"I too crave something more than I've been given," I said. "I don't want to sound too melodramatic, Janet, but my soul thirsts. I see emptiness around me, but I know there is more to life than this vacuum. I realize how meaningful my grandfather's life was. I want to understand what went into the making of a Naomi or a Shaindee."

Janet looked at me strangely. She did not say anything. I felt a tug in my heart. I loved Janet. She was the sister I have never had.

"Please try to understand me, Janet," I said. "I'm neither Jew nor gentile. What am I? Where do I belong? I know nothing of my Jewishness and am not accepted by Neal's parents because I'm not a gentile."

Janet was silent. I saw that she did not understand.

chapter sixteen

The stirring within me coincided with the changing of seasons. The trees, once heavy with leaves, were in their winter dress, bare and naked, stark against the open sky. As a mountain climber who realizes no precautions can offer perfect protection, I too prepared myself for the climb. A mountain climber's fall might cause his death, but if I were to fall, would it bring me life?

The spare moments I had were filled with reading. The more I read, the more I believed and the more confused I became. I decided to visit Naomi.

"How good to see once again, Marian." Naomi's warmth enveloped me. "How are you?"

"I'm fine," I answered. I waited for her to ask why I hadn't contacted her for so long, but she didn't. Naomi kept a loose tether.

"I apologize for not answering your note," I continued. "I know it was impolite. The truth is I tried to avoid you. Please don't misunderstand me. It was not to avoid you as a person or because of anything you did or said. I guess it was really because of myself. Naomi, I'm frightened."

Naomi's warm blue eyes looked concerned. They looked even bluer because of the blue kerchief covering her hair. She looked puzzled.

"So why did you come?" she asked.

"I feel like a fool," I said. "I can't even answer that. Well, maybe I can. I can't explain it, but there is something pulling at me. Look! My recent experiences have left me with so much I don't understand and so much I need to understand."

I told Naomi about Neal's parents and about the incident with the boys on our way to college. I also told her about Janet's father and about Shaindee and her family.

I had thought I had control over my emotions, but the last few weeks had taken their toll. I broke down.

"But most of all," I told Naomi, sobbing, "I'm concerned about Neal and his relationship with Kurt. Neal's changing. I don't want him to think like Kurt."

"He turned their hearts to hate His people, to scheme against His servants," Naomi quoted from *Psalms* 105:25.

"I don't understand."

"Everything you tell me points to the same thing: Neal's parents, Neal and Kurt. Marian, G-d is protecting you. Always in Jewish history, G-d tried to prevent assimilation by causing the gentiles to become our enemies. Decisions are being made for you. Don't you see that?"

I wasn't sure that I did, but it was a comforting thought.

We spoke about other things for a while. Naomi told me about the enslavement of the Jews in Egypt, about the miraculous exodus and about the giving of the Torah at Mount Sinai.

"Naomi," I said in a serious tone of voice, "do your really believe Moses went up on the mountain and received the Torah directly from G-d?"

"There is a joke which really isn't in place when discussing something holy but it will answer you," she replied. "It goes something like this. If you get two Jews together, you're bound to get three opinions. There were six hundred thousand men present at Mount Sinai, not to mention all the women and children. Marian, you can imagine the difficulty involved when you have such a multitude of people, and yet, each and every one was in total agreement about what they heard and saw. When you study Jewish history in depth, Marian, you will find something very interesting. Our heroes are human beings. Our leaders are not super-natural. They had human failings. Our history does not disguise this or rewrite itself. Now, after all these years, you will be reading the same, unchanged version as the original we received."

I looked at Naomi and then challenged her.

"Impossible," I said. "Even American history rewrites itself. Years ago, history books all showed the American Indian as our enemy. Now, we are beginning to hear more and more about the injustice the Americans did to the Indians."

"True." Naomi agreed. "That is exactly what I am trying to show you. Not one word has been changed in our Torah or Jewish history at any time. Time has proven its validity. In our history and laws, not one word has been changed in all this time because it is the truth and was given to us by G-d."

I tried to digest what she was saying.

"What a terrible hostess I've been," Naomi excused herself. "I got so carried away. I'll be back in a moment."

She returned shortly with a tray which had two cups of coffee, sugar and cream and a platter of cookies on it. Under her arm were some pamphlets and books.

"Cream and sugar?" she asked as she put the cup and saucer in front of me.

We drank our coffee in silence. The stillness of the room magnified all sounds. I thought I heard a baby crying in the background and someone trying to soothe the child.

"Is that a baby I hear?"

"Yes," Naomi answered. "It is my little boy."

"Really? Isn't that funny. I never thought of you as married."

"You're kidding," she said. "Didn't you realize it when you saw my wig and kerchief?"

"What?" I asked.

"I'm sorry," she answered. "I keep forgetting how much you need to learn. A married woman covers her head. That is why I wear this kerchief. But we'll leave that for another day and time. I want to bring the baby in so you can meet him."

She returned holding a baby in her arms.

"What's his name?" I asked.

"His name is Mordechai. Say hello to Marian, Mordechai."

The baby gurgled and smiled at his mother.

"How old is he?" I asked.

"Mordechai is seven months old," she answered as she cuddled him closer in her arms. "He is such a delicious little boy."

"May I hold him?"

Naomi handed the baby to me. I buried my nose in his neck and inhaled the clean smell of powder, soap and oil.

"He is adorable," I told Naomi.

Mordechai giggled and put his hands out to his mother. I returned the precious bundle to his mother's loving hands.

Later, as I was putting on my coat, Naomi asked, "When will I see you again? Oh, don't forget the books and pamphlets."

"I'll have to fit in a visit after I finish this load of reading matter and my college homework," I replied. "I'll get in touch with you. Thanks so much for all you've given me. Maybe, someday, you'll have . . . what is that word? Oh yes, that's right. . . much *nachas* from me."

chapter seventeen

W hat happens at a *Bris*, Mom?" I asked my mother. "Shaindee's mother had a boy, and I'm invited. Can you tell me something about it?"
The blood drained from my mother's face. She turned ashen.

"How fast things are happening," she said. "What your grandfather couldn't accomplish down on earth, he is managing to accomplish from the heavens. Thank G-d."

I looked at my mother. This speech was bizarre for her. Indeed, only lately she had been muttering under her breath, "We don't understand His ways. We just don't understand His ways."

I was living in two worlds. Where did I belong? I saw hate and prejudice at the Brennans, and I was ashamed because I still wanted to be accepted and belong. And now I was going to watch the joy in initiating a newborn boy into Judaism.

When I arrived at Shaindee's house, it was already filled with people. The men were in one room and the women in another. The melodious chanting of prayers could be heard. The men wore white shawls with something on them that looked like tassels. I recalled once coming upon my grandfather dressed like that.

"What are you doing, Grandfather?" I had asked. "Are you cold? What is that little black box on your head?"

"This is my *Tefillin*," he had said, pointing to his head. Then he pointed to the white scarf around his shoulders and added, "And this is my *Tallis*."

"Why do you wear it, Grandfather?"

"I wear one of the *tefillin* on the left arm opposite the heart and the other on the head above the forehead in order that it may influence my heart and mind to follow the Law of G-d and that I should love Him and obey Him with all my heart and soul. It also reminds me that we Jews were slaves in Egypt before Hashem took us out and made us free. It helps reinforce the trust I have in Him."

"I was never a slave," I answered. "We learned in school that the black people were slaves and that Lincoln freed them."

"My child," he said. "We were slaves to Pharaoh in Egypt, many, many years before there was an Abraham Lincoln."

It was just at that moment of reminiscence that I faced thoughts I had tried to keep submerged. I loved my grandfather, but during these past few months, I also found I resented him. He had let me grow up totally ignorant of something he held so precious. It wasn't because he was selfish or lazy. It wasn't that he just didn't care. In Shaindee's home, surrounded by the many "grandfathers," I finally understood. There are many ways to teach. Teaching is not only through preaching. The best way is by example, and this, my grandfather tried. I recognized my father's hostility. My father must have given him some sort of ultimatum that if he would deliberately try to influence me, he wouldn't be allowed to see me. I now realized how Grandfather tried, how difficult it must have been within the limits provided to him. That it had taken me so many years to become aware of this maneuver was the proof of my father's success.

Shaindee waved from the other side of the room. I watched as she made her way through the crowd. It was the first time I'd seen her since she'd been in my house. She kissed me on my cheek and turned to introduce me to some ladies at a nearby table.

"This is my Aunt Chava, my Aunt Penina, and this is my cousin Elisheva." She continued to introduce me to others, but there were so many faces, I could not remember the names attached to the people.

"Where is your mother?" I asked.

"She is in the room with the baby, but she will be out soon."

Azrial and Ovadiah saw me and came running.

"Can you say my name?" Ovadiah asked.

I deliberately mispronounced their names and enjoyed their laughter.

I noticed that everyone in the room wore long sleeved dresses. I tried to pull down the sleeves of my blouse, but the cuffs still remained above my elbow.

"*Mazel Tov*, Shaindee," a tall girl said.

"Marian, these are my friends," said Shaindee. "I would like you to meet them. This is Estie," she pointed out the taller of the two, "and this is Reva," she said about the shorter girl.

We nodded at each other.

"Please excuse me," Shaindee said. "You'll have to get to know each other without me. My mother is calling, and I'm sure she needs my help."

Shaindee's two friends were an interesting contrast. Estie was tall and thin with an exotic look about her, while Reva was plump and short with sparkling black eyes and a rapt interested expression on her face.

"Hi," I said. "Do you live around here?"

"I do," Estie answered. "I really couldn't live much closer. I'm Shaindee's neighbor, and Reva lives around the corner. How about you?"

"I live in Far Rockaway."

"Far Rockaway? How did you and Shaindee ever meet?"

Before I had a chance to answer, Estie said, "Sssh. They are about ready to begin."

I found Shaindee at my side. A solemn quiet descended in the room. The baby was carried in on a pillow and passed around. Someone moved into my path, and I couldn't see anything.

"What's happening, Shaindee?" I asked.

"The *Bris* is taking place," she said. "Come, let us get a little closer so you can see."

"*Mazel Tov! Mazel Tov!*" Shaindee's Aunt Chava exclaimed and kissed her on the cheek. "*Mazel Tov*, Shaindee. May Sholom Yisroel's birth be a *nechama* for you, and just as his name means peace, may he help bring you peace."

Shaindee's eyes were full of tears as she kissed her mother, and I heard her whisper, "Thank you. Oh, thank you."

I too wished Mrs. Josephs *Mazel Tov*. She thanked me and said, "*Simchos* by you."

Almost miraculously, food and drinks appeared. Shaindee's friends steered me to a table.

"Come. We'll wash," Estie said.

I followed them into the kitchen. I watched as Estie took a large cup, filled it with water, poured it on her hands and said some words. Reva handed the cup to me.

"I'm sorry," I said. "I never did this before. Would you please help me?"

111

They looked surprised but overcame it quickly and became very solicitous.

"Watch me," Estie said. "Then do the same thing and I'll say the *berachah* with you."

I followed along and did exactly as she did and repeated the words after her. She put her finger on her lips, and I did not talk. We sat down at the table, and Estie gave me a slice of bread dipped in salt, and again I repeated words after her. I bit into the bread, and then she said, "Okay, now we can talk."

While I ate a bagel-and-lox sandwich and had a cup of coffee with a cheese danish, Estie told me that Shaindee and Reva had been friends for a long time and that they attended the same school. I looked up when Shaindee returned and asked her if I could see the baby.

"Come," she said.

I followed her into the bedroom.

"This is Sholom Yisroel," she said, her voice caressing the words as she uttered each one. "You know, it is customary in the Jewish religion to name a baby after someone who died. This little baby is named after someone who was very close to me. His name was Sholom, which means peace, and he died in Israel . . . Yisroel. I thought that I would have to wait until I got married myself and had a son to see this name carried on. I'm glad I didn't have to wait that long."

I looked at the baby, a newborn, red-faced infant without any distinctive characteristics. He had just been welcomed into the brotherhood of the Jewish people. No! He was not just a newborn infant without any distinctive characteristics. He was really unique. Every baby carried a tremendous burden upon his shoulders. This tiny infant, just eight days old, could affect the destiny of generations. What he did with the pure soul with which he was born would determine the strengths and weaknessess of his children and their children and the children after them.

I know that when a child is born, he comes into the world with clenched fists and that when a person dies, his hand is open. We leave this world empty of material possessions.

Dr. and Mrs. Brennan were also infants at one time. They would not take their worldly goods with them. What would they leave? Possessions? Given in hatred. Meaningless.

I looked around the room. Utter simplicity. Shaindee's family did not have many physical possessions. But they had a legacy of love, culture, compassion and a tradition thousands of years old. Lucky baby, I thought. You will inherit millions, millions that have true value, and you will be able to give this to your children and to your children's children. I was proud of my new maturity.

I put my finger into the crib and the baby curled his little fingers around mine. I felt the softness of his little hand and the warmth of his skin. Softly, I murmured a little prayer.

"Dear G-d," I said. "I know I can also say my G-d, even though I came so late to understand You. Is it possible that the traditions this baby carries within him can be transmitted to me through touch? No! I have it also within my ancestry. I pray that the strength of this household fuse with the strength of my grandfather and ancestors to give me the vision to follow the correct road to where my future lies. Oh, dear G-d, help me. There is so much confusion within my soul. I want You, and yet, I want Neal. Please, dear G-d, oh, please, show me the way to go."

Shaindee looked at me and I at her. There were tears in both our eyes. She squeezed my hand. I felt her strength and support. Somehow, I knew she understood what was in my heart.

Shaindee and her friends walked me to the door. I said goodbye and that I hoped to see them again. I left the house with a trail of "*Mazel Tov, Mazel Tov,* good luck, good luck," ringing in my ears.

chapter eighteen

My world was growing more and more topsy-turvy. Even school was discouraging. I was disillusioned. My course in Educational Philosophy taught me that no one really knew what they were doing. Everything that was supposed to be the last word in education was just experimental. The Perennialists as exemplified by Hutchins felt that despite different environments, human nature is the same and education should be the same for all. The Reconstructionist movement was for individual freedom, and the Progressives were for something else. Some believed that moral training was the job of the school, and others felt it was the job of the home. Each one would claim that his views were based upon reliable, irrefutable findings, and then the next one would come along to refute the irrefutable findings by insisting his ideas were built upon reliable, irrefutable findings.

I was also disgusted with morality on the campus. Obviously, the homes were not doing the job, and neither were the schools.

Janet and I were trying very hard to keep our friendship cemented. It was built on trust and confidence, however, and now, there were too many things I could not share with her. I feared the consequences.

December arrived, and along with the chilling cold came vacation from school. As I walked along the streets, I now noticed which store windows and home windows had seasonal decorations. When I saw a *Menorah* in the window, a warm feeling of kinship would envelop me.

Neal had written when his plane was scheduled to land. I did not go to the airport to meet him. I knew his parents would be there, and I did not want to face them. Hypocrisy was never my cup of tea, and I couldn't smile sweetly at them when I felt such bitterness inside.

Neal called. His cheerful voice on the telephone told me that his parents had not yet discussed their "evening with Marian."

"See you at seven," he said.

But it was a totally different Neal at seven o'clock. The air between us was charged. We said "Hello" and "How are you?" and "It's good to see you again." There was no conversation walking to the car. I could not believe that my most conscious thought was of the weather. Yesterday, the wind had been howling all day, and the sky was filled with unbroken clouds; it was refreshing now to see the full moon breaking through the patches of pallor.

Neal opened the door of the car, and I stepped in. He started the car. The silence between us was deafening. I knew one of us would have to break this impasse, so when Neal stopped the car at an intersection, I made the first move.

"I guess your parents told you."

"I'm embarrassed and really sorry, Marian. It must have been a hateful evening for you. I apologize for my parents' behavior."

"They gave me quite a bit to think about."

"I'm sure! But they can talk from today until tomorrow. They won't be able to change things. I can't get over it, Marian. My parents objected to you only because you are Jewish. It is unthinkable. I never felt you were different from me."

I felt my heart lurch in happiness. I sat there basking in my feeling of pride. Neal was really unbiased. He didn't care that I was Jewish ... Was I crazy!? What had gotten into me? What had he really said? "I never felt you were different from me." But I was different. I was Jewish. There was no denying it, and suddenly, like sunshine bursting through a dark cloud, I finally realized I was proud of it. My religion was the father of all religions. My religion gave the world a moral leg to stand on. My religion opened the eyes of the world to the fact that a piece of wood could not be a god. If there was to be any future for Neal and myself, he would have to understand all that. He could not escape into his fantasy world and reject what I'd grown proud of.

"Neal," I said gently. "The truth is that I am different. You are a gentile, and I am a Jew. Your parents are not really wrong in their assessment that there is a basic difference between our heritages. I am proud of my heritage. It has always been an example for the world, and all religions have tried to take something from it to emulate. What your parents are wrong in is the senseless hatred which stems from your religion; your religion which is supposed to teach love and brotherhood has been the

115

cause of bloodshed throughout history."

"I can't believe this," said Neal.

"Neal, if you can understand that your parents will never accept me and if you yourself can fully accept the fact that I am a Jew, then there is something further to discuss. I have just recently discovered my roots and my identity and I glory in it!"

"What are you talking about, Marian? You never spoke or acted this way before. I know you are Jewish, but in a way, you really aren't. For gosh sakes, what made such a change in you?"

Neal continued driving. He drove over a bridge, and the traffic became heavier. Concentration caused all conversation to stop. His headlights illuminated the light snowflakes that had started to fall. It was a peaceful scene with a feeling of tranquility, completely devoid of the swirling currents of turmoil within the car.

I looked out the window. There was a vague familiarity about the area through which we were driving. The surrounding buildings on both sides of the narrow streets were filled with the sights and sounds of dim but not completely forgotten memories. I looked at Neal. His face was barely discernible in the weak street light which filled the interior of the car with shadows and faint pools of illumination. Neal was looking for a parking spot, but the holiday season made it difficult to find one.

He stopped the car near an open space littered with rubble. The light snowfall could not hide the disorderly sight. We were surrounded by tall houses known as "The Projects." There was a familiarity about it, but I knew I had never been here before. What was it?

Suddenly, I knew. Just before my grandfather had entered the nursing home, he too had lived in a similar complex. They all resembled each other, large buildings teeming with the young and the old. Even the young in these houses have an old weariness about them. Most of the buildings were lit with the twinkling lights on indoor trees which come with this season. One building was dark, except for one lonely candelabra with four sparkling lights. It seemed to be guarding the window in its solitary splendor. It brought me back to my grandfather's apartment, and I could almost smell and taste the potato pancakes.

"I think we have to talk," Neal said. "This tension between us is so thick, I can't handle it. I feel as if I'm walking a tightrope; one false move, and I'll fall. We must clear the air between us."

"Okay, Neal. Let's talk. What do you want to talk about?" My words came out harsh and unsympathetic.

"You seem so different," he said. "Why?"

"By the same token, Neal, I ask you the same question."

"Look, Marian, if we continue like this, we'll just go around and around in circles. If we want to get to the source of the problem, we have to start somewhere."

"You're right, Neal. Tell me about Kurt and your roommate."

"Why? Because Jeffrey is Jewish?"

"Stop being sarcastic, Neal. Then let's start with Kurt."

"What is it you want to know about Kurt?"

"Tell me everything. How you spend your day? What do you and Kurt do when you come home from school? What is Jeffrey like? So much has happened to both of us since you left, I guess we have to become reacquainted. Okay, let's start with Kurt. I don't really know him as well as you do. Tell me how you met him. How come you decided to room with Kurt? And what do you know about his background?"

"What does Kurt have to do with us, Marian? I don't ask you about Janet. This is between the two of us."

"But Neal, Kurt has become so much a part of you, and I want to know everything about you."

Neal seemed sickened by my tenacious insistence, and he expressed himself in no uncertain terms. My persistence paid off, however, and I received some of the answers I was waiting for.

"Kurt's father was a brilliant doctor in Germany. He came to America immediately after the Second World War and married Kurt's mother. She is an American and much younger than his father. My father and Kurt's father met when they were both practicing medicine in the same hospital. Dr. Smith is much older than my father, but my father respected his brilliance, and for that reason, the age gap narrowed and they socialized together."

"When did you meet Kurt?" I asked.

"I think I was about fourteen years old and Kurt fifteen when our parents sent us to Camp Wee-Hank-Inn. He drove the counsellors wild with his pranks. Most of the boys didn't have the nerve to follow him, but we all admired his courage. He was the first in everything he undertook: the best swimmer, runner, ball player. You name it. He became my hero, and I think I sort of worshipped him; you know, the little brother looking up to the big brother hero type. Of course, now that I'm older, I've learned to respect him for his positive qualities and accept those I consider negative as just being one part of Kurt."

"What would you consider his negative qualities?"

"Well, he has an arrogance and sureness about him. I always feel he knows exactly where he's going. No. Come to think of it, I don't think I would consider that a negative quality." Neal stopped talking and thought a while. "Well, he cannot accept criticism. He must always be in the limelight and is intolerant of inferiority."

"Can you give me an example?"

"Cut it out, Marian. You make me feel as if I'm on a witness stand being interrogated by the prosecutor. Are you also going to be the judge and jury?"

"I'm sorry, Neal. I didn't mean it to come out the way it did." I was groping for words to handle this delicate situation. "I'm really sorry. I didn't want to come across like this. Please, Neal, go on."

Neal shook his head as if wanting to deny the thoughts coming into his mind. "Well, in his intolerance, he doesn't seem to care whom he steps upon."

"Did he ever step on you?"

"Never. He wouldn't dare. Besides, we really get along great."

"Would you say he stepped on Jeffrey?"

"Marian, I told you about that. This conversation is becoming ridiculous. I wrote you all about Kurt and Jeffrey."

"Please, Neal," I attempted to placate him. "You wrote me about his plans, but you never did tell me how far he went."

"Well, he certainly cemented his relationship with the landlord. All it took was a beautifully packaged bottle on his doorstep every Saturday morning, courtesy of Kurt. The landlord is an alcoholic, and Kurt helps him support the habit. He has also sent Jeffrey ridiculous letters."

"What did the letters say?"

Neal squirmed in his seat.

"You know," he answered. "The usual hate letters. We don't want any Jews in Harvard. Get out of town, Jew, or we'll get you, and so on."

"What did Jeffrey do? Did he know it was Kurt writing the letters?"

"I don't think he realized it at first. He opened the letters, read them, tore them up and threw them in the garbage. Kurt stood there gloating, and after a while, it was obvious to any fool that Kurt had something to do with it."

"And Jeffrey is no fool. What did he do?"

"He totally ignored Kurt and the letters. Now he acts as if they don't exist. He doesn't even bother to open them but throws them directly in the trash can."

"Is Jeffrey still in the apartment?"

"Oh, sure. In fact, he has asked Kurt to move out."

"How about you? Did he ask you to leave also?"

"No. It was obvious who the culprit was. I told you Jeffrey is a whiz, and he zeroed in on it immediately."

"Did Kurt leave?"

"Are you kidding? Kurt said the only way he would leave would be over Jeffrey's dead body. In fact, this conversation took place the night before we left for vacation."

"What do you think of Jeffrey?"

"He is extremely intelligent and is at the top of the class. He has a natural brilliance. Although he studies hard and takes school very seriously, I think he could do better than average without applying himself as studiously. He is not much of a mixer and rarely socializes. It is as if he's in school for a purpose, and that's that. I think his family is poor, and either he is attending school on a scholarship or somebody is picking up part of the tab. He does get a lot of mail, so I assume he is not anti-social. The truth is that under other circumstances, I could like him."

"But in your letters, Neal, I seemed to get the feeling you didn't like him. Why?"

"Well, as Kurt says, 'They're pushy.' "

I tried to deceive myself that he didn't understand what he was saying. "How?"

"How what?" he answered.

"How are *they* pushy?"

"They want to get ahead," he replied.

"Is there anything wrong in that? Does it harm anyone?"

"Well, Kurt says—" He stopped abruptly as he realized what I was leading up to. "Look, Marian, you're different."

"Don't you realize what has happened to you, Neal? Kurt has brainwashed you into believing in a stereotype image of a Jew. No, Neal!" I shook my head. "No. I'm not different. If you accept that as a Jewish characteristic, I have it also. I am one of *them*. You should realize for yourself that there are Jews that are pushy and Moslems and Lutherans and Catholics and so forth that are also pushy. You are continuing to perpetuate a misconception."

"My goodness, what has happened to you, Marian? You seem to have become a flag waver for the race. Your defense mechanism is working full force. You never acted like this before."

Neal was angry, and I felt I had pushed him to the limit. He started the car, and I felt myself jerk as the car jumped ahead. I tensed against the pitch of the car. The silence between us was deafening.

Neal continued to drive. We exchanged no words. Between us, unspoken, was the memorized text of our disagreement. As the car continued moving slowly ahead in traffic, I shut my eyes. I could hear the pounding of my heart and hoped Neal could not hear it.

So engrossed had I been in our conversation, I hadn't realized that the snow had continued to fall. The streets were covered by the white glaze with a picture book beauty. Snowflakes clung to the bare trees, the whiteness against the stark outline giving it a ghostly witch-like effect.

Neal pulled the car up in front of my house. We were secluded, entombed on an island, surrounded by the purity of the fresh snow. Neal's tone of voice was conciliatory.

"We have to make a decision. Either we do not discuss religion or . . ." He stopped talking, and I recognized his hesitation.

"Or what, Neal?" Although my words sounded harsh, they were not meant to be.

"Or I guess we'll just have to call it quits. This is it!"

I had baited Neal. I wasn't ready to give him up. I did not want to give him up! My future and my dreams were tied up with him; the bigotry and hatred were something we'd have to overcome.

I didn't know where or from what reserve I got the strength to answer.

"The problem is not mine, Neal," I said gently. "It is your problem."

"Then as far as I'm concerned, we are not going to discuss this any further. The subject is closed."

"And your parents?"

Neal did not even give me the opportunity to complete my sentence.

"Marian, this is between you and me. Period!"

I laugh today at my innocence. I suppose that when a person wants to believe something, he accepts the impossible. I wanted so badly to believe that things would remain status quo. I wanted to believe his parents' feelings would not cause any future dissension between us. I wanted to believe there was no boundary between myself as a Jew and Neal as a gentile, and so, I returned to my fairy land. By mutual consent, we agreed to make no mention of this problem; we would try to efface it from our memories. We still looked forward to our future.

Ah, yes. But the mind cannot always be controlled. Emotions and thoughts can run amok. Although I tried to erase my thoughts, they kept strolling back insistently.

I realize now that we are the sum total of our past and of the present. Was it my mother who said that all happenings become part of us, changing us even if we are not conscious of it? Her words came back to haunt me, because as much as I wanted things to remain the same between Neal and me, I found myself reacting differently to a word said or to an expression. I became prickly and conscious of innuendoes, perhaps even manufacturing them if they weren't there. My thoughts were chaotic.

On the surface, our conversation became easier and although we did bid each other goodnight pleasantly, I recognized a gleam of mistrust. I knew a hairline of doubt would always be present.

I had been so certain of my future. I had been so sure where I was going and what I wanted out of life. I thought of Carol's brother. Had he felt like this at one time?

I lay on my bed, immobile, staring off into an uncertain future. A premonition of dread filled my heart.

chapter nineteen

The remainder of Neal's vacation proved uneventful. We both tried very hard and spent some comfortable evenings together. The Brennans had planned a weekend in their vacation lodge, and Kurt and his parents were invited. Neal sounded me out about joining them for a weekend of skiing, but I said I didn't think my parents would allow it. I hadn't asked them, but I knew I didn't want to go. I was happy Neal didn't exert any pressure.

When he returned from the weekend, we spent an evening together, and then Neal and Kurt left for Boston.

There was one more day left of my vacation, and I planned to catch up on a term paper I had neglected when Janet called.

"Marian, did you read today's paper?"

"No. My father usually brings it home from work, but he won't be home until late this evening. What is so earth-shattering in the newspaper?"

"I can't even begin to tell you. Go out right now and pick up the morning addition of *The Daily Times*."

Janet was not an impulsive person, and because of her insistence, my natural curiosity got the better of me. I quickly dressed, putting on my coat, hat and boots.

"Mom, do you need anything from the store? I'm going out now."

"It's bitter cold out, Marian. What is so important that you have to go now?"

"Oh, Janet said that there is an interesting article in the paper and that I shouldn't wait until this evening when Daddy brings the paper home. I'm going out to get one."

The car wouldn't start immediately. I hadn't used it for a few days. It took a while until it finally caught, and then it made the usual putt-putt sound until it warmed up. Driving was hazardous because ice was beginning to form on the snow. I had to concentrate on my driving.

I stopped at the first store I reached. It was difficult to walk from the car to the store, and I had to be extremely careful not to slip on the icy walk. Because of the inclement weather, cars were parked along the curb, abandoned by their drivers who walked the remaining distance to their homes rather than drive. I couldn't find a parking space and had to double park. I paid for the paper and scanned the headlines. There was nothing of special interest. I thumbed through the rest of the pages rapidly but again, I saw nothing unusual.

Mr. David, the owner of the store, made a comment about not having seen such a cold day for years. I agreed. The heat of the store indoors and the cold of the outdoors caused a mist of fog that clouded the window so that it was impossible to see out.

As I walked to the car, I found myself blowing smoke rings of cold air. Again, it took a while for the car to start and just as I was beginning to feel sorry for having listened to Janet and braving the bitter cold, I managed to get the car moving. I skidded on the icy road and was grateful to arrive home and enter its warmth and safety.

I searched the paper. It was full of the usual bizarre sensationalism to which readers have become accustomed.

I called Janet.

"You must be nuts," I said. "I went out in this cold weather to pick up a paper, and I can't fathom for what reason."

"Marian, hang up the phone and turn to the front page again. Look carefully and read everything."

I followed her instructions. I searched the paper again. There was an interesting article on the front page. I read:

Victim Points Accusing Finger at Dr. Zvilling
NEW YORK

Mrs. Y. Daniels had accused Dr. John Smith of being the infamous Dr. Hans Schmidt of the Auschwitz Concentration Camp. The alleged suspect was accused by Mrs. Daniels, a former inmate at Auschwitz, of being the doctor known for his experimentation on twins. The alleged crimes of Dr. John Smith, or Dr. Hans Schmidt, are well documented in the Allied records of the Nuremburg trials. Dr. Schmidt's specialty was the use of Jewish twins as guinea pigs for experiments. Twins from concentration camps in different countries were rounded up

(continued on page 30)

I quickly turned to Page 30 and the story continued.

and sent to the camp. Since identical twins are the closest blood relatives, he would allegedly use one twin for the various experiments he conducted and the other twin as the scientific control. The inmates of the concentration camp are reported to have called Dr. Schmidt by the name of Dr. Zvilling, which means Dr. Twin.

Mrs. Daniels claims her twin sister was killed in one of the experiments conducted by Dr. Smith, alias Dr. Hans Schmidt. She has called upon any twins involved or anyone who had knowledge of Dr. Smith's activities to please come forward.

Deportation proceedings are being considered.

I turned back to the front page and stared at the picture. I saw a well dressed man attempting to conceal his face with his hands as he was being led by two detectives.

I called Janet back.

"Janet, I don't understand your hysterics. Of course, this is a horror story, but for this, you made me go out in this weather? It could have waited until the evening when my father returns home."

"Marian, you nincompoop!" she answered. "Look again! That's Kurt's father."

"Oh, my gosh." I recoiled in horror. "I didn't realize. How horrible!"

I hung up the telephone. A slow burning fury began to take possession of me. I was heartsick at the evil of this man. I picked up the newspaper again and gazed at the picture in horror. The picture moved and danced before my eyes. I recalled Kurt's sardonic grin and sarcasm as he spoke to me. I even recalled his walk. I could now understand why I felt that he slithered like a snake. I recalled the red flush across his catlike face when we went to Coney Island. I remembered his ruthless war on his roommate who had offered him shelter. I now understood my innate rejection and repulsion. I wondered whether Neal knew. I felt betrayed by

Neal, and an insidious doubt of him continued to grow within me. I felt destitute and sick that Neal admired this man's son who so patterned his life upon his father's foundation of malicious hatred.

At dinner that evening, the atmosphere was tense. At first, I thought it was a reaction to my unusual lack of conversation, but then I noticed the agitation on my parents' faces. My mother, in particular, looked very upset. Her face was flushed and her eyes bright, hiding unshed tears. My father spoke to her softly. There was an increased tenderness in his voice. I searched their faces for the answer to the riddle. My mother's eyes were riveted to the fourth chair near the table. I looked to see what the magnet was that drew her eyes to that particular chair. It was only the newspaper.

I pointed to the newspaper.

"That article in the paper, that man in the picture . . . Dr. Smith, is the father of Neal's best friend Kurt. Do you think it's true?" I asked. "After all, a doctor takes an oath. His goal and the purpose of his education is to help humanity. They wouldn't treat people as animals to conduct experiments?"

"Oh, my G-d!" my mother cried out. Her face turned white as if she had suddenly seen an apparition. I thought she was going to faint. I ran to the sink and filled a glass with water. Gently, my father eased her head back. She sipped the water slowly. Her hands were ice cold.

"To these people, a Jew was not part of humanity. We were not considered human," she said, her face contorted in pain. Her voice was dull and each word seemed to be wrenched out of her. She spoke in a monotone, without highs or lows to express feelings or emotions. "When you think of a zoo, you think of animals in cages behind bars. Here, the animals were outside the cage. The Jew was behind the bars. The animal raised its eyes and looked briefly at the people behind the bars, planning the best method to destroy them. They killed people, babies, took lives, ruined lives just as easily as we pluck a petal from a flower."

And then she broke down. It was like water bursting from a dam. My very innards twisted at the sound. A cry of protest, of hysteria, a cry of hopelessness and despair, the eternal wail of mourning, for herself, for the dead, and for the future generations that would never have a chance to live. Her body shook, racked with torment, torn with sobbing. I felt my own body react with chills and trembling.

I threw my arms around my mother and cried. I pleaded with her not to cry. I stroked her face, her arms, her shoulders. I didn't know what to do. My father tried. Softly and soothingly, he spoke to her. Warmth and compassion surrounded my mother. I stood there helpless, a stranger to their world.

"Please, Mommy, please. Is there anything I can do? Is there anything I can say? Oh, my poor mother. Please. Please." I wasn't even conscious of my words. They just poured out of me. I felt I had to talk, to keep talking, to try to stifle the sight and sound of the scene before me.

Slowly, ever so slowly, the crying stopped and then, little by little, the trembling.

"We think, Marian, that we can bury the past but it comes back to haunt us," my mother said between stifled sobs. "We try to pick up the pieces and build a new life by just pretending the past never existed, that the events just never occurred. How many times have I told myself it was just a horrible dream, a nightmare, and that I will soon wake up? But everything comes back in vivid detail. Sometimes, it is a word, just a little word. Sometimes, it is a sound that makes the images return. Do you understand?"

I nodded.

"I don't think you possibly can, dear Marian," she said. "Once, I was walking in the street and caught a fleeting glance of a face in a store window, and once it happened with a passerby, a similarity to some face, to some monster, and I stop in my tracks, afraid to continue, and the horrors come back again and again. Tonight, a newspaper story made me lose control."

Now I understood the expression, "I felt as if my heart was breaking inside of me." I listened to my mother and that was exactly how I felt. She looked . . . perhaps like a broken doll or a child who had been whipped.

"Mom," I lowered my voice and, unknowingly, was talking in a whisper. "Was Kurt's father part of your past?" I put my hand over my mouth when a horrible thought entered my mind. "Mother, were you a twin?"

My father moved closer to my mother and took her hand in his.

"No, Marian," he said. "Kurt's father was involved in this specific type of heinous act. But other doctors were involved in many other forms of cruelty."

I waited. I saw it was difficult for her to continue. To repeat what she

126

had seen would once again become a visual act and would necessitate living through it all over again. I felt such tremendous pity for my mother.

My father put his hand out to me, and I too sat down on the couch and took my mother's other hand in mine. Her hand was trembling and cold. I took her hand and held it sandwiched between mine, hoping the warm blood flowing through my veins would warm her cold hands.

"I think I must have been about fourteen years old at the time it happened." Her voice was soft, barely above a whisper. "I was a little younger when I was taken into the concentration camp. It was hard to be torn away from my family. I told you we were close knit. My mother always worried about my eating, and would make special appetizing meals for me as I was a skinny child and a finicky eater."

She paused as if to try to get her thoughts together.

"In the concentration camp, our food consisted of a piece of moldy bread and a watery, tasteless soup. Sometimes the soup contained a drop of cabbage. We all suffered from one form of dysentery or another, and the cabbage did not help at all. At the beginning, I couldn't eat it. I would look at the moldy bread and the watery soup, and my stomach revolted at the sight and smell of it. But the other girls in the camp forced me to eat. They said this was all the food we would get, and if I wouldn't eat it, I would starve. They said that if I had no energy to work, the guards would report me, and the next step would mean certain death. And so," she shrugged her shoulders, "I guess you get used to anything. I ate this food just like all my friends.

"Some adventurous girls would scrounge through the garbage pails to find a discarded piece of real food the Germans had not eaten. I couldn't do that, either. That too revolted me. But you know, Marian, after a while, when I realized this soup and moldy bread would be the mainstay of my diet and that I could look forward to nothing else, I accepted gratefully anything they would give me."

I looked at my mother. How can I describe her? If a hair is out of place, if a spot is on her clothing, if the tablecloth is not snow white and the house and her person not neat as a pin, she gets agitated. Neatness and cleanliness are such an integral part of her.

"I became friendly with one of the girls in the camp," she continued. "Her name was Baila, and she sort of took me under her wing. She shared everything with me, every bit of food she was able to scrounge for. If it hadn't been for her, I don't think I would have had any energy.

She fed my body and my soul. Baila was a good scavenger, and on one of her hunts through the garbage, she brought back a piece of leftover meat. As she had shared things with me in the past, she again graciously shared this with me. I don't know if it was the meat. Baila ate it and it did not affect her. Perhaps I ate too fast. To this day, I don't know, but I doubled up with a horrible pain which persisted and would not go away. The other girls tried to cover for me the entire day, because if I couldn't work, it meant death.

"The pain persisted throughout that day and the entire night. Baila put her hand over my mouth so that my moaning would not be heard. I bit my lips, bit into my arms, stuffed the hem of my dress in my mouth. The girls tried whatever remedies they could think of, but nothing helped. The fear of the room they called 'The Hospital' was in all our minds. We knew that the function of the hospital was to complete the sequence of death. It was a known fact that of those who entered, hardly any ever came out alive. As if by mutual agreement, we knew I would have to suffer through this episode in quiet. But when I didn't show up the second day for the work squad, they came for me."

My mother stopped talking at this point. The tears were running down her face. She tried to compose herself to continue.

"Baila cried when I was taken to the hospital. Her arms held me tight. We clung to each other. We thought it was the end."

Once again, my mother stopped talking. At first she seemed in a trance; her eyes stared unseeing. My father left the couch and brought her a glass of juice. She held it in her hands.

"Maybe," he said, "I should continue."

"No." She shook her head.

"I guess I was one of the lucky ones," she sighed. "I survived and had you. I wasn't killed by air injected into my veins or subjected to hideous experiments."

She continued as if talking about a stranger.

"I was put on a table. The table must have had wheels, because I felt I was being wheeled into the operating room. I can still see the room clearly. It was a small room, perhaps a little larger than a closet. It was painted white, and wherever I looked, everything was white. Total cleanliness. Sterility. The German reputation for orderliness showed in the instruments. They were shiny and clean, all lined up neatly in straight rows.

"I was frightened. Fear paralyzed my vocal cords. But then, I was able to scream, to yell, 'I have no pain. My stomach is better. I feel fine. Please let me go back to work.' I strained against the bonds holding me down and tried to get off the table. I looked pleadingly at the doctor. He looked huge. His hands looked huge with long black hairs sticking out of the top of his hands. Germans are supposed to be blonde, I thought. Maybe I am dreaming all this. He didn't look like any doctor I had ever seen. He seemed larger than a stevedore. 'Please,' I begged. 'Please. Please.'

"The doctor laughed. Marian, for years I would wake up with night-mares and see his cruel face before me and his ham-like hairy hands. I can still hear his voice; a voice filled with malevolence and sadism when he spoke. 'Little one,' he said. 'Don't cry. You know you are only suffering from a stomach ache which may be due to a combination of cabbage soup and putrid meat, but I will see to it that you never have any stomach pains again. No. Never again.' He laughed. 'Your G-d made Eve suffer pain during childbirth. Remember, for the rest of your life, that this German doctor had compassion for you and eliminated all pangs that you might suffer in the future. You will never endure any childbirth pain. Ever.'

"I was only fourteen years old, childlike in my innocence, but I realized what he planned to do. I begged, pleaded and cried. My words fell on deaf ears. I don't remember anything after that until I woke up in pain. I never saw him again.

"There was a woman who came into the room afterwards. I think she might have been a nurse, but I'm not sure. I don't believe she was a German. She held me in her arms and rocked me as she comforted me. 'You'll be all right,' she said. 'You'll live. You have to be thankful for that.'"

I threw my arms around my mother, and we held each other tightly. Our tears mingled, blending together. Her tears were now mine, and mine were now hers. I thought I would choke on my feelings of compassion. I cried for my mother, and for my father. I felt cheated of the brothers and sisters I never had and of the children my parents so badly wanted and didn't have.

"And then, Marian, like a miracle, after many years, you were born," said my mother. "G-d was good to us. The Nazi did not complete his mission. We thank G-d for that and for you."

We couldn't talk. There was quiet in the room. Our silence was filled with emotion, with feeling, with pathos. I looked at my mother and father.

I broke the silence.

"How can a person go on, look a human being in the eye and believe in humanity again?" I asked. "Do you hate?"

"Hate?" she said. "Whom should we hate? The Nazis for their barbarious cruelty? The Polish people, the Ukrainians, the French, the Lithuanians, the Slovaks, the Hungarians or the Rumanians? They were all part of the cruelty of a world gone stark raving mad. They were ready, willing and able to assist Germany and become its accomplices in Hitler's master plan to make the world *Judenrein*. All they needed was a leader to light the fire, and they were standing there, only too anxious to throw their logs on the fire to make it a roaring one."

"Hate?" said my father. "Hate whom? Christianity?"

"Not Christianity," I interrupted. "The Church stands for compassion."

"My dear child," my father added. "The churches were accomplices."

"Oh no! You can't really mean that."

"Yes, Marian," he said. "That is exactly what I mean. The propaganda machines work full time making us believe white is black and black is white. How easily we accept it! The truth is that the churches, except for rare instances, were accomplices. Some of the rare instances were usually attempts to convert Jews to their faith. Yes, there were some people, wonderfully kind and compassionate, who were concerned with humanity, but unfortunately, they were all too few." My father paused. "The churches were accomplices in silence."

I shook my head. I just didn't understand.

"You said churches," I wondered. "Both the Protestants and the Catholics?"

"Yes, both," my mother said. "Your father proved it to me. I also didn't want to believe this hate extended beyond Germany. I made excuses for everything and for everyone. But wherever I looked, I found the Catholic Church's hands dripping with Jewish blood. Remember the Crusades? Remember its name? The Holy Inquisition. You heard of the Spanish Inquisition. Who instigated all the pogroms in Europe? Jews have suffered throughout their lives and into and through the Second World War. This hatred was constant and consistent. The Poles, Lithuanians, Austrians, Croatians, Slovaks and Hungarians were all fanatical Catholics, and all had unsatiable appetites for Jewish blood."

"Wait," my father told my mother. He walked over to the bookcase and took down a book. He turned the pages until he came to the part he wanted me to read.

"Here," he said. "Read it for yourself."

I looked down at the page. The words were blurred. My eyes couldn't focus.

"You tell her, Jack," my mother said. "It is too much for her to comprehend."

"There was this famous rabbi," my father said. "His name was Rabbi Weissmandel, and he was there. He saw from the inside what was happening and what Hitler's plans were. In his memoirs of his experiences in Slovakia, he told of two encounters with the Catholic hierarchy in that country. It was shortly before Passover of 1942, when one of the most respected rabbis in that country approached the Archbishop Kametke, a man whom he had known from happier days, to influence a man who had been his former private secretary and was now the leading Catholic priest in Slovakia. This infamous person's name was Tisso. Rabbi Weissmandel urged him to pervail upon Tisso to prevent the expulsion of Jews from his country. At that time, the rabbi was only worried about the threat of expulsion. The archbishop however, decided to enlighten him regarding what was awaiting the Jews in Poland. He said that this in no mere expulsion. 'There you will not die of hunger and pestilence. There they will slaughter you all, old and young, women and children in one day.' This, he said, is the punishment the Jews will receive for the death of the redeemer."

My mother continued where my father left off.

"Another time, I think in the fall of 1944, Rabbi Weissmandel, his family and hundreds of other Jews had been put into a temporary camp prior to deportation to Auschwitz. He escaped and made his way to the residence of the *papal nuncio*. He described the conditions of the families in the camp and asked him to intervene with Tisso. His answer to Rabbi Weissmandel's urging, pleading and begging was that since this was a Sunday, which was his holy day, neither he nor Father Tisso could occupy themselves with profane matters. You hear, Marian? Profane matters!"

I sat there, shocked. My illusions were destroyed. My youthful idealism was gone. I couldn't say anything. What was there to say? Their words were etched on my mind, soaked in the blood of my people and heart, and yet, slowly, it began to dawn on me. Passover, they had said. That was the holiday that made my grandfather so upset. I recalled his words. "If we don't eat the bread of affliction . . ." My parents seemed to deny G-d, and yet, my mother had said my birth was a miracle of G-d. My parents denied their Jewishness and did not care Neal was gentile, and yet, there was such a bitter hatred in my parents for what the gentiles had done to the Jews.

"I can't believe it," I said. "How could the blood of innocent men, women and children be considered a profane matter?"

"Listen," my mother answered. "Please let me continue. There is more. His answer was that there is no innocent Jewish blood. All Jewish blood is guilty. They have to die. This is the punishment awaiting them because of that sin."

"I'm sure that if America had any idea of what was going on, they would have stopped it," I said.

"That is how we all felt in the concentration camps," my mother said. "We lived each day, every hour, minute by minute, just waiting for the Americans to make a move. But after the war, we found out that America had many opportunities to help us, to bomb the roads leading to the concentration camps, to rescue many." A deep, penetrating, mournful sigh escaped from somewhere deep within the depths of her body, of her very soul.

My father read the disbelief mirrored in my face. It was impossible for me to even comprehend the possibility that America could have had an opportunity to help and didn't.

"Would you believe it if I tell you that the State Department, yes, the American State Department, suppressed information about the barbaric behavior of the Germans from the public?" he asked.

"Why should America do that?" I protested.

"We didn't know all this at that time," he said. "We found out much later. Why should America do that, you ask? It was because the State Department followed the path of isolationism and not humanitarism."

"But I'm sure that once they found out all about Hitler's plans, they did something to stop him."

"Which plans?"

"To make the world *Judenrein*."

My mother laughed. It had a hollow sound, and it echoed in the corners of the room.

"Marian, the Germans gave the world the opportunity to rescue Jews, to buy Jews like you buy a piece of cattle," she said. "They even offered to exchange Jewish lives for trucks, but there were no takers. The Germans were smart. When they saw a Jew had no value, they realized it was a silent acceptance of their mass slaughter, and they went ahead with their master plan. It was their go-ahead signal."

"I can't believe it. I just can't."

"I understand," she answered me. "We were also innocent and wouldn't, couldn't and didn't believe it."

"The world didn't yell? Wasn't there anyone?"

She paused and then said, "Yes, there were good people, individuals who tried, were concerned and helped save a person here and there. There were caring individuals who spoke up against the deportation of tens of thousands of Jews, but the message the Germans received was that mass murder was really just a domestic matter and completely within Germany's jurisdiction."

"But Mom, Germany was such a cultured nation. How could an educated people do what they did?"

My father answered in a bitter voice.

"Yes, they were a cultured nation. Germany was well known for its administrative order and skill, and they really used these well known achievements in outdoing themselves in planning death in the most organized manner."

"None of the Allies helped?"

"No," he said. "The Allies didn't help, and in particular, the British foreign office was riddled with terrible anti-Semites. The foreign office saw a tremendous problem if they would save Jews."

"What do you mean?"

"Oh yes. They had a serious problem." The sarcasm in my father's voice was so thick it could be cut with a knife. "If they would rescue people and save lives, what would they do with these people? After all, they would need a place to stay."

"Well, what about America or Israel?" I questioned.

"America? What would they do with so many foreigners? Israel? Palestine was the name at that time. That would bring problems with the Arabs. England? England didn't want the Jews."

"And so . . ."

"Yes, and so . . . forgive my sarcasm. The easiest way out was to let Hitler solve the problem. Let them die. No problem. Period!"

133

"But the children? Oh, Daddy, what about all the little children? Didn't anyone try to save them?"

"Marian," my mother said. "I learned about all this after the war, much after the war and much of this embittered your father as it did so many others. There was a resolution in the Senate to admit twenty thousand children from Germany to America."

"You see," I said. "I knew America did something."

"I said there was a resolution in the Senate, but the reaction to it was that the country would be flooded with foreigners. And most horrible of all, there were those who feared that if the United States of America were to admit such a large group of children, it would no longer be able to guarantee its own children their right to life, liberty and the pursuit of happiness."

I was bewildered by what my mother was telling me. I refused to believe this of my country.

"These little children," she continued, "all under fourteen years of age, were described as thousands of motherless, embittered, persecuted children of undesirable foreigners."

"Undesirable foreigners? What? What harm did they expect from them? What made them undesirable?"

She laughed bitterly. "They were considered potential leaders of revolt against the American form of government."

"Weren't there some Americans who fought?"

"Oh yes, but they were like grains of sand blown away by the wind. Can you think of a more hypocritical reason for not saving children from persecution and death than the one put forward by the American Legion?"

"What was that?"

"Tell her, Jack," my mother answered.

"The American Legion claimed it was traditional American policy that home life should be preserved, and the American Legion strongly opposed the breaking up of families. After all, taking the children to America would mean that the families destined to die could not die together."

"So instead of rescuing them, they sent them to death together," I completed.

"No, Marian. Even that was not allowed. Parents, mothers, fathers were all separated. Children were torn from their parents' arms. Each met his death separated from loved ones. Mothers held the hands of someone else's child, comforting that child and bringing it a little peace, hoping that if their child was in that same unfortunate position, someone was doing it for their child."

"How horrible." I looked at my parents with empathy. "You have lived with this all these years, and you have never told me. I feel so small. My gosh! All the petty things I wanted and argued with you about as I was growing up. I'm so ashamed."

"Don't, Marian," my mother said. "That was natural. This was unnatural. I was glad these so called petty things were important to you."

"I don't know what to say," I said. "I sit here and think, but I realize it is almost impossible for me to really understand the hell you both went through. I can feel for you. I cry in sympathy and understanding. I can share your feelings of hopelessness and helplessness towards the world, but . . . but . . . I just don't understand."

"What is it you don't understand, Marian?"

"After all this, after the actions of the gentile world to the Jews, I can't understand why you turned away from Judaism," I said. "I would think that it was the only shining star to follow after seeing the callousness of the world."

I felt the coldness in the room. It was as if a strong wind had blown the windows and doors open.

I looked at my mother. Her mouth was clamped shut. I looked at my father. Silence. His eyes were distant and cold. He pulled himself off his seat, his lips moved as if to say something, but he shrugged his shoulders and quickly left the room.

"Why was I raised without any knowledge of my ancestry?" I asked. "Grandfather, your parents, Aunt Leah and Uncle Meir held on to their faith and religion. What happened to you and Daddy? Why? Why?"

Stoic. No answer. I couldn't hold myself together any more. I couldn't control myself. I broke into hysterics. The sobs shook my body, wracking me with their intensity.

"Please," I begged. "Oh, mother, please."

So softly that I could hardly hear her, in a hoarse whisper, she asked, "Why is it important for you to know? Why, after all these years, is it tearing at your insides?"

"Mommy, I resent not having been given any choice," I said. "I resent your having hidden so much from me all these years."

The room hushed. The only sounds were our labored breathing and the hiss of the radiator in its attempt to keep the house warm. I shivered, not from the cold but from the torment and turmoil within me. We just sat there, our eyes locked, our form of communication a shared suffering. My mother's face softened; a teardrop emerged from the corner of her eye. Her shoulders heaved as if she had just wrested herself of a tremendous burden and decision. I realized that finally I had made a fissure in that solid brick wall of indestructibility my parents had built up during all the years since my birth.

"I'm sorry, Marian," she said. "I am really and truly sorry. We just never thought you would ever feel that way. Your father felt the best way to help you and protect you from hurt would be to build a soft cocoon around you. Now, I wonder if he was right. We wanted to save you, but I'm beginning to think we could have destroyed you."

"I'm afraid I don't understand. How could you have helped me by hiding all this from me?"

"I guess your father felt that by marrying out of your faith, by marrying a gentile like Neal, you would be safe, because then you would become part of the gentile society and would become submerged within that culture. In that way, all the ills that had befallen the Jewish race would not be yours."

I was angry. I couldn't help it. .

"First of all," I answered, "if anyone should know better, it is you and Daddy. I just found this out, but you lived through it. Hitler traced every assimilated Jew, and marriage out of the Jewish religion did not change the fact to him that a Jew was still a Jew. And there is something else. Are you trying to tell me that the only thing the Jews have behind them is a life of ills? I have met people who find joy and purpose in religion which has given them contentment. And we don't even have to look far. What about Grandfather?"

"Your grandfather had the strength of his fathers behind him."

"So my father had the strength of his father and fathers behind him. Why did he change?"

"Your grandfather refused to compromise. He drew his strength from his ancestors and from the books he constantly learned. The more he delved into them, the greater grew his belief and the stronger his stamina to overcome all odds. Your father became bitter, not at G-d, because He is always right and full of compassion, but he became confused and twisted by his lack of understanding of man's actions against the only thing that could help him live with it."

My mother kept her arms huddled tightly around herself as if the cold was more than she could bear. I watched her eyes shift to the lights, as if through them she could find warmth.

"And you, Mom," I asked. "And you?"

She looked beaten, dejected.

"And I, Marian, I took the easy way out. I took the coward's way of pacification. Peace at any price."

"Did you find the peace you craved?"

My mother wrinkled her brow and concentrated on the question I had asked her.

"No," she said. "I didn't find peace, and neither did your father. Oh yes, there were times we might have thought our lives were tranquil. There were times we thought we were living a life of serenity, but honestly, something was always missing."

"And that was?"

She didn't answer.

"When I was little," I said, "I didn't realize it, but in retrospect, I feel as if there was always a quiet war going on between Grandfather and Daddy. And I was somewhere in the middle, the pawn in the battle."

"How little we realize what is absorbed by the young," she said. "Yes, Marian, there was always a battle. Your grandfather tried constantly to bring your father back. He tried so hard to change his way of thinking. But please don't misunderstand me. Your father always had a tremendous respect for your grandfather. There was something pulling your father apart. He was like a big beautiful apple which had a tiny worm eating at the insides. Your grandfather used to call it the *Yetzer Hora* which had conquered the *Yetzer Tov*. He explained it by saying that a person is made up of good and bad and that your father was letting the bad overcome the good. Marian, I am just as guilty. I could have fought harder than I did. I didn't. I gave up."

"So Grandfather took on the battle with me."

My mother looked surprised.

"How did you realize that?"

"It took me a long time," I said. "It wasn't until after Grandfather's funeral that things sort of started falling into place. Mom, why can't I talk to Daddy about it? Why does he avoid me when I try?"

"Have you really looked at your father recently?"

"Yes. He looks terrible."

"You are the one now reopening his wounds, and all his sore spots are festering again. It is difficult to look back on your life and see wasted years."

I stamped my foot on the floor like a spoiled child having a temper tantrum.

"I don't understand it. I just don't. Tell me what made Daddy change. What did he go through to cause this? Maybe then I could understand him better."

"I'm sorry, Marian. Don't press me. Your father has to make his own decision. I just can't."

There was a sound like someone clearing his throat. I turned around sharply. I wondered how long my father had been standing at the door. How much had he heard? His face was a mask, hiding all feelings and thoughts. He walked to the couch and put his arm around my mother's shoulders, supporting her and comforting her. In silence, they walked up the curved staircase to their room. A chapter in the life of the Asher family had just been unfolded before me. My heart pounded within me at the uncertainty of what the pages would be filled with in my future.

I felt a restlessness within me. Sleep was out of the question. I opened the front door. A cold gust blew into the house, but the snow had stopped falling. It looked bright and refreshing. I closed the door and went to my room. I pulled on an extra pair of socks and put my boots on. I opened the drawer and took out my heavy turtleneck sweater. I tiptoed silently down the steps. I didn't want to disturb my parents. I found my fur-lined jacket in the hall closet and with a wool scarf over my head and my woolen gloves, I felt protected from the cold outdoors.

I left a note on the hall table as a precautionary measure, just in case my parents came down and wondered where I had gone. I wrote that I couldn't sleep and had gone for a walk. The door closed silently behind me.

I was surprised there were children playing outside. They had ventured into the snow after it had stopped coming down. Their cheeks were red and shiny. Our neighbor was shovelling his walk and waved to me. I waved back.

My mind was a blank. I walked without any thoughts. My thinking mechanism was smart enough to lie dormant and realize it was not wanted. There was an aimlessness and detachment as I went along. I was not consciously aware of any particular direction. Only when I heard the thundering of the breakers as they hit the shore did I realize where I was heading. The wind stung my face and whipped about my body. I welcomed the cutting bite as it brought back feeling to my numbness. I climbed up the snow covered steps and walked on the untouched boardwalk, my footsteps making indents in the whiteness of the snow. The waves were high and landed with a strange fierceness. Gone was the peacefulness of summer. Gone was the serenity of the past. The ocean looked savage and untamed, the blue turned into an inky black-ness. The warmth of the summer beach was replaced with the iciness of winter. I shivered from the cold, and my face started to tingle.

On the way home, I passed Janet's house. In her window was an electric candelabra with the eight lights shining brightly. Janet's parents' brush with tradition.

It was getting dark. I rushed home and went to sleep.

It my dream, Kurt was dressed in a Nazi uniform. He wore high black shiny boots. Tightly clasped within his hand was a whip. There were so many people, oh, so many people, squirming on the floor. The men, women and children were all mixed together. I recognized my mother and father in their midst. There was a sneer on Kurt's face as he lifted the whip to strike. I grabbed the whip before it could touch anyone.

"Don't," I pleaded.

"You belong on the floor with the others," he shouted. "Get down. Crawl. Beg for mercy."

"This is America," I answered. "It is not Germany. Who do you think you are?"

A woman walked over to Kurt. She also wore a Nazi uniform and boots. I thought she might help, and so I ran to her.

"Get down with the others," she shouted. It was Neal's mother.

The devil was standing on the side. He was laughing, laughing, laughing, an evil snake with a forked tongue. Smoke poured from his mouth.

"Help us," I shouted to someone . . . to anyone . . . to no one. "Help us."

I saw Neal coming towards me. I put out my arms.

"Help us," I pleaded.

He looked at me and turned his back.

Who is that stately young man walking with slow measured steps towards me? There is a smile on his black bearded face. Is it . . . Grandfather?

"Grandfather," I shouted and ran to him. He took my small hand in his large hands, and I felt the warmth comforting me.

"Don't worry, Malkala," he said softly. "Just hold my hand tightly, and you'll see. Everything will be fine."

I saw a mountainous cliff looming in front of us. There was no escape. We were locked in. Help! Help!

What was Grandfather doing? He put his hands in front of him. What were those strange words he was murmuring? Hebrew? A blessing? As one, men, women and children rose up from the floor. My parents, too. Grandfather looked at me and smiled.

"The future is in your hands," he said. "You make the move and G-d will help."

A miracle! The ground separated. A huge chasm. Kurt and all the evil people rolled into the unknown void. Down, down, down they went. They were like tiny ants. I couldn't see them anymore. We were flying, flying into the blue horizon, flying towards the warmth of the sun, flying ever higher.

chapter twenty

How can I describe how a friendship grows? My friendship with Janet had developed from our similarities, mutual need and dependency. Often, a friendship develops from seemingly contradictory roots. Sometimes, a friendship just flows naturally, and you wonder what helped it blossom. Shaindee and I were so different it was difficult to understand the drawing power, but we were growing closer.

Estie, Reva and Shaindee were giving model lessons, that is, sample teaching lessons in front of a class, in a school in my neighborhood. We decided it would be a good opportunity to meet.

"Terrific," I said. "There's a nice Chinese restaurant two blocks away from the school. We'll meet there for lunch."

Quiet. No answer. Pause.

"We only eat kosher, Marian," said Shaindee. "Would you mind if we eat at the kosher restaurant on Mott Avenue?"

"That's okay by me," I answered, and we decided that we would meet at one o'clock.

I recalled my mother mentioning that meat had to be slaughtered in a special way to make it kosher for Jewish consumption, but what was wrong with Chinese food or other dishes? I remembered that I hadn't read the pamphlet Naomi had given me that discussed eating kosher because I thought kosher meant clean and with today's stringent cleanliness laws, why should there be a problem? I had tossed it in the bottom of the closet with a few other items to be read on a rainy day. I fished it out of the closet after deciding there was no time like the present to begin.

Shaindee and her friends were already seated when I arrived.

"It's great to see you, Marian," Shaindee said. "This is a very special day. Estie just became engaged, and we're celebrating."

"*Mazel Tov*," I said. "That's what you have to say, right?"

"Right," Reva answered. "Please, let's leave all the talking for afterwards. I'm starved. Order and then we'll talk."

Indecisiveness was the order of the day. None of us knew what we wanted to eat.

"We have to make a decision," Estie said. "If I could make a lifetime decision, I'm sure we could or should be able to make one on what to order."

We decided on blintzes and sour cream. We also ordered four glasses of chocolate milk. It was a gleeful foursome that ate with relish.

"How did you meet your boyfriend?" I asked.

"I met him through another person," said Estie. "An introduction. Someone made our *shidduch*."

"In other words, like a blind date?" I asked.

"A blind date? What's that?" Shaindee asked.

"Well, a blind date is when, let's say, I know a boy and I have a friend. He calls her and then they go out."

"Do they have any common background or common interests?" Reva asked.

"No. Just two individuals who want to spend an entertaining evening together."

"Well, that's not exactly how we met. First, there has to be a common background and common interests."

"Just to go out on a date? You must be kidding!"

They exchanged looks. Finally, Estie spoke up.

"I know this is going to be difficult for you to understand," she said, "but we just don't go out on dates. When we and our parents feel ready for marriage, then any boy we do meet has to be a potential husband."

"Why?" I asked.

"If you go out with someone that is really not for you, there is always the possibility of becoming emotionally involved, and then, it is difficult to extract yourself from the situation. In this way, we avoid such a possibility. Marian, what is marriage about?"

"Marriage is about falling in love," I answered quickly and without hesitation.

"What is love?"

I tried to think of a description to answer her but almost every answer that came to mind seemed insipid.

"You see, when you come down to it, you really can't give an explanation," said Estie. "The media, books and our society have brainwashed us to believe that love is the hearing of bells or a purely physical attraction. If this is so, then what keeps couples together when they get old or if, G-d forbid, something happens in an accident and the former beauty queen is not a beauty anymore. No, that is not love."

"And what is?" I asked.

Reva answered.

"Well, I guess first of all, we really have to understand what marriage is all about. I haven't experienced it yet, but I am hoping. The way I see it, it's two people caring for each other, with each individual a member in a partnership that gives and receives respect. They form a home in which they grow as individuals, and together, they build a family. Throughout the centuries, the Jewish traditional family has been a model of what a family should be. The family bond is strong, and it develops through building a house on mutual respect, mutual interests and mutual goals. It is the joy of giving to another. The more we give, the more we love."

I laughed to break the tension and said, "Were your model lessons good? I would pass you all with an A plus. You do a great job. But what do you mean by the more we give, the more we love? I don't know that I can grasp that."

Shaindee answered me. "Look, Marian, when Sholom Yisroel was born, remember how cute he was? I loved him. My mother loved him. But Marian, the way we feel about him now is impossible to describe. The love we have is . . . maybe infinite. So let us take this as an example. When a mother gives birth to a baby, she loves the baby with a passion the minute it is put into her hands. But it just isn't the same love she develops for the baby after having had the child for a year. It is the getting up at night, the feeding and the diapering of the baby. It is the constant giving and caring for that little infant that creates a stronger bond daily. Now that love for the baby when it was first put into the mother's hands has developed into a totally different kind of love.

"The way I see it, therefore, is that love in marriage comes from the fact that each member of this union is incomplete without the other. Each gives to the other love, a home, children, and provides for the other member's needs. Mutual giving results in mutual gratitude; these are the things that true love is built upon."

"I guess," Estie added, "this means that sometimes the giving is on

143

the husband's part and sometimes on the wife's part." She thought for a while and added, "If love is the result of giving, like the mother with the baby—see, I didn't say taking but giving—then a part of you becomes invested in the other person. I expect to become part of my husband, and my husband will become a part of me, and the more we invest, the more our love and concern will grow."

"I'm going to ask you something which you may feel is a silly question," I said. "What do you feel about the entire concept of a woman being totally subjugated to a man?"

"Marian, that is such a wrong concept of the Jewish wife," Shaindee said. "When a couple marry in the Jewish Orthodox tradition, it becomes a holy bond. It is not just a social institution of marriage but a union blessed by G-d Himself. The word for marriage in Hebrew is *kiddushin*, which means sanctification. In fact, one of the prayers of the marriage ceremony is 'Blessed are You, O G-d, our Lord, King of the Universe, Who has created groom and bride, joy and gladness, delight and cheer, love and harmony, peace and companionship.' Our tradition expects a man to truly respect his wife, consult with her, and she is held in high esteem."

I looked at Shaindee. "I don't know if I can buy all this, but I do expect to find this with Neal, even though we did not meet, as you call it, through a *shidduch*. By the way, you haven't explained what that word means."

"We had to explain all this to you first or you would never understand the entire concept," Estie answered.

"Before meeting Neal," Shaindee asked, "did you go out on dates with other boys?"

"Of course. Why do you ask?"

"Why?"

"Why what?" I answered, puzzled.

"What was the reason for you to go out on dates?"

"To have fun, I guess. To enjoy a pleasant evening."

"In other words," Estie continued, "it had nothing to do with looking for a marriage partner."

"That's true."

"When you go out with Janet or with me," Shaindee added, "we have a pleasant evening, don't we?"

"Yes." I answered, not knowing where this was leading.

Shaindee looked like the cat that ate the mouse.

"In that case, if we were interested in just going out and enjoying a pleasant evening, then why go out with a boy?" she said. "We could just spend our time with girlfriends."

"Oh, come on, Shaindee," I protested. "Don't be so naive. It is not exactly the same."

"See, that is precisely what we are trying to bring out," she said triumphantly. "That type of dating does not follow the concept of having a pleasant evening or even having fun. There is a different reason for it entirely."

"I'm waiting," I said.

"Well, some kids date for status, so they can say they had a date with so-and-so. Some date because of peer pressure, and they haven't the inner strength not to do what their friends do. But most date because there is a different type of attractiveness between a boy and a girl. Because of this, platonic friendships are rare. The pull of opposites attracting is always there."

"So what?" I asked.

Estie answered this time. "The answer to the 'so-what?' is based upon what marriage is all about. It is easy to see that the very existence of a dating machine indicates how easy it is to be attracted to someone with different goals in life. We leave ourselves open to a purely physical attractiveness, and that does not help create the permanence of a solid marriage."

"And if a marriage is built upon—what did you call it, a *shidduch*?—how does that help?" I asked.

"The person who tries to arrange the marriage looks for similar family backgrounds, interests and goals," said Estie. "Only then are the boy and girl permitted to meet."

"I don't think that is fair," I answered. "Then the boy and the girl have absolutely no control as to who their life partner is going to be."

"You don't seem to understand, Marian. The boy and girl do meet, but only after all the other facets are investigated."

"It sounds too much like a business to me," I said. "Where do human relations enter into the picture?"

"The girl can reject the boy or the boy can reject the girl," she said. "It doesn't necessarily mean that this is the one you must marry. In fact, the Jewish faith has taken care of everything. We have a custom at a wedding called the *badeking*. The groom puts the veil over his bride before the marriage ceremony so he can ascertain he is getting the proper bride and that nobody is taking her place."

I was bewildered.

"Marian, please don't think that we planned this discussion," said Shaindee. "We really didn't, and we don't want you to feel we've ganged up on you. It is only because I care so much for you that I want you to understand. Look, Marian. Let us say a person was going for an operation. Would he just go to any surgeon?"

"Of course not," I answered. "He would check references carefully and perhaps even check the hospital where the doctor performs surgery."

"Exactly. Now I think you'll be able to understand what I'm trying to explain. We agree that when people go for an operation they wouldn't put their life into just anyone's hands. Marriage is your life. It is your children's future. Would you put that into anyone's hands?"

Things were a little clearer.

"Okay, I understand your point about marriage, similarity of interests and backgrounds," I conceded. "But what is wrong with simply dating?"

"You see, Marian," she said. "There really is no such thing as simply dating. No one has any guarantees a date with someone just for the 'fun' of it will not lead to marriage. Intellectualism and emotions are two different factors."

"But it can be fun," I insisted. "What is wrong with that?"

Reva answered me this time. "We had a teacher in seminary who explained this concept beautifully. She said the difference between a child and an adult is the ability to give up a present pleasure for the realization that there is something to gain in the future. She said that the pleasure of innocent dating is given up for a solid lifetime with a mature partner."

"I feel as if I'm in another world," I said. "I'm in culture shock."

"Your chocolate milk, ladies." It was the waiter breaking into our private thoughts as well as into our heated discussion.

"Let's make a toast," Reva said.

We all laughed. I said that I bet it was the first time a toast was made with chocolate milk.

"*L'chaim*, to life," said Reva. "To a wonderful life for Estie. May we all find our *besherte* . . . and for Marian's benefit, *besherte* means our predestined partner."

146

Once again, we were interrupted by the waiter, carrying in a beautifully decorated cake. Estie's eyes popped with surprise. She read the Hebrew words aloud, "*Mazel Tov*, Estie."

We dug into the cake. It was delicious.

"I feel it is almost sacrilegious to have so much fun tonight," Reva said. "Do excuse me, Estie. I know this is your *simcha*, but I can't control my thoughts. Did any of you see that article in the newspaper about that doctor?"

Shaindee, Estie and I all nodded that we had. Reva's eyes grew moist.

"My neighbor Mrs. Michel was so shaken she couldn't go to sleep alone, and so she spent the night at our house. You remember, Shaindee, when her husband died last year? It was so pathetic. They were inseparable. And last night, she told us such an eerie story. I just can't get it out of my mind.

"This was approximately the anniversary of the day she was chosen with a group of other woman. She remembered it because she can still hear the Germans and the Polish people singing carols. It was a bitter cold day and her only clothing was a thin, tattered dress. Oh, yes, and a shovel which all the women were given.

"They were forced to walk many, many miles through villages and towns. The cold was unbearable. Even the S.S. soldiers who marched along with them were shivering in their fur-lined coats and high boots. Her shoes were full of holes, and the warm, shiny boots of the Nazis were constantly in her view. But they had to keep going. If they stopped from exhaustion, they were shot."

"They passed through villages and towns," I commented. "Didn't they meet people on the way? Did no one offer help?"

"I asked her the same question, and she said that men were coming from work and the laughter of children at play was all around. The children looked at them. The men looked at them. The housewives opened their windows and doors, and the smell of home cooked meals wafted into the air. The men continued on their way. The children continued laughing at play. The housewives looked at them, then served their families supper. To the people in the villages and towns, it was as if an army of ants was passing on the road.

"Finally, they arrived at their destination. It was dark, and they couldn't understand why they were told to stop. There were no barracks, no tents to sleep in, just forest. They were told to dig a ditch. 'Faster, Faster,' said

147

the Nazi. '*Macht Schnell.*' She wondered why it couldn't wait until morning. Why dig a ditch after such a long trip? They were exhausted. But the ever present rifles prodded them, and they dug faster and faster. When the ditch was completed, they were lined up on the edge. Suddenly, an avalanche of bullets. Screams. Mrs. Michel says she can still hear them in her dreams."

I looked at Shaindee, Estie and Reva. Their faces mirrored mine. There wasn't a dry eye among us. I think we were all thinking the same thing. It could have, Heaven forbid, been us.

Reva's voice dropped to a whisper. "Mrs. Michel told us, 'Suddenly I felt warm. I hadn't been so warm, it seemed, for years. At first, it was an almost pleasurable sensation. Like the pressure of heavy covers. I thought of the down quilts in my mother's house and the wonderful warmth and coziness I felt under them. But the down quilts were light. This pressure was not light; it was heavy. It was very heavy. And the warmth, such a comforting liquid-like warmth. And I thought I was dreaming that I heard screaming and moaning and a barrage of bullets that did not stop. I heard them above me, and I heard them in the pit. And then . . . suddenly . . . silence. This must be what death is, I thought. Quiet and pressure of the earth and the warmth of liquid. I must be dead. It was hours later that I became aware that I was not dead, that I was alive. Alive, you hear. Alive. I moved my arms, my legs. The warmth was from the bodies pressing down upon me, and the stickiness and liquid warmth was blood. I wanted to rush out of the pit, to climb out and breathe fresh air before I would smother, but the fear of the Nazis restrained me. I lay still for hours. There were no sounds, no movement. I heard only the sounds of the forest. Finally, I climbed out. I looked down. Bedlam. Death was in that pit wherever I looked. I'm alive, I'm alive, I kept thinking. I didn't cry for the dead. I was too happy for myself."

The tears were running down my face unashamedly. I looked at the others and we were all sisters in this moment of compassion for poor Mrs. Michel.

"So she ran into the forest," Reva continued. "She said that she, who had always been afraid of a mouse, felt animal eyes upon her wherever she turned. Once, she brushed against something and wanted to scream, but she put her hand into her mouth to stifle any sound. She found herself wishing she had died with the others, because she did not want to die by herself."

Reva stopped talking and took a drink of water. She blew her nose and wiped her wet eyes with her handkerchief.

"What happened after that?" Estie asked. "How did she escape?"

"She remembers falling asleep," said Reva. "As much as she tried to stay awake, her eyes closed on her from exhaustion. Suddenly, she jolted awake. She heard a sound. She tried to shrink into the shrubbery and become part of the forest. She heard whispering. Now, she thought, they would get her. Now she'd be caught. The thought entered her mind that she should run so that they would shoot her in the back. It was the easiest way out. But it was a female voice. Two other women had managed to escape. They survived on shrubs, berries, roots and whatever they were able to find in the forest. They were there for weeks."

"How was she rescued?" I asked.

"I don't know. She broke down and couldn't continue. My mother gave her a sedative and put her to bed."

"My parents were also in the concentration camps," I said. "It has affected their lives very much. They are bitter because of the indifference of the world to the Jewish plight.

"I wrote a poem the other night after my parents told me a little about their experiences."

I walk along a street
  clean and neat
No more horrors
  at my feet
But I still hear groans
  misery and pain
This is the place
  where dead have lain
I am surrounded by
  apparitions, visions
World, remember! This
  was your decision

Voices still cry for dear hearts
  now dead
Hands wring for those
  poor unfed

nameless people
  nameless graves
The dead were once
  our brave

The sun's rays still warm the world
The blanket of stars remains unfurled
The scent of flowers is still the same
Unhampered by blood and pain
Bones make good fertilizer I'm told
Lying in the mud, left to mold

Silence is now
  their lot
Lying in the earth
  left to rot
Dead they lie
  feeling naught
You gave them death
That's what
  you sought

But know that where one man
  lies still and dead
G-d makes two more
  grow in his stead.

"Marian, you give me the chills," said Estie. "Whatever made you write something like that?"

"My mother's reaction to the newspaper story really shook me up," I explained. "Particularly when she told me about the lack of concern of the people in other countries."

Shaindee had been quiet all through this discussion. Something seemed to be bothering her. When I saw her leave for the ladies' room, I also got up and went to join her.

"I feel funny," she said. "There is so much lying and deceit in this world, I don't want you to ever think I'm part of it. I don't want any barriers between us, so I really have a confession to make.

"I told you the conversation about marriage and a *shidduch* was not planned. That is one hundred percent true. Although the girls know you come from a different life style, they like you and we all wanted you to become part of our crowd. However, once we did start this discussion, I was happy, because . . ." she paused. It was obviously difficult for her to continue. "I can't find the words. I don't want you to misconstrue anything that I say."

"Go on," I said.

"Marian, from the first time we spoke, we seemed to hit it off. I liked you, and I felt it was mutual. We were drawn to each other." She threw her head back and straightened her shoulders as if to give herself strength. She plunged ahead. "Marian, when your grandfather realized we knew each other, he asked me to develop our friendship."

I withdrew. I felt myself climb into my shell. I could feel the ice in my stare. I bristled with anger.

"So, because of my grandfather, we became friends," I snapped. "Because of my grandfather, you invited me to the *Bris*. Poor little Marian. Someone has to take her under his wings."

"I was afraid of this," said Shaindee. "Please understand. It was really in spite of what I knew and what your grandfather wanted that we became friends. I could never become close to someone I didn't like."

I ignored her remark and nodded my head as if I now understood everything.

"And this afternoon was a perfect ploy to break up my relationship with Neal, the gentile," I said.

"Please, Marian. You are making it sound altogether different from what actually happened. Believe me. This conversation was not planned. It really is the truth."

"Why did you have to ruin everything by clearing your conscience? Why didn't you just let things stay as they were?"

"Maybe I should have," Shaindee said. "But I didn't like feeling I was a hypocrite."

"Well, I hope your conscience is clear now," I answered. "It was an interesting discussion. Have a good day!"

I stalked out. I picked up my handbag from the table. Estie and Reva were engrossed in pictures of wedding gowns. They looked surprised when I said, in anger, "I have to leave now. *Mazel Tov*, Estie. It was nice seeing you both again. I'll pay my share of the bill at the cashier's window," and stormed out.

The glass window surrounding the restaurant was clean and sparkling. As I passed the other side to continue on my way home, I caught a glance at Shaindee as she was leaving the ladies' room. She looked pale, drained and hurt. Too bad, I thought. It was just too bad for her. She contrived our friendship and had put on such a big act. The nerve of her; the nerve of her. I was fuming, and my anger was not alleviated until two days later when I received the following note in the mail.

Dear Marian,

I prayed all night asking G-d for help to find words you would understand. I really know only one way and that is the truth. I hope you will find it in your heart to understand and forgive me so that there will not be any animosity between us.

Your grandfather saw us talking the very first time we met. The next time I visited the nursing home, he called me over. When he found out that I was Jewish and Orthodox, he couldn't stop thanking G-d. He said, and I'm telling you his words as clearly as I remember them, "Everything in life has a purpose. G-d must have brought you into our life to help my granddaughter Marian remove the blot that has come upon our family. My granddaughter has a heart of gold, and she is a good girl. I have confidence in Hashem that some day the veil will be lifted from her eyes. Everyone needs help and support. Please be that for her."

Marian, my personality is not that of a leader. I do not have a surplus of strength. I couldn't lead you, and I never tried. I never promised your grandfather anything. I just told him that I like you and I want to be your friend. He was happy with that. He also told me about Neal and the unhappiness it brought him. I visited him often, as I think I told you. I respected him and grew to love him as the grandfather I never had. He was a man of dignity.

In the restaurant, I wanted you to know I knew more about you and your family than you realized. I wanted us to have a clean slate. Perhaps I felt more of a need to tell you all this because I knew more about you than you did about me.

In all fairness, I hope to clear this matter up the next time we meet. I hope we can continue from here on.

Your friend,
Shaindee

I called Shaindee. Our conversation was somewhat strained. I think we both expected it to be. But I did feel that after such a traumatic breakdown, there was potential for a closer relationship. We agreed to meet on Sunday. I looked forward to seeing her once again.

chapter twenty-one

I felt drained when I awoke in the morning. I looked at the clock. There was still plenty of time to dress for school. I thought that perhaps a quick shower would be just the answer to perk me up. Even my hair felt limp and oily. I did a quick job, blow-dried my hair, dressed and went downstairs, feeling refreshed, clean and in a much better mood.

"Good morning, Mom," I said.

"You sound pretty chipper this morning," my mother answered.

"You should have seen me before my shower."

I went to the window and looked outside. The sun was shining brightly, and the melting snow was turning into rivers of water.

"It is January," I said, "but the sun makes it look like a spring day."

"I'll turn on the radio for the weather report," my mother said. The music blared. She changed the station, and we listened for the news. The announcer was talking about a bus strike.

"Good," I said. "No school would be welcome news."

The weather report came on, corroborating my initial reaction that it looked like a lovely spring day.

I watched my mother as she went to the bread box and took out a roll. She then took a can of tuna from the pantry. She put both items on the table.

"Thanks, Mom. I still have plenty of time. I'll make lunch myself. Is it okay for me to eat dinner tonight at Janet's house? We have an exam scheduled the end of this week. Janet missed school these past three days, and I want to help her catch up."

She nodded her consent, and I added, "Okay, remember. Please don't delay dinner for me."

I pulled my boots on. I took my coat from the closet and put it on.

154

"Goodbye, Mom," I said as I gave her a kiss on her cheek. "Have a nice day."

"You too," she answered. "Call when you're ready to leave Janet's house. Daddy or I will come pick you up."

The bus corner where Janet and I usually met was crowded. There were complaints about the poor service.

"An increase in salary they want," a gaunt faced man complained. "That means an increase in fares. I guarantee you the service will not get better."

I looked for Janet. She had not arrived yet. I turned to watch for her along the street of her route. The glare of the sun made it difficult to focus. It added glitter to whatever was in sight. Janet was almost upon me, only a few houses away, when I became aware of her waving to catch my attention. I waved back and watched her walk to meet me. The rays of the sun shone on her long blonde hair, creating a golden halo. As she came closer, I saw she was wearing brown pants, a brown pea-jacket and a brown cap. I admired the stateliness of her walk.

"Hi, Marian," she said. "How was your weekend? I'm sorry that when I called to tell you I wouldn't be in school for a few days I couldn't talk. We wanted to keep the phone free."

"My weekend was pretty emotional if you want to know the truth," I said. "My parents told me about some of the things that had happened in the concentration camp."

"After all these years!" she exclaimed. "What brought it on?"

"Believe it or not, it was the front page news about Kurt's father. Here comes the bus."

Politeness vanished. Shoving and accusations abounded as people wanted to board the bus and not risk waiting for the next. Conversation had to wait until we were on the bus. We were fortunate to find seats.

"What's doing, Janet?" I asked. "You said you would be out of school for a few days but you weren't sick."

"It's been crazy," she said. "You won't believe it. I was trying to put some sense into my brother's head. He has become peculiar, and there is no living with him. If I have succeeded, then there really is no reason to talk about it, but if not . . . We'll see. Anyway, I'm glad you're coming tonight. Boy! Do I feel rusty and unprepared for any test now."

It was only much later that I realized Janet was really more concerned about her brother than she let on, because she hadn't asked me any

155

further questions about what my mother had to say.

I, who had always shared everything with Janet, only told her I'd seen Shaindee. I was reluctant to tell her more.

Janet's house was as familiar as my own, and yet, that day the familiar had an unfamiliarity about it. The bright yellow shingled ranch with white shutters and white front door looked different. The melting snow left black watery puddles, giving the house a dilapidated, wilted look. The lone tree near the front walk, denuded of the green leaves of summer and the white dress of winter, stood there aloof, stark, shorn.

We removed our wet boots on the steps and carried them into the hall. There was a mat on the floor, waiting to receive them.

Usually, the radio or the stereo was the first thing to greet me whenever I came into the Abikoff home. Today, the door opened to silence. It was a solemn Mrs. Abikoff who returned my hello. Her usual cheerful smile was missing, replaced with a contemplative expression.

I followed Janet into the kitchen and watched her silently fill the tea kettle. She removed two cups and three saucers from the cupboard. She put a teaspoon of cocoa into each cup and placed a teaspoon near my cup and saucer and one next to hers. She put some chocolate chip cookies into the third saucer and sat down to wait for the water to boil.

"Is everything okay, Janet?" I asked. "Do you want me to leave?"

"No, don't leave," she said. "Stay. We have a family problem, but I feel everything will work out in the end."

I didn't press Janet. One thing about our relationship was respect for each other's privacy. We each knew when to keep quiet and when to share.

The tea kettle whistled and Janet filled our cups with water and added some milk. There was no conversation while we drank our cocoa, which was unusual for us. I helped Janet clear the table, and we picked up our books and went down the staircase into her basement.

I looked around.

"There is something different about the basement," I said.

"Yes, my brother blocked off a corner and made himself a retreat," Janet answered.

It was obvious Janet wanted tonight to be all business so I gave her the notes I had copied for her when she'd been absent.

During the years we'd been in the same class together, we'd worked out a unique way of studying. Janet and I would each review notes silently and prepare a list of questions to ask each other. We'd then answer the questions out loud and discuss them. We found this a pretty successful way of studying, and we maintained good grades throughout high school.

My concentration was interrupted by the doorbell. I heard a pair of feet going towards the door. Shortly after, there were two pairs of footsteps coming back, a murmur of voices and then all was quiet. I became absorbed once again in studying.

"Janet, Marian, supper. Daddy's home."

Mr. Abikoff greeted me warmly. He looked tired. The table was set for dinner for five, but there were only the four of us.

"Shouldn't we wait for Abe?" Mrs. Abikoff asked.

"We'll wait a few minutes," Mr. Abikoff answered, "but I really think he meant what he said."

I found the conversation around the table stilted and artificial. They seemed to have other things on their mind.

"I hope I'm not imposing," I said.

"Oh no, Marian," Mrs. Abikoff answered. "You are one of the family. Come," she said to Mr. Abikoff. "Let's eat."

We ate silently. The grapefruit had a tartness which the sugar I had sprinkled liberally could not erase. The soup was hot and seared my throat. I tried to help serve and clear the table, but Janet and her mother wouldn't let me.

"Enjoy the privilege today of being a guest," Janet said.

"Hi, everybody. I'm home," Abe announced as he marched in and took over the room. "I hope I haven't kept you back from your meal."

He was a tall, lanky blonde boy who had just outgrown his adolescent awkwardness and, even at twenty-one, always seemed happy-go-lucky Abe. I didn't think he had ever been confronted with any major problems except, of course, the time when the entire family had had to adjust to the loss of their sister.

Abe hung his coat in the hall closet and, still wearing his cap, sat down at the table. He tilted his cap back so that it remained on the tip of his head.

"How was your day, Abe?" Mr. Abikoff asked.

"Terrific," he answered enthusiastically. "That David is really something. He makes everything unusually clear."

"Were you in college today?" Mr. Abikoff asked searchingly.

Abe squirmed uncomfortably.

"Supper, Abe?" said Mrs. Abikoff. "Sorry we started before you arrived, but Daddy was hungry. Wash up, and I'll bring your dinner."

"Mom, I meant what I said," Abe said quietly. "Don't bother with me. I bought a corned beef sandwich, and tomorrow, I'm getting a small electric stove for the basement."

"You know, Abe. You're nuts," Janet said. "Come back down to earth."

"Janet, I'm the one that's down to earth," he said. "Open your eyes and you will realize things for yourself." He turned to his father. "What is your opinion on the Dr. Schmidt thing in the newspaper? Think he'll be sent out of the country?"

"I don't know," said Mr. Abikoff. "I wonder how many people are still alive today who can or are willing to come forward as witnesses."

"Monsters!" Abe said vehemently. "I tell you, Dad, there is just one answer. We don't belong here. Anti-Semitism is all around us, and you know it. We only have that little country, Israel, and we better get there before we are pushed there."

"Maybe, but that's not such a safe place either," Mrs. Abikoff answered. "The Arabs are a constant threat."

"Look. I don't want to start another argument, but the truth is that if we would all go in the correct way, keeping *Shabbos* and everything else, there would be no danger from anything. Okay, okay, Janet, don't start in on me. I'll go my way, and you go your way."

Mr. and Mrs. Abikoff looked upset at the turn the conversation had taken. It was obvious a family argument was about to begin.

"Janet, since you won't let me help with the dishes, I'll go downstairs and continue preparing the questions," I said.

"Go ahead, Janet," Mrs. Abikoff said. "I'll take care of everything tonight."

We went down the steps quickly and quietly. Janet picked up her notes, and I picked up mine.

"I can't study!" Janet slammed her books down on the desk. "He is driving us insane. He joined some youth movement last year and became close friends with a character, and now he wants to go to a *Yeshivah*. He doesn't show up in college, and my parents are upset. I can't imagine what got into him."

"You seem more upset than your parents," I said.

"I think they feel that if they'll protest or pressure him, he'll only become more determined," said Janet. "They leave him alone, believing he'll get over it. He is going through a phase similar to you, except that you're normal. You just want to learn about your roots. He knows all about roots. He wants to jump in with both feet. You know my parents aren't against anything. They have always been traditionalists. We were taught Jewish history and all that stuff, but he is on a totally different binge. He wants to turn the clock back."

Janet paused and at my puzzled expression, continued, "Well, he wants to become kosher. You know, only eat special Jewish food and so on. Now he always wears a hat on his head. He has gone all the way!"

"Really?"

"You see, that was our reaction. It's funny. My father's parents came here from Europe. In Europe, they had been very religious. In America, they were called old-fashioned. My father was brought up in a home that was part of two worlds. His home followed the European Jewish culture, and yet, at the same time, they tried to Americanize themselves by throwing off some of the Jewish limitations. My father has kept certain traditions but none of the limitations. Now, along comes my brother who wants to turn the clock back and bring back everything they discarded. Imagine," Janet scoffed, "eating kosher in this day and age. That is why he bought his own supper tonight. He told my parents that if they don't turn the house upside down, he will buy his own electric stove for the basement and prepare all his own food. Oh nuts! Maybe he'll outgrow it. Let's study."

The next two hours were spent doing just that. When we finished, it was quite dark outside. I called my home to tell my parents not to worry and that I would be ready to go home soon.

"Don't go yourself, Marian," my father said. "Wait for me. I'll pick you up."

I gathered my belongings, and Janet and I went upstairs. The Abikoffs and Abe were still sitting around the table talking. There was none of the anger between the parents and Abe that there was between Janet and her brother. The conversation seemed to be, if not friendly, at least cordial.

I had just pulled my boots on when I heard the honk of my father's horn. I picked up my books and thanked the Abikoffs.

"So long, Janet," I said. "See you tomorrow."

The car was parked in front of the house, the motor running.

"Hi, Dad," I said. "Thanks for coming to pick me up."

"I'm glad of the opportunity for us to be together," he said. "How is school?"

I prattled on about things of really no substance, just to keep the conversation going. When we arrived home, I looked around for my mother, but she was not downstairs.

"Where's Mom?"

"She was tired and went to bed early."

"Is she all right?" I asked.

"Oh yes," he answered, but I noticed that his lids seemed heavy with fatigue and his eyes seemed to be evading me. I felt he was trying to hide something.

I had a strong intuition that, just as my life was doing somersaults, there was much more going on between my parents than was visible on the surface.

chapter twenty-two

"Telephone, Marian," my mother called from the kitchen. "Would you like to take it in here? I'll be leaving in a minute."

"Thanks," I said as I took the receiver.

"Hello. This is Marian. Who is it?"

"Hello, Marian. Naomi. How are you?"

"I'm fine. So glad to hear from you. How are you and how is the baby?"

"We are all, thank G-d, fine," Naomi answered. "How are *you*, Marian?" I felt the concern in her voice.

"Pretty okay, I guess."

I think she detected my hesitancy because she responded. "But . . . "

"But, but, but," I answered. "What can I answer you? I'm okay, and I'm not okay. Sometimes, I feel things are going smoothly and I'm on top of the world, and sometimes, I get the feeling a mountain is pressing down on me."

"Would it help to talk?" she asked.

"That's all we do," I said. "We talk, and I've read the material you gave me, but I don't think I've found any answers."

She ignored my answer and said, "I really called, Marian, to invite you to spend a weekend with us. Perhaps this weekend. Would you like to come?"

"Why? How would that help?" I hoped my voice did not sound as surly as the words.

"We can make it just a pleasant weekend, friend with friend, or as a weekend of answers to any questions you might have. It's totally up to you."

I thought of Shaindee and that edge of bitterness was in my voice when I said, "The name of the book is *The Reform of Marian Asher*."

"Please, Marian," she said. "Don't take it like that. We would really love to have you. Both my husband and I have discussed it, and it was his suggestion as well as my own."

It was a tug-of-war. I wanted very much to go. I wanted to experience a *Shabbos*, but yet, I was afraid to go.

"Please come, Marian," pressed Naomi, noticing my hesitation. "I would very much like you to come."

Sometimes, a person crosses a road through dense traffic and when he looks back, he sees the swirling traffic behind him, and as much as he might want to, he just can't go back. I was afraid of that and yet, at the same time, daring enough to move.

"Thanks, Naomi," I answered. "I'll think about it."

Instinctively, I knew the approval of my father would be difficult to come by. However, once I had made the decision to go, I would do whatever I could to get it.

My mother's voice interrupted my thoughts.

"Marian, is everything okay? I called you three times."

"I'm sorry, Mom."

"Can you please go to the store? I forgot some things I need for dinner."

I took the list from my mother and picked up my car keys from the piano where I had left them. I opened the door. A refreshing burst of clean, clear, cold air helped me decide to walk the distance.

The snow was packed down tightly in the places where it had not been shovelled away. The sun was a ball of crimson and gold preparing for sunset. It must have been disheartened because even its beauty and warmth were unable to melt the snow. It had decided late in the day to break through the clouds, but the wind-chill factor had won this war.

By the time I left the store, the sun had set, and the sky was aflame with its afterglow.

When I came into the house, I saw that my father had already arrived. My parents were in the kitchen, and the murmur of angry voices stopped as soon as I entered. A grand performance was then initiated for my benefit, my mother and father again the actress and actor, the setting one of a peaceful atmosphere.

Dinner was quiet. My father seemed to be making a concentrated effort to be interested in what he was eating. Every spoonful was part of the dramatic act to deceive me into believing all was well. It was difficult to accept that this was the household I had been brought up in all these years.

I was afraid my next move would only cause further dissension, but plunge ahead I did regardless of the consequences.

"Naomi called and invited me to spend the weekend in her house," I said. "May I go?"

"Who is Naomi?" my father asked.

"Rabbi Isaac's granddaughter," my mother answered.

My father stiffened.

"Why should you spend a weekend with an almost total stranger?" he answered.

"She isn't exactly a stranger," I tried to explain. "I have met her, and we have spent time together. I like her and enjoy her company." I thought for a moment and then added, "I also appreciate her intelligence."

"I'd rather you didn't go," he answered.

"Please," I said. "I would like very much to go."

"Marian, there are many things in life we would like to have or to do, but we can't always have or do everything we like," he said. "I don't feel you should go."

I felt like a child once again who wasn't really sure she wanted the candy being offered, but when it was withheld, it became so tantalizing that she couldn't live without it. The more my father resisted, the more insistent I became.

"I want to go," I said.

"Marian, I don't feel you should go," he said. "It is just confusing you."

"I am confused now," I said. "Going won't make me any more so."

"Yes it will," he answered. "The more involved you get, the more conflicts you'll have."

"I'm beginning to realize that all living is a conflict," I said.

"That's not the same thing," he answered.

"Tell me," I said. "Why do you keep running away from issues? What happened to my strong father? What happened to the father I could always look up to and rely on? What has happened to you?"

"You won't understand."

"Try me. Maybe you will find that I can understand."

"Marian, you just don't know what life is all about," he said. "You think you know, but you don't."

"So tell me," I pleaded. "Tell me and show me."

He got up from the chair and paced the floor, each step measured and precise. He walked in a straight line to the opposite wall and then back to the couch, back to the wall and back to the couch. I thought of a caged animal caught in a trap. Although only minutes elapsed, it seemed it went on for hours. I looked at my mother. She looked unhappy; her mouth opened to speak, but then she closed it. She remained silent. My eyes pleaded with her for some response, for some support, but her awful solemnity assured me of no help. I heard the grandfather clock go bong, bong, bong; nine times it pealed. Nine o'clock. There was no reaction in the room. It was as if no one heard it. The silence continued, and the only sound was the muted pacing of my father's feet on the soft rug.

"No!" he said firmly. "I do not want you to go."

"Do you forbid me to go, father?" I asked. "Because unless you forbid me, I will go."

My father jumped. He was shocked. This was the first time I had ever talked to him in this manner. I wanted to cry. I didn't want to hurt him. It was the last thing in the world I wanted.

"Please," I begged. "Please let me go."

My mother broke the impasse we had reached.

"Marian," she said. "Please leave the room. I would like to talk with your father privately."

I walked up the stairs to my room. There was really nothing I could accomplish by remaining except further antagonize my father. My mother would either reinforce his views and the decision would be to forbid me to go, or she might persuade him to grant me permission. Either way led to conflict.

I pulled my chair over to the window and raised the blinds. The sky was clear and deep blue. The stars were twinkling brightly. I tipped my head and looked up at the millions of stars, bright against the sky. Why didn't they collide? I was amazed that every single star had a special place in the sky, each one kept to its individual sphere in the universe. Each followed a predestined pattern. Although they looked similar, each was unique and different.

My mind wandered and I thought about myself and some of the people I knew. I thought about my mother, father, Janet, Shaindee, Naomi, Neal and his parents. All of us are part of the same human race. Basically, we all seem alike and yet, we are different. We all have our

164

special shapes and individual roles.

As I peered fascinated at the heavens, I wondered why G-d had created the physical world. I looked at how high the stars were in the sky. Amazing, I thought again, how they stay in their path. How small I was in contrast to the galaxies.

Why does the world exist? Does it exist for my sake, or do I exist because of a purpose? If every star has a plan written out for it, then what about humans? I, Marian, have been endowed with the ability to think. What is my role?

I shook my head to clear it. Yes, it must be because of a purpose, otherwise I would be like the stars following a path predestined for me. I am more than only a grain of sand in the universe. I count!

Again, I thought of how much easier it would be just to ride the waves instead of fighting the tide. But I had a gnawing inside that just wouldn't stop. I felt old and tired and weary. Oh, so weary. I pressed my face against the window, hoping the cold would help revitalize me.

"Marian, can you please come downstairs?" It was my father calling to me.

When he spoke, his voice was hoarse and congested with emotion.

"Your mother and I have just discussed your request." I felt I was in a court of law and the verdict was about to be handed down. Guilty or not guilty. I looked at my father who was standing in front of me, stiff and unbending.

"I'm Marian," I wanted to shout. "Your daughter, Daddy. Your daughter. The same Marian you rocked in your arms and held on your knees. Look at me." But the words did not come out of my mouth.

His words, when they finally came, were frozen and icy. It was as if he was speaking to a stranger.

"I have to realize you are not a child anymore," he said. "I have tried to do what I think is for the best. Someday, you will understand. We cannot forbid you to go. Do what you want."

He turned and left the room immediately. I hoped he would say something in answer to my "Thank you," but he didn't.

My mother patted my cheek before she too left the room to follow my father.

"Be happy, Marian," she said.

I heard the door to their room close. I sat there alone with my thoughts. Be happy, my mother had said. I didn't know what would make me happy. It wasn't difficult to understand my parents' ambivalence.

I picked up the phone to call Naomi.

chapter twenty-three

I spent a quiet Saturday at home catching up on personal laundry and thinking about what the following weekend at Naomi's house would be like. I also thought a lot about my forthcoming meeting with Shaindee. I had said some harsh things to her. I wondered how we would feel facing each other.

Since Shaindee did not drive, we chose as our meeting place a small restaurant not far from her house. Kosher, of course. Traffic was heavy, and I found Shaindee already seated at a table in an unobtrusive alcove.

She looked pale. Our greeting to each other was hesitant. We were searching. I took the initiative.

"I'm sorry, Shaindee," I said. "I know you were totally innocent of any underhanded actions. I accused you unjustly. Please try to forget it ever happened. You don't have to tell me anything about your personal life. You really owe me nothing, so don't feel any obligation at all."

I watched the movements of Shaindee's fingers as she toyed with the silverware, making various patterns. She seemed lost in thought and didn't answer. The waitress took our order, and it wasn't until she left that Shaindee began. Her head was bent low and her voice was a soft whisper.

"You realize that these are not my real parents," she said. "They are wonderful people. I love them dearly, and they are truly as good to me as if I were their natural daughter. They have been as close to me as parents, but I have no parents, no sisters, no brothers, no grandparents, no aunts, no uncles. I am the only living member of my family."

"Shaindee, how awful." I put my hand over her hand. Tears filled my eyes.

"I'm not telling you this to seek pity, Marian. It is a fact I've learned to live with. At the beginning, I had hoped my brother might be alive, but

167

I've given up on that, too.

"My mother was born in Germany. My grandmother, her mother, was a very intelligent and perceptive person. She saw what was going to happen in Germany. It was no secret. Her husband and sons were killed on the streets on Kristalnacht and the other two by German neighbors who wanted their belongings. She realized that escape for herself out of Germany was impossible. In the middle of the night, she drugged my mother so she wouldn't cry and stole away to another city. She then made a radical move for an Orthodox woman. She deposited my mother on the steps of a Catholic Home for Girls.

"The next day, she went to the home, and they accepted her as an impoverished gentile when she begged for food and offered her services to clean, wash dishes or do any work they could give her. She watched my mother grow up. At the beginning, it was very difficult. She had to avoid my mother so that she should not recognize her and when she succeeded and my mother forgot her, my grandmother was able to breathe a sigh of relief."

"Shaindee, what a brave woman!" I marvelled.

"After the war, she kidnapped my mother from the Catholic Home and brought her to Israel," Shaindee continued. "She was an unusual person, Marian. Her faith and courage are something I try to emulate. When she died, I was heartbroken. You see, my parents met in Israel and we had a wonderfully happy home life until—" Shaindee's body shook as she lived through the trauma once again. "My parents, my brother and I were riding on a bus in Jerusalem when there was an explosion. It seemed some Arabs had placed a bomb on the bus in a shopping bag. My parents were killed immediately. I searched all the hospitals for my brother, but I could not find him anywhere. There were some tragically mutilated bodies, and I was told he must have been one of those. He would have been twenty-two years this Passover had he lived. I was not hurt at all. I was nine years old."

"Oh, my gosh," I said. "You poor thing. What can I say to you? I just can't find the words."

"On the same bus were a young couple," she continued. "They had been married for a number of years and had come to Israel to get blessings from the Sages and to pray at the Wailing Wall and at the gravesites of our great men. She had had three miscarriages and couldn't seem to carry a baby to full term. On the bus, my parents had become friendly with this young couple and invited them to our home for *Shabbos*, but then the tragedy occurred. The young couple also came out untouched. When they saw what had happened to my parents, they told me that because only the three of us of all the passengers on the entire bus came through unscathed, it must mean that we should be a family. They asked me to become their daughter, and that's my story in a nutshell. Oh, except that the baby is named Sholom Yisroel. Sholom meaning that there should be peace in Israel, and Sholom was my father's name."

"But your brothers?" I asked. "Are they also adopted?"

"No. A few years after we returned to America, my mother became pregnant. She had no problems and carried out a normal pregnancy. She said that she benefited two ways by adopting me. G-d was good to her and gave her the boys and gave me to her as a daughter. They are two wonderful people, and I am grateful and fortunate."

"Shaindee, how can you say you are fortunate? Grateful I can understand. But fortunate? How? To have lost everybody?"

"Yes. Fortunate. If what happened had to happen, I'm fortunate to have had these wonderful people give me a home. The entire family, aunts, uncles, all of them, have accepted me as one of their own."

"Shaindee, I'm so proud to know you. Maybe you can infuse me with some of your faith. I feel so small next to you, small and petty. Compared to you, I was born with a silver spoon in my mouth. How do you go on?"

"You just pick yourself up and continue with your life," she said. "You work on yourself and try to make yourself a better person and worthy to have G-d's help."

"You are really something!" I said and shook my head unbelievingly.

"No," she answered. "I get no credit. If you truly trust in G-d, you believe there is a purpose for everything."

"You sound just like my grandfather. But how? How do people believe after facing such terrible calamities in life?"

"Faith, *evmunah*, trust in G-d is something difficult to explain," said Shaindee. "People went to their deaths in the concentration camps, knowing they would be burnt to ashes, singing *Ani Maamim*, I believe. Marian, you do, too. You don't want to face it yet, because there is a conflict, a fight going on within you. But you do. You do. Every inch of me tells me you do. One day you will realize it."

"I love you, Shaindee," I blurted out. "I'm so glad G-d made our paths cross and that we met and became friends."

She laughed with joy.

"You see, Marian, you're getting there. You're getting there! I told you it would happen."

chapter twenty-four

I must organize myself better, I told myself for the umpteenth time. Leaving things for the last minute always caused unnecessary stress. I should have packed my clothes the evening before, but even last night I wasn't sure I would really go. I was so mixed up. I realized that each step towards Naomi's beckoning fingers created new problems for me.

Since I had left everything for the last minute, I had to get up while it was still dark outside. I stepped out of bed gingerly, expecting to meet the coldness through the rug that covered the floor. It sent a shiver through my body. The wail and sigh of the wind as it hit my window made a moaning sound. When I raised the window blind, I was surprised to discover a clear winter day with no sign of snow.

I am a girl, similar to other girls my age, although there might be turmoil churning within me. What to wear was my problem at this moment. I chose my heavy navy tweed skirt and red turtleneck sweater. Then my mind went blank, and to decide what to pack in my overnight bag for the weekend became a major obstacle. I pulled out my lavender wool dress and my gray skirt and couldn't decide between them. I turned on the weather report, and when I heard the prediction of fifteen degree weather and a wind-chill which would make it feel like zero degrees, I decided on my gray skirt and coral sweater. In the bottom of my overnight case, I put the box of candy for Naomi and a toy for the baby which I had bought just in case I should decide to go.

"Goodbye, Mom." I kissed my mother. "Have a nice weekend." Her hand lingered on me a little longer than usual. "Send my best to Daddy." I kissed her again and felt a rush of warmth.

I opened the street door and a gust of icy wind brought the metallic smell of salt from the ocean. My body met the onslaught with a tremor,

171

and I felt myself shivering head to toe.

I pulled my wool scarf over my head and around my mouth and went forward to brave the elements. Janet and I seemed to have timed it exactly as we both arrived at the same moment. The bus ride to school was not long enough to thaw out.

"Don't wait for me after school, Janet," I said. "I'm skipping the last two classes because Naomi wants me to come before sundown."

Janet looked at me oddly. Was I imagining it, or was there a frostiness in her voice when she wished me a nice weekend?

The short walk after school from the bus to Naomi's house seemed endless as the wind was blowing into my face, making breathing difficult. I felt the icy sting against my face. The wind blowing against my eyes made it difficult to see. I was forced to keep them half closed and squint. Finally, I reached Naomi's house.

The exterior of Naomi's house seemed serene. How a house should be able to give this impression is difficult to explain. Perhaps it was because it was set far back from the road, as if to render it unobtrusive. A blue station wagon with DD plates was parked in her driveway.

Someone had timed it just right. I lifted my hand to ring the doorbell, and even before contact, the door was opened. Rabbi Isaacs must have been standing at the window watching for my arrival. There was genuine warmth and pleasure in his greeting.

"Welcome, Malkala," he said.

I was taken aback. I thought for the moment I was dreaming. The voice, the accent, the warmth. I thought it was my grandfather, and it took me a few seconds to realize it was Rabbi Isaacs.

"You look surprised to see me," he said. "I had a bad cold, and Naomi insisted I come. She took good care of her grandfather, and now *Baruch Hashem*, I feel much better."

I felt disoriented. Bewildered. What was Rabbi Isaacs doing in Naomi's house? It took me some time to remember it was really through Rabbi Isaacs that I had made contact with Naomi.

"I'm glad to see you, Rabbi Isaacs," I said. "I didn't know you would be here. I really am so grateful to you."

"How are your parents?" he asked as he directed me into the living room.

I didn't answer immediately. I caught his searching glance and his intuitive remark.

"Problems, Malkala?" he questioned.

Naomi came into the room, and I was glad I was not given the opportunity to answer.

"Hi. Good to see you," she said as she took my coat and suitcase from my hands. She put the suitcase on the living room floor, hung up my coat and led me into the kitchen. "Here is a hot drink to warm you. It is bitter cold outside. You must be freezing."

There was a delicious aroma of freshly cooked and baked food. I looked around the kitchen. There was a sheet of metal covering the burners on the stove and on top of the metal were pots of assorted sizes and shapes. The kitchen table was covered with a white cloth.

Naomi put a place mat on the tablecloth and placed on it a steaming cup of coffee. I kept my hands around the hot cup until my hands started to warm up. The coffee and the hot potatonik hit the spot, and I felt much better.

"Come, Marian," said Naomi. "I'll show you your room."

I followed Naomi down a long hallway into a narrow room which contained a bed, dresser, chest and a chair. It was simply decorated, neat and clean.

"This is the closet," she said, and opening a drawer in the chest, she added, "The chest is empty. Please make yourself comfortable. I'll be back soon."

I opened my suitcase and hung my skirt in the small closet. I put my sweater and the other things I had brought into the drawers in the chest. I left the box of candy and the pull-toy on the dresser.

Naomi returned almost as soon as I had finished.

"Come, Marian, I'll show you where the bathroom is. Would you like to wash up? See, it is along the foyer to your right. Please leave the light on in the bathroom and in the foyer. We leave it on all night, because on *Shabbos* we don't turn lights on or off. I'll wait for you, and then I'll light the *Shabbos* candles. I'd like you to watch."

We went into the dining room. It looked different from what I remembered. Now there was a white tablecloth spread across the table, and gleaming silver candlesticks were in the place of honor on the table. I saw a blue velvet cloth covering a small mound. These, I later learned, were the *challos*.

Naomi explained to me that she was now going to light the candles which would bring the Sabbath into the house.

173

"I'm going to say a prayer in Hebrew," she said. "Here, Marian, is a translation in English so that you can understand what I am saying."

I watched Naomi spellbound. I felt a chill at the mystical feeling that stirred within me as she put her hands three times over the lit candles in a circling motion and then covered her eyes. The only sound in the room was the sputtering of the candles and Naomi's lips moving in prayer.

I read the translation she had given me. "Blessed are You, O G-d our Lord, King of the Universe, Who has made us holy through His commandments and commanded us to kindle the lights of the Sabbath.

"May it please You, O G-d our Lord, and Lord of our fathers that the Temple be rebuilt speedily in our own days, and grant us a share in Your Torah. And there shall we worship You reverently, as in the days and years of long ago. Then too, as in the days and years of long ago, all that Judah and Jerusalem offer to G-d will be pleasing unto Him.

"May it be Your wish, O G-d our Lord, and Lord of all who came before me to show all kindness to me and my loved ones, and grant that there be perfect peace in our homes, and that Your Presence reside among us. Make us worthy to bring up children and grandchildren to be wise and understanding, so that they may bring light to the world with their knowledge of Torah and their noble good deeds. May that light always brighten our eyes. And may Your glory too shine on us and help us in all we do. Amen."

Naomi turned to me. Her eyes were glistening with tears.

"This is my special time," she said. "I like to offer my private prayers to G-d. I hope they are all answered. You are part of them, Marian. I prayed that you find contentment and happiness."

I turned my head as I heard voices.

"*Gut Shabbos. Gut Shabbos.*" It was Rabbi Isaacs and a tall, young man who I realized must be Naomi's husband. He was carrying Mordechai.

Naomi introduced me to her husband.

"This is Rabbi Yehoshua Stern," she said. "Yehoshua, this is my friend Marian."

"*Gut Shabbos,*" he said. "I'm glad you could come. I do hope you enjoy your stay with us."

He bent down and put the baby on the carpet.

"Zeida and I will go to the *Shul* on the corner," he said. "I don't want him to walk further, because he had such a bad cold." He then turned to Rabbi Isaacs and said, "Bundle up carefully. It is still very cold outside. *Gut Shabbos*, everybody."

They opened the door to leave. The whistling and howling of the wind through the bare trees made an eerie sound. The gusts were so powerful that it was with difficulty that Rabbi Stern finally closed the door. The freezing cold outside made me appreciate even more the warmth inside, and I basked in the feeling of coziness.

I bent down and picked up Mordechai.

"He is just adorable," I said. "I find it difficult to believe this is the infant I left. He has grown so big in such a short time."

"You really haven't been here for a few months, and at this age, children grow rapidly. Would you mind keeping an eye on him for a few minutes? I would like to *daven*, to say some prayers."

"With pleasure," I answered.

I carried Mordechai into my room and returned, carrying the box of candy and pull-toy in one hand and Mordechai in the other. I put the candy on the table, and I put Mordechai on the floor. I sat down with him on the floor and showed him how to use the toy. I enjoyed watching him as he pulled himself up with one hand, using the couch for support and with the other he held the pull toy. I marvelled at the mental and physical development in growth that had occurred in such a short time.

"Come, Marian," Naomi said as she walked into the room and sat on the couch. "Would you like to see my wedding album?"

"I'd love to," I said. Naomi carried the album to the couch and sat down next to me.

"Naomi, you looked beautiful," I said. "You made such a stunning bride."

Naomi laughed.

"You know the saying that all brides are beautiful." She pointed to some of the people. "These are my husband's parents. These are his sisters and brothers. This is my mother and father, and here is my grandfather."

"Rabbi Isaacs looks so much younger," I said.

"Yes. These pictures were taken only two years ago. It is just during this past year that he has aged so much. I think it is because he has lost so many of his friends. Your grandfather's death, in particular, was something that he took very hard. Oh wait, there is a picture of your grandfather in the album. My father had someone pick him up at the Home, and they brought him to the wedding."

Naomi turned some pages and pointed to a picture.

"See, this is the *Chupah*, the marriage canopy and your grandfather was one of the witnesses. He is over there in the corner."

I stared at the picture of my grandfather. There was such dignity in the way he held himself.

"Grandfather," the cry was silently torn out of me. "I need you so badly. Why did you leave me now, of all times? It is now that I could appreciate you. It is now that I would be able to show you my love. But now . . . now, it is too late. It is too late for us, too late for anything and for everything."

I put my head in my hands and pushed my fingers against my eyes to hold back the tears I felt forming. Naomi put her arm around me in an attempt to comfort me.

"I'm sorry," she said. "Maybe this was not the time to show you the picture. It is still too fresh."

"No, it's not that," I said. "It's just that I miss him so much. I didn't realize when he was alive how much a part of me and my life he was, and I wish I could have shown him how much I loved him. But now . . . now, it is too late. Why is it when we have something precious we don't realize its value? Only when it is taken from us do we recognize and appreciate what we had."

"Unfortunately, that's life, Marian. In fact, that is why our wise men have said that we ourselves, not knowing how our days are numbered, should do repentance and good deeds as if each minute were our last. Enough! It's *Shabbos*, and *Shabbos* is not a time for mourning."

Naomi closed the album and put it back in the closet. She looked at me searchingly.

"Tell me, Marian, what's new with you? How are you really? How is school? Neal? Your parents?"

Naomi, with her intuitive ability, grasped my hesitation in answering.

"I guess you are going through a difficult time," she said. "When you are not sure in what direction your life should go, it is more difficult than when a person finally makes the move."

I laughed.

"Naomi, who do you think you are? A psychiatrist. Yes, it is true that you have me on the couch so now you want to analyze me. If you think you are so great, let's see you detect specifically what is bothering me."

"You know what it is, Marian. You don't need a psychiatrist to tell you your problem. Anyone with two eyes and two ears can easily identify and understand it."

There was a sudden metamorphosis in Naomi's face and voice. Her smiling eyes became sad, but they were warm and caring.

"Give up Neal, Marian," she said softly. "He is not for you."

I looked at her, shocked.

"What do you mean?" I said. "How can you possibly say such a thing. You don't even know him. How unfair!"

"Please don't get angry, Marian," she said. "You may feel it is none of my business, but everyone knows you can't mix oil and water."

"What are you talking about? What does Neal have to do with oil and water?"

"You know what I mean, Marian. A Jew and a gentile just don't go together."

"Oh, come on, Naomi. You know I have never practiced any religion and neither, for that matter, has Neal. There is no need for me to pretend to you."

"It really goes deeper than your realize, Marian. The spirit of a Jew lies dormant within you, but it is there! That spark is just waiting to come out. Being born a Jew links you to a chain that goes back thousands of years. It is a solid chain. Do you want to be the one to break it?"

"This conversation is totally ridiculous, Naomi. I am here today, not thousands of years ago. Really, this is a silly conversation."

Naomi was persistent.

"Look, Marian," she said. "Think of it this way. You are one person, and you are a Jew. You have two parents, each is a Jew. Together that means there are three of you. Your two Jewish parents between them had four Jewish parents which means there are now seven Jews. Continue this chain backwards and backwards and trace it into the past and keep it going on and on. You are a Jew and your birth designated you to keep this chain of ancestry going. Do you want to be the one to break this chain now?"

I didn't answer. I was angry, and I knew I looked sullen.

Naomi ignored my reaction and continued.

"Not one of your ancestors broke that chain," she said. "They could have done this at any time. My gosh! They lived through pogroms, the

Spanish Inquisition, the Crusades, through Hitler, in ghettos, and still, they kept their religion."

"That's not true, Naomi, and you know it. My father—"

She didn't give me the opportunity to complete the sentence.

"No, Marian. That is what is known as a drowning person clutching at a feeble straw. The ending hasn't been written yet about your father. As long as there is a breath of life in a person, you can't tell how he will develop. Jews have faced catastrophe time and again, over and over again. Yet, from each grave they arose and continued the function of our faith. Besides, you can't blame your actions on your father!"

I watched astounded as she cupped my hands within hers.

"Your destiny, Marian, is within these two hands," she said. "Let me tell you something. Your father is talking one way, but a person is born a Jew, lives a Jew and dies a Jew. Don't let him fool you. You'll see that I am right."

I breathed a sigh of relief when I heard the baby cry. Reprieve. Naomi got up to go to him but then turned back.

"Please, Marian. Do forgive me," she said. "I hope I didn't come on too strong. I was carried away, but I really mean it for your welfare."

In a few minutes, she came back with the baby.

"Do you mind holding Mordechai?" she asked. "I'm going into the kitchen to get him something to eat. I'll be right back."

She returned shortly with a baby's high chair into which she strapped Mordechai. She then left the room again and returned with a steaming plate of hot chicken soup with noodles and another plate containing a mashed carrot and small, mashed bits of chicken.

"I just can't believe it?" I said. "Was it just such a short time ago that I was here? He has grown so much. How old is Mordechai?"

"Almost a year old," she said. "Ten months to be exact. You know, you haven't been here since October, and it is now the end of January."

She put a paper plate with the chicken on the tabletop.

"He won't let me feed him, but watch how the floor eats too," she said with a laugh. "I'll have to wait for the soup to cool off a little. How is your friend Janet?"

"She's fine. If you're talking about people who are good Jews, you should meet Janet's father. He is very involved in Jewish causes and is knowledgeable and proud of his ancestry."

"What does that mean?"

I described Mr. Abikoff for Naomi and emphasized his sincerity, warmth and feeling for Jews.

"He sounds like a wonderful person, but I'm afraid I wouldn't call him a good Jew."

"Are you crazy, Naomi?" I said. "He is one of the most concerned people I ever came across."

"True. He is a good person, but there is a difference between that and a good Jew, Marian. A good Jew should be all those things plus. When a person is Jewish in heart only, I call him a cardiac Jew. He can open his checkbook and heart and feel a sentimental attachment to Judaism. Believe me, Marian, I'm not knocking that. It is important and has value but he really cannot transmit all his beliefs to his children. You can only transmit to your children what they see, and what they see should be a pattern for life. A child needs to see, feel and live a *Shabbos*, to wear *arba kanfos*, that's the fringes sticking out of my husband's jacket, to keep his head covered. This reminds him constantly that he is someone special. Only through all this living, thinking, seeing, learning, have Jews managed to survive all these years. Otherwise, Marian, we could have been swallowed up and disappeared, as other religions were in the past."

"Are you trying to belittle a person like Mr. Abikoff?"

"Oh no. Please, Marian. Don't misunderstand me. He is a caring person, and he must be a wonderful person. But he has found a substitute for religion . . . call it a pseudo religion. No. What I cannot call him is a good Jew, although I don't deny he is a fine person."

"People have the right to live as they want," I answered defiantly.

"No, Marian," she said. "I'm sorry we have to disagree once again. There is only one way for a Jew to live and that is as a Jew. You know, Marian, Jews have often substituted different idols for the idols we gave up during Abraham's time. We were always the first to take up a new cause. We have been in the forefront of all secular intellectual and social movements. We have worshipped these deities and poured our energy into everything except where we really belong."

"So what?" I answered.

"The answer to that 'so what?' is that the gentile intellectuals have shown us they knew the best way to gas our infants," said Naomi bitterly. "Did you ever wonder what happened to the social justice followers when the Jews were being slaughtered in the concentration camps?

They disappeared. No! We cannot ration how much of Jewishness we want. It cannot stay just in our hearts. It must fill our lives."

Suddenly, Naomi laughed and bent down to pick up something from the floor.

"See?" she said. "I told you the floor also eats when Mordechai eats. He won't let me feed him, but half his plate goes on the floor. The soup I insist on giving him. Come on, Mordechai, here is a spoon for you and one for me."

What Naomi said bothered me. It reminded me of something I had once read which was distributed to teachers by a principal in the public school. I repeated it to Naomi.

"Dear Teacher,

I am a survivor of a concentration camp.
My eyes saw what no man should witness.
Gas chambers built by learned engineers,
Children poisoned by educated physicians,
Infants killed by trained nurses,
Women and babies shot and burned by
high school and college graduates.
So I am suspicious of education.
Help your students become human.
Your efforts must never produce learned monsters
or educated Eichmanns."

"Where did you hear that, Marian?" Naomi asked.

"I don't recall, but when you were talking, I remembered I had read it somewhere, and I guess it pretty much sums up what you were saying. Naomi," I changed the subject, "exactly what is the meaning of *Shabbos*? What is it?"

"Remember I asked you to please come by a certain time? The reason was that I wanted you here before the Sabbath started, before the time to light candles came, because at that time we stop all work, all travelling, to usher in the seventh day of the week, our day of rest."

"You mean you live by a time clock?"

"If you put it that way, then the answer is yes."

"Well, it does seem ridiculous that, let us say at 4:00 P.M. you can do everything and that at 4:05 P.M. you can't," I said. "Naomi, our genera-tion is really at war with restrictions as well as clock watching. We try to do our own thing."

"Oh, how wrong that entire concept is," said Naomi. "Marian, the hippies of the Sixties felt like that. Therefore, they went unkempt, sang the same songs, dressed in clothing as far away from the Madison Avenue image as possible in order not to conform. But you know what? They were actually all conforming to the nonconformist image. Their mode of dress differed from Madison Avenue but they all dressed alike, sought the same music and pleasures. Don't you see that?"

"I suppose so," I said doubtfully.

"Marian, when you get up to go to school in the morning," she continued, "you have to be there by a certain time. When your father goes to work, he has to leave by a specific time. You too are ruled by the clock, but you are not manipulated for holy reasons. You watch the time because you are in a rat race. The religious Jew follows time because it elevates him."

I shook my head. I didn't understand what in the world she was talking about.

"To the Orthodox Jew, every moment is precious," she explained. "Most of our observances are followers of time. For example, the Sabbath can only fall at a certain time. *Rosh Chodesh*, the sanctification of the new moon initiating another month, and our festivals all follow a specific time cycle. We pray three times a day, morning, afternoon and evening. All this relates to a specific time."

"What does all this have to do with the Sabbath?" I asked.

"You see, G-d created the world in six days, and He rested on the seventh day. He gave us the seventh day to rest and also to refresh ourselves spiritually. We wait six days of 'time' until the seventh so that we can usher in the Sabbath. Marian, can you imagine the discipline necessary for a person not to look at what his cash register took in on Friday but, instead, to look at the clock and, no matter what he has earned, to close his business and go home for *Shabbos*? He leaves his work and any profit he might make for the remainder of the day, and what's more, he leaves without any hesitation but joyfully."

"I can understand that," I said. "So he goes home and does no work on Saturday because he has to take a forced vacation. Okay, anyone can do that. Anyone likes a day off."

"No. You don't understand, Marian. It is not a day to lie around the house or to drive to the beach. It is not a vacation. Yes, it is a release of the tension of everyday living. But it is a day of peace, a day of happiness, a day of rejuvenation. But most important of all, it is a day that shows our total *emunah* and faith in G-d."

"How does it show that?"

"Well," she answered. "It shows our complete trust that G-d will provide. We accept the loss of any profit we might make. Competition, the word which can be both a blessing and a curse, suddenly disappears. For six days we work, we cultivate the earth, wash, cook, clean, but on the seventh day we stop. Just like that! Imagine, Marian, that you are walking down a street. The sun is shining, and the gardens are blooming. You put out your hand and innocently, unconsciously pluck a petal from a flower or a leaf from a bush. Comes the Sabbath and you must refrain from doing that. How close you have come to G-d with just this little bit of self-control."

I guess Naomi saw my skeptical expression, because she dropped the subject.

"I always make special delicacies for *Shabbos*," she said. "I like the house to be permeated with the aroma of the cooking, and I want Mordechai to grow up knowing this special aroma as the aroma of *Shabbos*."

Naomi took the baby out of his high chair.

"I'm going to put him into pajamas," she said. "I'll be right back."

Naomi returned with Mordechai in her arms. At the same time the door opened, and Rabbi Isaacs and Rabbi Stern came in.

"*Gut Shabbos*," they both said.

"It is unbelievably cold outside," Rabbi Stern said. "I don't think I remember such a cold evening. Brrr, I'll warm up before I take Mordechai from you. My hands are ice cold."

"How do you feel?" Naomi asked Rabbi Isaacs, concern showing in her voice and in her eyes.

"*Baruch Hashem*," he answered.

He left the living room and returned shortly wearing something that looked like a lounging robe or fancy bathrobe. Rabbi Stern wore the same type of robe.

Rabbi Stern sat down with Mordechai on his lap. I sat next to Naomi.

As if at a signal, Rabbi Isaacs and Rabbi Stern broke into a melodious chant. Although the words were in Hebrew and I did not understand them, I still found it pleasant to hear.

"We are welcoming in the Sabbath as one would a queen," Naomi explained. "I feel my home is not just a home, but a castle."

Rabbi Isaacs and Rabbi Stern stood up and filled their silver goblets with wine. Again, they sang something, and Naomi told me that this was *Kiddush*. I was given a small goblet with some wine. Mordechai was cute. He licked his lips after being given a taste of the wine.

Although the washing for *challah* was not new to me, as I remembered it from Sholom Yisroel's *Bris*, I still felt like a child experimenting with a new toy. It wasn't Naomi's fault. She really tried in every way to make me feel comfortable. It was the newness and strangeness of everything.

Rabbi Isaac and Rabbi Stern sang through most of the meal. It was all so very different from any supper I had ever eaten. I was transported into another world.

Naomi put the baby into bed, and I helped her clear the dishes. I excused myself soon after. Although it was still early in the evening, I felt totally exhausted. The strangeness of everything was frightening to me. Was this what I really wanted? Although I lay in bed, physically exhausted, my mind could not relax. I heard a steady singsong melody and a murmur of voices from the other room. I reminded myself of my mother's reminiscence of her parents' household in Europe. This must be what she meant by the sounds of people learning. I had difficulty falling asleep. I tossed and turned for what seemed like hours.

I heard a baby crying. It woke me up and brought me back to the present. I wondered what time it was, and looking around the room, I realized I was in strange surroundings. Where was I? Then it all came back to me. The bedroom was warm and comfortable, and with great effort, I finally threw the covers off, washed my hands and face and dressed. I remembered not to touch the lights.

Naomi was standing in the corner of the room with a prayer book in her hand. She waved hello to me but didn't speak. Mordechai was in his playpen. When he saw me, he pulled himself up. I played a game of peek-a-boo with him, and he gurgled with joy. I released his little fingers from the edge of the playpen, sat him down and gave him a toy.

"*Gut Shabbos*," Naomi said. "How did you sleep?"

"Like a log," I answered. I looked at the clock.

"I can't believe it! It's ten o'clock already? I must have slept around the clock!"

"Come. Let me give you something to drink."

The glass of juice was just what I needed to help me open my eyes. It hit the right spot.

"Is it still so cold out?" I asked.

"The wind isn't quite so severe, but it is still quite cold."

"Tell me, Naomi," I said. "There is something that bothers me. How do you reconcile your way of life with the twentieth century?"

"I'm afraid I don't understand your question," she said.

"Well, aren't you old-fashioned in this modern generation?"

Naomi laughed. "Marian, do you think I'm old-fashioned? Remember how Abraham taught belief in one G-d. People who do not believe in G-d worship various idols, except that they are now dressed in modern clothing. You've heard the saying that there is nothing new under the sun. Believe me, it is true."

"What you are saying, Naomi, is that modern philosophy and religions are based on forms of ancient idol worship, but you really haven't answered my question about your way of life being old-fashioned."

Naomi didn't answer immediately. She seemed to be in deep thought.

"Marian," she finally said. "You are right. Yes, you are definitely right. If you mean that something out of rhythm with the times is old-fashioned, then yes, Judaism is old-fashioned. Just as in Abraham's time, Judaism was out of rhythm with the times and Abraham was branded a misfit, so are we today. Yes, we are misfits. We yearn for the days of old, for the past when we were in our glory. We are against the modern morals and values. Our homes have always been miniature sanctuaries. If this is old-fashioned, then yes, we are old-fashioned."

Naomi's remarks were so emphatically stated that I answered her in a conciliatory manner.

"Well, I didn't say that I was against it," I told her. "Just that it was very strange to me."

I did not want to continue the conversation, but some masochistic urge within me persisted. I felt I needed this point cleared up and hoped Naomi would be able to help me.

"Naomi, why are women looked down upon in Judaism?"

Naomi looked shocked, as if I had thrown a bucket of water in her face.

"Where did you ever get that idea, Marian?"

"In the translation in your prayer book, men thank G-d that they were not born a woman, and women just say that they are thankful for being created as they are. Look." I went to the bookcase and took out the book that said *Siddur* on the cover. "It says it here clearly in black and white for anyone to see."

"Oh, Marian," she sighed. "It is interesting how easily things can become misinterpreted or taken out of context. It is not because we are lesser people that we say these words. It is because women's role in life entails different work. Because of that we are freed from the obligation of certain *mitzvos*, good deeds, while the man thanks G-d for the opportunity of doing these *mitzvos*."

"Aha," I answered. "You just proved my point. You see, she does have a lesser role in society."

"No," she answered. "Her role is just a distinctly different one."

"Well, then," I asked her smugly. "Why should a woman's role be different than a man's?" I caught her on that one.

"Marian, are you different from a male? You know as well as I do that everything in life was created for a different purpose. Can you honestly say there is no intrinsic difference between male and female, and any law or religion which recognizes that difference is invalid? Let me assure you of one thing, Marian. It is not Jewish society that has given women a lesser role. It is the secular society that has done this."

"How?" I asked.

"You admitted that you believe G-d created Adam, the first man, out of earth. Right?"

"Yes," I said.

"Do you know from what woman was created?"

"No," I said, puzzled. "And what has all this got to do with what we are talking about?"

"Eve, the first woman, was created from Adam's bone," said Naomi. "Now I ask you, Marian, which has the potential for greater strength, earth or bone? Woman is the man's support!"

I didn't answer Naomi, because I didn't want to. Her arguments had the strength of conviction.

"I always find it ironic," she continued, "A woman who stays home and takes care of her children is looked down upon. After all, who can find satisfaction in the home? Let me ask you something, Marian. Is running to make the train every day, holding a nine-to-five job, being subject to employers' whims, the utopian life for which the liberated woman strives?"

"But there is no status in staying home, being exploited and looked down upon."

"Who is exploiting whom? Who is looking down upon whom? I am not saying a woman must never work. It is what is behind her reasons for working that is questionable. A woman's job is to be a full partner to her husband. In fact, Abraham's wife Sarah personified all this. Parenthood was first in her mind, and the total development of their son Isaac to the maximum of his ability was her main job. However, Abraham was busy teaching the Word of G-d, and our Torah tells us that Sarah worked right along with him, side by side, doing the same thing with women. And Marian, she did not hesitate to express herself if she had any difference of opinion. When there was a problem as to how to handle a situation that concerned their son, she spoke up and G-d instructed Avrohom to listen to his wife."

Naomi shook her head.

"No, Marian," she continued. "The Jewish religion honors women. We have no need to be liberated, because we are already liberated and respected. When my husband came home from *Shul* last night, he sang a song *Eishes Chayel Mee Yeemtza*. This is a song of admiration. It means that a woman of worth is prized above rubies and that the heart of her husband trusts in her for her words are words of wisdom. Marian, a Jewish husband treats his wife with honor and respect."

"So that's that on Women's Lib," I said. I threw my hands up in the air. "I give up. You win. Conversation closed."

Naomi smiled wryly. "I guess I'm winning some and losing others," she said.

I pulled the curtain away from the window to look outdoors.

"The wind seems to have subsided," I said. "It looks refreshing. I think I'll take a walk. The cold air may be just what I need to stimulate me after so much heated conversation."

I felt an unusual exhilaration. I didn't know whether it was the feeling of the wind on my face or because of the intoxication of our talks.

The wind was still blowing, the treetops bending to and fro according to the pressure of the wind, but it was without the fierceness of yesterday. I walked briskly, and it was a great feeing just to be alive. I looked around me. The streets were deserted for a Saturday morning. As I reached the corner, I heard voices, many voices, a multitude of voices, all in unison. It was coming from the *Shul* that Rabbi Isaacs and Rabbi Stern had attended the previous night. I pushed my tightly curled fists into my coat pocket and listened under the window. I felt like an intruder. These people were following a familiar routine. To me, it was a mystery, part of a vast puzzle

I went back to Naomi's house. I returned to the coziness and warmth which had surrounded me with a protective coat against the bitter cold of the outside world.

I returned to a *Shabbos* I would not forget.

I returned to a way of life both old-fashioned and with the magical ability to be contemporary always.

I returned to a life-style that had to make *Havdalah* on Saturday night before facing the week so that there could be a separation between the holy and the profane.

And after *Havdalah*, I returned to my own home.

chapter twenty-five

I returned home to find a letter on my dresser. I looked at the front and back. There was no return address, and the postmark said Brooklyn, New York. Who had written me without putting on a return address? I tore open the flap and took out the letter.

Dear Marian,

I didn't want to mail this letter from Israel as I did not want your parents to know I was writing you. I asked a friend to mail it for me when she returned to the United States.

Please tell me what is going on in your house. I received a rambling letter from your mother, and I can't make heads or tails of it. I answered her, but she hasn't answered my letter.

I heard from your father, but his letter was dry and non-committal. I get a feeling he is under some strain. Is he well? Please write and let me know what is going on. You and your parents are the only family from my side, and I worry constantly.

How are you doing, Marian? I haven't heard from you either. Have your problems been resolved yet? You will work them out. I know. Your grandfather had faith in you. His years of having a back-seat in your life did accomplish something. It had to, or his sacrifice of living in *galus* would have been in vain. No man wants to live his life in vain.

With all my love,
Aunt Leah

It seemed I had returned home to the additional burden thrust upon me by Aunt Leah which I felt was too heavy to carry.

I returned home to a tension and an undercurrent of anger between my parents. They spoke, but they were like strangers. My mother's eyes constantly had deep smudges of black underneath them. I knew she did not sleep well because I often saw the light on in the living room as she sat forlornly on the couch. Many mornings her eyes looked hollow and red-rimmed, as if she had spent the night crying.

Evening after evening, I watched them, my Aunt Leah's letter burning in my mind. They sat together in the living room. They sat together but seemed miles apart. They seemed strangers.

I watched my father. The newspaper was in his hands but his eyes rolled upward, looking towards the ceiling. He seemed fascinated by something there, staring unseeing at an imaginary point. His movements were almost predictable. They seemed to have formed a pattern. He would put the newspaper down and take a cigarette from a pack in his shirt pocket. He tapped the cigarette on the end table at the side of the couch, still staring at the spot on the ceiling. For a while, he seemed immobile, poured into that unseeing and unmoving position. Then, I watched him light the cigarette, take a deep drag on it, hold the smoke in his mouth for an interminable time, before releasing it in a cloud in front of him.

Just as he seemed completely immersed with the spot at which he looked with unseeing eyes, so did the few words my mother would utter fall on deaf ears. There was no response. He seemed to function automatically, eyes on the ceiling, cigarette to mouth, puff, release, tap of ashes into ashtray and then repeat.

Sometimes, I felt his eyes upon me. But here too, he looked at me sightlessly, as if he was looking through me. I felt terribly guilty. I wondered whether my basic rejection of his authority and wishes had affected him much more than I realized. My guilt made me feel it was I who had created a major trauma in our household, pitting my mother and father against each other.

I now knew what the role of a woman was in Jewish life, but I wondered what the role of a child should be to her parents. Was I right in creating a chasm between my parents? Wasn't I entitled to my own life, my own mistakes, my own search, my own needs?

The newspaper shook me out of my personal problems and out of my apathy with worldly affairs. One of the well known newspapers, anxious to cash in on the sudden resurgence of interest in the criminals of World

War II brought on by Dr. Schmidt's arrest, undertook a series of articles on the war and on war criminals.

My generation was fascinated. We really knew very little about the entire Nazi movement, and we read every word avidly. To further set the climate and maintain our interest, there were selected photos in the papers. Innumerable articles about the Nuremberg trial of Nazi war criminals were once again reprinted. Captured enemy pictures were flashed into homes for all to see. The horrors, cruelty and inhumane treatment seared young minds and opened wounds in old minds that had never really healed. The German meticulousness for detail in record keeping was proof of the magnitude of the deed. Old concentration camp pictures were splashed across the pages, and the pictures of the crematoria brought the tastes, sounds and smells vividly to us.

I shuddered when I read the details and descriptions of the tortures and the burnings. There was a picture of a building which said "*Bad*," German for bath, with a large pile of clothing left outside, clothing which would be issued to "poor Germans" as gifts from their leader. The deception was complete. The helpless were issued towels and soap before entering a room which had shower heads and concrete floors. Unfortunately, or fortunately, they did not know that as soon as the room was full, the doors would be sealed and instead of water from the shower heads, a deadly gas would pour out.

When I read the documentation of the medical experiments performed, I tried to picture Kurt's father, but instead, an older version of Kurt's face emerged. I cried for all Jewry when I read of experiments conducted on Jews to see how cold a human could get before he would freeze to death.

The callousness of the Nazi mind emerged. The newspaper quoted items from the book *A Profile of Simon Wiesenthal* by Joseph Wechsberg:

"Wiesenthal got his first insight into the mysteries of the S.S. mind soon after the war when he obtained some letters which S.S. men on duty in concentration camps had written home to their wives . . . One S.S. man described matter-of-factly how his unit had been ordered to repair a landing strip in Uman, near Kiev in the Ukraine, where a Russian bomb had torn a large crater. The S.S. mathematicians figured out that the bodies of one thousand five hundred people would just fill a crater of that size, whereupon they methodically procured the building material by shooting one thousand five hundred Jewish men, women and children and throwing their dead bodies into the crater. The bodies were covered with earth, a steel mat was placed on top, and the landing strip was as good as new. All this was described unemotionally, with much technical detail. On the same page of the letter, the S.S. man inquired about the roses in his garden and promised his wife to find a Russian servant girl who can cook and look after the children."

That same book offered more information for the newspaper. They quoted another letter an S.S. man wrote his wife and how he had described the method of killing Jewish babies, which was by throwing them against the wall. In the same letter, the Nazi went on to ask how his own baby was and if he had gotten over the attack of measles.

I closed the newspaper after reading this. My eyes once again clouded with tears that were constantly forming since the series began. I recalled Rabbi Isaacs' words at my grandfather's funeral and thought about my father and his little baby brothers. My father's anguished, pinched white face proved he was also involved in the series.

I surmised that the newspapers were anxious to bring Dr. Schmidt to trial and realized that because of his respected position, he had remained undetected for so many years. They wanted to insure that their battle would be successful and that his political pull would not save him. In order to do that, false sympathy and baseless compassion would have to be avoided. I was glad that for once, at least, the newspaper was involved in a fair battle.

It was open warfare. Members of the Nazi party still existed and their unsigned letters were published. Anti-Semites had a field day writing about the collective guilt of the Jews. Collective guilt, of course, included all children yet unborn.

The newspaper pleaded for witnesses to come forward against Dr. Schmidt. They stated that names and stories would not be printed. They wanted nothing to harm the prosecutor's case.

The Leipzig trials of 1920, which were held after the First World War, were raked with a fine-comb, and those of us who knew nothing about it realized the farce. It was because of the apathy of the Allies in bringing the criminals to justice that fair sentences for the prisoners came to naught. The reporter said that the Allies had had a list of two thousand war criminals but had submitted as test cases the names of forty five. Only twelve of these were ever brought to trial. Of the twelve, six were acquitted and the other six were given sentences averaging a few months. The reporter wrote that one defendant who was found guilty was immediately released because the time he had spent awaiting trial was deducted from his penalty. He wondered whether this had given the Nazis free reign with nothing to fear.

By this time, I knew that the black-booted S.S. had been the Nazi elite organization, a symbol of sinister terror. I learned it had originally been created to protect Hitler and other Nazi leaders but eventually became responsible for the deaths of at least eleven million people, six million of them Jews.

The story of the Queens housewife Mrs. Hermione Braunsteiner Ryan, who had been a guard and a supervisor at Ravensbruck and Majdanek Concentration Camp, was compared to Dr. Schmidt's situation. The similarity and problems were almost identical. After the war, she had immigrated to Canada and married an American citizen. They then moved to New York, and in 1963, she became a naturalized citizen of the United States. When she was found, she was "just a plain housewife."

Jurisdiction over war crimes was under the West German government. However, deporting her from the United States was not an easy matter. It was quite complicated.

I was surprised and angry to learn that in America there was no statute prohibiting admitting Nazi war criminals. The grounds for deporting her could only be based on proof she had signed a document that she was not a participant in the persecution of anyone due to race, creed or national origin. She had lied upon entering the United States, and this was the only basis upon which she could be deported. At the time of Mrs. Ryan's case, it was difficult to get witnesses, and the Immigration and Naturalization Service would have been willing to let bygones be bygones and forget about the approximately ten thousand women prisoners under Mrs. Ryan's command. It would be even more difficult to get witnesses against Dr. Schmidt, because people would be that much older and many might have died. Too many also just wanted to be left alone to continue their lives and forget. Old nightmares resurrected were too full of pain and hurt.

It took years of trying to bury the Ryan case before it was finally solved. It seemed the Nazis in America had bought, bribed and fought everyone to let her go free. The reporter stated that it was only because of a legal error that Mrs. Ryan gave up her citizenship. If not for that reason, she might have been able to fight extradition.

Another newspaper took up the fight for Dr. Schmidt. "Sensationalism," they spread across their headlines, claiming the only reason the first newspaper was so involved in the case was because they wanted to increase their falling circulation. "Nazi backing, Klan influences," yelled the first newspaper. It was total war, each newspaper trying to outdo the other.

The second newspaper ran a front page picture of Dr. Schmidt, looking the innocent, old humanitarian doctor; the middle section of the paper had pictures of him playing with children. Even I found myself pitying him. He looked close to eighty years old. I almost went along with the feeling that perhaps we should just drop it. But then I remembered what he was accused of and that if he would be freed, it would give free reign to others to believe Jewish blood is cheap.

In the midst of all this, I received a phone call from Neal. At first we talked about the weather. It was safe territory.

"How are you, Marian?"

"Fine, Neal. How are you? How are things in Boston?"

"It is ten degrees and freezing cold," he said. "Are the New York papers also carrying articles about Kurt's father?"

"Yes, they are."

"Don't believe everything you read, Marian. It could all be a mistake."

"A mistake? A mistake about what?"

"So many years have elapsed," said Neal. "How is it possible someone could still recognize him? No one could possibly look the same. No. It must be mistaken identification. You have to understand that in America a person is innocent until proven guilty. Let's not issue any verdicts on our own."

"Is Kurt there with you?" I asked.

"No. He requested a leave of absence from school, which was granted, until this sorry mess is straightened out. It has been very difficult for him to face the other guys in school. Everyone looked at him as if he was an oddball."

"Then who is in the apartment now?"

"Just Jeffrey and myself," said Neal. "I'll tell you something. Jeffrey is not such a bad guy, after all. Since Kurt has been away, I've gotten a chance to know him better and there is much more to him than meets the eye. I like him and we have become friends. Listen, Marian, I called to tell you that my parents are having a twenty-fifth anniversary party next Sunday, and they specifically asked me to bring you. I guess they have accepted the finality that I won't change my mind. I'm flying in Sunday morning and I'll pick you up at five. It's formal. Okay?"

"Fine," I answered.

Although I had answered in the affirmative, it was only after I hung up the phone that the question floated into my mind. I knew the Brennans did not want me and wondered what they had up their sleeves. In a way, I knew. They wanted to prove to Neal that I was awkward, gauche and couldn't possibly fit into their world. My social graces, after all, would not be acceptable. Although my anger was directed against Neal's parents, I recognized a subtle anger also against Neal. Was I beginning to put him into a separate category as part of the hostile gentile world, the world of Kurt's father, Neal's anti-Semitic parents and those monsters who had persecuted the Jews?

"Not fair," I said, not realizing I had said it aloud. It really wasn't fair to Neal to do that, to assume that because he was of a different religion he must be biased. If I could do that, then in a way I would be committing the same crime. After all, there were also good gentiles, and Neal had always shown himself to be just. Otherwise, I would have had no interest in him.

I knew my father would be happy to hear about Neal's phone call and about the party. I wanted to please him and to ease some of the strain that had recently become so obvious in his movements and on his face. I was right. His shoulders seemed to become straighter, and he even looked younger.

"Wait here," he said.

He went upstairs to his room and soon returned, carrying something in his hand. It was his checkbook. He took out his pen, and I watched him sign the check with a flourish.

"Here, Marian," he said. "Go buy yourself a pretty outfit."

"This is too much," I said, looking at the check. I handed it back to him.

"No, Marian," he said. "It is not. I want you to be a knockout. I don't want anyone saying you are a cheap Jew."

I looked at my father. I was astounded. Shocked. There really was nothing further I could say to him. I thanked him and put the check into my pocketbook. At least now I had given him something to look forward to besides the next edition of the newspaper.

The week flew by. My mother and I met in the city each day after school, and all I remember is that we shopped, shopped and shopped. In a flurry of excitement, we ran from store to store. Gradually, my outfit emerged, and I felt like Cinderella going to the ball.

There was actually an occasional smile on my father's face. Although my mother seemed very involved in the entire activity, she had a continuous pensive expression on her face. Many times I had the feeling there was something she wanted to say to me, but she would draw back before the words could emerge. I tried to be helpful, encouraging her by presenting openings, but for some reason, I was not successful.

At the most inopportune moments, Naomi's words would buzz around my head. "Give Neal up. Give Neal up." I shrugged her words aside and pretended I had never heard them. It was easy enough for her to talk. After all, it was not her life she was toying with.

chapter twenty-six

N eal came to pick me up in the now familiar Rolls Royce. He was wearing a tuxedo and a bow tie. I wore my hair up, in a sort of washerwoman style. There were tiny wisps of hair hanging down, and I had little sprigs of flowers woven into my hair. My gown made luxurious swishing noises as I walked. The top of the gown was white taffeta and the skirt a corresponding black. The thick belt made my waist look even smaller than it was, and with the swishing of the taffeta and the full bouffant skirt, I felt a little bit like the pictures I had seen of a southern belle.

Our conversation was once again strained and awkward. It was difficult to pick up the pieces, even more so for me since so much was happening in my life.

"It will be cocktail hour when we arrive," Neal explained, preparing me for what was ahead. "If I know my mother, she will give you a very gushy welcome. My father will also welcome you but in his staid way. I gave my parents, as a present, a silver tea service which I knew my mother wanted. Since I signed the card with both our names, I want you to know what it is all about when she thanks you."

I laughed. "I feel a little bit as if I am preparing for a performance."

"In a way you are," he said. "When you are dealing with actors, you have to fit in and be part of the scene. Right?"

"I suppose so," I said.

"You'll meet Uncle Nickie," he said. "Let me tell you something about Uncle Nickie. He is now about sixty years old but still thinks he's twenty-five. He drinks as if there was no tomorrow. By the time we arrive at the party, he will most probably be totally drunk, or not far from it."

"Is there an Aunt that goes with Uncle Nickie?"

"Four!" Neal said with a laugh.

"Four?" I repeated.

"There have been four wives, and I think he is almost ready for number five. He is the family's prize scandal. Anyway, that takes care of Uncle Nickie. There will also be quite a few doctors present."

"Will Kurt's father be there?"

"Most probably."

"And Kurt?" I asked.

"I think he'll be there," said Neal. "I know my parents invited Dr. and Mrs. Schmidt and Son."

"I'm glad I asked," I said. "This one really does need some preparation."

Neal pretended not to hear me.

"You'll also meet my great aunt Leslie," he continued. "She is my late grandmother's sister. Be prepared for her. She says whatever is on her mind. I'm very fond of her."

I looked out the window and began to recognize familiar signs. I remembered how I had caught my breath when I had come here that memorable evening and had been greeted by the magnificence of the Brennan's wealth. The house rose before me in its stately majestic beauty; the stark white marble columns shining. Everything looked brighter because of all the lights sparkling. We passed the pool; the colored lights reflected upon the surface. Sounds of music came floating on the evening air. I felt my pulse race and I thought that Neal could hear the pounding of my heart.

"I'm frightened," I said.

"Don't be," Neal reassured me. "Remember, they are all just people. Money does not make them different. They are just flesh and blood with the same positive qualities and pettiness of all human beings. Of course," he added with a trace of sarcasm, "some of them do think they are above the human race."

I don't think I had ever respected Neal as much as I did at this time. His normalcy gave me the security I needed.

The door was opened by a black-jacketed butler standing ramrod straight. I almost reeled as I was confronted by the bright lights, music and the multitudes of people.

"Easy, Marian," Neal said. "Remember. They're only people."

I smiled at him, thankful for the confidence he was trying to give me and for his calm in the face of the storm.

"Marian, how good to see you." It was Neal's mother, her voice particularly loud and each word clearly defined. I felt all eyes riveted on me. "You look stunning. Your gown is just lovely. Is it a Valentina? Her French designs are superb."

"I saw the label, Mom, and I can guarantee that it is," Neal laughingly answered. I caught his wink and accepted that for tonight it would be necessary to become conspirators.

"What would you like to drink?" Neal asked.

"Can I hold something in the cocktail glass that looks like a drink but is just plain soda or seltzer water?"

"One ginger ale with cherry coming up," he said as he left me.

"So this is Marian." A tall, well-built man with graying hair approached me. At one time, he must have been a pleasant looking person, but he now looked dissipated.

"Are you Uncle Nickie?" I asked.

"Yes, I am Uncle Nickie, the black sheep of the family," he said. "I see Neal has told you about me."

From the corner of my eye, I saw Neal coming to my rescue, and I breathed a sigh of relief.

"I see you have met Uncle Nickie, Marian," said Neal. "Uncle Nickie, how are you? I recognized you from afar by the glass in your hand."

"Is it my fault I inherited so much money that I have to drink it away? Listen," he lowered his voice to a conspiratorial whisper, "it is either drink it away or pay it out in alimony. My wives have gotten enough money out of me already." He turned around. "Look who is here. The great Dr. B. and his missus."

"Hello, Marian. How are you?" Dr. Brennan, ever the genial host, put on his perfect act.

"Marian, I forgot to thank you and Neal for the lovely tea set," Mrs. Brennan exclaimed. "Your taste is exquisite. Neal told me you picked it out."

I caught Neal's eye and answered, "I'm glad you like it."

Uncle Nickie added, "So is Neal's."

"Neal's what?" asked Mrs. Brennan.

"His taste is exquisite," he answered and then teetered away.

"Please excuse us," Mrs. Brennan said. "As host and hostess, we have to welcome our guests and, of course, circulate amongst all our friends. Do forgive us." She took Dr. Brennan's hand and led him away.

"Whew, I'm glad that's over," Neal said. "Now let's go and enjoy ourselves."

"Neal, this place looks like a massive ballroom. What changed since I was last here?"

"A door removed, a wall removed. Just small things that took weeks of preparation," he said with a laugh.

There was talk, talk, talk and wall-to-wall people. The combination of their voices trying to be heard above the music and the musicians wanting to be heard above the clamor of voices was deafening.

I looked around the room. It was decorated in red, white and blue. I assumed this motif was carried out because President Lincoln and President Washington's birthdays fell during the month of February. All the tables were covered with white tablecloths and the silver vases held red roses. In the far corner of the wall, heavy red drapes fell softly to the floor. I didn't recall seeing them the last time I was here. We sat down at the table and were served *hors d'oevres*.

A trumpet blast broke into the din. Conversation stopped. All eyes turned to the red drapery, where two little boys, dressed in red, white and blue, were standing. Each held a trumpet to his mouth. Each also wore a top hot and a false beard in an Uncle Sam impersonation. I watched, fascinated, as each boy took one end of the middle of the drape and while blowing his trumpet, swung the drapery open to reveal Dr. and Mrs. Brennan dressed as George and Martha Washington. Dr. Brennan wore a white wig and Mrs. Brennan's clothing and hairdo were perfect imitations of Martha Washington's. All the lights in the banquet hall were dimmed and a floodlight illuminated the Brennans. In the background, a painted screen depicted Mount Vernon, the Washington home.

While we had been engrossed in the spectacle, the tables in back were quickly and quietly cleared and reset. The lights went off and focused once again on the banquet hall.

Little black boys in old fashioned livery stood at attention behind each chair. They helped seat the guests. Each table now had a huge center-piece in the shape of the flag. It was raised and supported on feet. Each foot depicted the symbol of a state in the United States.

The two little boys blew their trumpets again, and the drapes fell back into place.

"Dinner is served," they announced.

Just then the Schmidts arrived. Their timing was all wrong. They must have thought that by arriving late, they would be swallowed up in the crowd. But since dinner had not been served as yet, and everyone had just been seated, they were conspicuous in their lateness. Conversation stopped completely. The lateness of their arrival, or possibly the patriotism of the decor, added to the embarrassing silence. A flush crept over Mrs. Schmidt's face. I could not see Dr. Schmidt's face.

Mrs. Brennan, the veneer of civility intact, walked up to the Schmidts, shook hands and led them to their seats. Neal followed his mother's initiative and slapped Kurt on his back in an obvious show of friendliness. I was disturbed to note that the Schmidts were seated opposite us.

I studied Mrs. Schmidt's face. There were remnants of beauty but her shallowness was obvious in her shrill voice and in her choice of clothing. She seemed over fifty years old, but she dressed in a style suitable to a much younger woman.

I tried not to look at Dr. Schmidt, but I kept being drawn there. My eyes couldn't leave his face. This was the face of a sadistic murderer and torturer. I wondered what sociological and psychological factors go into the makeup of a person who would experiment on a human being. How many lives had he himself taken? How many lives had he ruined? I could understand why a man might go to war. Perhaps he wanted to help his country expand and gain territory or settle other political differences. Wars were fought for independence or to gain technology. But I just couldn't understand what force could make a person put the human race into a test tube and, with the flick of a finger and as if brushing away an insect or fly, find an excuse to kill. Did he suffer guilt? Remorse? Was he able to sleep at night?

I remembered that one of the articles I had read dwelt on the mental makeup of people involved in atrocities. The author had given a two-sided review. On the one hand, he indicated that contrary to many views, Nazi leadership was not controlled by madmen. There was insanity in their actions, but on the whole, the people were of superior mental faculties. Another psychiatrist had disagreed, stating that this was an era in German history when pathological sadists were in power.

Basically, there are really two kinds of genocidal murderers. One kind never physically dirties his hands; he is a "white collar" killer, so to speak. All he does is sign his name to a paper giving permission for someone else to perpetrate the murder. The other kind actually performs the act; he is the "blue collar" killer. Schmidt personified both. He signed the orders, and he also devised and used new methods to destroy life.

All this time, I kept staring at Dr. Schmidt. I just couldn't tear my eyes away. He must have felt my eyes upon him, because he stopped talking to Kurt and looked directly at me. His icy steel blue cold eyes penetrated to my inner being. I was forced to lower my eyes.

"Hello, Marian," Kurt sneered. "You made it to the big time. You joined our society. It's temporary, you know. We don't accept your kind."

I looked to see whether Neal had heard, but he was engrossed in a conversation with someone else on his other side.

An elaborate dinner was served, but I could not eat. I felt as if every spoonful would choke me. Kurt and his father were looking at me; I could feel their hostile stare. Neal did not notice. He kept up a continuous joyful conversation with me.

After dessert, the trumpet sounds were heard once again. The two boys dressed as Uncle Sam opened the curtains and marched to the painted mural of Mount Vernon. It was amazing. The doors opened, and the two boys beckoned us to follow them.

We entered a tremendous tent, which had not been visible from the front of the house. Although it was February and very cold outdoors, the Brennans had arranged portable electric heating units, and it was as warm as if we were indoors. There were chairs lined up, and we were all seated.

The entertainment was diversified. We listened to a well-known opera star, a magician and a comedian. As soon as the entertainment was over, our coats were returned to us. I don't know how they managed to know to whom each coat belonged. The top of the canvas of the tent was opened and we watched dazzling firecrackers in the colors of red, white and blue.

I searched through the crowd for the Schmidts and was gratified to find them completely alone. Neal also noticed.

"Let's move closer to the Schmidts," he said. "It looks like they've been ostracized and are being totally ignored." Seeing my expression, he added, "Would you really mind?"

"I'm afraid I would," I said. "I just can't help it, but I keep looking for the blood on his hands."

"Please, Marian," he said. "Don't be like that."

"I'm sorry, Neal, but I don't want to have anything whatsoever to do with them."

We went inside to the banquet hall. Our coats were once again taken from us. An old woman approached us.

"Well, well, Neal," she said. "I've been waiting for you to do your duty, but I guess you've forgotten me."

She looked about ninety years old. Her face was totally wrinkled, but her smile was warm and her voice sparkled.

"You know I could never forget you," Neal said. He put his hand on his heart. "There is a very special place inside this heart that I hold only for you. No one else can occupy that spot."

He bent down and kissed her on the cheek.

"Marian, this is my very best friend. She is the best friend I have in the world and," he lowered his voice, "my secret admirer. This is my great aunt, Aunt Leslie. I have been in love with her since I was old enough to talk."

"Get away from me, you scoundrel," she jokingly scolded Neal. "Oh, oh, here comes the witch and her mate."

I turned around to see to whom she was referring and was astounded to see Dr. and Mrs. Brennan.

"So you've met our Marian," Mrs. Brennan said, her voice oozing with sweet sarcasm. "This must all be very strange to you, Marian, your evening out among us. I must say you certainly know how to blend in. I have to give you credit for that."

"Mom!" Neal reprimanded her.

"Your cat's claws are showing, dearie," Aunt Leslie said. "Are you jealous of her good looks? Or perhaps you are envious of her youth? Oh no! I know," she said with a mischievous twinkle, "I've heard it is because she is Jewish." Aunt Leslie ended her statement with peals of uncontrollable laughter.

She then turned and faced me.

"Don't let it bother you," she said. "She is an undisputed snob, even though she is my late sister's daughter. By the way, Marian," she continued, throwing a look over her shoulder at Neal's mother, "I guess you've heard the expression 'Some of my best friends are Jewish.' Well, I can truly say my best friend is Jewish. We have been friends for fifty years, and I have never met a finer person."

Neal's mother tried to interrupt, but Aunt Leslie didn't give her the opportunity.

"I'm sorry I can't say that about everyone," she added with a sigh.

Mrs. Brennan walked off in a huff, Dr. Brennan following meekly behind her. I couldn't help but contrast Naomi's marriage and this one.

"No one ever won an argument with this lady, Marian," Neal was saying. "Now you can understand why she has always had a very special place in my heart."

"Neal," Aunt Leslie said. "Do me a favor and disappear for a few minutes. I would like to talk to Marian and really get to know her." She looked at her wristwatch. "It is now eleven o'clock. Come back in a half hour. Now, remember. I don't want to see you even a minute before. Understand?"

"On one condition," Neal answered.

"And what is that?"

"That you don't tell her anything bad about me."

"At my age, Neal, I don't tell lies. I am too close to the accounting scale."

"I hope that means you won't say anything bad," Neal added with a smile. I watched him walk off.

"No comment, Neal," Aunt Leslie shouted after him.

They both laughed.

"Come, Marian," she said and took my hand. She led me to two chairs at the far end of the room. Her warmth enveloped me. She was so twinkly and spry it just made me like her. Her honesty was refreshing after the bitter pill I had been forced to taste.

"I'm going to be totally honest with you and I expect you to be totally honest with me," she began. "Remember, tit for tat. No pretenses. I had no time for them in the past and have even less time for them today. Okay?"

She put out her hand and took mine in hers in a gesture of shaking hands.

"How do you feel about Neal?" she asked. "I want you to forget he is related to me when you answer."

"I like him," I answered.

"But not enough to marry him," she stated.

"I didn't say that, Aunt Leslie. You did."

"Marian, when you have lived as many years as I have, people don't always have to use words. We have developed the ability to sense things."

"You can see that his parents obviously don't like me."

"Yes, they have made that pretty obvious, but if that would be the only barrier standing between you and Neal, would you marry him?"

"Is this conversation really necessary?" I asked. "After all, he hasn't asked me."

I did not say this rudely, but stated it softly. After all, the last thing I wanted was to be rude to this lovely lady.

"Yes, Marian," she said. "This conversation is very necessary, because he will eventually ask you."

"Well, there really is another problem," I said. "The difference in religion. His parents never fail to mention it."

"How about Neal?" she asked.

"It hasn't affected our relationship."

"And now, Marian, how do *you* feel about the difference in religion?"

Here it came. That nagging question I had been trying to push into the recesses of my mind. How did I feel about it? Could I honestly answer Aunt Leslie?

"I plead the Fifth Amendment," I answered.

"What is that?" she asked.

"Anything I say would incriminate me." I laughed.

"Uh, uh." She shook her head. "You are not getting away with that. I expect and will get an answer!"

"I guess I really feel it matters," I admitted. "If it is not a problem between us today, it will be some time in the future. And what do we do with our children? Yes, it concerns me very much."

She peered closely at me. There was a pair of glasses hanging on a chain around her neck. She put them on the tip of her nose and centered her eyes closely on my face so that absolutely no nuance of my expression would get by her.

"Marian, Neal is Jewish," she said quietly.

"What?" I reeled back as if she had hit me over the head with a club. "What did you say?"

"I said that Neal is Jewish."

"I . . . I don't understand."

"My sister could not have any children, and she adopted Neal's mother. She was Jewish."

I could not grasp her words. I thought I was imagining everything. It was just too much for me.

The music blasted away, drowning out her voice. She motioned for me to follow her. We went upstairs to a small room. Aunt Leslie closed the door.

"I'll start at the beginning," she said. "Try to follow closely what I am about to tell you. My sister, whom Neal thinks of as his grandmother, was a typical social butterfly. Since she did not have any children, her life became totally shallow. It was centered around clothing, dancing, parties and buying sprees. She decided that she needed a secretary to arrange her appointments and to manage her life. It was a dismal cold afternoon when the young woman came for her interview. When she walked in, it was as if a breath of fresh, clean air had arrived. Her skills were excellent, and my sister hired her.

"She thanked my sister and said, 'I need this job desperately but . . .'

" 'There seems to be something on your mind,' my sister said. 'Did I give you too many duties?'

" 'Oh, no,' she answered and then blurted out her story.

"Her husband had been killed in an automobile accident just weeks before, and she was left penniless with no family at all. The previous day, she had found out she was pregnant. Having a place to live and a job at my sister's home would be just perfect, but she didn't want to take it under false pretenses.

" 'I'm healthy and strong,' she said, 'and I'm sure I could work up until the time I give birth. After that, I'll make arrangements for the baby, and I'll continue working.'

"My sister had a soft and generous heart. 'You are hired,' she said. 'Just make sure you don't throw up on any of my rugs. I expect one hundred percent work out of you no matter what your condition might be.' She deliberately said this so that the young lady would not feel she was doing her a favor.

"Well, she was a wonderful worker and a brave person. To make a long story short, she died in childbirth. She gave birth to a little girl, Neal's mother, and my sister adopted her."

"You are telling me that Neal's grandmother was Jewish," I said. "How does that make Neal Jewish?"

"Young lady, don't you know anything at all about your faith?" she said. "A child born of a Jewish woman is automatically Jewish no matter what the husband is. Neal's grandmother and grandfather were Jewish. Mrs. Brennan, Neal's mother is Jewish, and that, therefore, makes Neal Jewish!"

205

"How did you find out she was Jewish?" I asked. "Were there any relatives?"

"She told me she was," she said. "And she had a typically Jewish name. If it wasn't her real name, I'm sure she would never have chosen it. After all, who would call themselves Yenty Cohen? And besides, we sent away for her birth records and for her husband's records."

"Does Neal know?" I asked. "Does his mother?"

"Neal's mother? Ha! It would kill the snob if she found out. But I think it is time I tell Neal. Who knows how much time I have left in this world? I wanted you to hear it from me so you would never think it was an invented story, and if your parents want proof, I'll give it to them."

I looked up and saw Neal coming towards us.

"Your half hour is up, Aunt Leslie," he said. "I'm taking over now."

"How did you find us?" Aunt Leslie asked. "I hid away with Marian so you wouldn't be able to."

"I sent my spy system out," said Neal. "It keeps a finger on everything for me."

"Sit down, Neal," she commanded. "I have something very important to tell you."

I watched Neal as she told him everything she'd told me. His face showed myriad emotions: shock, disbelief and then, slowly, belief. His face was white. He did not utter a sound. When Aunt Leslie finished what she had to say, Neal sat there, stunned.

"So that's that, Neal," Aunt Leslie said. "I'm waiting. No comment from you?"

There was no response from Neal. He looked at Aunt Leslie and then at me. He got up slowly and left the room. I started after him, but Aunt Leslie held me back.

"No, don't go, child," she said. "He needs time alone to get used to it. Give him a few minutes."

"I'm worried. How will he take it?"

"He'll live," she said dryly.

We went downstairs. Mrs. Brennan saw Aunt Leslie and me. I looked worried, and she shrewdly noticed my expression and that Neal was missing. A sly smile appeared on her face. She looked amused. I guess she thought we'd had a spat.

Neal was absolutely nowhere to be seen.

"Sit," Aunt Leslie commanded me.

"I just can't," I said once again. "I wonder how he is taking it."

"My goodness, Marian," Aunt Leslie said. "I didn't tell him he has cancer or something like that. He's not going to die from this. Maybe it will give him a chance for a happy life."

"I can't believe it," I said. "I have never met someone like you. Why are you so different?"

"Do you really want me to tell you the truth?" She didn't wait for my answer, but continued, "My neighbor changed my entire outlook. Most Jews I'd met seemed to be saying, 'Listen, gentile world. We are no different from you. We are just like you.' But the more Jews try to become like us, the more we resent them. But my Jewish neighbor *is* different. She keeps her distance where it matters. She is Jewish in everything she does, Orthodox Jewish, and I respect her. She is proud of her religion, not apologetic. Anyway, I think I must have a drop of Jewish blood in me, because I just never suffered from anti-Semitism."

The crowd was beginning to thin. I looked at my wristwatch. It was 12:30. Neal had been missing for at least a half hour. My eyes searched the room. He was nowhere in sight.

"I'm going to look for him outside," I declared. "Excuse me, Aunt Leslie."

"Go, child. I think he has had enough time by himself."

There were still a few couples strolling around the grounds, their collars pulled up tightly against the cold. I shivered as I felt the cold air penetrate my light dress. I was about to give up when I saw a young man walking quickly towards me.

"Neal?" I called out. But it was just another guest who brushed past me.

"Neal, Neal," I shouted. There was no response and no sign of Neal.

Helplessly, I gave up and returned indoors. Aunt Leslie was still sitting where I had left her.

"You didn't find him," she observed. "I didn't think you would. He'll come back when he is ready."

People were leaving.

"Lovely evening."

"Delightful party."

"What a bash!"

"The novelty party of the year!"

The words drifted back to me. We sat in silence, Aunt Leslie and I, a warmth between my new found friend and myself. Uncle Nickie came over to us.

"So this is where you've been hiding, Marian," he said. "I looked for you all evening. Where have you been?"

"I commandeered her, and I intend to continue to monopolize her," Aunt Leslie said. "Go!"

Like a child punished and sent to his room, Uncle Nickie did not answer and left.

I saw Kurt and his parents with their coats on, standing near the door, ready to leave. It had been a lonely, isolated evening for them. Kurt whispered something to his father. His father grabbed his arm, but Kurt shrugged it away and came straight towards us.

"We didn't kill enough of you," he spat. I thought he was going to strike me, but with a click of his heels, he twirled around and marched back to his father. They argued. Kurt looked at me with venom, and then his father looked directly at me.

"Nazi. Darn Nazi," Aunt Leslie said.

"Could you show me to a phone?" I said. "I would like to tell my parents not to worry. It really is quite late."

"There's a phone in the library, child," she said.

A couple was standing in the hall. I heard their whisper quite clearly. "Neal's girl . . . Jewish," were the words that drifted back. I lifted my head high. Aunt Leslie, bless her old heart, had helped reinforce my budding pride.

The library was dark. I searched for the light switch. I finally found it and flicked on the lights. I found the phone immediately and called home.

"I hope I didn't wake you," I told my parents, "but I'll be getting home much later than I thought. No. No problems. Everything is fine. Yes, it was a grand party."

I hung up the phone and looked around the room. Somehow, I sensed the presence of another person in the room.

"Neal! I've been looking all over for you."

He looked terrible. He reminded me of a little boy who'd had a precious object forcibly torn from him. His hair was tousled and his face pale. He put his head in this hands.

"So I too am a member of the clan," he said bitterly. "I've entered the fold."

"Is it really so terrible, Neal?"

"When you've lived for twenty-two years looking at life though different eyes, it is," he said.

"Neal, what difference will it make to you? Your life won't change. It will go on just as it did before."

At first, he didn't answer. I watched his hands fall, and then he looked directly at me. His face changed, and the tenseness seemed to leave it.

"You know, Marian, you are right. You are absolutely correct. There is one change though," and he smiled. "Now there are no problems between us."

I smiled back.

"You see, every cloud has a silver lining," I said. "Let's say goodnight to Aunt Leslie. I have to get home."

I kissed Aunt Leslie goodnight.

"You're really special," she said to me. "You're much too good for this family."

On the drive home, Neal joked around, but I saw through his pretense.

"I'm not leaving for Boston until Tuesday, so I'll call you tomorrow," he said. "Thanks so much for coming, and my apologies for ruining your evening by disappearing on you. I guess if it isn't my parents who kill the evening for you, then it has to be me. A Brennan always seem to manage it."

I ran up the staircase to my room. My mother called out from behind her closed door.

"Is that you, Marian?"

"Yes," I answered. "Have a good night."

I opened the door to my room, then closed it and turned on the lights. I looked in the mirror. My eyes were sparkling, and the blueness of my eyes shone clearly. I hadn't seen them so happy for a long time. My black hair tumbled to my shoulders, and my face looked wonderfully relaxed.

I felt lightfooted and lightheaded. I took one side of my skirt in my right hand and the other side in the left and waltzed around the room.

"Neal is Jewish," I sang. "Neal is Jewish. Neal is Jewish." I pivoted around and around.

The heaviness that had constricted my chest for so long was released. The burden I had been carrying on my shoulders was gone. I found myself singing and full of joy. I found myself dancing. I was full of happiness. Neal was Jewish!

chapter twenty-seven

I overslept the next morning. I had set my alarm clock, but my hand had automatically shut it when it rang. My mother tiptoed into my room.

"Marian," she said. "It's late. You'll miss school."

"I'm not going. I need sleep. Goodnight," I mumbled, and I turned over on my stomach and fell immediately back to sleep. It seemed like ages since I'd had such an untroubled night.

I was awakened by the ringing of the phone. Sleepily, I put my hand out and picked up the receiver.

"Marian, where are you?" It was Janet. "Why aren't you in school?"

"I can't talk," I answered. "I'm so tired. I'm so sleepy." Suddenly I jumped up. "Janet, guess what?"

"What?"

"Neal is Jewish," I said and returned the phone to its cradle.

The phone rang again. It was Janet.

"Are you okay, Marian?" she asked. "You sound out of it."

"I'm so tired I can't tell you the details but Neal is Jewish," I said. "We'll speak after school."

Once again, I put the phone back on its cradle but then took it off so I wouldn't be disturbed by further phone calls.

I awoke from a refreshing, completely untroubled sleep. I couldn't believe it! It was 2:00 P.M.

My mother greeted me when I finally came downstairs.

"Welcome, Marian," she said. "You slept as if there were no tomorrow. How did everything go last night?"

"Guess what?" I said, and again I sang and danced around the house. "Neal is Jewish. Neal is Jewish."

"Marian, are you running a fever?" My mother's concerned voice and

210

face brought me back to reality.

"Oh no, Mom. I don't think I have ever been so okay in my life." I told her about Aunt Leslie.

She smiled, and I was glad to see her face take on a glow. The gaunt, unhappy look she had worn for so long disappeared.

"So Mrs. Brennan does not know and is not to know," she mused. "What a turn of events."

"I'm going to call Daddy." I raced up the stairs to put the phone back on the hook so that I could make the call.

"Are you happy about it, Marian?" he answered. "If you are happy, then so am I. I'm so very happy for you."

It was most certainly not the answer I had wanted or expected, but under the circumstances, I guess I had to be content with that.

Later in the afternoon, I called Janet and told her the entire story from beginning until the end.

"What a weird turn of events!" She burst into peals of laughter. "If I didn't really believe you, I would say you had always wanted to be an author and that you surely made up an interesting twist to your story."

I waited all day for Neal to call. I made a thousand and one excuses about why he didn't. I watched the hands of the clock crawl until midnight, but there was no call. I lay on my back in the bed counting the tiles on the ceiling. I closed the light and pulled the covers over my head. Perhaps in that way I could smother my thoughts. I tried counting sheep. There was no sleep for me. My eyes remained open, and slowly, I watched daylight creep in between the edges of the closed blind.

In the morning, I got up and dressed. I had to wash my face over and over again with cold water to keep my eyes open. I went to school, but the raw edges of my nerves were twitching.

Tuesday evening, he finally called. His voice sounded out-of-breath and distraught.

"I'm sorry I couldn't call earlier, Marian, but I've had it. This has been some weekend! It is one for the books! Can you meet me at the airport? I just flew in from Boston."

"Boston? Why?"

"It's a long story. I'll meet you in Gate Eight Lounge at eight o'clock. Okay?"

I don't remember getting into the car or parking in the car lot. I can't even recall driving in traffic. It was as if another person had taken over the wheel of the car and driven it.

I saw Neal before he saw me. He looked worn and tired. His shoulders sagged, and when I came closer to him, I saw that his face had fine lines drawn all over it. He was pale and his clothing looked as if they had been slept in.

He could hardly talk. He just didn't have the energy. His voice was barely above a whisper.

"Let's find a corner where no one can hear us," he said, "and I'll tell you a story that will make your hair stand on end. Where do I begin?"

"I guess at the beginning, Neal."

"I don't even know what the beginning is myself. Marian, Dr. Schmidt is dead."

That caught me by surprise, but I recovered quickly.

"So what?" I said. "People die every day. I'm sorry to sound so callous, but I can't shed even one tear for him. What happened?"

"After I took you home Sunday night," he said, "I went to sleep and so did my parents. It must have about three in the morning. I had just closed my eyes when I heard the telephone and picked it up. My father was on another extension trying to calm a near hysterical woman. At first, I thought it was an emergency in the hospital, which in not unusual in a doctor's house, but shortly after the phone was hung up, I heard my mother's voice and movement in my parents' room. Curious, I got out of bed.

" 'It was Mrs. Schmidt,' my father said to me. 'Something has happened there. Throw your clothes on, Neal, and come with me, please. I'm not up to driving.' He turned to my mother. 'I'll call you as soon as I can.'

"When we came to the Schmidt house, Kurt opened the door. His face was a white mask. I couldn't understand what he was saying. At first, I thought he was drunk; his speech was slurred and each word ran into the other. There was a strong and peculiar odor in the room, like something burnt. Later, I learned the smell was from powder burns, the result of a bullet."

I listened to Neal, my face void of expression. I was calm, attentive, making the expected sympathetic sounds. I showed interest, but I really felt no strong emotion, neither sympathy nor anger. To me, Dr. Schmidt had been something twisted, degenerate, unhealthy and sickening.

"We went into the study," Neal continued. "The scene was appalling.

Drawers were open and turned over on the floor. Papers were strewn about. It looked as if someone had gone through the room with a fine comb. Dr. Schmidt sat at his desk, his head leaning on one arm, the other arm dangling by his side. He looked fast asleep.

"I asked Kurt, 'Why would anyone rob your father?' Kurt threw his hands up in the air in a gesture of helplessness.

"My father was leaning over Dr. Schmidt, checking his pulse.

"I asked, 'Heart attack? Is he still alive?'

"My father didn't answer. He didn't have to. I was able to tell from his expression. Dr. Schmidt was dead. I hadn't realized Mrs. Schmidt was in the room. She was so quiet. She stood by the door, her bulging eyes wide open, her bleached blonde hair hanging in strings. My father beckoned to me, and I came to him. He showed me his hand. It was covered with blood.

" 'Kurt,' he said. 'Take your mother to her room. Make sure she goes to bed. Neal, in my black case, you'll find a round bottle with a red cap. Give two tablets to Mrs. Schmidt. It will help her fall asleep.'

"Mrs. Schmidt protested. My father walked over to her and put his arm around her shoulders. 'He is very ill,' he said. 'There is no help you can give him right now except to go to your room and lie down. If you stay here any longer, I'm afraid you will faint, and then I will have two patients to take care of, which I will be unable to handle. Please understand.'

"Kurt took his mother's arm. She leaned heavily on him, and he helped her leave the room. I heard their slow steps going up the staircase.

"As soon as they were out of the room, my father called the police. 'My name is Dr. Brennan,' he said. 'I am calling from the home of Dr. Schmidt. I think there has been a murder. The address is 50 Logan Drive. No. I did not touch anything in the room. Yes. I'll make sure no one does.'

"My father and I sat there in silence. There wasn't much to say. We just sat and waited. Finally, the police came.

"Detective Inspector Morgan was a tall, husky, red-faced Irishman. There were three others detectives with him. While they dusted the room for fingerprints, I watched him walk to the body of Dr. Schmidt and look at it from different angles.

"Finally, he said to my father, 'What do you think? Which way did the bullet enter the heart?'

"My father indicated a particular path.

" 'Homicide or suicide?' Detective Morgan asked.

"My father looked bewildered. 'I think . . . homicide.'

"Detective Morgan shook his head, 'You take a real good, slow and careful look, doctor. I want to be sure, so don't make any mistakes. I think it is suicide. Come over here.'

"My father walked over to the desk. 'Look at his hands,' said Detective Morgan. 'Powder burns. Look at the angle of the bullet. See.' He pointed to the floor, bent down and wrapped a handkerchief around an object he carefully picked up.

" 'As sure as my name is O'Reilly, it's suicide,' said one of the detectives who'd been dusting the room for fingerprints. He held up two pieces of paper. 'Look what I found. One of these is the suicide note.'

"We hadn't heard Kurt come into the room. The soft carpet muffled all sound. Kurt grabbed the piece of paper from the policeman's hand and shouted, 'Let me see that!' Kurt's face turned ashen, even whiter than it had been before. He threw the note on the floor, stamped on it and tore out of the house. I ran after him, but he had jumped into his car and was tearing around the corner.

"I walked back into the room. The silence cut across the room like a scythe, occasionally broken by whispers, voices lowered in the presence of death. I broke the silence. 'I wonder why he did it?' I said. 'And why is the room in such a mess if he committed suicide? May I?' My father was holding the note, and I took it from his hand."

"Should I get you a cup of coffee?" I interrupted. Neal's voice sounded weak and tired. "Have you had anything to eat?"

He waved his hand, showing his disinterest.

"So what was in the note?" I asked.

"I'll try to reconstruct it as best I can," he said. "One note was to his wife and to Kurt, and the other to the world at large. To Mrs. Schmidt and to Kurt, he apologized for taking what might seem to be the coward's way out, but he couldn't live like an outcast and a hunted person. 'People look at me as if I committed a terrible crime,' he wrote. 'All I did was for science and the Fatherland. My career is finished. I called Heinrich Klaus. He'll help you get the money from Switzerland and from South America.' That was it."

"Isn't it strange that Kurt didn't find the suicide note when he first came into his father's study?" I asked.

214

"I guess the blast of the gun blew it onto the floor."

"And what did he write in the other letter?"

"It was an open letter to the world. 'You are bringing people to trial for crimes against the Jews. These sniveling cowards cry that they didn't act as individuals but on orders from the State. They deny all individual responsibility. I want the world to know that crimes against international law are committed by men and not by abstract entities. These acts are committed by the person with the full knowledge of the crime. Therefore, I take full responsibility for all my acts. Yes, I take full credit. I was a Nazi, I am a Nazi and I will always be a Nazi. I have killed myself not because I feel guilt in any way but because the longer the newspapers are filled with my trial and the more witnesses they get to testify, the more sympathy will be aroused for the Jews. With my death, the media will have a field day for two or three days, and then it will become old news. The issue will be closed. I thank the Fuehrer for having shown me the world's perpetual enemy. I hold my head high with pride that I had a share in destroying them. Heil Hitler.' That is the gist of it."

Neal stopped talking. I could feel the hair on my arms tingle, and a chill went up and down my spine. Dr. Schmidt felt no remorse and even after his death he still managed to hurt me.

I looked around me. I couldn't believe there was normalcy left in the world. People were walking and talking. Couples ran to catch planes. Others went to pick up baggage.

"I am tired," Neal sighed. "I feel a thousand years old. It took time, Marian, for it to sink in, for me to realize it was me he was talking about. Me! In another time and place, I would have been one of those he wanted to kill."

"Come, Neal," I said. "Let me drive you home. You look totally exhausted."

"Wait! I haven't finished," he said. "I still have to tell you how I ended up in Boston. The night was not over."

Neal took a deep, slow breath and then proceeded.

"By the time we returned from Kurt's house, it was morning. I didn't call you because you were in school. I fell into a deep sleep. About four hours later, the maid tapped on my door to announce that two gentlemen were waiting to see me. I wondered who it could be. I threw my clothes on and went downstairs.

"Two men were standing there. One was tall and thin with a hard face and dark, piercing eyes. He asked, 'Neal Brennan?' and put his hand out for me to shake. 'Tom Keegan,' he said. His grip was strong and firm. 'And this is my partner Jack Kirby.' Jack Kirby was short and squat with bright fireman red hair.

" 'We'll get directly to the point,' the man called Keegan said. 'Jack and I are members of the police force. We are here because of a call we received from the Boston police. You have a roommate in Boston named Jeffrey Fein, right?' He didn't wait for my answer but continued. 'Well, there is a problem with your roommate. He is missing and you are wanted for questioning.'

" 'How long has he been missing?' I asked. 'Because I really can't see how I can be of any help. I've been in New York these past few days. When I left Boston, Jeffrey was there.'

" 'Keep your shirt on,' he said. 'No one is accusing you of anything. No one is asking you for an alibi.'

" 'Then what do you want?' I asked.

" 'The Boston police have requested your presence in Boston so that they can ask you some questions,' he said.

" 'This is totally absurd,' I protested. 'How long has he been missing?'

"The redheaded policeman looked uncomfortable. 'Well, actually, only since yesterday,' he said.

"I laughed. 'Come on,' I said. 'If the police are looking for extra work, there is really plenty available. Let them ride the New York subways. A man goes away for a day and the police are called in?'

" 'It's really not quite as simple as that,' the tall one said. 'You see, last night was his mother's birthday and when she didn't hear from him, she called the Department.'

" 'Isn't that ridiculous?' I asked. 'So he forgot!'

" 'No, it is not ridiculous,' he said. 'She claims that since he was fifteen, he has never missed her birthday. He always sends her flowers, and no matter where he is, he calls to wish her a happy birthday.'

" 'Big deal,' I insisted. 'I repeat, so he forgot.'

"The red headed policeman answered. His voice was gentle and soft. 'When the police knocked on the door, there was no answer. They forced the door in.'

" 'They must be crazy!' I said.

" 'No, son, they weren't crazy,' he said. 'There were definite signs of a struggle and of possible foul play. The room was a total mess. Chairs were overturned. Books, furniture, and lamps were strewn all over the floor.'

"Now I began to be concerned. Jeffrey was a most meticulous and neat person.

" 'You mean it?' I asked. 'There were signs of a struggle? How can you b⌐ sure of that?' Now I was also really worried.

" 'We've said too much already,' he said. 'Come. We have to make the plane that leaves in a half hour. Hurry.'

" 'I must call someone before I go,' I said. I knew you were waiting for my call.

" 'Sorry,' he said. 'No calls. We leave right now.'

"We made the airport in record time. The flight was short. Practically as soon as we were seated on the plane we were ready to land. In Boston, there was a car waiting for us at the airport, and before I knew it, we were in front of my building. The door to the apartment opened even before we reached it. There was a murmur of voices coming from within.

"The room was crowded with official-looking men, some in plain clothes and others in police uniform. On the couch, a man and a woman were sitting. The woman was crying. Her hands covered her face. At the sound of our footsteps she lowered her hands and jumped. 'Jeffrey,' she shouted.

"Her eyes were red rimmed and her lids heavy with fatigue. The man was patting her shoulder, trying to comfort her.

" 'Neal Brennan.' The redheaded detective introduced me to those in the room.

" 'Please help us,' she cried. 'Do you know where Jeffrey is? There is no sign, no note. It is just not like him.' Her breathing was difficult. She huffed and puffed as she said each word. A mournful wail tore out of her very insides. 'And the blood . . . oh no, oh no. Not my Jeffrey. Not him. It couldn't have happened to him. My Jeffrey wouldn't hurt a fly.'

"She ran to me and grabbed my coat. 'Tell them,' she said. 'You know Jeffrey. Tell them what a good boy he is. What a good student he is. Never in trouble. He is a good son, my Jeffrey.'

"Marian, her piercing wails curdled my blood. She looked so pathetic. My heart went out to her, and every word she said was true. Jeffrey was a good son and a good student. And he wouldn't hurt a fly."

"Blood? What blood?" I questioned.

Neal ignored my question and continued.

"The police pulled her gently away and asked if I would mind looking around the room. They asked me to see if anything was missing. After a while I oriented myself to the mess.

" 'No,' I answered. 'I can't see anything missing.'

"They asked me to go into his bedroom and look around. I went into the room and stood by the door. After a quick glance around the room I told the policemen that I didn't notice any change.

" 'What seems to be the problem?' I asked. 'What are you looking for?'

" 'We don't know,' one of the men answered. 'Look in his closet. Can you tell whether any of his clothing is gone?'

"I went to Jeffrey's closet, but since I was not that familiar with his clothing, I could find nothing missing.

" 'Do you have any idea,' he asked, 'where he might have gone? Is there anyone who would want to hurt him?'

" 'Not the slightest,' I answered. 'No one would want to—'

" 'What is it?' He jumped at my hesitation.

" 'Nothing,' I answered.

" 'You stopped in the middle of a sentence,' he said. 'Remember. If a crime was committed here and you withhold any information, then you too are responsible for the crime.'

"I pretended not to hear and walked over to my desk to see if any mail had come for me during the time I had been away. There were a few letters, and I sorted them out and picked mine up. I looked for the letter opener. I was sure I had left it on my desk, in the right hand pocket of the ink blotter, but it wasn't there. I searched the top of the desk. I felt a sense of panic and broke out in a sweat.

"The detective was watching me. His eyes were constantly on me. I walked away from my desk and attempted a nonchalant pose.

" 'Something missing?' he asked.

" 'I'm not sure,' I responded. 'There was mention of blood before,' I whispered, not wanting Mrs. Fein to hear. 'What was that all about?'

" 'Look in Jeffrey's room on the far side of his bed. But be careful. Don't touch anything, and don't step in the roped off area.'

"I walked into Jeffrey's room and went to the opposite side of the bed, the side closer to the window and further away from the door. Although most of it had already seeped into the floorboard, there still was a puddle of blood on the floor. I tasted bile and thought I would vomit. I put my hand over my mouth to contain my words but they came out.

" 'The rug, the rug,' I said.

" 'Okay, son. Start talking,' he said. 'I watched your face when you went to your desk and when you went into Jeffrey's room. What's missing?'

"I hesitated, unsure as to whether to tell him my letter opener and Jeffrey's throw rug were missing. I didn't have to make that decision. He didn't wait for my answer but asked, 'There were three roommates who shared this apartment. You, Jeffrey and Kurt Smith. Before we picked you up, we were at Kurt's house. The house was locked and deserted. Do you know anything about that?'

"Leave it to the police. One hand doesn't know what the other hand does.

" 'Didn't the police tell you that Dr. Schmidt committed suicide?' I said. 'What do you think his son did? What would you do? He disappeared. He wanted to be alone. Wouldn't you?'

"The ringing of the bell interrupted us. A large black policeman strode into the room. He whispered something to the Chief Detective and they walked out together.

" 'May I make a phone call?' I asked.

" 'Sorry,' I was told.

"I was boiling mad. I sat down on the chair across from Jeffrey's parents. Poor Mrs. Fein. Poor Mr. Fein. They looked so lost. Mrs. Fein held a crumpled, wet handkerchief tightly in her hand, twisting and untwisting it.

" 'He is such a good son,' she said. 'When he didn't call me on my birthday, I got nervous. I hope he wasn't hit by a car or something.'

" 'Take it easy, Momma,' her husband said. 'The police are doing whatever is possible to find him. You see,' he turned to me, 'Jeffrey is our only child. He is our life.'

"I couldn't bear to look at them, but something bitter was eating away at me. My eyes functioned on their own volition. They kept turning back to Mrs. Fein. I was restless. I couldn't sit. I couldn't stand. I was exhausted from the previous night and emotionally drained. My eyes were burning in their sockets.

"I felt eyes piercing my back. I turned around. Sure enough, the redheaded policeman was watching me. My every move, my every expression was under close scrutiny and observation.

"My lids were heavy, but I knew I could not sleep. I closed my eyes, pretending to be asleep. The heavy footsteps on the staircase broke the monotony. It was the two policemen who had left before. I searched the chief detective's face, but his expression was inscrutable. He went into the kitchen and brought back a chair, placing the chair next to the couch. He took Mrs. Fein's hand in his own and said, 'Mrs. Fein, we found your son.'

"She pulled her hand away. 'Where is he?' she shouted. She jumped up, as if to attack him. 'Why didn't you tell me that as soon as you came in? He is okay, isn't he? Is he in the hospital? No. I know. He fell asleep studying in the library. He is such a good student. Right? Right? You found him sleeping overnight in the library. They didn't know he was there and they locked him in. Why didn't you bring him home? Why didn't you bring him to me? Why?'

"I watched the detective. His fleshy face turned florid. His eyes were soft. 'I'm sorry,' he said.

" 'You should be,' she shouted. 'Not to tell me he was in the library and to keep me in suspense all this time.' She turned to her husband. 'You see, I told you everything would be okay. Imagine, falling asleep in the library overnight. He always had to read. Remember when he was a little boy I would tell him no reading, but he would hide the book under his covers and turn the light on after we went to sleep?'

" 'Pesel,' he sobbed. 'Please take it easy. Remember, the doctor said you should not get excited. Here. Sit down.' He opened her pocketbook and took out a pill. 'Nitroglycerine,' he explained. 'Her heart. Please get a doctor. I'm afraid for her.'

" 'Remember when he was a little boy and wouldn't go to sleep how I used to sing those songs from the old country to him?' She sang, rocking back and forth. '*Auf dem pripichik, brent a fire'l un in shteib is hais.*'

"The detective motioned to one of his men to come over. He whispered in his ear, and the man went to the telephone. I heard the word ambulance.

" 'Come into the other room, Mr. Brennan,' he said. 'We have to talk.'

"I followed him into my bedroom, the familiar room suddenly unfamiliar. I felt like a stranger in a strange bedroom.

" 'To whom does this belong?' the detective asked. He unwrapped an object wrapped in a handkerchief. He was careful not to touch it.

"My eyes opened wide. It was my missing letter opener.

" 'It belongs to me,' I answered. 'Where did you find it?'

"His voice was hard. 'I'm asking the questions now. Do you have any idea how it left this apartment?'

"Puzzled, I shook my head. 'I distinctly remember seeing it on my desk before leaving for New York. I had just finished opening some mail. No. I haven't the slightest idea.'

" 'Well, you better think,' he said. 'Think long, hard and very clearly because this was the murder weapon.'

" 'So he is dead?' I asked. 'Poor Jeffrey. Why? Why would anyone want to harm him.' Then I turned on the detective in anger. 'Are you accusing me?'

" 'No one is accusing anyone,' he said. 'I am only trying to get to the bottom of this. Did Jeffrey have any enemies?'

" 'None that I can think of.'

" 'Has he had any recent arguments with anyone you know?'

" 'No,' I answered.

" 'Is there anyone who would want him dead?'

" 'I told you, no.'

" 'Do you know anyone with very light blonde hair?'

" 'Are you kidding?' I answered. 'I know loads of people with light blonde hair, medium blonde, dirty blonde, auburn, red hair, brown hair, black hair, green eyes, blue eyes—'

"He stopped me before I could continue. 'Listen fellow. This is murder. Quit horsing around.'

"I looked at him directly. 'Why do you ask?'

" 'Simple. Because there was blonde hair in his fist.'

"I reeled back, shocked. Suddenly, it hit me. 'Murder . . . dead . . . Jeffrey . . . Kurt.' I felt like a mechanical robot repeating these words again and again.

" 'What color hair does Kurt have?' the detective asked.

"I didn't answer.

" 'I was just testing you, buddy. You're hiding something. We know your friend Kurt has light blonde hair, and I just took some samples from his hairbrush and sent them to the laboratory. You better watch out. I warned you, and I'm warning you again. Withholding evidence is a crime.'

"I kept thinking about Kurt. No matter how he might feel about a person, he would not stoop to murder.

"The cry of the siren of an ambulance broke into our conversation. We rushed into the other room. A man came in carrying a little black bag. Following close behind him were two ambulance attendants. Marian, I can still hear Mrs. Fein as she was put on a stretcher. It was horrible. 'My son, my son. Our only flesh and blood . . . gone . . . No! No! It can't be. It mustn't be. I'm dreaming. Help me wake up. Please help me wake up from this horrible nightmare. Oh no, oh no, oh no.' Her cries ricocheted against the walls. Even the hardened detectives' eyes moistened. Mr. Fein pleaded, 'Please, Pesel. We need each other. I need you. Please try to control yourself.'

"Marian, I thought I was an unemotional person. But I had to remove my glasses. They became foggy. I couldn't see through them because of my tears.

"The detective then turned on me. He shot question after question at me. He tried every tactic—kindness, authority, fear—to get me to say that Kurt could have done the murder, but I refused to admit it. I refuse to admit it even now to myself. I just know he couldn't have done it.

" 'Look, sir,' I said. 'I've had a rough couple of days without much sleep. I'm totally exhausted. You brought me to Boston without breakfast, without anyone knowing where I am. If I'm correct, I can build a good, solid case against you.'

"I stood up and said, 'If you have something on me that requires my staying here, cough it up. Say it. Accuse. Otherwise, I'm going home.'

"He didn't answer me. He looked dejected. I knew I had won.

" 'Listen, son,' he said. 'I'm letting you go, because I have nothing on you. But you better keep in touch with the police in New York. The New York and Boston police must know where you are every minute. We have to know where you are twenty-four hours a day if we need you for anything. Otherwise, you are right. I have nothing to hold you on. You are free to go.'

"He put his hand out for me to shake.

" 'Thanks for coming,' he said.

"I laughed bitterly and said, 'As if I had a choice.'

"And that's it, Marian. I called you from the airport in Boston, and I flew back to New York."

I was silent. Speechless. Was this all real? It seemed as if we were living through a fictitious horror story one reads about only in books. Things like this don't happen to people you know.

"Neal," I said. "The truth. What do you think? Is there any possibility Kurt did it? He does seem the logical suspect."

"I refuse to think like that," said Neal. "Why would he do it? True, he was hostile to Jeffrey and showed it in many ways, but barking dogs don't bite. Just because people feel that way about others doesn't mean it leads to murder. No. It must have been a prowler. Let's go home, Marian."

"Neal, look across the aisle at the man over there. See. The tall, heavy-set man with the light hair. Light hair? Oh my gosh, Neal. Could it mean something?"

"What about him?"

"All the time you were talking, he has been watching us. He pretends to be reading the book, but watch his eyes. They are focused directly here."

Neal turned to look. The stranger dropped his eyes back to his book.

All around us, surrounding us, life was going on. A couple ran to catch a plane. A baby was crying, and his mother was attempting to calm him. An old couple were bidding each other a tearful farewell. Each group its own universe; everyone involved in his own world, unaware of the emotional turmoil in the next person's life.

"Let's get out of here," Neal said. "This is getting too complicated."

I wasn't sure exactly where I had left the car. We walked up and down the rows.

"Here it is, Neal," I said at last. "To the right. This way. Neal! That man is following us. I'm frightened. Maybe he is the murderer."

"Give me your car keys, Marian," he said. "I'll drive. We'll lose him in traffic."

Neal turned the key in the ignition, and I breathed a sigh of relief when I saw the car start immediately. We moved into the exit lane, but it was frustrating because the cars were moving at a snail's pace. It was bumper-to-bumper traffic.

"Is he still there?" Neal asked.

"No," I said. "Maybe this heavy traffic is to our advantage. I think we lost him."

"Good."

"What are you going to do about Boston?" I asked. "When are you returning to school?"

"I need a good night's sleep. Then I'll be able to think. I don't know if it

223

is advisable to stay in the apartment alone. I may have to look elsewhere. Hopefully, I'll be able to return tomorrow, and then I'll take it from there. Oh nuts, the windshield is fogging up. Where is the defogger on your car?"

"Right over there, Neal. I'll switch it on. How is the back window? Also fogged up?" I turned around to look. "No. It's okay. Neal!" I felt my throat clog on me. "He is in back of us. He definitely is following us."

"Let's wait until we get out of this maze and then I'll lose him in traffic," he said. "It is impossible now to budge even one car ahead."

Although we spoke calmly and tried to hide our fear from each other, our terror was close to the surface.

"Whew," I said when we left the parking area and made our turn onto the highway. Neal was driving in a zigzag fashion, cutting from lane to lane through every opening he could find.

"We lost him," I said excitedly. "I can't see him. Terrific driving, Neal."

"I'll drive myself home and then you'll take your car to your house," he said. "I'm too bushed to do it any other way. Is that okay with you?"

"Fine," I answered.

"I'm really sorry to have dragged you out to the airport and then to have to make you drive home from my house yourself. I guess I could have really called the chauffeur, but I wanted to speak to you face to face and not on the telephone."

"I'm glad you called me," I said. "If I'd heard about it from a different source, I would have been angry. I'm sure there will be something about it in the newspapers."

"Without doubt," Neal answered. "Dr. Schmidt's suicide, Kurt's disappearance and Jeffrey's murder are a chain of events the newspapers will quickly tie together. The happenings are too dramatic to let go."

When we arrived at Neal's house, I didn't even get out of the car. Neal opened the door and got out, and I slid right over into the driver's seat.

"I'll call you and let you know whether I'll leave for Boston tomorrow morning," Neal said. "I don't want to miss too much school. It is practically impossible to catch up."

I waved goodbye to Neal and turned down the driveway. I reached the end of the driveway and looked both ways to make sure the road was clear. My eye caught the glint of something shiny on the left, off the highway, almost concealed behind a grove of trees. It was the car that had been following Neal and me.

chapter twenty-eight

I was dressed and wide awake early the next morning when the phone rang. It was Neal. "Good morning, Marian," he said. "How did you sleep?"

"Surprisingly, I slept fine. How about you?"

"It's funny," I said. "I was totally exhausted and thought I would sleep right through, but it ended up being a restless night for me."

"Did you make any plans, Neal?"

"That was one of the things on my mind," he said. "I'll probably keep the apartment. I've given it a lot of thought and I keep remembering what a problem it was to get an apartment in that area in Boston. That was really such an ideal place."

"Aren't you afraid?" I asked. "Won't you feel eerie staying in the apartment all alone?"

"No, I'm not really afraid but then, of course, I don't think I'll be alone for long," he said. "Kurt should be back soon. He needs time to be by himself. After all, it is hard enough to accept death, let alone suicide and that of his own father. I'm sure he'll be back soon."

"You really feel sure Kurt was not responsible for Jeffrey's death?"

"Marian, you know I do. Kurt might have disliked Jeffrey, and it is true that he wanted to get rid of him, but murder? No! Never. Murder is a totally different story."

"Then who could it have possibly been?" I asked. "Do you think it could have been the man with the blonde hair? Aren't you afraid he might return to the apartment?"

"No, Marian. I think we're done with him. I don't think he had anything to do with this entire business. Besides, we lost him on the ride home."

"Neal, that's not so," I said. "I saw him hiding behind the trees when I left your house."

225

"Really?" he said. "It can't be. It must have been your imagination playing tricks on you."

"You saw him follow our car on the way home from the airport, Neal."

"For all we know, it might have been a detective," he said. "I guess we can just let the matter drop. I'm sure we are finished with it, and no one is following either one of us now."

"Neal, we didn't imagine his following us from the airport and I didn't imagine him following me from your house," I protested. "And what about Jeffrey's death? We are not imagining things. No! That's definitely not something we imagined. And aren't you afraid, Neal, that whoever was in the house and committed that horrendous act will return?"

"I told you I didn't get much sleep last night. I kept going over and over in my mind the various possibilities. I think what happened is that Jeffrey caught a prowler in the act and the prowler turned on him. No, I'm not afraid he'll return. I don't believe this murderer will return to the scene of his crime."

"If that was the case, why did he remove the body?"

"Perhaps to give him more time to escape. Really, Marian, I'm not trying to show any bravado or play big hero to you. I don't feel frightened. I feel sure Kurt will return soon and together, we'll just have to make some decisions."

"Like what?" I asked bitterly.

"Whether we want to take in another roommate or to just keep the apartment for ourselves. Listen, Marian, I have to get to the airport soon. I have an early plane to catch. Take care of yourself. We'll keep in touch. I'll call."

I wished Neal a good trip and slowly, thoughtfully, hung up the telephone.

I looked at the clock. It was late. I had to hurry. I was glad my books were already packed. I gulped some juice and ran.

I met Janet at the bus stop. She didn't look well. Her usual gaiety was gone, and she looked tired and listless.

"Are you okay, Janet?" I asked. "You look terrible."

"I'm okay . . . I guess."

"Is something bothering you?"

"We have a lot of catching up to do," she said, changing the subject. "Have you been following the newspapers about Kurt's father?"

I shook my head. Janet pulled some folded pages from her looseleaf folder and handed them to me. I read the articles rapidly. As usual, the newspapers had twisted the stories, and they were filled with inaccuracies. If I hadn't spoken with Neal, I would also have thought them accurate. Now I was able to realize how easily newspapers can mislead.

The newspaper article claimed Jeffrey's murder and Dr. Schmidt's suicide had taken place at the same time and that they were both part of a well-planned operation. They also stated that the police were searching for a missing witness. Another newspaper claimed there was a suspect in custody. Both articles were consistent in alluding to mysterious notes, although they did not claim any knowledge as to what these notes contained. The one fact in the newspaper was that Jeffrey was Jewish and that he was the only child of elderly parents.

I corrected the newspaper's version and told Janet the true story as Neal had told it to me. She reacted as I had.

"Do you think Kurt did it?" she asked.

"I do, but you know how I feel about Kurt," I said. "Neal doesn't think he did it. You know, Janet, I can't wait for this to be over. I thought these things only happen in newspapers and in fiction. They just don't happen to people you know. What has happened to our lives? Everything has changed. I wake up in the morning and can't believe what I hear, see and read."

"You took the words out of my mouth," Janet said. "Nothing is as it was. Marian, remember those calm, peaceful days at the ocean? I know we can't go back, but sometimes I long for those days. Our lives, my family's life, just everything was on such an even plateau. Now, everything is topsy-turvy."

I looked at Janet again. She looked hollow-eyed and pale, and there was a slight nervous twitch in the corner of her mouth. But she didn't elaborate, and I didn't press her.

When I returned home, I found my mother in the kitchen, an untouched cup of coffee in front of her.

"That poor boy," she said. "That poor boy. Those poor parents. What some people have to go through in life!"

"Terrible, just terrible," my father said.

I turned around quickly. I hadn't heard my father enter the room. I walked to the window and put my face against the cold windowpane. There was a foggy mist curling through the streets and the beginning of snow clouds. I felt my hands tremble. I couldn't control them. I held them straight against my body, but the shaking did not stop. It was as if my body belonged to someone else. The tensions of the past few months had finally taken their toll.

It is unfortunate, but sometimes it takes another person's tragedy to bring people closer together. For a while, we had been people, all living under one roof, family, yet almost total strangers. We were together now, commiserating with the poor Fein family.

And suddenly, I felt my parents's love surrounding me. It meant even more to me now since we had been somewhat estranged. I thanked G-d silently for letting us be a family again.

chapter twenty-nine

Neal called from Boston that evening. He spoke softly, his voice barely above a whisper. I felt a chill run up and down my spine.

"Are you alone?" I asked.

"No. Kurt is here."

"Neal! Don't stay alone with him. Call the police."

"Take it easy, Marian. Calm down. The police are here. They've been watching our apartment."

"Are they there now?" I asked. "You know it isn't safe."

"Please, Marian. Kurt has been questioned. He's been at the police station, and they've let him go. They have nothing to hold him on."

"But he is a suspect, isn't he? Can't they hold him on that?"

"If they let him go, it's obvious they have nothing to hold him on," said Neal. "Really, Marian, you do have to overcome your suspicions."

"Neal, that man with the blonde hair, have you seen him?"

"I'm . . . I'm not sure."

"Neal! Did you see him?"

"I think I might have, but I'm just not sure."

"Did you tell the police?"

"What can I tell them, Marian? They'll just laugh. That I think a man followed us from the airport? That you think you saw someone near my house? That I might have seen someone that looked like him in Boston and that he followed me from New York to Boston? It's ridiculous. I never saw him close up. I can't describe him. I didn't see his car in Boston. All I can say is that he has blonde hair." Neal laughed. "Marian, they'll throw my words back at me. Thousands of people have blonde hair."

"What does Kurt say? Does he talk about his father? Did he say anything about Jeffrey?"

I could barely hear Neal when he answered.

"I hope he's only talking this way because he's distraught, but he is venomous and blames the Jews for everything," said Neal. "It is ironic, isn't it? Dr. Schmidt thought his death would fill the papers for a few days and then it would all be forgotten. Instead, the newspapers are having a field day. The reporters don't leave Kurt alone. The minute he leaves the building, they surround him. He blames the Jews for everything under the sun, for his father's suicide, for Hitler's downfall, for the rain coming down or the wind blowing. It is impossible to reason with him. Uh, oh," his voice became conspiratorial. "I'll have to say goodbye. I think I hear Kurt coming out of the shower. I'll call you tomorrow."

I hung up the phone and breathed an audible sigh of relief that Neal had stopped protecting Kurt. Perhaps now he would see that Kurt was a malignancy on society. Kurt himself was bringing Neal out of his lethargy by his remarks, and Neal was now becoming aware that association with Kurt was dangerous.

I hoped the answer to this horrendous puzzle had come when I listened to the radio the next morning.

"We interrupt this program for a special bulletin," the announcer said. "A suspect was apprehended last night in the Jeffrey Fein murder that occurred in the Boston area. The Police Department has declined to mention any details until further investigation and lab tests are completed. They also refuse to indicate what type of tests are being conducted. We now return to our regular programming."

I tried to reach Neal on the phone. It rang and rang. There was no answer. He must have left for class. I was anxious to hear what further details and information he might have.

After school, I rushed home. I tried again and again to reach Neal but without success. I couldn't concentrate on my homework or keep my mind on anything else. There was nothing further on the radio or in the newspaper. It was frustrating to feel we were so close to the solution and, yet, still so far.

It wasn't until my third try that evening that the phone was finally picked up.

"Neal," I said. "Finally! I've been trying to get through to you all day. I heard something on the news this morning."

I heard heavy breathing on the other side of the telephone, but there was no answer.

"Neal?" I said, panic in my voice. "Neal? Are you okay? Is that you? If it is, please answer me."

There was no answer. All I heard was heavy breathing.

"Are you sick, Neal? Are you injured? Please answer me, Neal. Please."

What could I do? The phone hung limp in my hand. I was terrified. Was Neal injured and unable to talk? Should I call 911? Was the murderer in the room with Neal? Oh G-d, help me!

"Neal," I shouted. "Neal!"

Again, only heavy breathing and then a muffled cough. I fell into my chair, the phone still clutched tightly in my hand. Suddenly, it came to me. It came with clarity. There was no trace of doubt in my mind. I mustered all my courage and dignity, and in a clear, authoritative voice, each word distinctly uttered, I said, "Kurt, where is Neal?"

His voice was taunting and jeering at me.

"And who may I ask is it that wants to know?" he answered.

I knew then that I was locked in battle with a demented foe, and I did not know how to handle him.

"This is Marian," I said. "Kurt, where is Neal?"

His voice was pleasant, too pleasant. He was much too suave, and I understood why when he threw the Biblical phrase at me, "Am I my brother's keeper?"

He had accomplished what he had set out to do. I lost my poise and in blind fury shouted, "Kurt, put Neal on the phone."

I heard the scorn now in his voice. He laughed at me and made a few snide remarks, and then, the tone of his voice changed. There was a lilt in it, and I could just envision him smiling sadistically.

"Goodnight, Marian," he said. "Sleep well, Marian." Then he slammed the receiver down.

I tried to call again and again but received a busy signal. It didn't take me long to understand he had taken the phone off the hook. Kurt won that round.

It was a real predicament. In his maniac state, would he hurt Neal? Had he already done so? Think positive, I told myself, but telling and believing were quite a distance apart. Should I call the police? This inactivity made me feel even more helpless.

I tried to remember the name of the detective that had taken Neal to Boston. Was it Tom Regan? No. Something like that. What was the other detective's name? John Kirby. No. Jack Kirby. That was it! Jack Kirby. Where could I reach him?

I dialed 911, the emergency number of the Police Department.

"Hold on, please," a voice said. I slammed the receiver down and tried Neal's number one more time. I had made up my mind. If Kurt answered, I'd try another tactic. I'd speak to him kindly and without any rebuke.

I picked up the phone and dialed the number slowly. Each click of the dial vibrated in the silence of my room. The phone rang once. Twice. I was almost ready to put it back when I heard a voice on the other side.

"Hello," I said.

"Neal," I heard Kurt call in a high-pitched, intoxicated voice. "There is a feminine voice on the phone calling you."

Neal picked up the phone. "Marian?"

I burst out in tears. "Are you okay, Neal? I've been so worried. I called before, and Kurt played nasty games."

"I'm fine, Marian," he said. "I was in the library. I have a report due. What's new?"

"I'll ask you the same question," I said. "The radio said a suspect was picked up last night? Was it Kurt? What is he doing in the apartment? Why isn't he in jail?"

"I can't talk now, Marian," he whispered. "Keep your phone clear. I'll call you in about fifteen minutes from the street."

I sat next to the telephone, impatiently waiting for it to ring, and yet, when it finally did, I jumped at the sharp, shrill sound.

"It's this way," Neal said. "Soon after Kurt arrived, the police were here and asked him to go to the station with them. They said they had some questions to ask him. Kurt wanted to know if he was under arrest, and they said he wasn't.'

" 'Am I a suspect?' he asked.

" 'Everyone is, until the case is closed,' the policeman answered.

" 'Can my friend come along?' Kurt asked, and when they consented, I did.

"The police led us through a labyrinth of corridors until we reached a small room in the back of the Police Station. There were three detectives in the room and a woman.

" 'Who is she?' Kurt asked.

" 'She is a stenographer,' one of the detectives answered. 'She will take down your answers.'

" 'Are you here willingly?' he asked.

" 'Yes,' Kurt answered.

" 'You don't have to answer any questions if you don't want to,' he said. 'Do you want to call your attorney?'

" 'What for?' Kurt answered. 'I can handle myself. What do you want to know?'

" 'Do you have any idea why your father committed suicide?' a detective asked.

" 'Do you know why you are so fat?' Kurt retorted.

"The detective tried again. In a soft voice, he asked, 'We know your father was under terrific pressure, but can you think of any specific thing that happened that might have brought him to the act he finally committed?'

"Kurt did not answer.

" 'Did you kill Jeffrey?' The questions came rapidly.

" 'No.' Kurt answered.

" 'Did you ever threaten him?'

" 'I might have.'

" 'Did you kill him?'

" 'No.'

" 'Are you sure? Perhaps you did it in the heat of anger and you don't really remember.'

" 'No.'

" 'We know you threatened him. We have witnesses.'

" 'But I did not kill him.'

" 'There were a few strands of blonde hair, your color hair, caught between his fingers.'

" 'I did not kill him.'

" 'Did you want him dead?'

" 'Yes, I did.'

" 'Why?'

"Kurt did not answer.

"The detective tried again. 'Why did you want him dead?'

"Again, Kurt did not answer.

" 'Had he ever harmed you?'

"I watched Kurt's face closely. I saw the battle waging within him. He tried to control himself but couldn't.

" 'His kind have always harmed us,' he answered. 'They have harmed us before but not anymore. They won't have a chance. We'll take care of them. Because of them my father committed suicide. They drove him to it. They own everything, the newspapers, the radio stations . . . everything. They didn't let him live. They turned the world against him.'

"Marian, he continued along this vein for a long time, but he denied that he had murdered Jeffrey. I believe him. The truth of the matter is that although I kept telling you I was sure he hadn't done it, there were times I had my doubts. But I know Kurt well, and I would have known from his voice if he was lying.

"He has changed very much. He's become very bitter. I find it difficult to recognize the Kurt I knew from the old days."

"What you are seeing now, Neal," I said, "is the real Kurt. The other was a childhood illusion. He is and has always been a sadist. Do you know what he did when I first called? If it was his intention to play a game of wear and tear on my nerves, he accomplished it. He really did! My nerves are frayed."

Neal promised to call if there was any additional news and I had just gotten into bed when the phone rang. It was Neal.

"Well, I was right," he said. "Kurt is innocent. The detective just left. The strands of hair from the brush did not match the hair entwined in Jeffrey's fingers."

"Then I wonder who could have done it, Neal? It just doesn't make sense? By the way, I forgot to ask you when we spoke before, does Kurt know you're Jewish?"

I could practically hear Neal squirm.

"No," he answered. "I haven't told him."

"Do you plan to tell him?"

"Oh, come on, Marian. Cut it out. Not now. It just isn't the time. When the opening comes along, I'll tell him."

I fell into a restless sleep that night. I dreamed I was seven years old, sitting on the shore of a lake where we'd once spent an entire summer. The lake looked silver under the sun, and there were lush white lilies blooming on the water's edge. Under my eyes, the lilies grew taller and taller. They rose to an unusual height, towering over the trees. They surrounded me. I couldn't go forward, backward or sideways. I was just a little girl, and I didn't know which way to run. They were closing in on me. I felt I was drowning in their scent. They came closer and closer. "Help," I whimpered. "Please, someone, help me."

Then the scene changed, and it was nighttime. The air smelled of honeysuckle and roses. I thought I heard a whippoorwill calling, its cry lonely. I was sitting on the porch of our summer cottage, rocking back and forth on the wooden gray rocking chair. The scene was peaceful. I felt happy and secure. I watched the breeze stirring the leaves of the great maple tree in front of the house. There was a clatter of dishes and pots and pans in the background, giving me a feeling of security in the knowledge that my family was nearby. I watched my grandfather sitting under the bare and only light on the opposite side of the porch, a large book open in front of him. He swayed as he sang his special melody, the melody I always associated with him. I listened to the mysterious ancient words and watched him as he twirled the curl of his sideburns.

Suddenly, the peacefulness of the scene was interrupted. A long, dark towering shadow on the porch seemed to swallow up everything in its way. It inched along until it was behind my grandfather. He did not know it was there. Kurt's blonde hair shone in the moonlight. I watched as he tiptoed closer and closer to my grandfather. There was something in his hand. What was it? It was shiny. The moonlight caused sparks to fly off of it. Oh no! It was a knife. I screamed, "Grandfather, Grandfather," but I was too late. I saw the knife poised behind my grandfather's back. I put my hand over my mouth. I cried. The sobs tore at my breaking heart.

Wait! Look! With a tremendous effort, my grandfather wrenched himself away from Kurt. He stood up and walked towards me. I smiled and sighed, "Thank G-d, Grandfather, you are all right." My grandfather answered me in Yiddish. I couldn't understand his words. I jumped off my rocking chair and ran to meet him. I stretched out my arms towards him. I stopped short. Surprised. Shocked. The face was not that of my grandfather.

"You are not my grandfather," I screamed.

"No," he answered. "I am Jeffrey."

And then I heard it. It was maniacal laughter. The maniacal laughter of Kurt. He was laughing, laughing, laughing. It was the eeriest of sounds.

It took quite a while for the effects of the dream to wear off. I felt a terrible queasiness in my stomach. I reached out and turned on the lamp near my bed. Its rosy glow broke through the darkness and dispelled the horror of the dream.

I didn't need an alarm clock that morning to wake me up.

The snow I had anticipated had not come. It looked like rain. The patchy sky was threatening. I went back to the house for my umbrella, and because of the few minutes I lost, I had to run to overtake the bus at the corner stop. I felt a little like a commando with my umbrella rolled up like a bayonet.

Stop it, Marian, I said to myself. All this violence was getting to me. Enough is enough, I told myself. Don't add to it.

I saw Janet ahead. She was signalling wildly.

"Hurry, hurry," I heard her call.

I ran as fast as my legs would carry me and arrived panting and just on time. The bus driver had already closed the doors but opened them when he saw me.

Janet looked tired. Her skin was pallid and her eyes red-rimmed from lack of sleep.

"Janet, you look terrible," I said. "Are you okay?"

"So, so," she answered. "Don't wait for me after school today. I have to take care of some things."

This secretiveness was so unlike Janet it disturbed me. When she called the same evening to tell me she wouldn't be in school the next day, I was really worried.

Two days later, it all came out.

"Well, I lost," she said. "Abe finally did it."

"Did what?"

My thoughts were as far away from Abe and his life as I was from actually sitting near the silvery lace of the lake that had been part of my dream.

"He moved," Janet said. "Moved as far away as possible. He went to Israel."

"You're kidding," I said. "Really? Why?"

"He said he felt he wasn't getting enough of a background here in America and that living at home with constant strife wasn't helping," she said. "He said he was going to join what he called a *Baal Teshuvah Yeshivah* and become a real, Torah-observant Jew. I tried everything, Marian, to straighten him out, but the more I tried, the further I seemed to drive him away. Now I think we've lost him to that crazy way of life."

Janet's eyes filled with tears.

"How are your parents taking it?" I asked.

"Much better than me," she said. "They said they are thankful he

236

hasn't chosen a harmful way of life and as long as he doesn't infringe on their way of living, he has the right to make that choice."

"I don't understand you then, Janet?" I asked. "Why are you taking it so hard?"

"Because I know we've lost him," she said. "He'll never come back. Never. Never. Never! He didn't just take a sabbatical leave to get an education in another country. He dropped out of college and has made a major decision to embark on this totally different path. Don't you realize what it means, Marian? He'll marry a girl going in the same direction as he is. We will have nothing in common, his wife, Abe or me. Our families won't meet; our children won't be cousins."

"Janet," I said. "It really isn't the end of the world. You won't lose your brother."

She rejected my effort to comfort her.

"We were so close, and now we're worlds apart," she said. "We'll live totally different lives. I hate him for doing this to me!"

I was frightened at her outburst. More and more, I was becoming aware of the differences building up in our outlook towards life. I could not tell her I was reading constantly. I had finished everything Naomi had given me and I had found a Jewish book store not too far from my house to satisfy my insatiable appetite for more knowledge. Neal's Jewishness gave impetus to my search, because now I felt that together, we could grow in our eventual development towards Jewishness. More and more, I found myself thinking about the kind of home life I really wanted for myself and my children. I now included Neal in all my thoughts and felt closer to him since Aunt Leslie opened the secret door.

Upon my return home, I found an envelope on my dresser. Inside was a folded card. On one side, there was writing in English and on the other side in Hebrew. It was an invitation to Estie's wedding. I answered the response card immediately.

"Miss Marian Asher would be happy to come," I wrote. "*Mazel Tov* and thank you for the invitation."

I was proud of myself. You're getting there, old girl, I thought.

Neal called in the evening.

"From where are you calling?" I asked.

"The apartment," he answered. "Kurt left a few minutes ago. He flew out of the house as if it was on fire after receiving a phone call."

"Who called him?" I asked. "Do you know?"

"No," he said. "But when I answered the phone, it was someone with a deep, guttural accent who asked for Schmidt. At first, I found it difficult to understand him because of the accent. Kurt looked surprised when the caller identified himself, slammed the receiver down and ran out of the house. He said he might be gone all night. I wanted to know why, but he didn't say. Well, that's his business, I guess."

Thoughtfully, I hung up the phone. My musing was interrupted by the faint murmur of voices in the kitchen. I hadn't realized my father was home. I opened the door to the kitchen. My father looked tense, his voice filled with urgency.

"What should I do?" I heard him say. He was breathing fast . . . much too fast.

"Think about it," my mother answered. "Perhaps you should lie down for a while. You don't have to answer immediately."

My father sat down on a chair. He closed his eyes. Although I was reluctant to leave, I moved back through the shadowy hall into the dining room. I didn't want to eavesdrop, but their voices floated back to me.

"I think you should go yourself," my mother said. "She's right. You need time to think. Papa's death and all that has happened has shaken us all up. Maybe you should go yourself without Marian or me."

"I don't want to leave you both here alone," my father answered.

It became quiet in the room. I deliberately coughed so that they would hear me.

"Marian," my mother called out. "Supper is on the stove. Would you please set the table?"

"Certainly," I answered.

I went into the kitchen, just in time to catch a glance at my father's face. Again, I was shocked to see how much he had aged in such a short time. His hair was gray, and the stubble on his face had also turned gray. When did all this happen? Had it crept up on me while I was unaware? How selfish I had become in my search for fulfillment. Had I lost my sensitivity?

My parents left the kitchen. I looked around. Supper was warming on the stove. I opened the refrigerator and took out two grapefruits. I cut them in half and put one half back in the refrigerator. I put the three halves on the table and then took out the silverware. I made a tossed salad and also brought that to the table. It was then that I noticed the piece of paper on the floor.

A TIME TO LIVE

I had no intention of reading something not meant for me, but, at first, I didn't know what it was, and once I started, I couldn't put it down.

Dear Yankel,

Remember the game we played as children? We called it "Let's Pretend." You would pretend you were one of the *Gedolim* and I would have to guess who you were. Those were wonderful times, because we really knew who we were, are, and always would be.

Then you grew up, Yankel, and did not outgrow childhood games. This time, you are playing "Let's Pretend," and your partner is the Devil. We hope to grow older and much wiser. Instead . . . instead . . . what?

Yankele, my dear brother. Yankele, my only brother. Yankele, my blood relative, son of our father and mother. And what a father! And what a mother! Stop playing your game of "Let's Pretend." What has happened to you? And what are you doing to Malkala?

Are you pretending you are not Yankel? Have you worn the clothing of Jack for too long? Wake up! Wake up, my dear brother. We are not getting younger. We are only getting older, and each day brings us closer to the final day of reckoning. Somewhere, deep within your frozen heart, within the recesses that have became abscessed, you know what I mean. You know there is a G-d in Heaven. Stop hiding your head in the sand like an ostrich and pretending you don't see!

I refuse to accept that you don't believe. I remember my brother from our home only too well. You didn't deceive Papa, and you haven't deceived me. You have only deceived yourself.

Come back, Yankel. Come home to our people. You know that deep down within you, that is where you want to be, where you belong.

Come home, Yankel. Come home to Eretz Yisrael. Come home and *daven* at the *Kosel* and beg forgiveness from our forgiving G-d. Come home and give your body a chance to be re-injected with the vitamins of which your mind and heart have become depleted. Come home so you can give your daughter Malka the encouragement she needs to become a true *Yiddishe tochter*, so that she can have a chance to raise a generation of *kinderlach* true to *Hashem Yisbarach*. Come home.

Come home, Yankel, my brother, and give yourself time to think about what you have done and are doing.

I have a room waiting for you and your wife, your wife who is like my sister, and there is also a bed waiting for Malka. Please come for *Pesach*. Please come. I beg you . . . please come.

> B'Ahavah,
> Your sister who loves you,
> Leah

"So you found the letter," I heard my father say. "Maybe it is better that way."

I hadn't heard my parents come in, and I dropped the letter guiltily on the table.

"I'm sorry," I said. "I found it on the floor, and once I started to read, I couldn't stop."

"That's okay, Marian," he said. "I would have given it to you to read, or at least I'd have told you about it. The lack of communication between us has made us grow too far apart. Without realizing it, or meaning to, we have hurt each other."

I ran to my father. I didn't feel like an eighteen-year-old, but like a little girl once again, pleading and seeking succor, looking for someone to soothe her wounds. My father's needs were forgotten in my selfishness. He enclosed me in his arms, and I felt his warmth and caring.

"What are you planning to do?" I asked. "Please, let's go."

I was jumping with excitement. What an opportunity this was, a chance to see Israel and meet Aunt Leah.

"It's great," I added. "I would love to go to Israel."

"I don't think it is such a good idea," my mother said.

"Why not, Mommy? I think it is a wonderful idea."

"It is better for Daddy to go himself," she said. "There are times for a family to be together, and there are times a person needs to be alone. I think this is one of the times Daddy should be alone."

"Besides," my father added, "you would miss too much school."

Here it was, my opportunity to tell my father my feelings about school, but I didn't take it. The wire of our emotions was strung too fine, and this was not the time to cause it to snap. I kept quiet.

"When would you go?" I asked my father.

"I can leave work before the Passover holidays," he said.

"But there won't be any school during that time," I offered enthusiastically.

"Marian," my mother said firmly. "Daddy is going to Israel himself. You and I will go to Uncle Meir."

"Terrific," I answered in a conciliatory manner.

I was thrilled! Finally! A chance to meet my uncle, aunt and cousins.

"I must share this good news with my friends." I ran to the phone to call Shaindee. It was only afterwards that I realized I had called Shaindee and not Janet.

As soon as I put the phone back on the cradle it rang again. It was Neal.

"Am I glad to hear from you," I said. "Is everything okay? I've been so worried."

I sensed his hesitation.

"I really don't know," he answered. "Something strange is going on. I don't know what to make of it. Kurt was out all night and came back today with a wild expression in his eyes."

"Really? Did he say anything?"

"He kept muttering. It was difficult to make out what he was saying. He mentioned a lot of dates. I thought he had gone completely off his mind. He was irrational. The suicide of his father has him up a wall."

"Dates?" I asked. "What dates?"

"As far as I can recall, he mentioned the following dates: January 30, 1933, September 15, 1935, November 9, 1938 and January 20, 1942."

"Does it have any meaning to you?"

"It didn't at first, but then it became significant and quite clear. January 30, 1933 was the date Hitler became Chancellor of Germany. September 15, 1935 was when Germany passed the Nuremburg laws which took away Jewish citizenship rights. November 9, 1938 was the infamous Kristalnacht, when synagogues were burned, Jewish homes looted and countless Jews beaten and killed. And January 20, 1942 was the date when Hitler and his leading officers met at Wannsee outside Berlin and decided on what they called the Final Solution, their official plan to kill every Jew."

"What a monster! What did you say to him?"

Neal understood what I was getting at. I could practically hear him squirming over the telephone.

"No! I didn't tell him I'm Jewish if that's what you mean," he said. "You know, Marian, you're constantly harping on one track. I don't have to flaunt it. I found out about my mother being Jewish, and that is difficult enough for me to accept. You don't have to bring it up at every opportunity!"

Neal hung up in anger. I picked up the phone to call him back but changed my mind. What could I say?

I waited for the phone to ring. One day and then another went by. I refused to call him. If he didn't call me because he rejected his roots, then maybe it was for the best. At least, I tried to bolster my spirits by thinking it was so. I felt stranded and lonely, deserted by my two anchors of friendship, Janet and Neal. I couldn't talk to Neal, and I couldn't talk to Janet. I wallowed in self-pity and resorted to my journal to write.

Loneliness
Captivates
Weaves from spider's thread
An outer covering of silk
Smooth, tangled and cold.

chapter thirty

T he March winds tore at my clothing as I walked through the streets. I felt an aimlessness in my movements and thoughts. I looked at the desolate sky, heavy with clouds. A stiff wind whistled past my ears, making my breathing labored.

My mind was filled with worries. Janet was drifting out of my life. We were still warm and friendly to each other, but I felt us growing apart. I knew it was my doing, but that didn't help. It would take me a long time to get used to it. I was happy to be drawing much closer to Shaindee, Naomi and their friends, but Janet and I had gone through so much together.

I decided to call Shaindee and talk about Estie's upcoming wedding. "What shall I wear to the wedding?" I asked Shaindee and listened as she explained, delicately and carefully so as not to hurt my feelings, that I was to wear long sleeves and a dress that covered my knees and a high neckline. The concept of *Tzinus* was completely alien to the world in which I had grown up, but I assured her I would conform.

When Neal finally called, our conversation was stilted, or would chilled be a better word? I refused to ask about Kurt, and Neal offered no information. The entire conversation lasted two minutes.

My father was going full swing ahead with his plans to visit Aunt Leah. There was a new springiness to his steps, and he seemed younger; his face was now wreathed in smiles where once there had been so much sadness. And my mother? Well, she seemed much more reserved, as if afraid that any movement on her part would rock the boat.

When I told my mother I had looked through my closet and couldn't find anything really suitable to wear to the wedding, she suggested a store where I could find a dress suitable to an Orthodox function.

"If you find two more dresses there you like," she added, "buy them.

You'll be more comfortable in long-sleeved dresses in Uncle Meir's house."

As I was dressing for the wedding, the phone rang.

"Well, it's all over," Neal said, as I picked up the phone.

I felt my heart lurch. Was he telling me that this was the end of our relationship?

"Kurt returned late last night and went immediately to bed," he continued. "This morning, when I awoke, I found him packing his suitcase."

I sighed with relief. It wasn't over between us. It was Kurt he was talking about. Neal continued.

" 'What's happening, Kurt,' I asked him. 'Are you moving out?'

" 'I was going to wake you before I left,' he said. 'Promise me not to repeat what I tell you to anyone.' He didn't wait but continued, his words coming out in a torrent of hate.

" 'I'm leaving,' he said. 'I'm leaving this country. Now I know why I was born. Now I know why my father had to die. It is so I can step into his shoes. I will become the next leader. The world's fate is now on my shoulders.'

"I swear, Marian, he clicked his heels and threw his shoulders back as if he was a soldier ready for battle. The expression in his eyes was maniacal and his words were that of a fanatic zealot.

" 'Kurt,' I said. 'Sit down. I'll get a cup of coffee. Relax!'

" 'Don't you understand a word of what I am saying?' He looked at me, making me feel stupid and ignorant. 'What do you know about heroics and missions in life? You've always been a spoiled rich boy raised in America. What would you know?'

"Marian, he got my back up, and I was ready to punch him one. But I realized he wasn't really aware of what he was saying. He seemed to be in a trance, murmuring parrot-like words he had heard someplace.

" 'Calm down, Kurt,' I said. 'Start from the beginning. I can't seem to follow you.'

" 'I'm leaving America,' he said.

"I spoke softly to him. 'And where are you going, Kurt?'

" 'To the Fatherland. To Germany.'

" 'Are you crazy, Kurt? Not you! This is not the Thirties or early Forties. This is today. You are Kurt Smith, and you are a medical student in Boston.'

" 'Look, Neal,' he said. 'That call last night was very important. It was from my father's friend. We are going to Germany to build up the Nazi party. There is an active neo-Nazi group there now, but it needs strong leadership. We have to show them that they are a bunch of weaklings, afraid to twist some arms or to make ripples.'

"I looked at Kurt, wide-eyed and astonished. I couldn't believe what I was hearing. He kept talking.

" 'Imagine, Neal, how proud you will be when you will hear that Kurt Schmidt, your friend, your roommate, is the new Fuehrer of the New Germany.'

"He was mad! His father's death mush have pushed him over the fine point between sanity and insanity. I decided to humor him.

" 'All that requires money, Kurt, lots of money,' I said. 'How do you intend to finance such a movement?'

"He looked at me, puzzled that I didn't understand. Then he shrugged his shoulders and laughed.

" 'You are just like all the others, Neal,' he said. 'No vision. Just a plain mortal. We have money, loads and loads of it sitting in banks in Argentina and Switzerland. The money is just waiting for this time.'

"I spoke to him softly. 'Listen, Kurt,' I said. 'Your father put that money away for your mother's and your security, not to squander on a losing movement.'

"He threw a tantrum, stamped his feet, and banged his fist on the table.

" 'Don't you understand, Neal?' he shouted. 'It is not for a losing movement. This time we will win. I guarantee it!'

"A sly expression crossed his face. 'By the way,' he said cunningly. 'Do you know where that money came from?'

"I shrugged my shoulders.

" 'My father put that money away for just this purpose, for this moment, for the movement,' he said. 'He thought he would lead the movement himself, but he was too old.'

"I felt I might as well go for broke and get the entire story, so I asked him how much money was involved and where it had come from.

" 'Think, Neal," he said. 'How much do you think could be involved here?'

" 'One million,' I ventured. I thought that the figure was ridiculous, but so was this entire conversation. He laughed and shook his head.

" 'Ten million,' I said.

" 'Now you're getting warm,' he said. 'Go better.'

" 'Twenty-five million?'

" 'Over one hundred million,' he said and smiled smugly.

" 'You're kidding, Kurt,' I said. 'You're just trying to pull my leg.'

" 'If it's proof you want, let me show you.' He walked over to his suitcase and took out bankbooks listing phenomenal amounts of money. Then he pulled a key from his pocket and added, 'And here is the key to the vault where millions more are stashed away.'

"Marian, he was not boasting.

" 'Where did all this money come from, Kurt?' I asked.

" 'You see, Neal. You never believe me. I've been telling you all the money is in Jews' hands.' He smiled complacently. 'My father and his friends tortured those animals, and they got all the information that they wanted. They confiscated their valuables,' and then he laughed, his voice escalating in insane glee. 'They even took the gold from their teeth.'

"I looked at him. I couldn't believe these words were coming from my friend Kurt's mouth. He mistook my silence as agreement and continued.

" 'This money will help us to make this world *Judenrein*,' he said triumphantly."

I interrupted Neal. "Oh no!" I said. "Oh no! Did you stop him?"

"I didn't get the chance, Marian. The phone rang and when he hung up, he said, 'Something has come up. I'll leave tomorrow. You wouldn't mind if my friend sleeps here tonight, Neal, would you?' I answered that of course I wouldn't, hoping he might talk some sense into Kurt. And that's the story up to date."

"How long ago was that?"

"Kurt left about a half hour before I called you," said Neal. "I expect them back soon."

"Did he say which friend he is bringing home?"

"Not really. But anything is better than this. He needs some stabilizing influence," Neal said before he hung up.

I looked at the clock. It was almost six o'clock. If I wanted to meet Shaindee at the special bus which would take us directly to the wedding hall I would have to hurry. I quickly put a few touches to my hair, refreshed my lipstick, waved goodbye to my mother and hurried as quickly as my new high heels would allow.

Shaindee looked refreshing. I needed that! She wasn't wearing any makeup, and there was a naturalness about her face. I felt a little overdone next to her and took a tissue out of my purse to wipe off a little of my blush.

The bus was full of people, and the talk was in a mixture of languages. There were a number of men sitting in the front. I saw one single seat and another in the adjoining row and headed for them. Shaindee took my arm gently and led me to the back of the bus.

"Those seats are set aside for the men," she said. "There is a separate women's section in the back."

Here we go again, I thought. Women in the back. We are not good enough to sit next to the men! Shaindee read my thoughts and hastened to explain the concept of modesty to me and that it had nothing to do with delegation to the back but rather to separation. I wondered whether she realized how far from understanding and accepting I was. This is going to be some evening, I thought bitterly.

The bus pulled up in front of a well lit building. We checked our coats, and then Shaindee steered me towards the music. We entered a tremendous hall. On either side were long tables lavishly set with a variety of food. There was a crowd of people gathered towards the front of the hall.

"There's Estie," Shaindee said. "Let's wish her *Mazel Tov*."

Estie looked beautiful. We wished her *Mazel Tov* and moved aside to give others the opportunity to do the same. Shaindee told me that Estie hadn't eaten yet and neither had her groom, because the wedding day is like a private *Yom Kippur* for the bride and groom; they would break their fast between the ceremony and the reception. This part of the evening was called the *Kabbalas Panim* or the greeting of the bride and groom.

"Where's the groom?" I asked.

Shaindee continued my private lesson.

"The *Chosson* and *Kallah*, the groom and bride, remain in separate rooms where they greet their guests. Some people sign the *Tenaim* or betrothal agreement at the time of the engagement and others sign it at this time. The *Kesubah* or marriage contract is also signed by the groom and two witnesses."

The beat of the music drowned out her voice. All I was able to hear was "Come, let's dance," and she pulled me to join a group of girls dancing. The steps were totally unfamiliar to me, but before I realized it, I was following along.

"*Mazel Tov,* Marian." At first I hadn't recognized Reva. She looked different dressed up.

"*Mazel Tov,*" I answered.

"Let's get something cold and refreshing to drink," she said.

"Hurry," said Reva. "It's time for the *badeken.*"

"What's that?" I asked.

"Watch and you'll see," she said. "After the *Kesubah* is signed, the men will dance with the *Chosson* toward the *Kallah.*"

I stayed close to Shaindee and Reva, because I didn't want to miss even a second of this very different experience. I had been either uninvolved or an observer as far as traditions were concerned my entire life. This time, I wanted to be a participant and to really understand everything that was happening.

I watched as the groom was led into the room amidst singing and dancing. The entire procedure went so quickly that, as much as I wanted to get a glimpse of the face of the boy that was to marry Estie, I just couldn't.

We went upstairs. I looked around. It was a large room with seats lined up. There was a separate section for the men and another section for the women. There was a beautiful canopy decorated with flowers. The flowers fluttered in the breeze. Reva explained that it is preferable for the *Chupah,* or nuptial canopy, to be placed under the open sky and that there was an opening in the ceiling for just this purpose.

I listened to the background of murmuring voices around me. The words were indistinguishable. It took a while before I realized it was because they were speaking a foreign tongue.

"Hebrew?" I asked. "Is it the custom at Jewish weddings to speak in that language?"

Shaindee laughed.

"No," she replied. "It is not the custom for the guests to speak Hebrew, unless of course, they are more comfortable in the language. Actually, the reason you hear so much Hebrew at this wedding is that Estie's husband is from Eretz Yisrael."

"Really?" I said. "How did she ever get to meet someone from across the ocean?"

"The Jewish world is really not so far away," Shaindee explained. "Although we are scattered all over the world, you'd be surprised at how small the distance becomes and how much of a community we are. Actually, Estie went to a Beth Jacob school in Eretz Yisrael after she graduated from high school."

I looked puzzled.

As if she read my mind, Shaindee continued. "Just as I went to a Seminary here in the United States to continue my education, Estie did the same thing by going to a Seminary in Eretz Yisrael. Her older married sister lives there, and it gave her the opportunity to spend some time with her sister's family. It was her sister who was really instrumental in the *shidduch*."

"The boy has a wonderful reputation," Reva said. "He is supposed to be just great. He lived in the house of his *Rosh Yeshivah* and is a real scholar. Big things are expected of him in the future."

"Where will they live?" I asked.

"For the first month, they plan on staying here, and then they will make their permanent residence in Eretz Yisrael."

"Whew! I give her credit," I said. "Imagine picking up and moving to a country and culture foreign from your own."

"Actually, it is really not that foreign, nor is the culture basically different," said Reva. "Oh, ssh. The ceremony is about to begin. I'm so excited for Estie."

The music began. The groom marched down. I couldn't see his face. His head was bent in prayer. He wore a coat, and I saw a white robe between his coat and his suit. There was a man escorting him on the right side and one on the left.

The room was quiet. The usual joviality and chatter I had heard at previous weddings was missing here. I couldn't see Estie's face as it was covered by a lace cloth. Her head was bowed. The solemnity of the occasion came through to me. I watched as each step unfolded just as Shaindee had described.

"What do we do now?" I whispered after I heard the *Mazel Tovs* echoing throughout the room.

"We eat and dance," said Shaindee. "Let's go upstairs."

The room looked regal. The tablecloths were decorative, and there were flowers on each table. We picked up cards with our names and table numbers, and I followed Shaindee as she led me to our table.

Once again, I saw men and women separated by a partition. However, reluctantly, I do have to admit that I had an enjoyable evening. Estie was the picture of effervescence, and she looked ecstatic. I was giddy with happiness and on Cloud Nine, because of the wedding and also because of my father's planned trip. And ours as well. Shaindee, who knew about the upcoming trips, seemed to read my mind. We exchanged swift, triumphant looks. It was an evening I knew I would not easily forget.

As soon as I opened the door to my room upon returning home from the wedding, I heard the phone ring.

"Neal," I said enthusiastically. "This was some night!"

I wanted to share my enthusiasm for my night and without giving him any opportunity to respond, I began babbling about the wedding.

"Marian," he interrupted me. "You'll tell me about it some other time. I've had an unbelievably grueling evening. Yes, this was some night!"

I stopped abruptly.

"I'm sorry, Neal," I said. "Did something happen with Kurt during the time I was at the wedding?"

"Did something happen?" he echoed. "Oh nothing . . . only that the world caved in."

"Don't be sarcastic, Neal. Tell me."

"Well, Kurt brought his friend. He introduced us."

" 'Neal, this is Heinrich Klaus, a very good friend of my father's and now my good friend,' Kurt said. He paused and then added, 'It's good to have my two best friends with me at this very important time in my life.'

"Marian, the name Heinrich Klaus had a familiar ring to it, and Kurt must have seen the expression on my face as I tried to recall where I had heard it.

" 'Don't you remember, Neal, my father's letter?'

"It was then that I recalled the words in Dr. Schmidt's suicide note. *My career is finished. I called Heinrich Klaus. He'll help you get the money from Switzerland and from South America.* It was only then that I began to realize that Kurt wasn't all bluster but that he really was going to Germany. Still, I tried to hold him back.

" 'Glad to meet you,' I said to Heinrich. 'Can't you do something with Kurt? He has this crazy idea about going to Germany and that he'll be the next Fuehrer. He's just upset about his father's dying. We must do something to help him.'

"He stood there, this massive blonde man, his powerful hands placed firmly on his hips, his legs astride. He threw back his head and laughed. In a voice with a deep guttural accent, he said, 'Kurt is right. Yes, he is right. Every word he says is true. Look at him. Look good. You will be proud one day to be able to say that Kurt Schmidt was your friend.'

"I became swept up in their madness. 'This time,' I said, 'the world will not turn its' back and let you do that to the Jews. The world has learned its lesson.'

"They looked at each other amusedly and laughed.

" 'Foolish boy. Foolish innocent boy,' Heinrich responded. 'Do you think the world cares one little bit about the Jews? I don't understand you. Wake up! Wake up! Did you think the burning of Jews was something new? They were burnt at the stake during the Inquisition and burned by modern technology during the Fuehrer's time. What is so different? Anti-Semitism has always existed. Don't you know history? Many popes were really enemies of the Jews. Why, even here in your own country you have the Ku Klux Klan, white hooded men burning crosses on the lawns of Jewish and black homes. Even in literature authors are anti-Semitic. Look at Dostoyevsky, Hemingway, Dickens, Fitzgerald, Melville and, of course, Shakespeare. I can go on and on. Do you think this is something new?'

" 'Come on, Neal. Wake up!' Kurt added conspiratorially. 'Look! Although you are not a German as we are, we'll take you along, right Heinrich?' Kurt looked smug. 'Neal is my friend, Heinrich. We've been friends for ages and ages. We'll make an exception with him.' He looked pleased with himself when he added, 'You'll be my right hand man.'

" 'I'm telling you Kurt, this is ridiculous,' I said. 'Get this nonsense out of your head. Cut it out!'

" 'Aha,' he cried. 'You're worried about your poor little Jewish girl Marian. Come on. Forget about her. What you need is a real wife, a blue-eyed blonde German. I'll pick one out for you when I get to Germany.'

" 'Hold it a minute, Kurt,' I said. 'You'll do no such thing, I think there is something you should know. You'd better sit down, or I'm afraid you'll tumble over when I tell you.'

"I pushed him into a chair and told him about Aunt Leslie and how I found out that I was Jewish.

" 'And, Kurt,' I said. 'If you plan to kill all the Jews, you might as well start with me, because I am one of them.'

"His face went through a metamorphosis. I could see the change in him. He became red and purple, his anger and wrath aroused by what I had just told him. He went into a rage and was actually frothing at the mouth.

" 'You dog, you!' he said. 'You hid it from me all these years.' The hatred spewed out of him.

" 'Kill him,' he said to his friend. 'Kill him just as you killed Jeffrey. Quick. Do it quickly while I watch, so that I can sleep freely from now on.'

" '*Du redst zu vill*,' Heinrich said angrily to Kurt. '*Schveig!*'

"I don't know. I guess I should have been terrified and in fear of my life, but I think my anger only strengthened and fortified me. I was unafraid. I turned to Heinrich, my voice steady. 'So you were the one who killed Jeffrey,' I said. 'Why? How? What did he ever do to harm you?' And then I felt the impact of my thoughts. Suddenly it dawned on me. 'Were you the one following me in the silver car?'

" 'So you saw me,' Heinrich answered. 'Yes. I followed you, because I was looking for Kurt and I thought that you might possibly lead me to him. When Herr Dr. Schmidt called me, he told me to give the money to Kurt, to explain to him everything that had happened and to advise him of our plans for the future. But he forgot to tell me where the bankbooks were. I searched Dr. Schmidt's office thoroughly, but I couldn't find them. I thought maybe Kurt took the bankbooks and went to the Boston apartment. When I came to Boston, no one was home. I forced the door open and searched the drawers. I was sure Kurt wouldn't keep it on his person. I wanted to make sure it was in the proper hands.

" 'And as far as Jeffrey is concerned, I mean, Jewfry, the stupid Jew, as one would expect, did not know when he wasn't wanted. He came in and found me going through the drawers. He was no match for me, although I must admit, he put up a good fight.'

"Now I was really frightened, Marian. I'm no hero, and I was all alone with these two crazy nuts. But I knew that with this type of person, if I showed fear, I was a goner without any chance to live at all.

" 'You better leave,' I bluffed. 'Just before I came up to the apartment I saw one of the detectives in the building. He told me he was going out to eat and would be back shortly.'

"I refused to cower and hoped they would fall for my bluff. But they didn't. I felt my knees get shaky when I looked at their menacing faces.

I'm not ashamed to say that when I thought of what had happened to Jeffrey I was frightened. Slowly, I backed up towards the door, my eyes never leaving their faces. Like prizefighters in the ring, we sized each other up.

"The real danger was Heinrich. Kurt, like most braggarts, had a bark that was worse than his bite. He would be afraid to fight me. Little by little, I inched towards the door. Kurt's eyes were upon me. He was about six feet away. But Heinrich was another matter. He was right next to me. He was so close I could feel his stale garlic breath on me. My arms were behind my back sliding along the wall behind me, and at last, I felt the cool metal of the door knob. I murmured a silent prayer that the door wasn't locked and with all the strength and force I could muster, I turned the handle, jumped aside and swung the door completely open, hitting Heinrich directly in the face. He let out a bloodcurdling scream of pain. From the corner of my eye, I saw him throw his hands over his face. This gave me just the time I needed to run down the steps. I ran as if the Devil himself was after me and as if my life depended upon it. Which it did.

"I heard them cursing, and then I heard running footsteps behind me. Believe it or not, I ran straight into a detective's arms. So now, Marian, meet Neal the hero. Newspaper reporters were here for interviews. I'm going to be on the front pages in tomorrow's newspapers."

"Neal," I said. "I'm so proud of you, but that was some risk you took. Thank G-d it turned out okay."

"Wait. I'm not finished yet. Our apartment was bugged."

"Bugged?"

"The police had wired the apartment and everything was taped, so Heinrich's confession of how and why Jeffrey was killed is on record."

"And Kurt?" I asked.

"He'll most probably go free," said Neal. "He really did nothing criminal." After a pause, Neal continued, "You know, Marian, I've been thinking. When a bear is born, everyone knows it will grow up to be a bear. When a serpent is born, we all know it will grow up to be a serpent. But when a child is born, we never know what kind of a man it will grow up to be. You were right all time about Kurt. He was born a child but grew up a serpent."

"Thank G-d you realize this now, Neal," I said.

"It is not G-d that made me realize it, Marian," he said "It is just pragmatic events."

chapter thirty-one

M any thoughts passed through my mind as we arrived at the airport. Intuitively, I felt this trip to Florida to meet my family for the first time was a truly momentous occasion. I believed the circle of my life was nearing completion. I was happy my mother was coming with me. I clutched my handbag tightly and glanced at my parents walking beside me.

My father looked different somehow. Happy? Perhaps. I couldn't tell but there was a look of contentment on his face.

"Remember," he said as he saw us off at the gate. "I love you both very much. We've been through some difficult times together, but everything will work out for the best."

The image of my father standing there alone still lingered in my mind as I watched my mother attach her seat belt in the seat next to mine. She also seemed different, as if my father's words had enveloped her in an airtight bubble of happiness. I hugged myself as I had done as a child. I was euphoric. The love I felt for my parents brought tears to my eyes.

After the few hectic days of preparation, the plane ride was just what we needed. What with getting my father packed for Israel and getting ourselves ready, my mother and I had had no time to talk. The time together on the plane was just the interlude we needed.

The plane settled down to a slow, rocking motion. The stewardess distributed the headphones to those who wanted to watch the movie. Some passengers turned out the lights and huddled in their seats in a sleeping position. I was wide awake and so, I saw, was my mother.

"You know something, Marian," my mother said. "The last few months have been very trying on your father. I think he is frightened."

"Frightened? Of what?"

"I think he is frightened of losing you." Then softly, she added, "Of losing me also, because I just can't continue acting anymore. I wanted our marriage to last and went along with him all these years, but the last few months have been impossible. I lit candles, and he protested. I kept *Shabbos*, and he protested. But I sensed his protests becoming weaker and weaker. I really think he wants to go back, but it is hard to admit he was wrong, that he wasted all these years."

"I can understand that," I said.

"Well, Marian, Grandfather's death has shown him that life is fragile," she said. "Also, the changes in your life have made him realize that the tower he built was really quite frail. Basically, Daddy is a reticent person. It is sometimes difficult for him to express himself. The years in the concentration camp and the years in Israel when we were first married were very hard on him. He lost faith in people, especially those in positions of authority. After having lived with German barbarism for so many years, he yearned to be among his own people and Yiddishkeit, but then to be offered Jewish duplicity? It is then one really perishes. It is difficult for me to explain this to you, to make you understand the strangeness and bitterness in life. I hope you never experience it."

"I think I've already experienced a bit, Mommy," I said. "I've seen much of the darker side of life these past few months."

"I'm sorry about that, Marian," she said. "I wish you hadn't had to go through that."

"Sometimes it's better not to be so protected," I said with a sidelong glance at my mother. "It may be easier but not better. And in the long run, it is not even easier."

My mother smiled ruefully and nodded her head.

"You're right, Marian," she said. "You are the one who had the courage to face the realities of life. Your father and I will always owe you a debt of gratitude for it. You know, I'm sure your father will have a wonderful *Pesach* in Israel. *Pesach* commemorates the release of the Jews from slavery in Egypt. I pray this is also the time of the freeing of your father and myself from our bondage of blindness and that we will be freed from our spiritual famine. But enough of this talk! Let's talk about your uncle, aunt and cousins in Florida. We're going to have such a marvelous time. I can't wait."

chapter thirty-two

I looked out of the maze of windows in the airport and saw a blue sky full of promises. My life had been filled with cold drifts and blizzards, but now, I felt only singing excitement and warmth. And I knew it was not only from the Florida sun; it was music from the heart.

The encounter I had anticipated for so long finally materialized. I recognized Uncle Meir as soon as I saw him. His bright eyes glittered when he met mine, and happiness was written all over his face as he greeted my mother, his sister. He was such an outstandingly distinguished figure that, at first, I was in awe of him. His beard was coal black, and he was so tall that I had to run to match his every step. I was shy and couldn't talk, but my mother and uncle didn't notice. They spoke incessantly, trying to make up in minutes for years of separation.

The porter delivered our luggage at the curbside, and a car pulled up shortly after. Uncle Meir introduced me to the driver, my cousin Yitzchak, who looked a lot like Uncle Meir.

The car stopped at a low-slung ranch house, very Spanish in architecture with its picture window, red tile roof and wrought iron trimming and gates. At the corner, we had passed a large building with marble steps. My uncle had pointed it out as the place where the family *davened*.

I saw the drape that covered the window fall back in place, and the door flung open by Aunt Sarah, a chubbier Aunt Sarah than my mother had described but with the same bubbly warm personality. Aunt Sarah encircled me in her plump arms, holding both my mother and me at the same time. My mother and Aunt Sarah continued laughing and crying for ten minutes, and I couldn't even grasp one word of what they were talking about.

The house was teeming with people, and it seemed as if every corner was taken. I was introduced to cousins, their wives or husbands and their children, but they remained just one mass of faces. It took me days to decipher and remember names and who belonged to whom.

My cousin Shmuel and his wife Chavie gave me a tour of the house. I couldn't believe all these people slept under one roof.

"Where does everyone sleep?" I asked. "There aren't enough rooms."

"This house is like the *Bais Hamikdash*," my cousin Shmuel replied. "Its walls expand to accommodate everyone." Of course, he had to explain *Bais Hamikdash* to me.

It was a long time since I had seen my mother so happy. Her face was flushed and her eyes sparkled as she went about helping Aunt Sarah with the cooking.

"Everything would be just perfect if Yankel, the old Yankel, could be here," Aunt Sarah said.

The house was run with modern business directives and division of labor. Everyone seemed to have a job to do.

"Can I help?" I asked, and my cousin Rechie put me to work helping her polish the silver.

My cousins Shmuel and Yitzchok left to deliver the *maos chittim*. "It is a custom in every Jewish household," my uncle explained, "to provide for those in need. After all, how can we enjoy a *Yom Tov* meal knowing there are others who can't afford their own?"

I was glad my mother had explained to me on the plane what was involved in the preparations for *Pesach*, otherwise, I would never have understood the flurry of excitement as pots, pans, china and silver that had been used throughout the year were packed away. Now, I was able to understand that they too are considered *chametz*, and since it was expressly forbidden to eat *chametz* during the eight days of Passover, they too had to be put away.

I was enthralled as I observed my aunt distribute crumbs of bread throughout the house. Then I watched my uncle take a wooden spoon, a feather and a lit candle and, accompanied by my cousins, make a complete round of the house, searching every nook and cranny for the slightest trace of leaven. I listened as he explained the prayer he made nullifying whatever *chametz* might have escaped his detection, and I watched as he made a bundle of the *chametz* he had found and put it away to be burned the next day.

As a student majoring in education, I marvelled at the *Seder*. I thought of the components of a lesson plan I had been taught in school, and I was amazed. It was all there in the *Pesach Seder*, from the methods of motivation, the use of visual aids, stimulation, and the involvement of the entire "student body," old and young. Everyone participated, learning through a system of questions and answers. What is the meaning of this, or what is the meaning of that? The story of our deliverance from Egyptian bondage is reiterated year after year in every Jewish household and serves as reinforcement. Every man, woman and child in the family is imbued with the same spirit of unity. We all live through the experience of our forefathers and believe that just as our fathers were helped during the times of persecution, so too will we be helped.

"O merciful Father, we thank You for Your loving kindness and never-ending goodness to the house of Israel. Our ancestors languished in Egyptian slavery and ate the bread of affliction, but You led Israel from bondage to freedom, from darkness to light, from despair to hope."

And you, dear Hashem, will lead me also from bondage to freedom, from darkness to light, from despair to hope.

chapter thirty-three

O
n the second day of *Chol Hamoed*, I looked out my window and admired the pristine sky and the clear, warm weather. It was six o'clock in the morning, but the house was already active and alive. I dressed quickly and picked up the registration and the keys for the car from the marble counter in the kitchen where my cousin had left them for me.

It took me less than an hour to arrive at the beach, and as I sat in the car, I watched the sun rise, a red ball of fire on the horizon. I admired the palm trees standing tall in their majestic splendor along the street near the beach.

After a while, I opened the door of the car and was met with a sprinkle of raindrops. I put my face up, and the refreshing drops tickled it. The rain lasted all of two minutes, and the same way it had come, it disappeared, leaving no sign behind.

I went down to the edge of the water, took off my shoes and walked along the beach. The white coral lying in the sand looked like skeleton faces, in a sharp contrast to the green seaweed beside it. An airplane flew overhead, an intruder amidst the sounds of nature.

I sat down on the dry sand on the empty beach, pulled my knees under my chin and wrapped my dress tightly about my legs. I recalled that on the airplane I had looked out the window and observed that the clouds resembled an ocean of waves. Now and then, the sun peeked through the thick banks of clouds for an occasional glance at the beach.

There was only water as far as my eye could see. I admired the colors, a dull pea green and a light green outlined in blue which met the sky with its white fluffy clouds underlined with gray. The green-blue of the water was a different, unusual color, unlike the color of the waters I was familiar with in New York. The view reminded me of a painting, a lone rider on a surfboard riding the waves and a white sailboat on the horizon looking as if it would fall over the edge if it sailed any further.

The waves seemed fierce that morning, with a ferocity that made the whitecaps look like white glaring teeth. I watched the white foam well up at my feet in a bubbling froth, like a tub full of soap suds. I turned away from the water and saw the modern skyline of hotels, but even then, my gaze was caught by the numerous seagulls, with their gray backs, white breasts and spread wings, cawing loudly as they landed on the beach.

And I thought. I thought about college. I had really looked forward to going. It was not only something my father had wanted for me but something I had wanted for myself. But I was finding my readings on Judaism and my college experiences in conflict. Little by little, I was learning what the Torah expects of a Jew, but I was finding that college was the propagator of a totally non-Jewish culture. Many of the basic required courses were anti-religious. Was the growth I was experiencing strong enough to fight this deluge of indoctrination from college?

I thought about Pavlov's experiment. The ringing of the bell conditioned the dog to expect food, and his salivary glands would be trained to function at the sound of the bell. Could people likewise be conditioned? Would my college courses condition me? Change me? I know people were created with the ability to think and be responsible for their own actions, but they are also the product of their environment. Could a daily diet of sacrilegious ideologies do damage?

I thought of the discussion yesterday during lunch in my uncle's house. My cousin had said that Science was becoming a god and man was worshipping at its feet. "Science may have made changes in our society through great technical progress," he had said, "but it has also opened the door to chaos. It has brought us forward technically, and at the same time, it has set us back morally to the time of Noah and Sodom and Amorah."

Education should make us better, but the world was becoming more and more perverted and without morality, I decided.

When we read the *Haggadah*, we thanked Hashem for taking us out of physical slavery. I couldn't help but think that slavery still existed in different forms. People were now enslaved by their passions, by their fears of walking the streets or being accosted by terrorists. We are all enslaved by our need for money and the luxuries we have grown to depend upon.

My thoughts turned back to my college courses. What about Darwinism which believes man is descended from apes. I smiled when I recalled Janet's response during class.

"Professor, if you want to believe your grandfathers were apes, it's okay with me," she had said. "Mine were descendants of Adam and Eve."

And what about Freud, a Jew who stated that man cannot control his own nature? Ridiculous. I now know that each person is responsible for his own actions.

There is so little substance to these theories, yet unbelievably, they are taught as fact. I realized I was wasting my time. I wanted to quit. But could I make the move? What would my father say? What about Neal? I could just hear his mother's voice. "She wants to be a doctor's wife. It is bad enough she is Jewish, but no college degree either?" I felt like slapping my own face. Marian, I said to myself, this nastiness is unbecoming.

And how about Janet? What about our friendship? She was thriving in the college atmosphere, enjoying the permissive social mores. Janet . . . my friend . . . my sister.

And then there was Neal. How about Neal? I realized that the ultimate decision about whether to marry Neal was mine. I now knew what marriage meant and what it entailed. Did Neal and I want the same things from marriage? Were our values similar, our ideals, goals and aspirations the same?

I had read in the Torah that Isaac took Rebecca as his wife and loved her. I had previously thought that one fell in love and then married, but now I questioned the meaning of love. Marriage, I realized, meant a shared destiny.

I thought about the world in which I lived. This was the Age of Anxiety. Why were we all so anxious? We had great wealth, technological advances, and yet, our arteries were hardening, our stomachs developed ulcers and the psychiatrists' couches were full. We were a restless, dissatisfied generation searching for security but not really knowing the meaning of security. We ate too much, drank too much, indulged our senses too much. We worked very hard and played so hard that play also became work. This mid-twentieth century society in which I had grown up was built on competitiveness, on getting ahead, on achieving. And even if we made it to the top, the pressure still wouldn't stop; there would be the pressure to remain at the top.

We needed a "macho" image, I realized, an image based on externals, with people judged by what they have and not what they are. We had become slaves of instinct. I thought of how easily a mob could get carried away, proving that man can become a fiend and everything we call civilization could easily result in the cruelest violence. I realized: What is life without Torah?

I thought about my uncle. His measure of prestige was knowledge of Torah. His life was filled with compassion, charitable deeds, stability of purpose. I considered him and his life a success.

I returned to my uncle's house and sat down to write a letter.

Dear Neal,

You know I am not a verbal person. To express myself in spoken words is more difficult for me than in writing. Where do I begin? How? Let me see. I'll start by telling you a story about a boy named Jack and a girl named Jill.

Although their economic backgrounds were different, that was basically the only major dissimilarity. Jill met Jack, and they really hit it off. A casual friendship led to an urge for more companionship which then led to plans to marry and live happily ever after. But is it so easy to live happily ever after? Remember that nursery rhyme?

Jack and Jill went up the hill
to fetch a pail of water.
Jack fell down and broke his crown
and Jill came tumbling after.

The problem is that Jill was the one who had a terrible thirst and went for water, but Jack did not have the same urge and did not come after.

What am I doing? Really, I guess I'm talking in circles, Neal, and I'm really messing things up. But I'm not going to rewrite this letter or even reread it. I'm just going to put down my feelings as they come instinc- tively in my head.

We always hear the expression that if you want a happy marriage, then marriage has to be based upon the theory of fifty-fifty. This, in my opinion, is totally ridiculous because if a marriage is based on fifty-fifty, then each person is really pulling for their fifty percent and marriage becomes a tug-of-war. Marriage sometimes has to be ninety-five on one side and five percent on the other, or vice versa. Then there is no tug-of-war, each person vying for his share.

But what happens if each person wants something different from life? I'll admit we both don't have to be exactly the same. We are individuals with different personalities and the right to be different, but we really must want basically the same things and have similar goals. You might answer me that since the times we have spent together in the past were good, therefore the future times we will spend together should also be good, but I would have to refute that. You see, Neal, I am not the same girl I was when I first met you.

I look at our friends and our contemporaries. What are their lives like? What was our life like? We call ourselves children of a liberated generation, but our liberated generation has become empty. We have become seekers of pleasures and material goods, the Now Generation. We have turned the value system upside down. Restraint is now called inhibition and "doing your own thing" is the order of the day. This is not a healthy blueprint for life; it is hedonism. If we, you and I, accept this as our way of life, then we will bring it into our home. I don't want a G-dless home. I want a home that contains the three most precious gifts G-d has given us; wisdom, understanding and knowledge based upon belief in G-d.

You see, as corny as it may sound, I have found and recognized G-d. I love Him, worship Him, and am in awe of Him, in awe of everything He has given me. I wake up in the morning and thank Him for being alive and go to sleep praying I will once again see a new day. I have stopped taking things for granted and believing everything is due me. I look at a blade of grass and recognize why it sprouted and who made it grow.

Neal, I am aware that this life would demand limitations and discipline on my part. I am ready to accept this because I now realize it is this readiness to forfeit comfort and even one's life that has kept the chain of our ancestors intact.

I was looking through some books in my uncle's house, and I was deeply affected by an explanation of the source of a prayer in a book. The name of the prayer is *U'nesaneh Tokef*. It was written by a Rabbi Amnon of Mainz, Germany, about one thousand years ago and is said on the High Holy Days.

Rabbi Amnon was a good friend and advisor to the bishop of Mainz who, one day, insisted that his friend convert to Christianity. In order to buy time, the Rabbi asked for three days in which to think about it and to make his decision.

The Rabbi spent these days alone and in prayer, begging to be forgiven for the sin of procrastination as he had not immediately refused the bishop's request. When the bishop demanded an answer, the Rabbi asked that his tongue be cut out for the sin of saying he would consider the matter. The angry bishop chopped off his feet, joint by joint because he said the sin was not in what he said but in not coming as he had promised. The same thing was done to his hands. Needless to say, he died, but not before he sanctified G-d's Name in the synagogue with his moving prayer.

Neal, I find a message in this story for me. I can't wait any longer. I shouldn't. Each individual must decide for himself whether the Torah is true or not, and belief also means action. I believe our forefathers stood at the foot of Mount Sinai and received the Torah from G-d through Moses, our teacher.

In making this most crucial decision of my life, Neal, I recognize all your good points and they are many, so please understand that I am not rejecting you personally. I am really rejecting my former self.

Neal, you have, as I have, only recently found out about your Jewishness. Join me, Neal, in a search for our spiritual roots. After all, my people are your people, my G-d is your G-d. This is the only life for me.

May G-d guide us and give us strength.

Sincerely,
Malka

chapter thirty-four

I t was difficult to leave my uncle's house. Knowing it really was not a final goodbye did help soften the departure, but we cried a river of tears. The ray of sun on the horizon was that my father too would be home the following day. Our luggage was loaded with Aunt Sarah's delicious delicacies left over from *Pesach*.

When we arrived home, my mother prepared a shopping list for me, and while she took care of the unpacking, I drove the few blocks to the shopping center. I switched on the radio to a classical music program. They were playing Beethoven's Fifth Symphony, the heavy beat portending the future.

The radio announcer broke in.

"We interrupt this program to say that a plane on its way to America from a mid-eastern country has been hijacked. It is not known whether any Americans were on board. We repeat, a plane carrying some three hundred passengers has been hijacked. We will bring you further reports as we receive them."

The music returned, and I hummed the dum, dum, dum, dum along with it as I parked the car at the shopping center.

When I returned home, the fragrance of the food from Aunt Sarah warming on the kitchen stove greeted me. My mother was reading a letter.

"I found two letters from Daddy in the mail box," she said. "Daddy must have sent them with someone, because there are no stamps on them. Oh, I'm so happy. Daddy sounds just wonderful. And he's coming home tomorrow! I can't wait to see him. Here's your letter, Marian."

I hastily tore the envelope open and read.

A TIME TO LIVE

My dear daughter,

I have you to thank for giving me back my life. I have been dead for so long. It took your delicate hands to reawaken me and six thousand miles of travel to bring me back to where I belong.

Malkala—you see, I can now call you by your proper name so easily—I realize how much you have been tormented by your lack of understanding, and I was no help. You wanted so to comprehend the differences between Grandfather and me. It is no easy task for me to explain my shame. How could I, with the great father I had who guided me throughout my youth, follow the devil's path? Perhaps a person with great innate strength could have come through untouched. I fell apart. Now, when I look back, it is difficult for me to excuse my actions, but feeble as you may find my reasoning, I do owe you this explanation.

Where shall I begin? I'll start at the beginning. First, let me tell you something about us, you and me and our Jewish nation.

For hundreds of years, Jews lived in Europe, mostly in *shtetlach*, small villages, some in poverty and almost always under the shadow of persecution. Money was not the measurement of a person's achievements, but his ability to learn Torah was what won him respect and esteem. Religion was a living thing, a daily reality. The family structure was strong, and *Shabbos* always had a special glow. This was how I was raised. This is what your grandmother and grandfather gave me, because this is what they believed in. They also taught me that each person is responsible for his own soul. I seemed to have always known that we have to answer to a greater Being.

Today, as I sit in Aunt Leah's house and look out her window at the white stone houses of Jerusalem, and smell the special fragrance of flowers carried by the breeze, I can't believe that there was a Dachau, Treblinka, Auschwitz, Bergen-Belsen and other Nazi extermination camps. I can't believe I witnessed the murders of some of the six million. I can't believe I was once a slave laborer, a sub-human. I can't believe your mother and my friends were objects of medical experiments. Sometimes, I think: Am I going berserk? Did I really see my friends killed before my eyes?

Life does strange things to people, and the concentration camp was no different. I thought it was impossible to survive, but I guess the will to live is strong. I survived.

Yes, I survived. I didn't think I would. The Nazis took away everything, even our individuality. They made us into one human mass of numbered, filthy, shaven-headed excuses for humans caked with dirt, lice,

mud and feces. They thought that by bringing us to the lowest defile-
ment, degradation and humiliation, they would destroy our souls
before they killed our bodies.

Would you believe me when I tell you they failed? My soul lived
through this. Some people died because they lost the will to live. I had a
strong will and lived through everything.

Was my job once to pull the gold teeth out of gassed mouths? Oh,
my G-d!

But the more they tried to kill all signs of humanity and dignity in me,
the more I became strengthened. You know what kept me going,
Malka? An image and a haunting melody. I saw my father in *shul*, his
tallis wrapped around him, his face uplifted, tears streaming down his
eyes in concentrated prayer on *Yom Kippur*, and I kept hearing the
mystical melody of *Kol Nidre*. A nation that believed with unswerving
faith had to survive. We were the people of G-d. We would remain alive.
I would remain alive.

I remember the taunts of the Nazi guard. "No one will believe
genocide existed on such a scale," he boasted. "No one will believe
humans could be used as guinea pigs."

It is true there were times I wanted to just close my eyes and blot out
the oppressive evil around me, but it was a luxury I did not permit
myself. I had to be a witness.

And then the war was over, and we survivors tried to pick up the
pieces of our lives. I met your mother, and we got married and started a
real Jewish home.

I didn't know Grandfather was alive and had immigrated to America.
It was only afterwards that I found out Rabbi Isaacs had had family in
America who brought him over and that he, in turn, had brought
Grandfather to America. Your mother, Aunt Leah and I went to Israel,
then known as Palestine. Believe it or not, Malka, getting in was
difficult. The British were in control and limited Jewish immigration.

And it was in Israel, in Eretz Yisrael, that my world really began to
cave in. It was there that truths emerged.

I had seen the inhuman face of man in the concentration camps of
the Germans. I did not expect to see the inhuman face of man in the
land of my people. Little by little, I began to hear whispers that became
louder and louder. Could anyone believe that "selectivity," that frightening word that pulled us from our exhausted half-dead sleep in the
Nazi camps, would be used in dealing with problems of immigration to
Palestine. Could I believe that "selectivity," meaning the choice of
whom to save from the ovens, was based upon the ability of the person

to withstand the difficulties of life in Palestine, which immediately doomed to death the old and very young? Could I believe that a Jew, with the blood of Avraham, Yitzchak and Yaakov in his veins, could say that it is necessary to sacrifice a few in order to save many or that only those trained in agriculture and industry were worth bringing to Israel?

Could I believe that, although many wonderful American Jews gave millions of dollars to save their brothers from the Nazis, there were also American Jews in positions of importance in the United States who could have helped save some of the six million but preferred to be recognized as Americans and not Jews?

Could I believe that, since all was serene in their domain, Jews betrayed Jews to the British to be hanged in my Eretz Yisrael? Could I believe that governments made up of Jews were refusing to take other Jews out of the cauldron of Europe?

And then, with the opening of the doors of Israel, lo and behold, Operation Magic Carpet. Yemenite Jews were brought to Israel on "the wings of eagles" and this same government of Jews took the Yemenite Jews, who had kept thousands of years of tradition intact, and cut off the children's *payos* and told them that now that they were in Israel it was unnecessary to eat kosher or keep *Shabbos*.

Malkala, my soul became an inferno and I ran from these seeds of destruction, from the bitterness and hatred of religion I saw in some of my own people. You see, Malkala, I was able to retain my mental strength throughout the war because I knew the Germans were animals and animals did not have a Torah to guide them. But when I saw my own people tearing apart more than five thousand years of Torah, after everything we had been through, it was then that I ran away from Israel, from my people and from my traditions as if a plague was after me. I ended up blaming G-d for man's inadequacies.

Only now has this sickness in my soul healed. Only now have I realized my mistakes. I know G-d accepts one who repents. I pray He will accept my *Teshuvah* and forgive me.

I thank you, my dear daughter, for helping bring me back where I belong, and I love you.

Daddy

The call came the next day. We went to bed early, planning to arise at five o'clock so that we could pick my father up when his plane would land at seven, and so we had not heard the radio or the phone ringing. It was only afterwards, in bits and pieces that we were able to put together the entire story.

It was my father's plane that had been hijacked and forced down in the desert. And it was my father who had emerged the hero. It was he who shared the food packed for him by Aunt Leah with everyone on the plane, not knowing how long they would be interred and knowing there was no other food. It was my father, my dear, wonderful, compassionate father, who had kept up everyone's spirits with songs like *Ani Maamin* and *Min Hametzar*. It was my father who had given the others the courage to persevere until they were rescued. And it was my father who was in an American military hospital recovering from his ordeal.

My mother reminded me that today was my Grandfather's *yahrzeit*. As she lit the special candle in his memory, I stared at the flame burning brightly.

"Oh Grandfather," I cried. "What could have been and what should have been."

My mother put her arms around me and we cried together. I cried for my grandfather, my father, my mother, but I also cried for myself, for all those precious years that had been wasted.

Dear G-d, I prayed, help our family pull through this difficult period in our lives. Grandfather, wherever you are, pray for your son, your only son, and for his wife and daughter. But even as my tears stained my cheeks, I felt a strong surge of hope and happiness in my heart. And I knew, I just knew, that all would be well. Just as there is a time for everything under the sun, there is also . . . a time to live.

Acknowledgments and Dedications

When it comes time to give thanks for accomplishing a dream, where do I begin? I thank the *Ribono Shel Olam* for everything. I pray I should continue to be worthy of His goodness and that I should have the *zchus* to see it.

I would like to dedicate this book *Lezecher Nishmas*: My beloved father, אבי מורי, Yaakov Yosef Eider ע״ה, my teacher, guide and mentor who showed me the true path. Moshe Mordechai Stavsky ע״ה, who took up where my father left off and continued as my teacher, guide, mentor and friend. Shulamith Atkin ע״ה, who by her example taught everyone who came into contact with her the meaning of respect of parents, and who always had an open heart and an open hand.

I would also like to dedicate this book *Lehibodel Lechayim* to the following people:

My dear mother, Brucha Eider שתחי׳. Not until I walked in your footsteps did I really comprehend your worth and realize how impossible those footsteps are to match. May you live for one hundred and twenty years and be well and enjoy *nachas*.

My dear father-in-law, HaRav Chaim Zvi Stavsky שליט״א. Your *Emunah* and *Yiras Shomayim* set an example for all of us. May you continue as the Patriarch of the family with much *nachas* from the entire *mishpachah* for one hundred and twenty years.

My children, their spouses and my grandchildren who give me *nachas*. I pray they be blessed with the same from their children and grandchildren.

Yitzchak Isaac and Miryam Stavsky: Thank you for being son, daughter and father. I'll never forget it.

Chaya Sura and Meir Gross: Thank you for showing me that it is possible to make time to make my dream of writing a reality. You showed me how you find time within your hectic schedule as parent, exemplary teacher and author to do this, and by your example, you encouraged me to start this book.

Penina Pesel and Avrohom Dovid Feigenbaum: Thank you for bringing me cheer, for the special touches of thoughfulness, for caring and always being there and available, no matter the time of the day or night; and thank you for *Havdalah*.

Esther Reva and Shmuel Dovid Florans: Thank you for your encouragement, suggestions and belief in me and in this book. You were my constant "sounding board" and consultant throughout. I really owe this book's completion to you.

Yaakov Yosef and Layah Stavsky: Thank you for always being available to "hammer" away those problems that may seem small to others but which caused me frustration and sometimes seemed unsurmountable. And thank you for doing it with such willingness.

My brother-in-law and sister Jack and Jean Fogel and my brother and sister-in-law Rabbi and Rebitzin Shimon Dovid and Shifra Eider: Thank you for making yourselves available during those trying years.

And last but not least: Rabbi Simcha Eliezer Rubin שליט״א, my best friend, who exemplifies true *Avodas Hashem*. Thank you for your patience and support. And to the children, Naftoli Shmuel and Chani Rubin, Meyer and Devorah Rubin, Leibe and Rechi Purec, Dovid Rubin and the grandchildren: Thank you for the warm welcome and for caring.

An author, while writing a book, becomes very involved in the book and may not always see "the trees because of the forest."

Therefore I offer my deepest thanks to: Rabbi Joseph Elias, principal of Rika Breuer Teachers Seminary and Beth Jacob High School, for setting aside valuable time from his busy schedule to review this manuscript and for his practical suggestions and constructive criticisms. Rabbi Noson Scherman, Editor of Art Scroll, who was kind enough to read this manuscript and offer suggestions. Rebetzin Felice Blau, principal of Beth Jacob Academy, for her review of the book, for always having a listening ear and for her encouragement. Rebetzin Toby Handelsman, principal of Beth Jacob High School, for her gentle critique and literary expertise. My niece Chaya Sarah Fogel for her helpful comments and suggestions.

In closing, I would also like to express my gratitude to the editorial and graphics staff at C.I.S. Communications Inc. of Lakewood, New Jersey, for the high degree of professionalism they have brought to the production of this book.

C.S.R.